The Bull Option

Sameer Garach

MARE PRESS

The Bull Option
Cover Design by Canva
Stock Photo: Man with Umbrella | ID 24386574 Copyright Anetakwiat | Dreamstime.com
Author photograph by Sameer Garach
Copyright © 2019 by Sameer Garach
All rights reserved.
ISBN-10: 0-9990574-1-3
ISBN-13: 978-0-9990574-1-4
Library of Congress Control Number: 2018915188
Published in the United States of America by Mare Press, Houston, TX
MARE PRESS and MARE PRESS Design are trademarks of Mare Press.
Social media logos on the cover are trademarks of Facebook, Pinterest, and Instagram.

For my readers and supporters.
You give me a reason to continue writing.

If you can't do it, write about doing it.

ACKNOWLEDGMENTS

Thank you for reading *The Bull Option*. It was a long, arduous journey, roughly three years, from idea to publication. The very act of creation required a substantial amount of will power, plugging into depths I had no knowledge of existence.

There are a great number of people who contributed to this work. After performing a sample edit, Author Jen Blood first rejected my manuscript for editing because it was not a good match for her. Nevertheless, she pointed me in the right direction, so that I could compose a serviceable, editable novel. She provided honest feedback, suggested I join a writing group, and advised I read books in my genre to get a better understanding of how to write a novel. Though she never edited my final work, her little guidance went a long way.

I owe a debt of gratitude to Author and Professor Sasha Troyan, who requested that I thank her without getting into the specifics, and Author Michael Garrett, Stephen King's first editor and publisher, who provided an extensive copyedit without dampening my spirits. Incorporating their guidance made my work of professional grade.

I reserve a special thanks to my Monday evening critique group—Sonja Cassella, Desmond White, Margo Catts, and Ali Tareque—and my Thursday morning critique group—Mark Andersen, Alicia

Richardson, Lynn Long, Tassie Kalas, and Mandy Broughton. They found flaws in the development of my story that no single editor could find on his or her own and made suggestions for improvement. At Scribendi and Skylight Editorial, I'd like to thank the talented team of editors for providing manuscript critiques and proofreads, respectively, at an affordable cost. I'd also like to give a big shout-out to my friend Peter Kozlowski for his review.

I can't say thank you enough to STREBER Weekly at www.streber.st for granting me permission to use the website for research.

Finally, on a personal note, I'd like to thank my family. This would not have been possible without your support.

I hope you enjoy *The Bull Option*. Thank you.

CHAPTER 1

Manhattan, New York

At the New York County Civil Supreme Court, Robert Prosperi, a husky man with dark brown, curly hair, swallowed his loss. The head of The Prosperi Organization, a real estate development firm, and RP Capital Management, a hedge fund, anticipated the publicity that would follow. He closed his briefcase and stormed out of the room.

Several people, mostly reporters and camera operators waited for two men to emerge from the courthouse. The defendant and plaintiff exited, one after the other. The camera operators taped a live feed of reporters stuffing microphones and recorders in the interviewees' faces. The paparazzi snapped and scrabbled for space, adding to the raucous congestion.

The defendant, David Lemon, a fit man in his early fifties with white-and-gray hair, a broad forehead, sideburns, and a receding hairline, wore a suit and answered questions behind a podium with a buoyant smile. A brunette with rosy cheeks and raspberry pink lips stood next to the elder man and held his arm.

The plaintiff, Robert, tossed on his sunglasses, scowled with his mouth open, and spewed profanities with his right arm extended, ready to knock over the camera operators. He raced down the stairs of the courthouse to his shiny black Maybach Exelero, felt a raindrop hit his head, and glanced at the dark, steely gray skies indicative of a heavy pour down.

"How's it feel to miss the train, Rob?" A reporter stuck a mic in the large man's face.

"Get that shit out of my face, you fucking ass wipe," Rob yelled with a classic New York accent as he entered his chauffeured vehicle.

Yawn. In an old, broken-down, graffiti-laden subway train, Kannada Khan, a bearded, homeless Indian man in his mid-thirties, woke from his much-needed slumber, as his head and spine never quite acclimated to the pile of tomatoes he kept for a pillow, nor the hard, merciless floor. He stretched his arms toward the ceiling and smiled as he took in the scenery; colorful markings and initials, photographs displayed in lightboxes, and poetry in unused advertisement fixtures slots. He appreciated the moment; this moment was his life.

Kannada adjusted his dark gray beanie and slowly circled his head around his possessions. The tin can, used for begging, red plastic milk crate, employed as a chair, and three bags, filled with clothes and papers, were still there, and so was his breakfast, lunch, and dinner—nut bars. A few business books he had checked out from the Science, Industry and Business Library lay near his head. *I need to return those.*

The business resources reminded him of his recent accomplishment—a novel. He clasped his hands behind his head and reminisced on his writing journey. The former investment banker never wrote much, but since he'd hit rock bottom, writing became a tool to express his pain and frustration with an unexpected job loss at a hedge fund. Eventually, he turned to producing fiction and made the New York Public Library, in particular, the Rose Main Reading Room, his office. The room's ambience softened the realities of poverty, especially the mural on the ceiling, vibrant skies and brilliant clouds, and had him coming back for the last twenty months. He sighed. *I can't believe I wrote a book.*

A light scuffle from his right distracted him. A woman wearing a dirty, white dove, ivory pendant was covering her small boy with an army jacket while he cuddled under her arm on the floor, sleeping, at the other end of the train car.

The world is cold. Kannada knew all too well that New York was a city where cutthroat capitalism shined forth, where competition for success, for those who defined it as money, was, is, and always would be fierce.

He recalled the words that brought him to New York several years ago. "If I can make it there, I'll make it anywhere," Liza Minelli sang in *New York, New York*. Over time, he learned for every winner, a plethora of losers watched and saw life too clearly, moved on with their lives, and found a different way of functioning.

Kannada sniffed his distinctive scent, a combination of perspiration, garbage, pollution, and grime, and returned to viewing the ceiling a little more dejected. *When will things change? I'm doing what I can. How come it's not good enough?* A feeling of constraint gripped him as he mulled over his condition.

There were two prisons in this world. One was visible, situated far away from society, and housed criminals who overstepped the boundaries created by humankind. The other was invisible, omnipresent yet rarely seen, and sheltered those who had been displaced by some unexplainable power.

Although Kannada never saw anyone emerge from poverty unscathed, there were exceptions to this rule. He reminisced on movies made about such folks and newspaper articles written about them; then he remembered the phrase that kept him going all these years, Liza Minelli's inspirational words in *New York, New York*. "It's up to you."

Kannada removed his blanket but remained still; he needed to mentally prepare himself for the day. Today would be different from his normal routine—selling tomatoes on the side of the road—because he had a job fair to attend. Though the former investment banker had polished his resume and rehearsed what he would say in interviews, he knew that all the preparation in the world couldn't guarantee him a job, much less a career. *Get up.* He slowly rose to his feet with a few cracks of the joints, grabbed some undergarments from a small luggage bag, and took his belongings, a backpack and briefcase.

He sneaked through a hidden passageway thread only by subway rats and similar rodents and moved to one of the scattered restrooms in New York City's subway system. Under dim lighting enclosed by sage green walls, he shaved his black beard clean and pristine just as it had once been with an old-fashioned razor blade knife previously used to cut foodstuffs, as classical music played outside.

Next, Kannada brushed his teeth with a toothbrush, snipped his black hair with a pair of scissors to an Ivy League cut, and washed himself by caressing his tan body with hand soap from a soap dispenser. He smiled in the smudgy mirror from start to finish, taking his sweet time. Kannada splashed himself with water from the sink, rinsed away the soap and the agonies of poverty, and flooded the floor with soapy water; there was no need to worry. Finally, he pat dried himself with paper towels and toilet paper.

He moved to a dry corner of the lavatory to complete his transformation. Kannada opened his once clean briefcase, now tattered, on a baby changing station, looked at its expensive contents, a dress shirt, black slacks and coat, a black belt, a shiny red tie, good-as-new shoes, and a leather satchel, remnants from a different life, and traded his dirty rags for another shot at success. Kannada slipped on his new attire, smeared his body with fabric softener tissue, and smelled the result—fresh. The new and improved look had few wrinkles in the mirror, which was a relief, and required a minor straightening of the tie.

The chic stud checked his wallet, which held a few hundred dollars and a couple of expired credit cards, and then stuffed his papers and backpack into the shoulder bag. As he picked up his worn-out suitcase, it fell apart. *Not so fast, hot stuff.* He sighed and tossed the briefcase into the garbage. Kannada felt something in his pocket, took it out, and looked at it—a picture of him and his fiancée, Amara Sanon, an Indian woman with black-and-brown hair and a fair complexion. He replayed the moment the image was taken.

"Oh, look, there's a photo booth," Amara said.

Kannada started to walk away, camera shy.

"No." Amara tugged his arm. "You're taking this picture with me. Come on." She dragged him to the memory room during a date at Navy Pier in Chicago a few years ago.

"We already have a bunch of pictures," he argued without choice.

"It's what couples do."

Kannada fought back. "Why?"

The woman paid no attention to his wishes. "So I can show you off."

"I'm not a novelty act, you know." He was now inside the photo pod.

She reached across him and closed the curtains.

Kannada looked at the camera lens with one eyebrow raised while his lady friend, shades on, turned her face and kissed him on his right cheek. The camera flashed.

Looking at the picture reminded Kannada of Amara's desire to make memories, lots of them, often taking selfies, sending them to him, and nagging him that he didn't take enough selfies for her to view.

He put the picture into his wallet, opened the door of the changing room, and stepped out.

A homeless man waiting to use the restroom, playing the music Kannada heard, abruptly turned off his boom box.

"Nice music," Kannada remarked.

"Nice suit," the poor guy said.

"Eh." Kannada shrugged and went on his way.

A few miles away, Rob had reached his destination, the Empire State Building, the headquarters of his hedge fund. On the 81st floor, he sat at one end of an elongated, mahogany oval table, worth several thousands of dollars, in a conference room, viewing a report before him. His closest advisors surrounded him.

Mallory was a sorority girl. Her resume had far more extracurricular activities than career accomplishments, but Rob couldn't say no to her cute smile, nor her rich daddy's money. To Rob's surprise, she worked her way up to a commendable position via assmosis. Bryan the Beard and Bald Bill, yes-men to a fault, were persistent Ivy Leaguers; using bold tactics such as name repetition, personality mirroring, and firm, unbreakable handshakes, they had a way of getting into Rob's head. Karen rounded out the group; she was Chinese and smart. That combination had Rob begging she work for him, as he revered the Asian community.

Having put the demanding trial behind him, Rob thought he could relax. Instead, he became irate; the company report failed his expectations. "Mallory, we didn't see this coming?"

"Well, there's been an accumulation of negative factors." Mallory innocently twisted a lock of her long, glossy hair.

"Explain."

"Poor performance, dwindling investor interest, and an outdated fee structure, according to some in the media."

Rob stared the bearer of bad news down. He didn't like the announcements or her tone.

The woman stared at the papers in front of her. She cowered before the great man.

"Recent market conditions have proven difficult for our short/long-term, middle-market-focused investment strategy." Bald Bill glanced at Mallory, the corners of his mouth turned up.

Mallory smiled as she looked at him.

"Rob," Bryan the Beard said. "Nowadays, investors are interested more in passive investing. Alternatives like robo-advisors, ETFs, and ETNs."

Rob put down his papers and sipped his stress-reducing joe. He felt the sweet, warm liquid run down his red lane and empty into his stomach, soothing his nerves.

"I think it all started nine months ago," Karen said, "when we faced legal charges. The costs to clear the firm from allegations of possible fraud have put a dent in the perception of our fund."

"Nine months ago?" Bryan the Beard sounded incredulous. "It has more to do with our business model. It doesn't fit today's market."

"Well, that wouldn't—" Karen started to argue.

Annoyed, Rob cut off the woman. "Maybe an organizational shift would do the trick."

The advisors froze, their roles and responsibilities on the line.

"Where're we year-to-date?" Rob questioned, in control of the meeting again.

"We've lost twenty-seven percent this year so far, and fourteen percent last month alone." Mallory seemed to have regained her courage.

"How does this compare to the previous year?"

"We only had a four percent return last year."

Rob nodded.

"Some of our portfolio managers are resigning," Bald Bill said. "Anand Kumar is leaving in the next two weeks and Hank Deaton

6

will be out by the end of the month."

Rob looked out the window to his left and saw rain. *Great, now I'm losing quality people.*

"With all due respect, sir," Mallory said, "we don't have any choice but to close down. There has to be a compulsory withdrawal of all investors at the rate we're functioning."

Rob drank his afternoon mocha. Suddenly, it tasted bitter. "Do you have a timetable?"

"We expect to return about eighty percent of investors' money by the end of the third quarter and the rest in the next month," Bryan the Beard said.

Rob made a note of the recent news on his report.

"There's already been a good amount of redemptions from investors," Karen informed. "In fact, Met Jay Pension and Bar Roades Industrial have already pulled out."

Rob sighed, then stood on the two-inch-thick, lush carpet. He walked toward the window to his left, leaving footprints behind, and looked at the many skyscrapers amid lightning, weighing his circumstances, hands in his pants' pockets. *I could jump.*

He felt the board members watching him. "I want to suspend our investors' right to redeem their capital by the end of the week; we don't want everyone pulling out at once."

"That's a good idea," Bald Bill brown-nosed.

"Excellent idea," Bryan the Beard echoed.

Rob noticed the others' reflection in the window. They were nodding in agreement.

"We were planning to file Chapter 11 bankruptcy protection as part of the liquidation process," Karen stated.

"Look, tough market conditions are a part of the game, and we didn't navigate this better?" Disappointed, Rob spun around to face the group.

The boardroom was quiet. Some looked down at the table, while others stared at each other.

Rob returned to the window and viewed his reflection.

"Before we do all that, do we have any other options to pull ourselves out of this hole?"

"Maybe we could diversify more," Bald Bill proposed. "I mean, focusing on global technology, media, and telecommunications is simply not enough. Those sectors have been doing terribly. These are risky bets that were okay last year, but not this year."

There was a moment of silence as Rob considered the proposition.

"We can run through our database of applicants. Some Ivy Leaguers may be interested in joining us and turning the firm around," Mallory suggested.

"They're all the same, useless shit," Rob said, distressed.

The reflection of the Ivy Leaguers in the window showed them looking at each other.

Rob sensed the displeasure generated by his response. "I'm not feeling well. I think I need to get some fresh air."

The soothing sound of a guitar being played by a *Music Under New York* program street performer, rivaling that of professional nature, came and went, as did the decorations, gaudy ceramic tile artwork, mosaics and murals, and sculptures. Kannada weaved through a stagnant crowd in the metro's stuffy corridors, amid the stench of body odor, urine, and dead rats, as a couple of New Yorkers grumbled, "Where's the train?" and made it to the stairwell at the other end. As he walked up the stairs, against light traffic, he came to a halt midway; it was raining. *Just my luck.*

He looked around, thinking of what to do next, and spotted a bright green umbrella next to a man leaning against the wall, preoccupied with his phone. Kannada eyed the sunshade for a moment and bit his lip. He slowly descended the stairs, went to where the man was standing, and nabbed the bumbershoot as he dashed up with the crowd, never once looking back. He stood at ground level at one of the subway stations and opened his new possession as though he were Mary Poppins. At the entrance to the subway, above his head, white letters on a black background read, "Times Square 42 Street Station."

As Kannada set off to the job fair in The City of Dreams, he hesitated to go right, then tried his left; a pair of women sharing an umbrella were coming at him. *Which way do I go?*

"Ah, I want a dog, but it wouldn't be fair to the dog," one woman commented to the other. Their umbrella ran into Kannada's.

"Oh, sorry," he said.

The girls smiled at his handsome appearance; he smiled back. He was the same man that people ignored yesterday. A part of him was grateful for the attention, the other part was frustrated that they judged a book by its cover. It didn't matter; no one could take away a person's spirit. This was what he'd learned living underground.

A few steps later, the clouds ceased their downpour, and the warm, humid air brought by a late summer sun opened his sweat glands. The streets were at a hornless mellow, unusual for this hour, except for a growing ruckus. He craned his neck to the right to observe the distant commotion. The source of his distraction was a group of Occupy Wall Street protesters picketing and striking outside some building. The people-powered movement was still alive in September 2014 but had waned over the years. Only three stooges wallowed in the First Amendment today.

A short, stocky man repeatedly shouted as a few executives walked out of the building. "Whose street?"

The other two demonstrators completed the chant. "Our Street!"

The executives made a break for their chauffeured vehicles and ignored the hecklers.

Kannada didn't think much of the uproar and its purpose. *Does protesting even work? Do the rich even care?*

Times Square sprang up. In the most densely populated region of America, Kannada was missing the personal space he had moments ago as Manhattanites rushed to get somewhere, overrunning intersections and sidewalks, bumping into one another. *Ugh, New York.* Carefree tourists hindered his path, as they gawked at all the colorful, fluorescent signs of multinational corporations—Coca-Cola, McDonald's, Samsung—on the strip as though it were a national holiday. *Yeah, New York.*

Kannada studied the flyer for the career fair as he walked resolutely down the street. Upon seeing the several industries that would be present, he became hopeful. It seemed like all of New York, from mom-and-pop delis to fashion and modeling agencies, was ready to hire. He paused at an intersection and looked at the street signs to determine the fastest route to his destination.

Rob vented his courtroom rage and boardroom despair to his friend Niles, another hedgie, over the phone as he strode down the sidewalk.

"Fuck Lemon! We're planning to shut down. Two years in, and we're already finished."

"It's okay," Niles said. "Hedge funds have been closing down everywhere amid poor performance. People are saying they may become obsolete in a couple of years."

Rob bumped into a man's shoulder and continued onto the road, unaware of the crosswalk signal. "Yeah, well, my investors—"

"Watch out!" a man yelled.

A car's horn honked repeatedly, and Rob snapped out of his trance. His eyes dilated, and his heart fluttered, as the yellow taxi charged at him. A stranger pulled back Rob in the nick of time— another moment and he would've become roadkill. Rob and his savior hit the ground hard, and Rob watched the cabbie from Where-the-Fuckistan zoom away.

"Are you crazy? That car almost flattened you!"

Confused, Rob ran his fingers through his own dark brown, curly hair then stared at the stranger, a well-dressed, good-looking man with onyx eyes and an imaginary halo over his head. "Thanks." Rob was still in shock. "Oh my God, you saved my life."

"Yeah, yeah, you would've done the same for me."

"No . . . I wouldn't." *I'm not that heroic.*

The stranger raised one eyebrow and frowned. "You should really watch where you're going. First, you bump into me. Then you jaywalk." He picked up his closed, bright green umbrella.

"Sorry . . . I was somewhere else in my head." Rob looked for his phone but couldn't find it.

The stranger stood and extended his hand. "Come on."

Rob hoisted himself up with the man's assistance, though he could easily have done so without it, and readjusted his Star of David necklace, as he recalled the higher power that ultimately saved him. He glanced around at the surrounding bystanders, who resumed their business as though nothing had happened.

The stranger dusted off his black suit and leather satchel and straightened his red tie.

An unfamiliar feeling of indebtedness bound Rob. He put his hand out and introduced himself.

The stranger shook his hand. "Kannada." He started to walk.

"Wait!" Rob couldn't let him off that easy; he was used to having the upper hand in everything, especially in providing gifts and favors, as most people were not as well-off financially as him. He stood face-to-face with Kannada. "I owe you one."

"Don't worry about it."

"Let me at least buy you a beer, or lunch, or something."

"Uh, I'm kind of busy right now."

"Dinner. Anywhere you want." *That should make us even, I think. He saves my life. I give him a free meal.*

Kannada smiled, and they exchanged emails.

CHAPTER 2

Long Island, New York

Its market value was $90 million, in stark contrast to the $21-million price tag he paid two years ago. For sellers, the collapse of the housing bubble was a nightmare waiting to happen. For buyers, it was manna from heaven.

The property rested on eight acres of serenity in Great Neck, New York, twenty-five miles from Manhattan, as Gatsby-esque as one could get. It was a sixty-thousand square foot chateau articulated with twelve bedrooms and thirty-three bathrooms and besieged by a dense forest and beautiful plants. It had a private pier that could accompany a two-hundred-foot yacht, and did accompany a yacht, multiple swimming pools, several fountains with white marble statues, and an indoor lazy river. Gargoyle lampposts lit the pietra dura styled stone pathways as gargoyle statues watched. It possessed a magnificent garden with a birdbath fountain as its centerpiece. A tennis court outside and a ballroom, bowling alley, and casino inside capped off this masterpiece. No one knew that Rob lived here.

In his great living room, Rob lounged in a single-person sofa chair with his feet on an ottoman. He held a glass of brandy in his right hand, which rested on top of a built-in coaster in the chair's armrest, as he watched television.

A white-haired news correspondent reminiscent of the late Walter Cronkite in appearance was seated on a wooden stool in a black room on the other side of the glass surface. "On this week's segment of 'Where Are They Now?' on *Weekly News*," the news correspondent said, "We caught up with some of Caldwell Investments' victims, both employees and clients, five years after Wendell Caldwell topped Bernie Madoff and committed the largest Ponzi scheme in history. First, we'll speak to Walker Mays, a former worker who has had his fair share of trouble after the collapse."

The screen changed to a bright living room in which the news anchor sat across from the interviewee, a black, athletic man with a goatee. "Tell me. What was your previous position with the firm?"

"Well, I was a stockbroker down at the Exchange." Walker had a deep voice.

"The New York Stock Exchange?"

"Yes."

"And how much were you making?"

Walker hesitated. "About one-hundred thirty K."

"That's quite impressive."

The subject nodded.

"After Caldwell Investments went down, where did everyone go?"

"Nowhere in particular, but one of my colleagues was homeless last time I checked."

The interrogator nodded, arms crossed, holding his chin with his left hand. "And what about you?"

"Well, it's been difficult recovering, but I found something."

"What's that?"

"I'm a personal trainer."

"Wow! A personal trainer. Look at you, that's great! You've certainly rebounded."

The interviewee smiled. "Mmm hmm."

Rob chuckled.

The display suddenly returned to the black backdrop with the interviewer seated on the wooden stool. "And there you have it, a man once managing portfolios and earning six figures is now developing bodies and producing six-packs. When we return, we'll be speaking to a few of Wendell Caldwell's other victims, his former clients, and see how they're doing now."

Rob's twenty-four-hour analog wristwatch read 19:11. *Where is this guy?*

Kannada arrived at Rob's tony estate in the evening, courtesy of a driver arranged by the burly man. He gaped at the pearly gates, the well-groomed gardens, and the gray stone mansion as he rolled up to the front door.

A butler, an elderly man with Harry Potter glasses and white hair and whiskers, greeted him with a Cheshire Cat smile. As Kannada followed the butler through the elaborately decorated hallways, he paused at the sight of a contemporary sculpture. A bird with ribbons for wings and a transparent cube for a head flew under an umbrella attached to its nape. He sighed. *All Greek to me.*

They moved into the high-ceiling dining area, where Rob met him and apologized for his wife's absence. The fat man—in wealth and size—sat across from Kannada at a long wooden table and made small talk as the butler prepared their meals.

"Did you have trouble finding the driver?" Rob asked.

Despite his even demeanor and John Goodman appearance, Rob's accent had been conjuring up the image of Tony Soprano for some time. "No . . . I haven't had a good home-cooked meal for a while."

"You travel a lot for work?"

"Yeah." *Only in New York.*

The butler approached. "Would you like some wine?"

"Uh, yeah, sure," Kannada said.

As the butler filled his glass, Rob stood, walked toward the fireplace, and uncovered a small rectangular box from behind a portrait on the wall. *Interesting*, Kannada thought. The large man removed a stogie from the humidor and returned things to normal. He lit the cigar with a lighter from his pocket as the butler went back into the kitchen.

Rob faced Kannada. "You smoke?"

"Only second hand."

The high roller took a puff of his cigar. "Ah, that feels good."

"Stressful day?"

"You could say that."

"What happened?"

The cigar aficionado hesitated, then took a drag and loosened up. "I lost to my rival." He shook his head then turned toward the fireplace, his back facing Kannada; smoke rose. "David Lemon. The Chairman and CEO of the New York Stock Exchange."

Kannada remained quiet.

"He's a hedge fund giant, the leader of Lemon Group, and a real ugly son of a bitch," Rob continued. "He's always one step, or rather several steps, ahead of me. I just don't get it." He shook his head as he walked from one end of the fireplace to the other.

"Well, there's always someone better than you," Kannada said. "I heard that guy was a charitable man."

"Yeah, after stealing from people like me." Rob snickered. He tapped his cigar with his fingers, and ashes fell into the fireplace. "I've been relishing the chance to make lemonade out of that bastard since he outbid me for some newly laid fiber-optic cables, traded ahead." He sounded livid. "More like stabbed me in the back. The deal was made after I officially won the auction. Now he'll get the trades I want faster and sell them back to me at higher prices. My hedge fund can't compete; we're due to shut down in a few months. In this business, if you're not first, you're last."

Kannada said nothing. The Tony Soprano in Rob came out. The hedgie seemed to be a man plagued by a nervous tic; he'd been talking since Kannada entered the dining area. Perhaps it was the roller coaster nature of the market racket. Perhaps it was the frenzied lifestyle and extravagant Gatsby-like parties akin to those 1920s ones on the nearby East and West Eggs. Regardless, it made Kannada feel comfortable; even rich folks had problems.

Rob turned around and faced his guest. "Pardon me. Sometimes I start talking and don't stop. I shouldn't have burdened you with my troubles." He sighed. "You never mentioned what you do."

Kannada hesitated, wanting to lie. "I . . . sell tomatoes, hustle." He couldn't brag about or fabricate his status as easily as he once did; poverty had humbled him.

Rob narrowed his eyes. "Like at a bodega?" He put the cigar back into his mouth.

"More like on the side of the road. I'm . . . out of work."

"Ah. Well, we all got bills to pay."

"Uh, yeah . . ."

"What part of town you stay?"

Kannada avoided eye contact and wavered. *Should I tell him?* "The subway." A feeling of relief swept over him; saying that took courage.

With furrowed brows and an open mouth, Rob stared then exhaled smoke. He looked away, out the window, and appeared to dismiss his guest's words. "That's kind of hard to believe. Homeless people don't wear suits, nor do they look as sharp as you do." He glanced at Kannada. "And I say that with staunch heterosexuality."

Kannada chuckled.

"That's a sweet suit. How much do you make selling tomatoes?"

"I cleaned up for a job fair today. That's where I was going this morning."

"A job fair? Those things don't work. Some of my businesses make appearances and give a good face. We get tons of resumes and toss them out the door."

Kannada was annoyed. "I know they don't work, but I have to try something."

Rob nodded, his brows furrowed. He looked toward Kannada's satchel. "Do you have any resumes in there?"

Kannada glanced at his bag on the table. "Yeah, I have a few." He opened his sack and sifted through the papers for a précis of his life as Rob discarded his cigar in the fireplace and reoccupied his chair.

"Hold on. One second." Kannada continued to search his bag anxiously as Rob waited. The cigar's lingering scent was good. *Maybe I should start smoking.* He took out a stack of papers.

"What's all that?" Rob asked.

"Nothing. Just my work."

"That's a lot of paperwork for selling tomatoes."

Kannada looked up and laughed. "I've been trying to write a book." He returned to his bag.

"I have a friend who published a novel; writing a book and getting it out there is a lengthy process."

"Yeah, I know."

Rob remained quiet as the papers ruffled in Kannada's bag. "What's the genre?"

"It's a financial thriller."

"Oh, what's it about?"

"It's a heist on the New York Stock Exchange."

"How can you rob the NYSE? There's no money."

"It's a long story." Kannada didn't want to bore the man. "Here." He handed Rob a resume.

Rob glanced over the document then sighed. "Hmm. Math background, yeah, this isn't bad. I'll tell you what your problem is. You have a big employment gap. Don't tell me you've been selling tomatoes for over a decade."

"I used to work for Caldwell Investments as an I-banker. I left it off since, you know, the Ponzi scheme."

"I always wondered how he kept getting good returns for his clients." Rob shook his head and returned the resume. "So, what made you want to write a book?"

Kannada looked at the table then faced Rob. "When you can't find a way, create one. That's kind of how the main character functions." Kannada put the paper into his satchel. "He recruits a group of people and tries to get into the NYSE. Ultimately, they jack a bunch of securities and flip the shares for a profit." His ego jumped, bucked, and kicked like an untamed rodeo bull for Rob's attention, as most people ignored him. He held back the details to avoid going off on a tangent even more.

The hedgie's eyes lit up. "How?"

Kannada sighed. "That's the long part."

Rob looked toward a grandfather clock in the corner. He faced his guest with glowing eyes. "No, I want to hear this. It's the least I could do for you saving my life."

Kannada smiled and expressed his pent-up enthusiasm as the butler brought them dinner.

One hour later, Kannada asked, "So, what'd you think? Bush league, right?"

With a wrench in his hand, Rob rolled out from underneath the hood of a forest green 1938 Chevrolet Master Coupe in a dimly lit, oversized garage. He appraised the plot carefully and blindly stared at Kannada who was leaning on a car, arms and legs crossed.

"No, that's . . . ingenious."

"Oh." Kannada sounded surprised. "It's unconventional, I guess."

"Yeah," Rob said slowly. *This is my solution.* "Don't lean on that car."

Kannada followed orders.

"This kind of thing isn't in the playbook. You'd make some good trades, someone would try to steal your traders. Wine and dine. But this . . . this is something else." Rob rushed his words.

The broke author grinned.

Rob envisioned a sucker on a stick replace Kannada's head and neck, then searched the floor. "I want to make you an offer."

"For what?"

"Your book."

Kannada's eyebrows rose. "My book?"

"I want to make it a reality."

"Well, I'm flattered, but . . . I haven't typed it up yet."

"No, no, no. I want to do it—put the rubber to the road. It's perfect."

Kannada tipped his head to the side and scrunched his eyebrows together.

Rob looked down. "Of course, nothing ever goes to plan, but a few tweaks along the way, and we're good." He confidently looked at his answer, waiting for a response.

Kannada maintained his confused facial expression. "Um . . . okay."

"Look, you have the experience, you know what you're talking about, and the heist makes sense. I'll be your sleeping partner—not literally." He needed to be clear; being gay on Wall Street was frowned upon. "By the end of this, I'll have recouped my entire investment, and then some."

Kannada's brows rose then came down and joined together. "Look, Mr. Wonderful. That sounds great, but who's going to do all of this?"

Rob grinned at his recognition of Kevin O'Leary, a business magnate on *Shark Tank* and a friend. "You're the one who'll do it. You told me you were looking for a job. Well, here it is."

Kannada glanced at the many cars, antique and modern, lined opposite one another.

"At the Friars Club, a few weeks ago, my friend Niles mentioned that he took a chance on some po'boy to resurface his hedge fund," Rob reflected. "He said if someone like you came along, it was up to me to take a risk. Well, I'm ready to go out on a limb."

"You'll get caught and go to jail."

"That won't happen." *At least not for me. Minimal involvement, my lawyers, I'm okay.*

"There're NoGo blocks, Delta barriers, and cameras, everywhere. The NYSE has enough security to arm the Great Wall of China."

Rob flashed a toothy grin.

"Okay, maybe not that much, but everything's tracked at multiple sources and the damn SEC will hunt your ass down!"

Rob smirked at his thought of the Securities and Exchange Commission. *The SEC? Fuck them.* "I used to sit on the board at the NYSE a few years ago and know a thing or two about its security."

"But still, I don't know where everything is inside."

"That's the least of our problems. I'm in the business of real estate," Rob pushed. "I have access to the Surrogate's Courthouse building, where the NYC Municipal Archives are."

With a wrinkled nose, Kannada raised one eyebrow and the corner of his mouth below the lower eyebrow.

Rob connected the dots for him. "I can get the floor plans to the Big Board."

Kannada smirked. "I don't know . . . It's not possible. We'd have to anticipate everything. The markets are won by those who know what'll happen before it happens."

"I agree." Rob envisioned gaining revenge against Lemon with Kannada's story as the smell of black oil and harsh chemicals reached his nose.

"You're pissing in the wind. It's too risky."

"Well, it's your opportunity to take."

The bait paused before responding. "Let me guess. You have too much money and you're looking for the next adventure."

"Far from it. The riskiest thing I've ever done was get married."

Kannada rolled his eyes and snickered. "Yeah, that's pretty risky."

"It's crazy, I swear." Rob leaned over and spoke earnestly. "I have no freedom."

Kannada nodded as Rob returned to his normal posture. "Look, positivity and hope are wonderful drugs. It makes people believe they can do anything." He shook his head.

Rob fought back. "And doubt kills more aspirations than failure ever will. I can see why you're homeless now. It's your attitude."

Kannada had met his match and stared at Rob. He chided his new friend. "You can't be serious."

Someone opened the door to the garage. "I smell smoke in the house, Rob. Believe me, you'll get cancer," Rob's wife yelled with a Long Island accent.

"Cancer my ass," Rob shouted back.

The wife slammed the door close.

Rob put down the wrench, leaned forward, and sighed. "You see what I mean?"

Kannada nodded.

"How'd you come up with that idea?" Rob asked.

"I have a lot of time on my hands."

Rob observed his hands; there was a lot of lubricant on his. He started to wipe the grease off his chubby fingers with a blue towel while considering Kannada's fictitious plans. He shook his head repeatedly, rubbing harder and harder to get the oily residue off his hands, as his wife's prudent nature came to mind. She was a good complement to his hasty personality. He sighed.

"I may have jumped the gun earlier, but you're underestimating what you have—the payout has size, real size." Rob paused with a face of disappointment. "I'll run this past my lawyers and I think they'll agree with me. If you can assemble some people like yourself, nothing to lose, this can actually happen."

Kannada grinned and stared at him. "I don't get your angle, Rob."

Rob rubbed his fingers together and felt a trace of grease. He stood for the first time. "Look, it's for a noble cause. Lemon deserves his fate."

With slightly puckered lips, Kannada slanted his eyebrows inward and moved his mouth to the side, creating a crease in his cheek. He turned to leave down the long, domed parking lot decorated with colorful, fancy cars of every kind that spoke of the man's status in this island of money.

"Hold up!" Rob yelled. He removed a few Fast Orange wipes from a cylindrical container that rested on the trunk of the car he was working on. "You're right. Publishers are probably dying to get a hold of your manuscript. It most likely doesn't need to be edited, but what do I know?" Rob's latest comment stopped Kannada dead in his tracks. "You could go to a commercial publisher, and hope they accept your plot. That'll take a few years and a lot of luck. Or, you could believe in the Magic of Niles, and see where that takes you in a few months."

Kannada turned around. He grinned, waved one last goodbye, and began to walk down the hallway toward the garage door.

"Where're you going?" Rob asked.

"Back to shaking a can."

"Wait!" Rob yelled. He realized this man wasn't lying about being homeless earlier.

Kannada stopped.

"When I started out twenty-five years ago, my father gave me one million dollars, not much by today's standards, to make something of myself. I know what it's like." Rob and his silver spoon met an unpopular stare. "Sort of. All you need is the right people."

Kannada nodded slowly. "And where're you going to get this dream team?"

Rob finished wiping his hands, placed the towelettes on the Chevrolet's rear, and walked toward the man who was warming up to him. "You'll find and recruit them."

"Me?" Kannada sounded shocked.

"Well, it's your story, not mine. I can't get involved; I'm too busy with my real estate holdings and hedge fund." Kannada looked away as Rob continued. "I have a rental property in the Plaza that's hard to find a tenant for; we could use it."

Kannada glanced at Rob, then looked away again.

"Contingent on my lawyers' approval, I'll even give you a weekly paycheck for your headhunting efforts until about Thanksgiving; that's three months' pay. I'll supply you with a cell phone and you'll be employed. Tell me who you get, and I'll confirm."

"You'll pay me?"

Rob nodded with a Grinch-like smile. "Mmm hmm."

The prey's eyes drifted to the floor.

"Think about it," Rob said.

After a pause, Kannada looked up with narrow eyes. "I have."

CHAPTER 3

Manhattan, New York

Later that evening, after meeting Rob, Kannada returned to Manhattan and walked up the four stairs leading to the welcoming doorway of the world's best bar, the Dead Rabbit Grocery and Grog. The green-trimmed, heavy glass door stood propped open, next to a porch with a wooden bench laced with green seat cushions and under two flags, one for the tavern and one for the country.

When his ears heard the bustle of the market news circulating the noisy room, every nerve became attentive as if he were ready to trade down at the NYSE. As he looked around, a feeling of loneliness took hold of him for a moment; every person appeared to belong to some faction.

Nevertheless, he dove headfirst into the drinking room and listened to the buzz generated by people, his kind of people. All these traders and market specialists were talking a good game, sharing tips and stories. He absorbed all of it, the sight of wealthy high rollers chugging down shots, the sound of glasses hitting each other, the smell of alcohol, the feeling of the fast-life returning, and the taste of intoxicating beverages that could have a man taking the riskiest, most daring trades ever.

He made his way through the crowd and took a seat on a bar

stool. A waitress possessing a cute face and massive boobs greeted him with a smile from behind the bar, and Kannada ordered, undistracted. As she prepared his beverage, Kannada pulled out his wallet and extracted a crisp bill, careful not to tip or pay more than necessary, as his budget was limited to tomato sales. He tossed the money onto the mahogany and saw it replaced with the desired glass of alcohol; she stared at him with her mouth closed, void of emotion.

Kannada grasped the cocktail, a Manhattan, and the ice banged against the glass as if the opening bell had just been rung. He walked back past a group of friends goofing off, and settled at a table for two, on which a newspaper lay.

Kannada perused a folded-back copy of *The Wall Street Journal* as he searched for someone. He covertly listened to conversations not meant to be heard, determining what would be a good bet to make.

"L.M. Barrels Bank will be heading up soon," a man commented.

No, it wouldn't. Its financials were in the red after the recent acquisition of an insolvent bank. It would take a few years for it to be where it used to be.

"Buy arms and defense contractors," another man stated.

That was a terrible idea. The war was over. If anything, a couple of put options would be worth something.

"Oil's a good bet," a woman mentioned.

Maybe. The oil industry was cyclical. It could still go down, though it had already hit rock bottom in 2009.

Kannada knew how the markets worked. Was there any doubt? The calculating brain of one of the best had been restored.

A second bartender, blue-eyed and blond, joined the first and started serving drinks. Kannada recognized him as Paul Hansen and smiled. He was Kannada's old trading pal and the man who helped him land a job in New York several years ago.

"The usual, Tommy?" Paul asked an approaching patron taking a seat.

"You read me like a book." The customer sounded elated.

"One black velvet coming up." Moments later, Paul produced the beer cocktail.

This Norwegian bartender's customer service made him a gem in the best bar in New York. People flocked to this watering hole not just for the drinks and service but for an unfair advantage.

The Bull Option

Kannada continued to peer over his newspaper from a distance as Paul cleaned behind the counter.

As Paul wiped the bar top with a rag, a thick man with a scar over his lip grabbed a seat at the bar away from the other customers. The man directed Paul with his head, and Paul stared, an uneasy warmth coursing through his body, before tending to him.

"Here's a little extra." The man winked and slipped Paul a couple of hundred-dollar bills.

As Paul turned around to fix the man's usual, he viewed the reflection of the people behind in the bar's mirror. The coast was clear. Paul faced *his* customer, drink in hand.

"Kingdot Games beat its second quarter estimates for EPS. They'll announce it the day after tomorrow," Paul said.

The requester of insider trading information grinned and nodded.

Paul resumed his cleaning duties at the other end of the tavern. A few minutes later, the shadow of someone cropped up on the bar top.

"Hello, Paul," the person said.

Paul Hansen, the assisting bartender, glanced up at the man who addressed him, making eye contact with a face of bemusement. He squinted, like an old man with poor vision trying to make out the words on a newspaper. He looked away, skeptical. He didn't want to offend the patron by mistaking him for his old friend, Kannada.

"What's on the beat?" the man asked, as the music from the DJ played.

Paul recognized Kannada's signature line for acquiring insider information as a pair of male police officers, who looked out of place compared to the other customers, grabbed seats next to Kannada and stared hard at Paul.

Taking note of the boys in blue, Paul quickly rebounded for a sharp response. "What happened? Extreme Makeover: Kannada edition?"

His friend laughed.

"Where'd the beard go? And this suit?" Paul was wide-eyed. "You're welcoming my customers rather than scaring them away like last time."

Kannada smiled. "When's your shift over?"

"Midnight. Are you going to stick around?"

"Yeah."

"Outside?"

"Sounds good."

Paul wanted to continue the discussion, but with cops nearby and maybe even a few others undercover, a bartender sharing information he had inadvertently picked up? That was a huge no-no for anybody in this town. It was a life ender, whether you received it or gave it.

"I'll see you in a few," Kannada said.

Paul nodded.

Kannada had a couple of hours to kill. He stuck around, trying a few different drinks, flirting with the female bartender.

The Taproom of the nineteenth-century tavern on the ground floor served craft beer, whiskeys of the world, and bottled punch in a colloquial setting. Opposite the bar's taps, artwork from large murals to smaller framed pictures decorated the soft white walls. Midway down, the art gave way to dark wood panels that met the rich brown carpet. The ceiling had original wooden beams covered in mostly black-and-white photos of Americans from long ago. The bartender's table stretched long with attractive servers and shelves of glassware on one side and brown, padded bar stools on the other.

A similar layout, except for a change in colors and long-plank flooring in place of carpet, transcended the floors, first with the Parlor, then the Occasional Room even higher. The sumptuous Parlor focused on communal punch and served several cocktails, seating guests on brown upholstery to the tune of whoever wanted to play the piano.

Kannada made it up to the Occasional Room and reminisced on his past as he walked around aimlessly. The Occasional Room was equipped with ideal audio-visual amenities for private events, training seminars, and after-work team-building parties—events Kannada had attended when he used to work around these parts. The Room kept up with the nineteenth-century atmosphere, with interiors inspired by traditional whiskey distilleries.

There was a cozy feeling about this joint, sheltering New Yorkers from the frigid cold or even the melting heat. It was a place where people could unwind, loosen their ties, and be themselves. It was like *Cheers* all over again.

Kannada returned to the Parlor, opened his wallet, viewed the picture of him and Amara taken in the photo booth, and brooded for a moment.

Hearing a glass drop and break, he snapped out of his longing for her and put his wallet away. Recalling that his watch had stopped working, a seated Kannada asked the last patron in the Parlor in passing, "Excuse me, sir. Do you have the time?"

"Ten 'til midnight."

"Thanks."

"No problem."

He went down and checked the long table nearby in the Taproom. Half-a-dozen tired corporate wigs rested at the bar while a young woman covered in several layers of makeup growing up too quickly tended to them.

The conversations were a low mumble at best interspersed with lengthy yawns. Only a few night owls kept the drinks-a-coming. *Sure, you have work tomorrow, but you people aren't unemployed and homeless. Cheer up.*

Maybe the set of first college exams during the fall semester infected the southern tip of Manhattan as it had other college towns, changing the environment from youthful exuberance to hackneyed fatigue, bringing in adults who were too old to keep up with the city.

Whatever happened to The City That Never Sleeps, The Capital of the World? Where were all the big players?

The financial world of yesterday had been dying thanks to the speed of computers and automated trading while he was underground. Maybe their eyes were tired of staring at screens.

Kannada made his way outside and nursed his cocktail on a bench with green seat cushions in front of one of the bar's windows. He stared into the glass and sighed at his watershed moment. *Are you sure you want to go through with this?* The thought of doing the unthinkable sent chills up his spine. *Don't think. The more you think about it, the more you'll talk yourself out of it. You can do this; it's only in your mind that you can't.* Regardless of his pep talk, doubt filled the void, the silence that had the answers.

"I thought you died and went to hell," a man's voice said.

Kannada turned his attention toward the man. Sitting next to him was Paul Hansen, the late arrival, no drinks in his hand.

"The devil forgives," Kannada quipped.

"Ready to make money the old-fashioned way?" Paul said.

Kannada smiled and hesitated. "Ready to take money a new way." The words were out of his mouth; now all he had to do was walk the walk.

Paul looked Kannada over then stared at his nearly empty glass. "Back on the stock market roller coaster."

Kannada grinned.

"How've you been holding up?"

"All right," Kannada said. "What about you? Still on the lookout for cops?"

Paul sighed. "With the crackdown on insider trading, every moment." He shook his head. "The tips are nice, but how else can I compete against all these Wall Street sharks?"

"When's the last time they busted you?"

"I'd rather not remember."

Kannada rolled his eyes. He already knew why Paul was sweating bullets every time he saw the police. It had to do with Paul's history. If Paul wasn't careful with whom he spoke to, he'd be hanging out with the hobos in Central Park.

Paul heard things, lots of things being in Manhattan, and banked on that knowledge. That was why he worked only part-time, and that was for the camaraderie and his interest in knowing every mixture possible.

The bartender was the perfect ally to get an unfair advantage. There were strict rules for making sure he didn't act as an intermediary to Wall Street hawks. Any scratches pertaining to the markets on a prospective employee's resume could get him struck from the list of trusted insiders.

"You look like you're back on your feet," Paul said. "Where do you stay now?"

"Same old place." Kannada watched a pair of patrons exit the bar to his right.

Paul lowered his head and frowned. "My apartment's still open."

"I think I'll take you up on that offer for a while."

"What'd you do today?"

"Oh, the usual, save a hedgie's life and get repaid with a job that requires me to break every law. You?"

Paul grinned.

Kannada sipped the whiskey and sweet vermouth drink with a dash of bitters and drained his glass clean. He stared at a couple of people smoking across the street as Paul watched him.

Kannada smiled at his friend, then placed his glass on the armrest. "Let's take a walk, Paul." For some unknown reason, the more he contemplated his plans, the more he believed in them and himself.

Kannada and Paul walked out to Battery Park, a few minutes away on the southern edge of Manhattan, catching up on old times. Kannada had the gait of a financially independent man, at ease, viewing the lampposts and benches along the Hudson River like a tourist.

"So, what're you going to do, hit the bid?" Paul was standing, arms crossed, backside against the railing.

"I could just pocket the money and skip town," Kannada said.

"That's not a bad idea. Take the bonus and leave."

Kannada and Paul shared a laugh.

After they regained their composure, Paul said, "You're living off dreams."

"Ha," Kannada said. "The poorer you get, the bigger your dreams. Five years and no real job prospects, can you believe that?"

Paul studied him. "Nothing to lose, right?"

Kannada met his stare indifferently, then looked away. Of course, he had nothing to lose. "I can't keep selling tomatoes on the side of the road. And slinging hash or working the register at Duane Reade won't cut it. It's not who I am."

Paul nodded. "Getting the same advantage as Wall Street has isn't worth it. Believe me. You know my history."

Kannada grinned faintly.

Paul turned around to face the ocean; he put his hands on the railing. "It's more challenging now, cheating the system." He studied the waters in the distance. "Too much regulation, too much automation. Main Street just can't catch a break."

"Maybe." A gust of wind smelling like clams, scallops, and metal hit Kannada's face.

He also peered over the railing; a few chips bags floated in the unattractive, dark water. Kannada shook his head vigorously, as the alcoholic beverage coupled with the ocean waves made him nauseous. He looked up and vaguely discerned what appeared to be a lit boat. There wasn't much to see at this hour.

Paul remained quiet.

"I know it's crazy, but . . .." Kannada said.

"It's not totally absurd. Word is the NYSE is hiring for bug bounties," Paul said.

Kannada's motion sickness disappeared; there was rationality in his response. "Yeah." He narrowed his eyes on the distant object. *Maybe the Statue of Liberty; it hadn't moved for a while. Ellis Island wasn't too far off.*

"When?" Paul inquired, finally.

"A few months." A late-night runner passed behind Kannada. *Definitely the statue.* "Let me tell you how it'll happen."

Paul smiled, nodded, and occasionally probed and summarized the plan to understand Kannada's intentions, as they continued to walk along the riverfront, passing *The Sphere* sculpture. They gradually left the park and came to a halt near the split in the street.

"There's one problem. I need people," Kannada said, frustrated.

"He was freezing his ass off in the Windy City last I heard," Paul said, "running some schemes on penny stocks."

"Who?"

"Ben Wu. He could help you assemble a team."

Life always had a way of rearranging itself for one's destiny, and Kannada's fortune was already changing.

"So, you in?" Kannada said.

Paul laughed and smiled.

Kannada had the response he wanted.

"You're going to need him more than ever," Paul said.

Kannada smiled. "I know. He's the network."

The *Charging Bull* sitting in the cobblestoned fork of Broadway and Canyon of the Heroes accentuated the close of their conversation and the opening of a new chapter in Kannada's life.

CHAPTER 4

Chicago, Illinois

Kannada departed an Uber ride in suburban Oak Brook, then stared at a four-story brown building with tinted windows under cloudy skies. It was situated in a beautiful, cozy area of west Chicago surrounded by tall trees, flower beds, and groves of bushes in the heart of a couple of rare apartment complexes, and was occupied by Bright Future Investments, LLC, an international boiler room operation.

The pleasant environment didn't fool him; he knew what went on inside, as he had some experience with sleazy joints. This innocent-looking building was where the stock, real and fictitious, of micro-caps was sold, such as those that traded on the Pink Sheets or the over-the-counter bulletin board, as both these exchanges required little in terms of disclosure and regulation.

His friend, Ben Wu, worked in the building, most likely in an inexpensive office space, where armies of young, naïve telemarketers hoping to realize visions of Scrooge-like pools of green paper and gold coins cold called unsuspecting, innocent Americans and Europeans out of phone directories.

He frowned at the thought of the workers. Most of the salespeople and brokers weren't even qualified to work in the securities industry, but that didn't stop them from using high-pressure sales tactics and providing false or misleading information to hype their products. They'd go to great lengths to swindle folks to sell the coveted stock and claim too-good-to-be-true commissions.

How'd Ben get involved with this garbage? Kannada took a deep breath and walked toward the entrance. He opened the glass door and headed for the elevator at the end of the long foyer.

Ben was on the phone with his top button undone and a loose tie, taking up residence in a chair near the front of an office. He'd been lying to customers since the morning and was weary, given that he had skipped lunch today. He viewed those seated around him with half-open eyes as he waited for the person on the other end of the line to finish complaining.

An aging Hebrew legend, the team's leader, a senior broker, sat at a desk orthogonal to two long tables, one of which was Ben's. Sales from the group at his station went to him. These other people were just making his name. His tongue was perverted, to say the least, spitting out racial and sexual epithets whenever he found an opening. Anyone had to be able to take that kind of rousing to work here. He liked to take the other members out to strip joints and bars, and even had escorts visit them. It kept them happy, blind to what they were doing.

Inexperienced newcomers occupied three of the other seats in this deceptive and coercive scam. The first held a twenty-something-year-old Italian playboy, who was there for one reason—women. He operated under the notion that more money equated to more women. The second chair held a black man—had to have one of those around to meet the company's quota, according to management. The last of the trio was a knucklehead Irishman who needed the money to pay off the cops every time he got into nosebleed fights with some rival at Chicago's crazy bars.

"Hey, listen to me. Listen to me. You don't want to sell a stock when it's down. Buy high, sell low? You'll never make money like that," Ben talked into his phone. He turned to his right, where a rookie, the sixth punk, Jason Capers, had his table set perpendicular to the two parallel ones that held the other four. The Hebrew legend sat across from him at the other end.

Ben leaned over and instructed. "Is that the bitch? Remember, if

31

they don't have balls, they're not worth the calls."

Jason nodded, smirking.

"Ma'am, is your husband, Mr. Howard, home? . . . Yes, I'll wait," the wannabe broker said.

"There you go. Stay in the game. Trust me; you won't regret it," Ben said on his line. "Talk to you later. Buh-bye."

"When he gets on, fill him with piss and vinegar. Give him more wood than a porn star could," Ben taught again.

Jason was the baby-faced kid in the group. He hadn't even finished college. Working for a hotshot guy, the Hebrew legend, could make him feel he had promise. Jason was here to learn the ropes, as he was a rube being introduced to a cold world run by ruthless greed. The Series 7 was all Jason needed to be a real broker. He hung with the financial-minded whenever possible, learning, calculating, and networking all the time.

"Hey, Mr. Howard, how're you doing today? . . . Great, my name's Jason Capers, and I'm vice-president of Bright Future Investments"—he was picking the game up fast—"and do I have something for you."

While Jason continued his sales call, Ben began to go over some company's prospectus that he would send out later. He leaned over again to Jason, listening.

"Oh, you're not interested," Jason said.

"Tell him to hold," Ben whispered.

"Can you hold for one second? . . . Thanks," Jason said.

"No, no, no," Ben murmured, shaking his head in disappointment. "What the fuck are you doing, asshole? You're going to get a lot of rejection; it's part of the job. You can't give up that easily. Keep the dickhead on the line. Say whatever you have to to turn a buck."

Jason grinned, but the corners of his mouth stayed down. "All right, all right, I got it."

Ben stared at him coldly. "Don't give me that damn lip; I'm teaching you how to fish, and your ass better learn how to survive. Understand?"

Jason nodded. He was new but knew when to get serious and take orders. The newb had a good hold on which clients to chase, the whales who could bring in the money, but still needed refinement to have the presence of a smooth operator.

"Let me see the phone," Ben said impatiently.

Jason took Mr. Howard off hold, ready to learn. It wasn't about putting in the effort; it was about being clever. Jason watched as Ben put Mr. Howard on speakerphone.

"Mr. Howard. Thanks for waiting. My apologies," Ben said. "Let me ask you something. Do you have any kids?"

"Why yes, I do," Mr. Howard answered.

"Great, I do, too. Let me fill you in on what lies ahead. I love kids. But, you know what? They're expensive, and they get even more costly when we try to get them out of the house. College, you know what I'm talking about?"

"Yes, you're right."

"The cost is going through the roof today. I mean, what are these politicians planning to do? Nothing, like always. But, there's a way, a better way, and I'm going to show you." Ben had Mr. Howard's attention. "This stock here that I'm showing you today is what you're looking for. The company is Com Coffee. It's the next Starbucks."

"Well, I'm sort of in the middle of something right now, have a couple of friends over. Plus, I'm not in the market for that kind of thing."

"And that's why you're sweating bullets for your child's education; am I right?"

"Well, actually, yes."

"Look, it doesn't have to be that way. I wouldn't be telling you this today if it wasn't for my own child's sake. This stock could blow any time now. I put my money down for my kids—you know why? Because I know. I know. And I want you to know. You want your children to succeed, don't you?"

"Well, I was planning on taking out a HELOC, so I don't need to invest."

"A Home Equity Line of Credit? Why?"

"Simple. Lower rates than fixed loans and lower closing costs."

"Sure, HELOCs sound good, but your interest rate will fluctuate. And they come loaded with fees. Did you know that?"

"No . . . what was the name of that stock again?"

"Com Coffee. It has locations in all the major cities. The company is so hot that it's undergoing a reverse merger as we speak, which means a private company is about to buy it over and grow it even more. When it's acquired, guess what? You'll have a new friend. Hello, Mr. Benjamin."

Mr. Howard laughed.

"I can send you information if you'd like, but just keep in mind that if you wait until the press release, you're too late. So, what do you think?" Ben waited while the man thought it over.

"Okay, put me down," Mr. Howard said.

"Great, let me transfer you to a senior broker who'll take care of everything. Just one moment." Ben transferred the call to the Hebrew legend.

"Shit! That was awesome," Jason remarked.

"That's what the fuck I'm talking about," Ben said, his eyes widening as if this kid had better recognize.

Ben checked the clock on his computer and rose in response. "I need to take a monster shit after that." He walked out of the loud room through the quiet hallway and to the john.

In the meantime, Kannada approached the boiler room. He came out of the elevator, walked across the hallway past the big booty secretary, and entered the mahogany door without permission. His well-groomed appearance, haircut and suit, said he didn't need approval.

An office filled with alpha-males pumping stocks in a ruckus was in full swing, just as he'd expected.

In the background:

"I own this stock myself," a seller lied.

"Look, the stock is in high demand," another exaggerated.

"You don't buy stock? You want a retirement, don't you?" a standing man pushed while holding his phone set.

In the front near the entrance was a table comprised of five pushers, with five telephones held between tilted heads and scrunched shoulders, and five sales tickets waiting to be filled. He could tell this was stressful stuff and that no one who worked here failed to close. He spotted an empty chair and approached it.

Kannada was hardly noticed.

Ben jammed the toilet with some Mexican food from the previous night, washed his hands, and dried them with napkins. By the time he finished pat cooling his rectangular face with the wet napkins, checked his appearance, especially his dark brown, short, spikey,

Asian hair, buckled his belt, and zipped his XYZ, twenty minutes had passed.

As Ben returned from the bathroom and opened the door to the cacophony awaiting inside, the rookie, Jason, ran into him, the door not having to be pushed by his shoulder's press.

"Dude, you gotta see this guy!" the kid said. "I don't know who this big swinging dick is, but he just closed two sales and opened an account."

Ben went to his designated section and saw the back of a man in a black suit with black hair sitting in his chair. He was at the new employee's table when he turned to look.

The newcomer nodded and gave a wink. "I hope I can work here." He discreetly slipped his sales tickets and new account paperwork to the Hebrew legend. "An ad in the paper mentioned there were some openings."

Ben couldn't believe his eyes. *How'd Kannada get in here?* The transactions on his behalf weren't lost on Ben. This guy had come for a job. "You can definitely work here. What's your name?"

"Kannada Khan."

"Ben Wu."

The other telemarketers enviously stared with closed-mouth smiles. Kannada was the perfect candidate.

"Is this your seat?" Kannada asked.

"I kept it warm for you," Ben said, grinning.

Kannada smiled.

Ben retrieved a chair from another table in the room as everybody else welcomed the new trainee. He placed his seat next to Jason and made use of it.

The next round of phone calls from the table began anew.

"Jason, Mr. Williams is on Line 2," the receptionist sorting incoming calls said.

Jason went after his phone. Kannada blocked him from picking it up.

"You're in a meeting," Kannada advised.

"Wanda," Jason yelled to the receptionist, "tell him I'm in a meeting."

She nodded. Jason turned to Kannada with glowing eyes.

"They want to argue with you about why the stock didn't go up. Remember, you don't want to sell, no matter what. They'll make their pleas, cry, but you have to hold your ground."

Jason nodded.

"Learning from the master here," Ben said, referring to Kannada. "Certainly, you have some experience doing this, correct?"

"Well, I've been known to jam product, mostly commodities, you know, like tomatoes." Kannada picked up Ben's phone and rummaged through a stack of business cards on the table.

"They're doing that with tomatoes now? Sounds fun," Ben said.

"It's decent. Just a bunch of buying and selling, back and forth."

"You must be making good commission?"

"I get by." Kannada looked beady-eyed. He placed a phone between his head and shoulder and started to dial a number on a card he found.

The other telemarketers studied his approach as they kept their free ears alert to his conversation and their bound ears searching for new suckers to reel in. Their phone calls ignored, they paused to watch.

"Hi, can I speak to Dr. Ahluwalia?" Kannada turned on the speakerphone. "Yes, I'll hold." He took a pile of business cards from Ben's desk and put it into his coat's inner pocket.

Dr. Ahluwalia addressed the call a short time later. "Hello?"

"Hi, Dr. Ahluwalia. This is Satish Singh with Bright Future Investments," Kannada started the attack.

"See what he's doing?" Ben said to Jason quietly. "He's matching personalities—an Indian with another Indian. People trust their own kind."

"I've got a lot of patients today. My hands are completely tied," Dr. Ahluwalia stated.

"I understand. I'm busy myself, but I have a trade idea, just one, that could help you with that vacation you're planning or retirement. A few minutes now could change your future forever," Kannada laid the trap.

"Who is this?"

"Dr. Ahluwalia, have you ever heard of the shipping company, FrontRidge?"

"No."

"Listen, listen. This company is about to make one of the largest dividends in history, a yield of twenty-seven percent on its stock. Today is the last day for you to get in on that dividend."

"No. Now, wait. Hold on a second. What was the name of that company again?"

"FrontRidge."

"I don't know. My wife and I are planning to retire soon." Dr. Ahluwalia sounded hesitant.

"Well, congratulations! You could still be earning while you're in retirement, you know? Why let that hard-earned money sit? Listen, my sister is a cardiologist, but while she's making her money, I'm putting it to work for her. You see what I'm saying?"

"Yes, I see."

"So, why keep your money stagnant? You work for the money. Now let it work for you."

"That's a good one, but I have a qualified workplace retirement plan."

Some people in the room frowned, while others shook their heads. Ben remained confident; he knew Kannada could bullshit with the best of them.

"Good, a lot of people do," Kannada said. "But are you maxing out your contributions to the plan?"

"No."

"Then you're missing out. Do you have a non-qualified retirement plan?"

"Yes. In fact, I have a mix of investments, and my nest egg is just fine, thank you."

"That's great. When you diversify, are you aggressive or conservative?"

The doctor hesitated. "I'm aggressive."

"Well, that's the wrong way to go. Being aggressive only makes your savings more susceptible to market fluctuations."

"Oh . . . Actually, I'm probably more conservative."

People in the room started to nod, and smiles began to form.

"Then you're limiting your potential for growth," Kannada said.

"Oh . . ."

Kannada smirked at Ben. "First you say you're aggressive, then you say you're conservative. Dr. Ahluwalia, there's no doubt you know medicine, but it's clear you don't know money. You're in a tough situation."

"But I'll be getting Social Security, so I probably don't need to invest."

"Social Security? Are you kidding me? Social Security won't secure you. Social Security is about to collapse any day now. The U.S. is suffering its worst recession in decades. The debt is astronomical. Banks are creating inflation. You've seen the news, haven't you?"

Ben grinned. He liked Kannada's style.

"Yes," Dr. Ahluwalia said.

"The government is going to break in half anytime. Did you know that the City of Detroit filed for bankruptcy just a while ago?" Kannada said.

"Yes, I saw that." Dr. Ahluwalia sounded concerned.

"I'm telling you, as an insider, this country is no longer what it used to be."

"Yes, but I still don't know. I've never heard of Bright Future Investments."

Kannada yawned; this looked too easy for him. "We're a private company that serves only high net-worth individuals like yourself. Normally, people have to search for a broker, but since we cater to a better society, we cut that part out and find you, the buyer."

"I see. What does FrontRidge do exactly?"

"It's involved with shipping oil. With the recent wars, the U.S. has gained a surplus of oil reserves. So, naturally, they made a huge profit, and they're giving it out as dividends to their loyal shareholders. It's the perfect time to take advantage of their generosity."

"What's the price?"

"It's about two dollars."

"Why's it so cheap?"

"They recently did a stock split. Do you know what that is?"

"Yes, I'm aware. It causes the price to drop dramatically."

"Perfect. Well?" Kannada looked over to Ben.

After a quiet moment, Dr. Ahluwalia said, "Okay, put me down."

Kannada slowly pumped his fist. "All right, let me transfer you to a senior broker. He'll take care of the rest for you."

"Thank you."

"My pleasure. You have a wonderful day. I know you will, with so much money coming to you."

"Hahaha, goodbye," Dr. Ahluwalia said.

"And that's how you bag the elephant." Kannada addressed the group of fans surrounding him and transferred the call.

The people in the room applauded.

"Hey, kid, give them something to fear, and before you know it, they'll do exactly what you want," Kannada instructed Jason, the student. "Now, if you'll excuse me, I need to take a break, get some fresh air."

Ben and the other telemarketers watched him move toward the exit with the luck they wished they had.

"He's only been here for half an hour. Where's he going?" Jason said.

"He's done for the day," the Hebrew legend responded in a raspy voice, a clear indication of his years of smoking. "You perform like that, your ass can go home, too."

Ben stood shaking his head, smiling, as Kannada walked out the door.

Kannada struggled to keep his shirt on for Ben. He shook his head and sighed with crossed arms and feet as he leaned against an old, silver Camry in an open-air, half-filled parking lot. A resurgence of interest in trading and a whatever-it-takes attitude swept over him after exercising his long-lost selling abilities in the boiler room.

"Hey, Kannada, you—" Ben said.

Kannada cut him off and glared. "What took you so long?"

"You could've given me a heads up."

"What's the fun in that?"

They entered the vehicle, and Ben started the ignition and reversed out. "How long's it been?"

"About four years."

"Time flies by."

"It sure does."

Ben looked at his friend. "Are you on vacation?"

Kannada lowered his head and pressed his lips together. "A long one. I haven't found much since Caldwell tanked."

Ben's eyebrows rose. He merged into traffic, then gave Kannada a quick sideways glance. "You could work here if you wanted."

Several black, unmarked SUVs, some with flashing lights, raced past them and turned into the boiler room's parking lot. *The authorities.*

"Or not," Ben said.

Kannada took a deep breath and shook his head. "Even then, I'd need Viagra to keep up that performance every day."

Ben laughed. "Well, you have to do something."

"I'm taking time off."

"That's some luxury you got. I just spent seven hours straight in that shithole. I'm tired."

Kannada glanced at Ben. "Yeah, you got one of those 7:00 AM toilet faces. How long have you been doing that?"

"Three lousy months. It's just odd job after odd job, from one boiler room to another. Nothing else out there. Damn Caldwell."

Kannada smiled as Ben stopped at a red light. A Cadillac hooptie came to a halt next to them and blared hip-hop music through rolled-down windows.

"How many whales did you reel in today?" Kannada asked.

Ben snickered. "Not enough."

"Not enough dishonesty?"

"Hey, it's not the liar who's at fault, it's the believer."

Kannada started to respond but stopped short and shook his head swiftly. He looked Ben over as his friend grinned. Ben had been laying the bait for gullible whales since he was of drinking age. A quinquennium later, passing as a licensed broker, he started working for Caldwell Investments. At thirty, he was axed from the company when Caldwell robbed Peter to pay Paul. From then on, every law-abiding investment firm closed its doors and directed him to the underground world of boiler rooms.

"You cheat people," Kannada said.

"I practice the craft of manipulation," Ben reasoned.

Kannada tilted his head and scratched his eyebrow. *Interesting rationalization.* Ben was a creative, strategic thinker full of bullshit, who could manage to find a backup to the backup to the backup. Assertive and outspoken, driven to lead, he was exactly what Kannada needed.

The light turned green and Ben continued.

"Young guns. They want to make it rich fast. They don't know what they're saying. They don't even know what they're doing. They expect me to teach them how to swindle. The people I meet," Ben said.

"How is it, Ben, that you know so many people?"

"Hey, I only know six people."

"That's it, huh?"

"That's all you need, and the world knows you."

"That's such BS."

"It's true."

Kannada smiled, pulled out a stack of Ben's business cards from his coat's inner pocket, and rolled off the rubber band. "A couple from your sucker list." He sifted through them, searching for one. "I was surprised to find this in here." He handed one crisp linen-stock card across to Ben.

Ben viewed the card in front of him near the steering wheel, multitasking with his eyes on the road and the card. "Robert Prosperi. Real Estate Developer, The Prosperi Organization. CEO and Founder, RP Capital Management . . . Old money won't take the bait. I've done business with him before."

"I'm not talking about that boiler room garbage," Kannada said.

Ben glanced at Kannada, then continued to navigate the road as he should. "You going somewhere with this?"

"I'm not just going somewhere. I'm trending in a direction," Kannada said in stock jargon.

He gave Ben a quick tour of what he had in mind as they drove past a series of tourist attractions on Lake Shore Drive.

As the misty night descended, the two of them stopped at *Cloud Gate*. A constant cool breeze from Lake Michigan enveloped them as they sat on wet benches across the sculpture amid fall foliage, lit lampposts, and a dark blue sky. Surrounded by puddles, with a cup of mint chocolate chip ice cream before him, Ben held a spoon filled with the frozen dessert near his face.

"So, you want to rip-off the booshi on Wall Street?" Ben asked.

Kannada took a spoon out of his mouth and nodded. "Look, if you're not inter—"

"I'm interested."

"You are?" Kannada sounded amused.

"I just lost my job, didn't I?"

Kannada nodded, then dug into his vanilla treat with chocolate sprinkles.

"Look, money talks. Just how much do you think this could rake in?" Ben asked.

He and Kannada stuffed their respective mouths with ice cream, simultaneously.

"Ah, too cold." Kannada winced.

Ben shook his head and handed Kannada a napkin. He licked his spoon and stared patiently as a couple of gulls talked to one another nearby.

Kannada swallowed and wiped his lips and the surrounding area. "It'd be nothing like the chump change that boiler room makes."

"What're we talking about?"

"F-You money. Like one big ass jelly bean."

Ben looked at *The Bean* sculpture across from him as his brows rose. He searched his friend's eyes.

"It has potential, but it could be a dud. We'd have to anticipate everything," Kannada warned.

Get to the point! "You going to give me some color on this?"

Kannada hesitated. "An IPO."

"An initial public offering?" Ben sighed. Suddenly, he felt a bit queasy, and it wasn't because of the foul scent of fresh gull poop circulating the air. He looked carefully at Kannada, then shifted his gaze out to the left toward the skyline, high-rise buildings and skyscrapers, but none too high.

As they walked the streets of Chicago, near the Marshall Field and Company Building, toward Petterino's Italian restaurant, Ben noticed the recent rain had silenced the pavement and cleared the crowds, dampening the vibrant nightlife.

"I need people, specifically, talented people that can be trusted," Kannada said.

"Honesty's not my cup of tea, but if a team is what you want, I can get you a team," Ben said.

Kannada smirked. "All right. Where should we start?"

"What you need is a grease man."

"Right, a grease man." Kannada nodded.

Ben stopped and stared at a lost ball in the high weeds.

Kannada bit his lip. "What the hell's a grease man?"

Ben rolled his eyes. "A guy who can get you in, make things run smoothly, a hacker."

Kannada nodded. "They're underground. You know any?"

"There's this one guy I met a few years back at a trading conference. We got to talking about computerized trading. He was studying to be a Wall Street quant, algorithmic developer. He can code in pretty much any language."

"What's he doing now?"

A couple walked past them, their arms around each other. Kannada and Ben paused their conversation and stared at each other. They waited until the potential eavesdroppers were no longer within earshot.

"He led a couple of friends in running a startup hedge fund," Ben said. "They made a fortune in high-frequency trading before anyone could catch up to them, but because of some order type mishaps, they struggled to compete."

"Why isn't he doing it anymore?"

"His systems failed. So, I think that plays a large part in how the industry sees him. Plus, it doesn't help that he's on the outside now, no longer part of the inner loop of hearsay."

"So, where can we find him?"

"He keeps a low profile. Last I heard, he shot off on his own and started one of those websites for leaked documents. But nobody knows his exact whereabouts. Come on."

They continued to stroll on the sidewalk.

"Don't know his name and don't know where he is. Sounds like your typical hacker. Okay, so then who else?" Kannada said.

Ben stared at a sculpture of an elephant under the green clock affixed to the building ahead of them, thinking, as a whiff of fresh air touched him. "Smarty Gonzales." Ben passed the street art, sure of himself.

CHAPTER 5

Las Vegas, Nevada

Ben sighed as he waited for his bag to fall onto the conveyer belt at a baggage claim in McCarran International Airport. Kannada had no checked luggage, only his backpack.

"Rob wants revenge; I get that. But you, I don't get. What's the theme of this story?"

Kannada scrubbed his hand over his face, then rushed his speech. "It's about leveling the playing field. It's one for Main Street. Why? Because Wall Street takes advantage of schnooks, like you and me, every time. They skim the cream off the top and give us the leftovers while Uncle Sam says they're too big to fail."

Ben nodded.

"People are suffering. Just look at everyone around you." Kannada sighed heavily.

Ben glanced around; a couple of people claimed their bags with smiles, a few kids played peek-a-boo between their guardians' legs, and a pair of airport employees joked with each other. He faced Kannada. "They look okay to me."

"On the surface." Kannada pointed at Ben. "But inside, they're hoping for their misery to end."

Ben nodded slowly, smirking. "That's deep."

Kannada smiled and playfully patted his own chest. "It comes from the heart."

"You sound like you read that off some teleprompter."

"Well, I try my best to not think for myself."

Ben grinned. His bag arrived, and he picked it up.

Kannada and Ben inserted their mid-size rental car in a garage, then sprung forth onto the Strip. They bounced around like a pinball on the Strip's glitzy allure, casinos, gambling, nightlife, and flyers for escorts, before they rested between two bumpers, the Bellagio and Mirage.

The Black Hat USA Las Vegas Conference took place at Caesar's Palace with its group of programmers, information security analysts, and cryptographers as guest speakers. The meeting sought to train, brief, and award security practitioners. A full house listened when required, laughed when prompted, and applauded when appropriate.

Kannada and Ben, outsiders to cyberspace, sat front and center, surrounded by security and hacking enthusiasts, intent on catching every detail.

Kannada's cell phone, courtesy of Rob, rang. "Yes, Rob, everything's going fine. You got the information I sent you, right? . . . Great, this thing's about to start. I'll talk to you later. Buh-bye."

"Big cheese coming down on you?" Ben asked.

Kannada sighed. "I miss being unemployed and free-loading off people."

"They say it's a glamorous life."

"That indeed." Kannada viewed the time on his phone. "Where is this guy?"

"That's him right there."

Kannada looked up at the man behind the podium, the man who they would gamble on to gain unauthorized access to trading data in the NYSE.

The speaker's jet black, curly hair and brown skin shined brightly under the spotlight. "I'd like to welcome all of you today. Hopefully, you haven't lost too much money gambling." A scant amount of laughter followed his joke. "Tough crowd."

Kannada, unimpressed, leaned over to Ben and whispered, "He's not a funny guy."

"What're you here for, jokes?" Ben said.

"Just saying."

"My name is Iago Gonzales. But, before I begin, let me tell you a little about myself. I hold a BS in Electrical Engineering and Computer Science from UC Berkeley."

Smarty Gonzales, Iago, stopped to take a drink of water as he adjusted his black, full-rim plastic glasses.

"You think a white hat could become a black hat?" Kannada asked.

"Mmm . . . I think so," Ben said.

"You know anyone else?"

"Just wait."

"I've held many different positions during my time as an IT specialist," Iago said. "At Google, I revitalized their security program with innovative technology and products. However, I'm more known for exploiting MD6 collisions to create a rogue certificate security, skirting the browser exploitation alleviations of Windows 8, and creating the Gon Tyco exploitation technique."

Kannada twisted his mouth to the side. *Big words can't scare me.*

"Currently, I'm an independent consultant, working with a few colleagues." Iago coughed.

Ben leaned over to Kannada and spoke softly. "He also runs an education charity for kids in Nicaragua."

"Okay, he's too good for us," Kannada said.

"Oh no, too bad for us. That's another way of saying, 'mail and wire fraud.'"

The truth startled and impressed Kannada as a latecomer with refreshments walked in the aisle in front of him. Iago was morally bankrupt, but he had the right experience.

"That's your black hat," Ben said.

Smoothly changing direction, Iago gave a Black Hat briefing, a fifty-minute speech on security vulnerabilities facing web browsers and operating systems, followed by a discussion on open-source security tools and designing reliable systems. Seated directly in front of the speaker, Kannada and Ben had to listen to avoid being rude.

Iago moved a cleaning cart parked in front of his hotel room in Caesar's Palace out of the way, opened the door, and walked straight in, looking at the floor.

A plastic bag ruffled as he passed the bathroom to his right.

Maybe it's the house cleaner. He looked up as he entered the open area where his bed lay. Just as he had left the room before giving the speech, clothing strewed everywhere, and empty soda cans and Cheetos bags littered the tables. The door slammed shut.

Iago's adrenaline spiked and the hair on his nape and arms rose, as he stared at two uninvited male guests, one Indian, with onyx eyes and an Ivy League cut, the other, Asian, with dark brown, short, spikey hair. He flinched, as the Indian man opened a bag of munchies.

"Hey, I was saving that," Iago said with a shrill voice. He pointed at the humongous bag of Cheetos.

The man holding the bag wore a black suit and red tie, stood near a nightstand, and smiled. "Well, today is your lucky day."

Iago's heartbeat started to return to normal, as the men failed to pose a threat. He pointed at the man who addressed him. "Um, who are you?"

"Kannada Khan at your service." He shook Iago's finger and walked toward the desk.

Iago looked at the other man and squinted. "I've seen you somewhere."

"Ben Wu. Fast Futures Trading Conference," Ben said.

Iago nodded. "Yes, now I remember. How'd you get in here?"

"Sorry about the entrance, but we didn't know how else to reach you." Kannada leaned against the desk. "Would you like a Cheeto?" He handed one to Iago.

"The singular form is Cheetos snack." Iago took the orange puff and the bag politely, then placed them on a desk.

Kannada and Ben looked at each other.

"We like you," Ben said, standing in front of the king-size bed. "We think you're one-of-a-kind, and we'd like to maximize your potential. We'd like to talk to you about a special job we're doing."

Iago wandered a short distance toward the door, then returned. He tilted his head to the side, pulled his ear, and pursed his lips. "Uh, what kind of special job is this?"

Kannada and Ben traded glances.

"It's right up your alley," Kannada said.

Iago blinked and raised his eyebrows. He eyed the exit. "Uh, I don't do that kind of thing anymore. What're you, law enforcement?"

"Don't you think we would've arrested you by now?" Kannada said.

Iago looked from one set of eyes to the other. "All right, what do you guys want?"

Kannada and Ben smiled before they let Iago in on their plans.

An hour passed. "So?" Kannada observed Iago's every move, as well as the orange fingerprints on his clothing.

"Getting a job at the Big Board isn't a walk in the park, you know." Iago snacked on some Cheetos nonchalantly, standing in his hotel room. "You have to know somebody."

"I know somebody." Kannada stood near the window, holding a coffee cup filled with the orange, puffed cornmeal snacks.

Ben glanced at him with an elevated eyebrow and a smirk, then looked away.

Iago repeatedly crunched the cheese-flavored corn products loudly. "But even then, Wall Street is impenetrable."

"From the outside." Kannada wiped the orange dust off his fingers on his suit. "But not the inside, if you know what you're doing."

Iago stared at the two of them. "It's fascinating." He looked away. "But it's not an overnight affair, you know."

"You're right." Ben smeared the white comforter with orange lip marks as he sat on the messy bed. "It's not. And we don't expect you to be there one night, nor two, nor three—"

"I still don't know." Iago cut off Ben.

"Think of it this way," Kannada said. "The return will last you no matter how many times you reincarnate."

Iago looked up quickly, alert. "The money doesn't motivate me. I have a decent life." His gaze drifted away again as a door closed in the hallway.

Recruiting Iago's a closed door. The smooth, even noise from the air conditioning unit was putting a stumped Kannada to sleep.

"Why do you study hacking and programming?" Ben asked.

Kannada glanced at Ben. *Here comes the sales pitch.* Ben's search for an emotional reason gave his intentions away.

"It's interesting, challenging work." Iago added another set of orange streaks on his shirt as he smoothed away the powder.

"Are you challenged now?" Kannada followed Ben's lead.

"What do you mean?" Iago licked his fingers.

"Intellectually, are you challenged by what you're doing now?" Kannada said.

"Finding clients, yes. The work, no, not really." Iago finally decided to use a napkin on the desk to wipe his hands.

"You just gave a speech on how to stop hackers, but when's the last time you hacked?" Ben said.

Iago sighed. "I'm retired now. I used to hack to see what I could get away with, but I haven't done it forever." He leaned against the desk, feet crossed.

"Isn't hacking complicated?" Ben said.

"Look, hacking isn't all that it's cracked up to be. It's simple. People are complicated. People perceive what their senses show them." Iago cocked his head, then shook it. "They don't perceive what their intellect already knows."

That was over Kannada's head. He was certain that it was over Ben's, too.

"Well, if you're not challenged, and you think hacking is simple, why not test your knowledge?" Kannada said.

Before Iago could respond, Ben intervened. "Do you have it in you?"

Iago stopped munching and put down his Cheetos bag on the desk behind him. He crossed his arms, sighed, and stared at the floor. "All right." He looked up to face them. "I'll take you up on it."

"Are you sure? You could do some heavy time with the law and mess up your career." Kannada recalled Wendell Caldwell's future time in jail and his own subsequent years in the subway.

"Obey the law?" Iago said. "Obedience is slavery."

That was music to Kannada's ears. He smirked at Ben as the inner hacking rebel in Iago had been incited.

Ben returned his grin similarly.

A short while later, Kannada and Ben, their clothes and fingertips stained orange, exited, maneuvered the hallways, and headed to a parking garage at the end of the Vegas Strip.

Kannada passed a couple of scattered tourists posing for pictures in front of a fountain near Caesar's Palace on a sunny day. He was anxious to see what Iago could do for them in the coming weeks.

Ben stopped in front of the human-made geyser. "We need

Dilip."

Why'd he bring him up? The mist from the fountain touched Kannada's face. "He won't agree. He's leaving his post."

"Got a new job?"

"Got bribed." Kannada walked straight ahead and left Ben standing. "He's all yours."

CHAPTER 6

Washington, D.C.

As soon as Ben deplaned at Ronald Reagan Washington National Airport, his search for the group's next accomplice began.

Dilip was an absolute necessity. As a traveling attorney for the SEC, Dilip went after the small fish to curry favor with the big fish—any big Wall Street firm. It wasn't uncommon for him to land a nice, cushy job with such a company and lobby on its behalf, screwing Main Street every time. He was *the* model SEC regulator; he had the ability to make settlements outside of court. That was what had him passing through the revolving door, back and forth between too-big-to-fail banks and the SEC.

At the airfield, Ben caught the yellow line, unusually congested for this hour. *Where'd all these people come from?* he wondered. Picket signs, painted faces, American flags, and a couple of happy Hare Krishnas. *Eh, what're you going to do?* After all, it was D.C. He certainly never saw that much national pride in Chicago, except for on Independence Day. He was uncomfortable as he scrunched between people, coughing, sneezing, and rubbing their clammy bodies against him. A few minutes later, he exited, with the rest of the train it seemed, at L'Enfant Plaza Station at 7th and Maryland.

He headed toward Lincoln, prying himself apart from the crowd and moving in the opposite direction. The National Mall was Dilip's getaway on the weekends; Ben could make a fortune placing wagers on Dilip doing a couple rounds near Honest Abe. It never changed. The same old routine, the same time—he never got tired of it.

The brisk walker, accompanied by a golden lab, seemed a little vigilant as he walked past the Washington Monument; certainly, he looked more alert than usual thanks to his recent planned job swap. Dilip Patel, dressed in running shorts and a shirt with an American flag, sweated—more because of his nerves than the heat—while he picked up his pace with his mutt on a leash. They moved along one of the walkways near the Lincoln Memorial Reflecting Pool on the side of Independence Avenue.

Ben, dressed for a semiformal meeting, watched from a distance, behind one of the colonnades of the D.C. War Memorial. Dilip's uneasiness was indicative of one problem: where his loyalties lay.

His retirement from the SEC to join a big bank, again, had made Dilip a difficult sell. He couldn't turn any of them in to the police.

Ben approached as Dilip went up a flight of stairs toward the Lincoln Memorial.

Dilip settled down at the base of the memorial, at the top step leading down to the Reflecting Pool. He pulled out a towel from the back of his shorts and started to cool himself.

Ben moved toward him, his dress shoes tapping on the pavement.

Dilip stopped and turned around. The sixty-two-year-old's sweaty, salt-and-pepper hair matched his stubble, and his gold stud earring shined under Lincoln's light.

"What's up, Dilip?" Ben asked.

"Inflation, that's what," the old man quipped.

Ben sat next to him. "When'd you get a dog?"

"Since the recession began. All these damn liberals keep me up at night." Dilip patted his face with the towel.

"Is that the only thing keeping you up?"

Dilip looked at Ben. "What're you, an ethics professor?" He sounded pissed.

"I managed to come meet you. Come on."

The hum of an electric vehicle approached. A police officer on a Segway passed by at the base of the Reflecting Pool.

"Aren't you going to say hello to your friends?" Ben asked.

"A man should keep his friends close, his enemies at a distance,"

Dilip said.

Dilip was always difficult to talk to; he had too much to hide.

I think he phrased that wrong. "Which side are you on?"

"I play to win." Dilip spat a gob of phlegm to his side.

Ben tilted his head and smiled with his mouth open. "You getting sick?"

"Getting old."

A full moon set over the Washington Monument and glistened in the human-made, rectangular pool in front.

The sexagenarian remained focused on the reflection. "You here for some business, or what?" He wiped the sweat off his forearms. "Should I just go through the door without you?"

"Dilip Patel," Ben said, "The definition of corruption. You're here in D.C.; then you're at some bank. How much is the asking price?"

"You can't buy me," Dilip said. "This is an art form. It's about making relationships, keeping a bond, holding a silence. Others don't know about it. That's the beauty; they never know about it. And they certainly can't do anything about it."

"Me and you, we need a certain figure. We go where the offer is better. There're no hard feelings. Heck, there is no feeling."

"A big bank crushes feelings."

Ben counted the ripples in the water. "Nice night . . . peaceful. No people. How come?"

"Demonstrators," Dilip said. "They're protesting at Capitol Hill. Don't ask me what, but everyone's there."

The zealous patriots in the subway.

"How long are you going to wait?" Dilip stretched his feet out and rested on his elbows. "What could possibly be better?"

Under the stars, Ben made himself comfortable. Following Dilip's reclined position, he began to inform him without concern in the lonely night.

"We're trying to pull off a heist on—" Ben said.

"Lower. What're you, a billboard?" Dilip cut off Ben from being overly loose. "The FBI—and, God forbid, the damn NSA—aren't too far from here. They'd love to bust my chops any chance they get."

Ben adjusted, as Dilip *ooh*ed and *aah*ed with occasional glances over his shoulder to make sure no one was spying. The noise of the protesters came trickling down Constitution Avenue. The group of misfits, hippies, and folks who had nothing better to do than let out their frustration marched toward the White House.

"You in?" Ben said.

Dilip coughed and spit more mucus out. "Who put you up to this?"

"Kannada."

Dilip sighed and shook his head. "Nephews and mischief; a match made in hell."

Ben had an arrière-pensée. "You guys are related?"

"I'm not saying that."

Too many secrets. "I thought he'd come to you first."

"That lousy hobo. I can't help him."

Ben reminisced on Kannada's past. He was broke and ready to go out on a limb. "You end up helping us, you won't have to ever again."

He stood and walked away slowly. Dilip's golden lab followed for a few feet, then stopped to wait for its master. A pair of security guards on Segways zoomed behind them to the President's abode.

Dilip ruminated for a moment. He could go to a big bank, get paid the old-fashioned way, through the revolving door, or he could do something he should've done a long time ago.

Fido barked. Dilip was getting old; he might as well go out on a high note. Dilip grabbed his dog's leash and followed what man's best friend already knew.

CHAPTER 7

Coney Island, New York

Kannada received his order at *the* hot dog restaurant, a heavily trafficked, fast-food eatery on Coney Island, and walked to an outdoor table and bench where Ben was waiting.

A few gulls flew away from Kannada's designated spot as he approached. He inhaled sea air, a fishy, tangy, iodine-like essence from the Atlantic Ocean, as he placed his food on the table and took a seat.

"Okay," Ben said. "Who do we have so far?"

"Paul's in." A cool breeze brushed Kannada. "The insider. We've got the angel investor, the hacker, the backdoor revolver, and the network."

"And the bum with the master plan," Ben said.

Kannada grinned in acknowledgment under sunny skies.

They had rendezvoused at Nathan's Famous, in South Brooklyn, the most exotic ethnic enclave of New York. Situated between overridden roller coasters and far enough from Brighton Beach, where flabby-skinned geriatrics in Speedos and empty bottles of Baltika beer lined the shore, they discussed their candidates' roles over lunch as a few gulls squawked overhead.

"Rob's closing down his hedge fund." Kannada sipped his Coke through a straw.

Ben shook his head. "The SEC rehired Dilip. He's working in New York now."

Kannada removed the straw from his mouth and shooed away a fly that hovered over his food with his hand. "Iago got a job at the NYSE. Turns out the Big Board is hiring hackers for bug bounties. He went through a grueling background check under a new ID, Mr. Diego Sanchez. I had him contact Napoli for the fake ID."

Iago Gonzales had mentioned to Kannada the closing down of his business and his false charity, the Hope Nicaragua Fund, supposedly aimed at eradicating illiteracy and providing education in Nicaragua.

Manhattan, New York

Iago was getting ready for his first day in the Securities Cyber Fraud Department in the NYSE building. He straightened his tie in the restroom, explored the many corridors with his escort, and entered one of the circus-like trading floors.

Across from the opening bell, he stopped, stared, and smiled with pleasure, as it rung. His credentials were more than good enough and his ties to the mail and wire fraud, fronted as a charity, were completely severed.

His escort led him to his office.

Coney Island, New York

Before Kannada took a bite of his hot dog, the creamy, tropically floral fragrance of suntan lotion caught him by surprise, as a pair of women with smooth, long legs applied the protectant nearby. They reminded him of his past flame's flawless skin, aromatic scent, and soft voice. "Iago was hired with my connection."

Ben nodded. "I meant to ask you earlier. Who's your friend?"

"Amara."

"Oh yeah, I forgot she worked at the NYSE. She still hasn't added me on any social media site."

"I don't think she likes you." Kannada was trying to be nice. Amara didn't like him at all; she thought he was a sexist, anti-feminist asshole because he had a few choice words for supporters of equal pay at a party.

Ben showed one index finger. "I made one pass at her, and that's before I knew you two were dating."

Kannada shrugged.

"How's she doing?" Ben asked.

Kannada thought of the picture of Amara in his wallet. He hadn't looked at it in a while, but he didn't need to, as her image was etched on his heart.

"Okay . . ." Ben said. "Fight? Breakup?"

"Things are fine."

"Are you thinking about proposing?"

"It can wait."

Ben laughed. "I don't blame you. Once you're locked in, you're locked in."

"Yeah, yeah," Kannada said. *I miss being told what to do.*

Ben dipped a French fry into a cup of ketchup and mustard, then bit into it.

Kannada surveyed his own food. "What about a pilot?"

Ben glanced at his friend, then looked toward the counter with narrow eyes and put two fingers on his chin. "I texted Alan McGill yesterday."

"The Whiskey Delta? He's always behind the eight ball."

"He's at the Grand Canyon." Ben took a sip of his Sprite.

Grand Canyon, Arizona

At a deserted, red rock helipad, a white, dusty EcoStar 130 deluxe helicopter, its rotor blades rotating before liftoff, was ready to show the foreign tourists on board the magnificence it had witnessed time and again. The helicopter's engine revved loudly, though it was barely noticeable to the passengers, softened as it was by the Fenestron tail rotor and their headphones. They faced forward in stadium-style seats with plenty of personal space and a 180-degree view, courtesy of the large windshield.

Nearby was an infinitely smaller drone, but in black.

The pilots stared at each other; Alan McGill, carrying real people, and some bystander, carrying an intention to disrupt, remote control in his hands.

The child's one, manned by a kid for an adult, flew up straight.

The actual, life-sized copter buckled and rose with reflexive jerks toward the sky before steadying for a smooth ride.

Coney Island, New York

"Can he fly in narrow spaces?" Kannada asked.

"The question is: Can he stay sober?" Ben said.

Grand Canyon, Arizona

The pilot, Alan McGill, a tan blond with matching mustache, planned on giving his patrons great views as the sun was rising. They would shoot the shit over an aerial view of the Grand Canyon's endless desert, outlined by picturesque landscapes of red, orange, and purple cliffs and a winding gorge in the middle of it all.

The miniature chopper had different plans, cutting off Alan midair.

He removed the hip flask from his lips. "What the . . . ?"

As the EcoStar lowered past several-million-year-old rock layers and flew through the airways, the black drone zoomed overhead. It pestered Alan and his customers and was headed for the landing pad. Alan couldn't let this radio-controlled drone win; he had passengers, international guests, seeing the country for the first time. He had to show them how Americans dealt with menaces; he moved his joystick and shredded the machine into pieces.

"Take that, you son of a bitch!" Alan exclaimed.

The tourists clapped.

"Real American," one Asian tourist said to another.

Coney Island, New York

"I got the feeling," Ben said, "he's not going to fit in too well in New York."

Kannada nodded as two men were fixing to square off for a hot-dog-eating contest at a table to their rear. One hefty black man and one equally big white man sniffed up the aroma as the plates were put in front of them.

Kannada went to his phone. "We need some muscle."

"Walker Mays," Ben said. "I saw him on *Weekly News*. He's a personal trainer. It hasn't been working out, though. No clients, no money."

Kannada looked up. "Yeah?"

"He's all jacked up now and has been earning a living fighting."

Philadelphia, Pennsylvania

In the City of Brotherly Love, two no-names with quick jabs and dreams of being the next Rocky Balboa paused their fight, as a bell signaled the end of a boxing round at the dimly lit, uncrowded Blue Horizon boxing venue.

Walker Mays, a well-built workout junkie and victim of bouts of anger, since losing his job at Caldwell Investments, crouched low in his corner while his trainer fed him water. Walker, exhausted and sweaty, his eyes half-open, his lip busted, chugged down the refreshment. He was shirtless, exposing his light black skin, but was wearing red boxing gloves and shorts.

He was flanked by his two trainers, one of whom tried to spark some fire in him.

"Come on," his first trainer said.

"I can't," Walker said in a deep voice.

"You gotta." The second trainer patted his bloody lip with a white towel.

"No, no, I'm done," Walker mumbled.

"He just called your mother a—" the second trainer finished in his ear.

Walker's eyes widened, reddened. The bell sounded.

He rushed up and, with one sucker punch, knocked his opponent cold. The referee motioned his arm in odd circles, trouncing his hand on the floor for each count. One. Two. Three. Four . . .

The referee raised Walker's hand and exclaimed, "Winner!" while the opponent's gang tried to wake up their man.

Coney Island, New York

"How's Walker's power?" Kannada put down his phone and followed Ben's eyes. Their attentions turned to the competition underway.

"Decent," Ben said. "He could do some damage."

"He's a phone call away."

Kannada and Ben stared at the ruckus nearby until the large white man choked and threw up his obstruction, giving himself a seated Heimlich maneuver. They turned back around and looked at each other, their eyes in agreement. It was time to go.

The two men continued their discussion while heading to enjoy the largest attraction on Coney Island, the Wonder Wheel. Kannada marveled at the century old Ferris wheel as he approached the carnival ride. The metal screeched as the lift came to a halt.

Just before entering one of the eight white stationary passenger cabins on the circumference, Kannada waved to the owner, who was standing less than twenty-five feet away at a corner.

The owner gave a slight nod with a grin and kept a focused eye on the wheels of the red and blue swinging cars in the space enclosed by the large circle.

Inside the passenger capsule, "Con man," Ben said.

"Antonio Garcia." Kannada surprised himself; he knew a con artist.

"Mexico."

"Running from the law?"

"Running from Trump. Sold him paintings."

"Any contact?"

"Nah."

Kannada frowned as his muscles tensed. He went silent and tried to put the upsetting information out of his mind.

"He's not what we're looking for," Ben said. "We need a scammer, a financial type."

The Ferris wheel elevated as Kannada reminisced on what would become of Antonio. His genre of fraud was artwork. The man scored millions, as his newly created works of famous paintings lost through time hit auction blocks, galleries, and museums.

Riding in the Ferris wheel's moving cabin after eating made Kannada nauseous. "Well, I'm out of fresh ideas."

Ben crossed his arms, one arm propped up, hand stroking chin. "Ricky."

Kannada's shoulders slumped. "Ben, I said talented people. The guy's a ham actor."

"The guy's a con man now."

"Really?"

Ben nodded. "Didn't make it on Broadway, so he went the wrong way."

"Huh." Kannada turned away. "I could see that happening."

Ben informed Kannada how Ricky was a better fit. After failing to make it on The Great White Way, he became legendary in his own right, as a confidence trickster and impostor. It all started with the death of Duke Henry Williams, a fictitious creation. Ricky developed a legal association for the Williams' heirs, open for a fee to anybody sharing the last name "Williams" to pool their money for the legal battle that was to recover their share of the inheritance. From that point on, making shit up became a living.

One of his more impressive feats was when he learned that the Taj Mahal needed repairs; he produced fake government papers, showing that he was an authorized seller of the mausoleum's white marble. It wasn't long until a couple of dealers slipped him a $400,000 bribe to get the coveted contract, and all that within America's borders.

Ricky had left the authorities baffled again and again, wowing Kannada repeatedly. Ben said he had developed a knack for conning folks, gained an encyclopedic knowledge of how to do it.

Ben checked his phone. "Come on, we better get to him before he moves."

"What's he up to?" Kannada followed Ben out the ride.

Miami, Florida

It was Friday afternoon. Separated from the glittery nightlife, just inland, a few feet away from the waves hitting the beachfront and surrounded by palm trees, the location was a hospital in South Beach, Miami.

"Paging Dr. Kravitz," a nurse said over the intercom. "Please report to room 305."

The game began. Ricky Tennyson strutted along one of the many hallways nonchalantly, wearing a lab coat with the name Dr. Eli Kravitz embroidered on it, a stethoscope around his neck, and a brown hairpiece atop his pale head. He was bald by choice; the lack of hair enabled him to wear toupees easily.

Ricky reported to the designated room. The smell of rubber gloves and alcohol prep entered his nostrils. "Yes, what seems to be the problem?"

"The man is suffering from a dry cough, chest pain, and fever, and is experiencing trouble breathing. Strep results are negative," Nurse Wang said as another physician, Dr. Carter, stood across the open doorway filling out some paperwork on a clipboard.

"Well, let's see here." As Ricky snapped on his gloves, a sick woman discussed her problems through the ultra-thin wall. The white paper on the bed crinkled, as the sufferer sat up from a reclining position.

Ricky looked at the patient, a senior with pink eyes.

The sick man repeatedly coughed loudly, covering his mouth with a paper towel.

Ricky grabbed the man's jaw and turned it one way, then the other, and nodded several times with, "Mmm hmm."

"Well, my diagnosis is that the man has a problem, a serious problem," Ricky said, "and there's a solution, a good solution, now isn't there, Nurse Wang?"

Nurse Wang loosened her posture and looked at the doctor with narrow eyes. She blinked rapidly, then bobbed her head up and down slowly. "Yes . . . yes. He may need a chest X-ray."

Ricky wore a deceptive smile. *Can't you tell I'm a quack?* Nurse Wang was fresh off the boat and recently licensed in her profession; the perfect recipe to be conned. He became more encouraged to continue his charade, as Dr. Carter glanced up from his clipboard to watch through the doorway.

"Then order one. Look, if you want to be a doctor one day, you're going to have to pick it up," Ricky said. "Now, what is it?"

"Possibly pneumonia and treat with amoxicillin?" Nurse Wang responded.

"Wow. That was so . . . professional."

"Pneumonia and amoxicillin," Nurse Wang said assuredly.

"That's the spirit." *Sucker.* Ricky smiled and turned to leave the nurse and patient.

"Excellent job teaching her," Dr. Carter commented.

"Hey, she's got to learn one day. I can't be everywhere at once."

"Amen," Dr. Carter said as Ricky walked away.

Moments later, as the workday was nearing an end, Ricky met a female receptionist in the bean counter's office. She handed him a check.

"Thank you, Mary," Ricky said.

"You're welcome. It's two weeks' pay."

Ricky smiled and left the hospital for good. He returned to his two-star hotel in a hurry and spent the next twenty-four hours preparing for a visit to the bank, as one fraudulently acquired check was just enough to get the ball rolling.

Ricky, leather bag in hand, sporting a tropical shirt and a panama hat, walked up to a teller sitting behind the glass at a nearby bank the next day. He was a man on a mission.

He opened the bag on the counter and slid a stash of envelopes in front.

"How can I help you, sir?" a young male teller asked.

"I'd like to cash these checks." Ricky smiled, his eyes twinkling. Check forgery was his latest passion. Mastery lay in manufacturing the check, a perfect copy of an actual payroll check. To accomplish such a task, he had to gain the confidence of his victims by posing as someone else. So far, he'd gotten away with being a lawyer, a police officer, a teacher, and a physician.

"All right, sir, just give me one moment."

Ricky leaned on the granite top of the bank teller's workstation. A few minutes later, the teller returned with another person, a Hispanic male with a Harvard cut.

"Hi, I'm Miguel. I'm the manager here. Sir, can I ask you why you want this much money?"

"I'm buying a new car. I need it for the down payment."

The manager nodded, then turned around and spoke with the teller privately. He returned to Ricky. "We'll have everything ready for you in just a moment. Thank you for banking with us today."

Ricky nodded with a smile. He watched the manager leave, then analyzed the teller's every move for any red flags that could arise. The man went through the motions, processed the checks and, within a matter of minutes, produced hard cash.

The teller gave Ricky his goods. "Is there anything else I can help you with today?"

"Well, there is this one thing," Ricky said hesitantly, placing the money into his bag. "Can I tell you something?"

The man behind the glass nodded.

"I love brown hair. It complements your eyes."

The man stared. "Thanks . . . I guess." He slightly blushed.

"Are you free this weekend?"

"I'm sorry, I'm not . . ."

"Come on," a voice said from behind, accompanied by a tug of Ricky's arm.

Ricky turned, and his mouth fell open. *Where'd they come from?* Standing to his side were two loyal supporters from his acting days, emotionless, in dark suits. Ricky grabbed his bag and joined Kannada and Ben in walking to the exit.

"Give Kannada the bag," Ben ordered.

"Why?" Ricky wondered.

"And put these on." Ben gave Ricky handcuffs.

Ricky shook his head; something was amiss. He handed the bag over and snapped on the cuffs. "Using the Find My Friends app?"

"It came in handy for once." Ben held Ricky's arm.

Ricky glanced at Ben's hand, the one around his arm. "Have you switched teams yet?"

"Nah. Just wait a second. You'll see why we're here."

Kannada and Ben escorted him to a black SUV with government plates. As they exited the building, several men came running from both sides, as to ambush someone.

"FBI. Drop it," an FBI agent with a thick, dirty blond mustache said, holding a gun. "Hands up. Hands up. Hands on your head."

Ricky stared, but didn't see, as things moved too quickly to process. His leg muscles tightened, ready to run.

"Relax," Ben said calmly as Kannada took to the driver's side.

"Pat him down," the mustached FBI agent said to a bald, Hispanic agent.

"Relax, Captain America." Ben raised his voice. "We got all the evidence we need."

Kannada lifted Ricky's bag above the SUV for visibility.

Ricky smiled slowly. *That's why Ben wanted me to put on the cuffs and fork over the dough to Kannada.* Within seconds, the air rushed out of his body, as the bald FBI agent firmly patted him down, examining the contents of his clothing from head to toe. "Ooh. You have strong hands."

The bald agent stared at Ricky, then turned away.

Ben shook his head. "Mr. Tennyson doesn't use weapons."

"Who the hell are you?" the mustached FBI agent demanded.

"We're the NSA," Ben responded.

The agents paused, looked at each other, and shrunk.

Higher authority, bitch. Ricky smirked.

"What? You think this is FBI property? Think again," Ben said.

"What're you talking about?" The mustached FBI agent sounded innocent. "You guys are international."

"And he's not local. We've been on to him for some time. Let me guess; you want him on payroll checks, government checks."

The FBI agents looked at one another and nodded.

My friends sound legit.

"Well, did you know he's been playing with foreign checks, even dabbling with cyber scams abroad?" Ben said.

They shook their heads.

The mustached FBI agent narrowed his eyes and raised his chin. "You got some ID on you?"

Ben flashed a fake NSA ID.

Ricky rocked back and forth slightly. *My friends even look legit.*

"It's over, boys. He's ours," Ben said. "Now, if you don't mind, we'd like to have a discussion with Mr. Tennyson, isn't that right, Ricky?" He sounded stern as he twisted Ricky's arm and stuck him into the back seat of the black SUV.

"Wait until I get my lawyer," Ricky mouthed off.

"Lawyers?" Ben shook his head. "We're going to have a little fun today." He shoved him into the back seat, shut the door, and took the passenger's seat.

"Where'd you get those government plates?" Ricky asked from behind Kannada.

"A friend of mine works at a body shop," Ben replied as the engine started.

"Okay, but how'd you guys know the FBI was on my tail?"

Ben turned his head toward the central armrest. "You got to fight fire with fire. They keep tabs on you. Well, I've got some inside men who keep tabs on them."

Ricky squished his brows together as the SUV started to roll. *He sure knows a lot of people. I should keep in touch with him more.*

Ricky took off his wig and shackles and relaxed in the middle of the back seat.

"Glad we got the Cadillac." Kannada steered the vehicle.

"Can't go wrong with American." Ben smiled.

"Damn straight," Ricky said.

CHAPTER 8

Manhattan, New York

Kannada and Ben staggered into Prince Street Pizza, the "Home of the SoHo Square," in Nolita, or North of Little Italy. They skimmed the menu, made their requests, and stood in line in front of the counter, where brick-lined walls began, made their way to the back, and wrapped around to cover the right wall.

As they counted on the workers to get their orders right, Kannada became nostalgic and thought of Amara because of the environment. He absorbed the aroma of freshly baked, hand-tossed dough and zesty tomato sauce permeating the air and received his square pizza slice and personal dipping sauce. He hardly noticed the portraits of visiting Italian-American celebrities, like John Travolta and James Gandolfini, which grazed the walls, as he grabbed a Coke bottle from the soda fridge and took a seat on a bar stool at one of the centrally-located pub tables, the only empty table, a few feet away from the fridge.

His mind drifted back to that fateful summer.

Kannada sprinkled parmesan cheese on his slice. "How is it?"

"Perfect, like always," Amara said, absorbed in a savory bite, the cheese stretching out before her.

"You know this place should expand?" He held the pie near his face and sniffed it.

"I know, right."

He adjusted an olive that hung off the side, then watched her eat. "Maybe that wouldn't be a good thing."

"Why not?"

"Because that's all you'd eat."

She grinned. "Fine dining every day? No prob-lem-o."

"Then you'd gain all this weight and become a salad dodger."

Amara frowned and avoided eye contact. "Wow . . . well, you're not getting any action tonight."

Why'd I say that? Kannada groaned.

"Doesn't matter what I eat, my figure doesn't change," she said.

"Youth is such a beautiful thing." He tasted his pizza.

His woman nodded, homing in on another bite. She stopped short and stared at him.

"What?" He said with his cheeks stuffed.

Amara smiled. "You did it again."

Kannada grabbed a napkin and tried to wipe himself. He missed the smudge of tomato sauce on the side of his face, over and over.

Amara reached for the napkin. "Give me that. Thirty and still no table manners." She wiped his face for him.

He smiled.

"Kannada?" Ben said.

Kannada stopped daydreaming. "What?"

Ben had taken a seat across from him. He directed with his eyes. Kannada looked down at a folded-back copy of *The New York Times*. The newspaper had an article titled, "FriendBin Corp. set to go public in December." A photo of the founders of the new social media company celebrating was embedded in the story.

Kannada nodded and looked at his accomplice. *Everything is falling into place.* He positioned a slice of pepperoni pizza in front of his mouth and spoke softly. "We're still not done, you know." He bit down.

Ben showered his slice with Parmesan cheese.

"We need someone with class and elegance. Someone with a killer instinct who always gets his way." Kannada chewed heartily, wiping the ends of his mouth with a paper napkin before things got out of hand.

Ben shrugged, sprinkling red pepper now.

Kannada waited on the edge of his seat, searching for a response.

"You won't succeed without her." Ben put down the pepper shaker, picked up his slice of the pie, and took one humongous chomp as a pizza pan banged against the floor, breaking the smooth sound of low, indistinct voices of strangers nearby. A few customers looked in the direction of the noise.

Kannada momentarily forgot all else, leaned in, and grimaced. "Her?"

Beverly Hills, California

Surrounded by the cities of West Hollywood and Los Angeles, Beverly Hills, "90210," was one Indian woman's paradise. From five-star, five-diamond luxury retreats to neighborhood boutique hotels, nearly every place on earth looked like the slums compared to this niche abode for the affluent.

In the heart of 90210, three blocks of Rodeo Drive were home to the epicenter of fashion, luxury, and lifestyle. With crisp paved roads, palm trees, and blue skies, it had an atmosphere of no worries. Lamborghinis, Ferraris, Rolls-Royces, and Bentleys lined the sidewalks and teased outsiders with their sun glare. Visitors luxuriated in lavish spas, indulged in world-renowned shopping along famed Rodeo Drive, and, if they were lucky, caught glimpses of celebrities.

On Via Rodeo, a European-style, pedestrian concourse that resembled a movie set with high-end stores and fantastic restaurants, one shopper kept her poise as though she were on a fashion show runway. Rather than a runway, her stage was the lightly packed handbag section toward the left on the ground floor of the spacious Versace store.

With sea green eyes that complemented her wavy, chestnut, balayage hair, she was the *crème de la crème* of women. She was also a sugar baby, serving as arm candy and companion to some sucker of a wealthy guy. If it wasn't for the on-and-off twirling of gum around her fingers, which drew hard stares from the employees, she might have been mistaken for a model.

Zara Sethi was her name, and modeling didn't give her the same rush as teasing men.

A couple of guys gawked, nudging their buddy to enjoy the spectacle, and some took quick peeks, even in the proximity of their wives or girlfriends, who were busy yapping about whether something fit their wardrobe. The hapless women didn't realize that Zara had the attention that they sought from their men.

There was a small chance the other patrons would realize the trap Zara was laying, her countenance focused. She gingerly caressed the leather purse in her hand.

"What do you make of this, honey?" Zara inquired of her partner.

"It's perfect, like you." The rich man molded his lips into a kiss as he held three shoe boxes under his arm.

She denied him the pleasure of a peck. "Thank you. I'd like these other two as well."

The man winced as he examined the price tag. "Well, that's more than ten thousand dollars just on purses."

"Oh." She turned her head away. "I guess I'll never meet a respectful, caring guy."

The man swallowed. "It's really not that much."

"Ah, you're so sweet." She hugged the man and kissed him on the cheek.

The man blushed.

Zara, a high-class escort, just got away with murder. She smirked as the pathetic man followed her wherever she led him. She had him wrapped around her fingers just as she had that gum every few minutes.

A few minutes later, Zara and her client exited the store. As she paused at a prime tourist photo spot under the intersecting street signs of Via Rodeo and N. Rodeo, she noticed a text message. The message:

THE Blvd Restaurant. Regent Beverly Wilshire Hotel. 6 PM. Your admirer.

Zara stared at her cell phone, then looked around the street. *Which way is the hotel?* The men glancing at her were nearly caught; they swiftly faced their partners and remained inconspicuous.

She replied to determine her admirer's involvement with law enforcement, the necessity of a non-disclosure agreement, and his interest, a dinner date. After some light screening, she excused his lack of references and texted back in agreement.

When the clock turned 6:10, she walked into the Regent Beverly Wilshire Hotel, past the opulent foyer with a chandelier hanging over a round table of flowers, and into THE Blvd Restaurant, her eyes searching for a sign. A perky blonde hostess greeted her at the front.

"Are you Zara Sethi?"

Zara nodded, twirling a red lollipop in her mouth. It was still daylight. It was in public. *Couldn't be all that dangerous.*

"Right this way. He's been waiting for you," the hostess said.

She led her through the sophisticated dining spot with lofty ceilings and large windows overlooking the intersection of Wilshire Boulevard and Rodeo Drive. They walked past the modern lounge, centered on a magnificent backlit wine display and an illuminated onyx bar, to the outdoor sidewalk patio, a perfect place for people watching. There, she saw a calm, cool, and collected man, well-dressed, wearing the classic Wayfarer Ray-Bans and enjoying a slice of tiramisu next to a window.

This lone man had to be her admirer, so she believed.

"Hi, Zara. I'm Kannada from New York. So glad you could make it. For a second I thought you were going to flake on me."

"I'm sorry I'm late," Zara said.

"No apologies necessary. I'm a friend of Ben Wu. Please have a seat." He took off his shades and showed his onyx eyes.

Zara's encounters with men ran the gamut; she didn't have the slightest idea who Ben Wu was. All she knew was that Ben wasn't a cop; she hadn't been caught yet.

She raised her threaded brows, expecting. "Do you have my roses?"

"Roses?"

Her posture deflated. "Didn't you read my ad?"

"I got your number from Ben."

"It's a six-hundred-dollar donation for thirty minutes, and nine hundred for the hour. No kissing on the lips. And you have to pay for the meal."

Kannada's mouth dropped. "Can I write you a check?"

She looked sternly at him. She wanted cold, hard cash. It was the currency of her trade.

"Don't waste my time." Zara didn't hesitate. She wasn't going to give him a choice; if he tried to negotiate, she'd leave.

Kannada pulled out his wallet from under his coat and opened it.

She observed the crisp hundred-dollar bills in his wallet, took a hunch to trust him, and sat down. She touched fluid on the recently washed table and put her Coach bag to the side.

Zara watched his every misstep. "You're a first-timer."

"No, I'm not."

She sensed hesitation in his response. "Yes, you are. It's okay."

"I've done this plenty of times, so many times I can't even keep track. In fact, I'm a seasoned veteran."

She smiled. "I love first-timers. You're cute."

Kannada bent his neck forward and opened his mouth but gave up and opted for a sigh. "Ben mentioned you." He laid six fresh hundreds on the table. "He said you were one of the best-looking women he'd ever met. He said you were independent."

She collected the money. "Thank you."

"Said you were high maintenance, too."

Zara chortled in disbelief. "I resent that. Do you even want to do this?"

"Only kidding."

She narrowed her eyes, then relaxed them. "I'm sorry; who's Ben Wu?"

"Let me guess, too many clients?" He put away his wallet.

Her attention gravitated toward a waiter making a table a few feet away, then settled on Kannada.

"Yeah, I'm sorry," Zara said. "What else did he say?"

"So, how come you're not in Chicago anymore?" Kannada put his hands on the table and interlaced his fingers.

"I don't like cold places. Chicago is just too cold. I like it here. The weather is warm; the people are friendlier and more generous. I like to travel to other places, too, tropical and temperate climates, like San Francisco—"

"I love San Francisco. I could definitely live there."

Zara stared and finished her sentence. "But I stay away from the cold cities. Have you done this before?"

Kannada stared at the table as silverware clanked against dishes in a bus tub. He opened his mouth to say something, then closed it.

"Yeah, of course," he said at once. "Ugh, I hate L.A."

"That's because you're from New York."

"You know what? Actually, I feel like I could live in L.A."

Zara rolled her eyes; she didn't think he could. "You know what I really like?"

"What's that?"

"Shopping. Do you want to go shopping later, then maybe back to your hotel room, or mine? We can have some fun," Zara said with a naughty smile.

She rolled the sweet lollipop against her dick pillows, reddening them, then stopped to place it on a small plate. She smiled and stared.

"What're you doing?" Kannada asked.

She held her tantalizing gaze.

"That doesn't work on me."

Zara tilted her head down slightly and showed him a pair of sexy bedroom eyes, her eyeliner, eye shadow, and mascara in full effect. She gently caressed his hands.

"Stop. Enough already." Kannada retracted his hands. "I want you to come work for me. Come to New York."

"I'm kind of busy here." Zara's gaze flicked upward. She crossed her arms and tried to think of an excuse to leave. *He's even worse than the last guy I met.*

"How much do you make doing this?"

"That's my little secret," she said flirtingly.

"I know your gig is pretty sweet, a couple of hours of work, then you can pay your bills and buy, or get someone else to buy, whatever you want. That's great for the short-term, but I'm talking long-term. Either you can continue to pick up some money here and there, or you can make the big bucks, right now. What's it going to be?"

I already make the big bucks. How much does he rake in?

Kannada pulled out his cell phone and placed it in front of Zara with its display on.

"What's this?" She unfolded her arms and leaned forward.

"Your boarding pass."

Zara stiffened her posture. She wanted to share this experience with her friends, other escorts. "That's some wishful thinking you got."

"Ben told me you were underrated, a hidden talent. We just want to put you to good use."

"Look, I don't do porn or anything like that. I'm an upscale

luxury companion, only available for 'time and companionship.'"
She chose her last words wisely; he could still be a cop.

"No." Kannada sounded distressed. "This isn't about that. It doesn't happen very often that you get a chance to make some real money. It's either now or never."

Zara frowned. "Aren't you even going to tell me what this is for?"

He searched the table. "A hedgie wants to get revenge on his peer based on my plans. Your good looks could help us. I'll give you more details when you come."

Zara squinted for a moment. She leaned forward, rested her chin on her hands, elbows on the table, and stared deep into Kannada's eyes. "For how long?"

"Three weeks."

"Three whole weeks?" Zara's mouth fell open, and her thoughts became fuzzy. "You'll have to pony up."

"How much?"

"Well, two thousand bucks a day, times twenty-one days . . . I guess sixty thousand," Zara said, calculating in space.

His chest caved in. "Well, aren't you a pretty penny? The math says forty-two thousand. Where'd you come up with that number?"

She smiled. "Nights and weekend rates."

"Sixty thousand?" Kannada held his elbow while the opposite hand made a fist against his mouth. He pressed his lips together in a small grimace. "That's it?"

Zara hadn't the slightest idea to whom she was talking, but he sounded less and less like a police officer. "Well, I mean—"

"I'll make sure you get at least a hundred times over."

She stared at him. *Who is this guy?* "And what if I don't want to?"

"We'll move on, make our money, and you can keep meeting guys for 'time and companionship.'"

Zara slouched back in her chair, folded her arms, and reflected. She stared at the QR code in front of her, then looked at the people walking along the open thoroughfare of Rodeo Drive.

This man is serious. No drama. No cop.

A blond waiter approached. "Can I take your orders?"

Kannada whispered, "In a few," waving him off.

He nodded and left the two alone.

"New York?" Zara said, undistracted.

"New York is always a good idea." Kannada smiled.

CHAPTER 9

Manhattan, New York

Rob had invited everyone to join him at the Plaza Hotel, his baby under The Prosperi Organization. Located at Fifth Avenue and Central Park South, the centuries-old luxury hotel had all the splendor, grandeur, and opulence of a French chateau. It was once said that, "Nothing unimportant ever happens at the Plaza," and if everything worked smoothly, that maxim would hold true. It was the hotel to view and be viewed. Political dignitaries and stars of the big screen had all visited the Plaza.

Rob made sure to treat his guests. With a hefty price tag, roughly sixty million dollars, the one-of-a-kind "attic" penthouse, a magnificent, triplex apartment at the top of the building, on the residential property side, would be the group's residence for the next few weeks. It contained four bedrooms and six bathrooms, advanced home automation, and a 31-foot terrace overlooking Central Park. It was accessible only by private elevator, providing the privacy they needed to carry out their mission.

Paul was already there, an early arrival, sporting a black Dead Rabbit T-shirt and talking to the female bartender, drink in hand, at the custom bar.

Rob was there, naturally, trying to figure out how the thermostat worked on an iPad.

Upon hearing knocks on the door, he bobbled the iPad and nearly dropped it. He looked up, expecting the guests to start pouring in one by one as the doorman addressed his call for duty.

On the twentieth floor, five men came in all at once, jackets on, with a bellboy in the back carrying their luggage.

"Hey, Rob, nice place you got here," a black man said, low-pitched.

Rob stood to meet his guests; he started by welcoming and thanking Walker for his compliment, then exchanged introductions with a pale bald man taking off his jacket.

Ricky gave his warming garment to the doorman, then faced the host. "Why's it so chilly in here?"

"It's this iPad. It's supposed to control the room's ambiance." Rob stared down at the device as if some old geezer out of touch with the day's technology.

"Perhaps I could be of assistance," a brown-skinned man with plastic frames said.

"Why not? I'm getting nowhere," Rob said.

"Iago 'Smarty' Gonzales." He introduced himself with his hand extended.

"Nice to finally meet you." Rob stared him in the eye and firmly shook his cold hand.

While Iago flopped onto one of the sofas, Rob greeted everyone similarly and gave them an unforgettable taste of the Big Apple, his New York accent.

Near the custom bar, Alan the desert pilot rubbed the red chapped skin on his face.

"What happened to you? You look like a sunbaked cheddar chip," Paul remarked.

"It's this damn sunscreen. It says up to eight hours of protection, more like two," Alan said.

"Hey, there's a fitness room in here!" Walker yelled from the back.

After styling his short-and-spikey Asian hair, Ben came down from the master bedroom, which occupied the entire third floor of the penthouse. "There's a buffet in the dining room," he said to Paul and Alan. "If you guys aren't aware, this is a white-glove building. Rob made some arrangements, so you guys have access to the spas, restaurants, food halls, and everything the hotel offers. You can eat all you want here: twenty-four-hour in-room dining and a twenty-four-hour butler service. There's a complementary Bimmer, too."

Paul and Alan glanced at one another and smiled.

The posh master bedroom overlooking Central Park was decorated in a romantic palate of creams, beige, and gray. In the generously sized en-suite bathroom, adorned with marble mosaic tile and 24-karat gold-plated fixtures, Kannada was getting ready in front of the mirror. The master bedroom would be occupied by him and Ben, as Rob would continue living at his Long Island residence.

The gaudiness of the penthouse and Rob's generosity made him believe Rob was flaunting his wealth to an outsider, but it didn't matter; he hadn't felt this good in a long time. The environment, the people and the nice townhouse, was doing wonders for his spirit, even if his plans amounted to nothing. A few minutes later, he would make his appearance.

At the custom bar, the sound of a machine disrupted Ben's flirty conversation with the barmaid. He checked his watch to determine whether it was time to start the meeting. There was no need to worry. To investigate the jarring noise, he walked down a curved, wooden stairwell to the nineteenth floor and saw Walker in the fitness room. *As I expected.*

In gray cotton sweats, his head covered with a black beanie, just like Rocky Balboa, Walker was working out on a treadmill.

Ricky walked into the luxurious dining room; it seated up to fourteen, more than enough space. The table at the center of the room was lined with foods of all kind; he selected a banana and peeled it.

"Have you ever visited the Grand Canyon, Ricky?" Alan the outdoorsman said, holding a plate of steak, under a chandelier.

"No, never been out West." Ricky, the ham actor turned con man, took a bite of the banana. His salivary glands went to work with the sweetness. The smoky scent of Alan's food permeated the air, and he considered trying some.

"It's great. You could get away from it all." Alan put down his dish and grabbed a napkin.

"Would you say it's a good hiding place?" Ricky said, his cheeks stuffed with fruit.

"Heck, if you hid there, no one would ever find you." Alan wiped the rim of his mouth.

Ricky nodded. "Precisely." He'd visit the Grand Canyon for only one reason; to hide.

In the exquisitely designed living room, fitted with a grand piano, Rob noticed Iago playing on the sofa with the iPad and called his name a couple of times to get his attention.

Iago finally looked up. "Yes?"

"I called you twice."

"Sorry, I'm oblivious to people when I use Apple products."

"You and the rest of the planet." Rob rolled his eyes. "Did you figure it out?"

"Not only that, I jailbroke into the iPad. Now, you can do more with it."

Rob furrowed his brows in confusion.

Outside, on the balcony, on his own with glass in hand, Dilip marveled at Central Park, his body leaning over the glass fence. He lived in a different world, unfamiliar with this group. His nephew, a market man turned homeless over the years, had kept him at arm's length since he started working on Wall Street. Dilip was aware of the unwritten code of silence on Wall Street; you just don't go to the SEC.

Rob looked around the living area. "I think that's everyone. They've had enough time to get to know each other. Should we begin?"

"No, there's still one more," Ben said.

"Who?"

"Ma'am, would you like me to take your bags up to your room?" a bellboy asked.

Zara, filing her nails, glanced at the man as the driver of her vehicle waited. "Sure." She readdressed her nails, feeling cold.

She strode into the Plaza in a midriff and short skirt with knee-high leather boots, her very own sexy style. Zara had no need for winter clothes living in The Big Orange.

The receptionists' heads, male and female, turned as Zara walked to the elevator.

When she reached the townhouse in the sky, the doorman opened the door and let her into the room. The bellboy followed with her luggage.

Though Zara knew the score, she dropped her jaw and widened her eyes upon seeing the assembly of men. *I am not fucking all these guys for three weeks. I'm not a Dutch wife. Where's Kannada? What's he trying to do, get a group discount?*

Zara swallowed, and her belly fluttered. Despite her reluctance, she pointed to a spot near a wall. "You can leave them right there."

The bellboy started to unload the bags.

"Hi, boys." Zara grinned with an air of bravado.

The newly assembled gang ogled at her hourglass figure.

"Maybe we should get to know each other a little longer," a husky man with dark brown, curly hair remarked, from the side of his mouth.

"Sounds like a good idea," a blue-eyed blond man wearing a Dead Rabbit short-sleeved top said, his mouth open.

The attention flattered Zara as the bellboy patiently stood by the door, waiting.

"Oh, I almost forgot." She kissed the bellboy on the cheek, then smiled. "Thank you, sweetie."

The bellboy broke out into a goofy smile, blushing. "Absolutely." It was more than good enough.

Rob witnessed Kannada coming down the stairwell a short while later with Ben at his side. Kannada stood at the front of the living room on one side of the fireplace; Ben took his position next to him on the opposite side of the mantel. Rob waved off the attendants, the doorman and the barmaid, to leave.

"Gentlemen and lady, welcome to the Plaza," Kannada announced.

Rob surveyed the room; Kannada appeared to have everyone's attention, except for Dilip, who was missing.

"Everybody ready? We'll be starting shortly," Kannada said. He and Ben set up the PowerPoint while the rest of the group settled down.

With drink in hand, Rob searched the floors for the old man with salt-and-pepper hair and matching stubble and found him standing on the terrace of the master bedroom. "Hey."

Dilip turned to face him. His gold stud earring shined because of the light indoors.

"You're the regulator, right?" Rob said. *A little intimidating, this Dilip fellow.*

"Yeah."

"All the way from D.C.?" Rob took a shot of alcohol.

"Yeah." Dilip hocked a loogie over the balcony.

Rob's eyes widened. *Some poor sap below is going to be hit with a wad of phlegm.* He shook his head. *Not my problem.* "The SEC headquarters is there." He took another sip. "You're here to take Lemon down?"

"Yeah."

"That's fantastic." *At least he's on our side.* "I still hate you guys."

Dilip smiled. He walked right in, descended one floor, and moved into the living area where he took a seat.

"I hope you guys had a good Thanksgiving," Kannada said, as everybody was present, then looking at Zara, "and a good Black Friday." She smiled. "I'm glad all of you could make it. So, are you people awake? Anybody feeling jet lag?"

A few people chortled; some grunted.

"All right," he went on. "Some of you have worked with each other before when we were at Caldwell Investments together. And the rest of you met each other tonight. You probably haven't met Zara before; she's Ben's friend from the Golden State."

"And Dilip," Ben added. "He's Kannada's acquaintance from D.C. A backdoor revolver."

Kannada wasn't going to acknowledge his uncle; Dilip never returned his calls when he needed a job.

Zara glanced around the room; every single pair of eyes met her.

Dilip stayed stone-faced, as usual.

"Okay," Kannada said. "I'm assuming all of you are in for this ride. That's why you're here, or you just wanted to stay at the Plaza for free."

A few people laughed.

He paused to appreciate the moment. This was the first time he stood in front of an audience in five years. He could feel his voice returning, as he was important again. The attention was beautiful.

"When we met earlier with you, we gave you a summary of what was expected. Now that you're here, we'll discuss the specifics and answer any questions you may have." He paused again, anxious. "All right, let's begin."

CHAPTER 10

Manhattan, New York

Kannada stood in the living area of their Plaza Hotel penthouse and absorbed the setting before he described the nature of the caper.

A chandelier hung in the lavish living room. A giant skylight met a row of awning windows on the sidewall, all facing Central Park. One large TV monitor perched atop a solid, cherry oak wood stand, and a grand piano stood in the corner. The room was equipped with two sofas, soft woven upholstery rendered in a neutral beige, one rectangular, wood-and-glass centerpiece table situated between them, and a couple of accent chairs that matched the sofas' decorative pillows, all on top of a Kashmir pure silk, floral rug.

As nice as the penthouse was, the group seemed to barely notice, as their eyes were more interested in discovering what was under a cover, masking some structure, on the central table. Under the blue-and-gold cover, the vague outline of a complex structure was barely discernible. They looked as though they had been waiting to see what it was since they arrived.

"At 11 Wall Street, we have the New York Stock Exchange, also known as the Big Board," Kannada said. "It's the country's oldest stock exchange and the world's largest stock exchange by market capitalization."

Ben removed the cover from a model on the central table. The team inched closer, captivated. Under the cover, revealed for the first time, was the NYSE, made of Taskboard and plastic and similar in tone. He raised the rooftop and exposed the main elements of the building, the trading floors.

A moment of silent captivation took hold as the team gazed at the model.

"That's what you used the floor plans for?" Rob asked.

"Yeah," Kannada replied. "Pretty neat, huh?"

Rob parted his lips and widened his eyes. "You even got the trading posts and broker booths in there. You must've gone to some trouble to get that piece."

"No kidding," Ben remarked.

"Gentlemen and lady, the trading floors," Kannada said. "Within the heart of the NYSE lie the four trading floors, the Blue Room." He pointed to one of the floors. "The Expanded Blue Room." A similar motion specified the area. "The Garage, which is being renovated and will be called the Buttonwood Room." He indicated another trading floor. "And the Main Room." He pointed for the last time. "Financial instruments are traded. There is no money, no gold, and no vaults. Nothing physical to rob."

Half of the room frowned. The other half voiced their concerns to one another.

Walker shook his head with a distraught gaze. "This is exactly why I wasn't sure about this."

Dilip crossed his arms and turned his head slightly toward Walker. "You're not the only doubting Thomas."

"Is this a joke?" Zara asked Ricky.

He shrugged. "That's what I'd like to know. I *had* to come after they saved my bacon."

"And we're going to go in, take some shares, and get away with it," Kannada continued.

Zara coolly put a red lollipop into her mouth as everyone gasped and murmured.

"Just walk in and make a couple of trades, huh?" Walker said, in a low tone.

Ben sighed. "I wish."

"The first obstacle, getting into the building," Kannada said. "The Big Board has a security system so tight that not even Jack

83

'Superthief' MacLean could get in."

Eyes bulged, and heads jerked back. The sound of effervescence slipped past them, as Alan the elbow bender pried off a beer cap with a bottle opener on his key chain.

Kannada's mouth ran dry and his nose twitched, catching the smell of food from the dining hall; he hadn't eaten yet. He became lightheaded, and his fingers involuntarily twitched toward the rations.

He shook his head and continued. "Seven intersections were closed to protect the NYSE since 9/11, making the entrances nearly unapproachable."

"The front door, 18 Broad Street." Ben pointed to an entrance. "The back door, at the intersection of New Street and Wall Street." He motioned again. "The side door, 20 Broad Street, which may no longer be an option because of luxury rental properties taking over." He pointed to another door. "And the VIP entrance at the corner of Broad Street and Wall Street." He indicated the last entrance.

Kannada swallowed. "This isn't the same as simply walking in. It's like the Ring of Steel but worse."

Looks of whoa marked most of the faces in the room. Some furrowed their brows. Alan cocked his head back and chugged down beer. Zara swished the lollipop around in her mouth.

Kannada continued. "There are steel barricades preventing anyone from getting within twenty feet of the building. NoGo blocks on sidewalks, bronze pillars on turntables, Delta barriers, and operable bollards make vehicle passage obsolete. Unless you have a special permit, you're not allowed to drive within a few blocks of the NYSE, and they search every car that comes in."

"Which means we'll have to get creative," Ben said.

Kannada paused to see how the gang was taking the news, but his attention quickly turned to the growls in his belly.

"New York's finest, twenty-four hours on the ground," he said.

"Which we won't pass," Ben quipped.

"Homeland Security helicopters in the air," Kannada said.

"Which we can't hide from," Ben remarked.

"Cameras and license plate readers."

"Which puts us on *America's Most Wanted*."

"No regular tours inside, not since 9/11."

"Which spoiled my vacation."

Kannada stopped. They were still there, and so were his obsessive thoughts of food. "Okay. Now for the bad news." He pulled out the remote from his pocket and switched on the TV.

"Thanks to Iago Gonzales, new bug bounty hacker for the NYSE, we have the security details inside the building." He stepped back and watched with the other nine members.

On the screen, a video played. A man in his late fifties with thin brown hair combed to the side stood emotionless in an empty lobby of the NYSE, surrounded by old tickers encased in glass.

"Welcome to the New York Stock Exchange. I'm Richard DuPont, Head of Security and Managing Director of Cybersecurity at the New York Stock Exchange, or NYSE. At the NYSE, we take great pride in ensuring the safety and security of the financial markets. As an employee, you'll be issued a universal security badge, like this one." He lifted the badge on his lanyard, then put his hand to the side. "It will provide access to most, if not all, areas of the building. Certain individuals will be provided with a higher security clearance for restricted areas depending on the nature of their work."

DuPont suddenly appeared in the mailroom, where several workers sorted mail behind him.

"Furthermore, all incoming persons, mail, packages, and parcels are subject to physical and x-ray magnetometer inspections. All messengers delivering mail, packages, or parcels are screened. All visitors and employees are required to have unified photo ID badges."

The next scene positioned DuPont at a security post inside the NYSE. Several brokers and traders scanned their badges and hurried through turnstiles in the background.

"Now, though we have security guards set up at different posts, you—yes you, the employee—play an integral role in securing the markets. Let me explain. As an employee, you will be issued a cell phone with two-way radio capability and given access to emergency contact telephone numbers. It's your responsibility to report any fraudulent or suspicious activity.

"To maintain a smooth flow of the markets, access to a password-protected contingency website, which provides directions and information in case of a disruption or incident of any kind, will be provided, as well as laptops with cellular modem cards and remote connection software to wirelessly connect to the NYSE's resources wherever cellular coverage is accessible."

The screen showed a close-up of a worker logging into a computer and a trading account.

"For those of you who will be trading on the trading floors, two passwords are required. A daily password, issued at the start of each trading session and good for one day, will be used to log into your computer station. The other is a password that your firm will provide you with to trade on your firm's account."

The camera slowly moved from right to left and showed a busy trading floor.

"In the event that damage is done to the trading floors, the NYSE has a backup trading floor at—"

Kannada paused the video and sighed. *Damn, that was long*. He examined the room to see what his guests thought. No one was sweating bullets, at least not yet. So far, so good.

"Once you're in the building, you'll meet the usual, cameras, security posts, etcetera," Kannada said. "Just fit in with the crowd, act like you know what you're doing, and you'll be fine."

The group remained silent, frozen. Either they had questions, unsure where to begin, or held their objections, sure this wasn't even going to work.

"Do we have to contend with biometrics or voice activation?" Ricky asked.

"No," Ben answered.

The room was quiet again. Kannada swallowed. *Ricky's conning skills will come in handy. He's interested. I can tell.*

"It's not the time to be shy," Ben said.

The attendees may have been coy, but the unexplainable creaks and cracks of an aging edifice weren't. Kannada smiled, as his presentation skills were still on point.

"All right, now our objective. The market reacts to the news, any news." Kannada started to walk around the room, as if giving an imaginary son a lecture to remember. His limbs quivered.

"Stocks," he continued, "can start off high in the day, and end up low at the end. Or, they could start off low, and end up high. It doesn't take a day. It could be a matter of minutes, even seconds, if the conditions are right. Oil goes up when there's war. Pharmas go up with new drugs. An acquired company goes up when it's taken over. That all occurs over time or, in the case of an acquisition, without notice."

The potential accomplices smiled and nodded.

"But, on a highly-anticipated, hyped-up IPO, initial public offering for those of you not familiar with stock jargon . . ." Kannada looked at Zara who was sucking on a lollipop. He licked his lips. "The company's shares skyrocket."

Zara's sea green eyes lit up with dollar signs, and her pouty lips smiled with pleasure. Kannada stopped in the front, where he originally was, and stood beside the monitor.

Ben intervened, "So, just to give you some background, the shares are bought by investment banks at the IPO price minus commission; then, they're sold to their institutional clients at the same IPO price after the company goes on a road show to market their business. The initial buyers submit subscription requests for the IPO a few days prior to the IPO date. And if history is any indication, Lemon Group will 'subscribe' to FriendBin's IPO."

The group was dead silent. A bag of Cheetos crinkled and unmuted the room, as Iago opened the bag.

Where'd he get those? Kannada's stomach grumbled. *Speed this presentation up.*

"If you haven't been paying attention to the news, FriendBin, or F-B-N, as it will be listed on the NYSE, announced months ago it would offer two hundred million shares on the public market," he said.

"Once the shares are released for trading," Ben said, "all hell breaks loose. Orders start coming in from all over the world. The first trade, and subsequent trades, will be settled much higher than the IPO price paid by the institutional clients. So, the rich, the institutional clients, get richer, selling shares at double, even triple, the IPO price."

Alan removed the beer bottle from his lips. "What price did the company set for its IPO?"

"Anticipation has been building since they made their announcement," Kannada said. "Some think the offering price will be in the $20 to $25 range, a few weeks later, analysts were saying it would be between $23 and $28, but we won't know until opening day."

"Any other questions?" Ben asked.

"Who're the institutional clients?" Iago put a Cheetos snack into his mouth.

"Jews like me." Rob grinned, his hands atop his large gut.

Ben smirked and took over. "They're the important clients, the big players, of the underwriting banks, such as large mutual funds, hedge funds, high net-worth individuals, and long-time clients."

Iago paused crunching. "What about in the gap, from the time the institutional clients get the shares until they're released?"

"There's no opportunity in the gap," Ben said. "It's an auction, with the demand generated from the outside, with tons of market orders driving up the price."

Kannada smiled at Ben, as the group bristled with anticipation.

"How do they get the shares? Does someone just give them a slip of paper?" Iago asked.

It was Kannada's turn. "The transaction between the client subscribers and the investment bankers happens only in the accounts at the investment bank. The cash is debited, and shares are credited to the client's account, all at the same time. So, no client can get a head start on any others. Then the shares are released."

"The institutional clients," Ben added, "are given first dibs on the shares because they provide 'stability' in the markets, as they function as long-term investors. They usually don't flip the stock immediately. It's frowned upon in the industry."

"But we will," Iago observed.

"Right on," Ben said.

Kannada checked on Zara; she addressed her phone, her head down. *Poor hooker. Probably doesn't understand a damn thing.*

"Now there're ten of us." Kannada rubbed his stomach. "You all have a special part to play based on your talents, so each gets an equal share. Depending on where the market opens and how much investors push the stock up, we can either be rich, or filthy rich."

With dreamy eyes, the guests glanced at one another to see if others experienced the same feeling. Some sat at the edge of their seats, while others smiled. Everyone whispered with hushed, excitable tones.

Ben looked at the old man. "No more going through the revolving door."

Dilip cleared his throat. "Let's say we get into the NYSE, make our trades, and so forth, but isn't there still a possibility the shares don't go up?"

The group stared at Kannada, waiting for a response.

"Yes, there's a small chance that the shares don't pop. In fact, they may even go below the offering price paid by the institutional investors," he said.

The group muttered collectively.

"Calm down," Ben said. "The likelihood of that happening is slim, and the underwriters would probably add support by purchasing additional shares to save face."

The room came under order.

Iago adjusted his black, full-rim plastic glasses. "How're we going to operate?"

"We'll be operating as a private partnership called The Main Street Company," Kannada said, "and it will have an account with one of the major investment firms."

"Shared expenses?" Iago snacked again.

"Yes, this is a real partnership," Ben said. "They'll be taken care of by Rob initially, but will ultimately be shared."

With sweat on his forehead and hands, Kannada stared at the Cheetos bag in Iago's lap, the bottle of alcohol in Alan's hand, and the sucker in Zara's mouth, and sighed. *This is it. If you cheat those folks down at the NYSE, you can get drunk all you want and live a sweet life.* He cleared his throat before he posed the big question. "We got three weeks to prepare. So, what do you think?"

The members of the group looked at each other.

"Better than any tip I'll ever make." Paul started things off on the right foot.

"Cheaters can finally prosper." Ben added to the good vibe.

"No risk, no reward." Rob was ready to try a new way.

"I look forward to the challenge." Iago smeared the sofa with orange dust.

"What the hey? I'm going to croak any minute now." Dilip's cough returned. He stood and walked toward the kitchen, ready to expectorate mucus.

I wonder if this old guy can keep up. Forget about him. What about you? Kannada returned to attaining the remaining responses.

"Heck, I'm ready to knock the shit out of someone right now," Walker said.

"This will be the greatest con job I'll ever do," Ricky remarked.

"You know me. I'm too drunk to know what I'm doing." Alan resumed drinking.

"Zara?" Kannada waited for the last but not least important member of the group.

She took out the lollipop from her mouth. "My best advance yet." Zara, possessing the finest killer instinct, winked with a devilish smile.

Kannada beamed; they approved, and he could finally go eat. "All right. Get a good night's rest. We start tomorrow."

CHAPTER 11

Manhattan, New York

The next morning, Kannada sat at the head of the dining table and addressed Walker, Alan, and Iago after breakfast.

"First step, access to the NYSE," he said to Walker. "I want to know about the entrances to the building for both vehicles and people. Find out where the guards are stationed."

He turned to Alan, the desert pilot. "Everything the hawks in the air can see, I want to see."

Kannada looked at Iago, the white hat turned black hat. "And most of all, I want a rundown on whoever makes the NYSE run—traders, brokers, janitors, etcetera."

Walker, with his ability to home in on punching targets, focused on his task as he made his way around the Big Board. Dressed like Rocky, wearing a black beanie, a pair of black Chuck Taylors, and gray cotton sweats, he could've easily been mistaken as a tourist or freelance photographer, and some might say a hobo, if it weren't for the professional DSLR camera dangling from his neck.

Away from the Big Board, large trucks squeaked, and luxurious cars smoothly accelerated as they stopped at the retractable posts and continued. Guards approved the entrance of vehicles, and drivers subsequently smiled with relief. Walker lurked among the pedestrians, marked the location of entry points on a miniature map, and took a few photos.

He approached the NYSE and put the camera to his face to take a picture, but hesitated, as a police officer came into view. He held the device near his chest and looked around; the financial district was swarming with the New York Police Department, or NYPD. There were cops and cameras everywhere. Somebody was watching everywhere. It was like a beehive. Anyone attempting some mischief was sure to get stung. He ignored his worries; he was only taking pictures.

He looked at the skyscrapers that flanked the NYSE on all fours. The Exchange was conceived as short and stout to keep people from getting in, getting too close, and disrupting the flow. Though he had worked here many years ago for Caldwell Investments, he hadn't noticed how low the building lay until now.

When he saw businesspersons enter and exit the building, he reminisced on his glory days as a stockbroker. He had worked, lived, and smoked on the Exchange grounds, chasing paper, for nine years. His former job required him to be vigilant as to what was happening in the world, anywhere, anytime. *Ah, those were the days*. His sentimental longing for the past ended abruptly, as a man in a hoodie bumped into him, hard.

Watch where you're going, asshole! Walker gave the man a dirty look as the idiot stopped at a corner, looked over his shoulder, and kept his head down. Walker became suspicious and put his camera to his face to get a better look. The hooded man pulled out a small package from underneath his jacket and handed it off to a well-dressed person for some money. *In daylight?* Walker was familiar with the way Wall Street worked; soon, the fashionable player would distribute the contents of the package, drugs, to his buddies at parties.

Aside from terrorism and regular criminal activity, the financial district was home to a peculiar crime, one that went amiss, or the cops turned their heads to more often than not. Players in the high-stakes stock game had an infatuation with drugs, cocaine, speed, or whatever kept them focused and trading. They were running ragged, with fifteen hours of work done in eight hours to get that mansion, yacht, and private jet. It seemed as though they lived by one mantra:

get rich or die trying.

Walker snapped a few pictures of the drug runner and his dealings, then returned to scoping the area out. The first entrance he researched was the front one at 18 Broad Street; it was the most recognizable, lying under an architecture dating back to the Roman Renaissance. There were six columns and a pediment above them that contained six figures. A female character stood in the middle and was surrounded by two smaller men, which received and took note of the products brought to her by the others.

Of all the three thousand or so workers, only a handful glanced at the façade. Hardly anyone used this entrance. Workers gossiped and smoked as visitors passed by. Walker paused taking pictures and smirked, as their eyes followed women in short business skirts, tights, and stilettos along the street.

He moved south to 20 Broad Street, though he had been advised not to, as this address was being renovated for luxury rental apartments and retail space. He looked at the entrance with nostalgia; time was changing the building in which he had left his salad days and made his career. Walker paid little attention to the entrance and continued onward.

The entrance at the corner of Wall Street and New Street, the back door, just behind 2 Broad Street, was the most interesting and gave Walker more insight into NYSE life, as it was used by most of the individuals who worked at the Big Board. Everyone used badges or passes to gain access, even if a person stepped out for a moment. During the day, the entrance was crowded with employees taking a quick smoke, meeting colleagues, or searching for a little privacy from the floor.

Capping off the four main entrances, more like three with 20 Broad Street disappearing, there was the seldom-used VIP entryway at 2 Broad Street. It was the only gateway to touring the Big Board nowadays. If a person wanted to get in, he or she had to know someone. Fortunately, Walker and his team had Iago. He recalled his conversation with Kannada during the recruitment phase; Walker had made it clear that if the group didn't have an insider, he wouldn't come along for the ride.

He took some photos, then observed his miniature map; he had all the main entrances down. Walker searched his memory for other doors he had utilized when he worked here; nothing came to mind.

He looked up at the pediment and experienced an aha moment. There was another entrance no one used, no one knew about—the rooftop. The NYSE building was affixed to two large buildings, one to its left and one to its right. Both skyscrapers had entry points, but better, the Exchange had an entrance, too, several stories down: a spectacular thirty-foot square skylight. *The group needs a rooftop entrance, but will this do? Better check with Kannada.*

He snapped a picture of the pediment above the columns to remind him of the skylight when he presented his work to the group, then noticed a police officer staring at him. He looked elsewhere; another officer was watching him.

Walker needed to make the impression that he was just a friendly neighborhood Negro. He let the camera hang from his neck and smiled and waved at the vigilant officers to avoid looking suspicious. He checked the quality of the photos he shot, then left the scene.

Standing outside a high-rise hotel near the Big Board with a suitcase in hand and a camera bag over his shoulder, Alan spotted a Department of Homeland Security (DHS) helicopter flying above him. Maybe aerial security was needed. Maybe the Big Board just had too much money and wanted to spoil itself. Maybe the government was exercising its might and power, sending a clear message that the backbone to U.S. wealth wouldn't go down without a fight. Maybe it was a combination of these and more, but Alan couldn't say. He lowered his gaze to street level and twisted his mouth to the side.

Hardly any of the commoners who maneuvered around him on the streets noticed the chopper. It'd be best if they didn't know what Big Brother was up to. To the unsophisticated, the whole idea of aerial security was daunting. Who wanted to mess with the DHS? Who wanted to deal with the national government? If there was any indication of terrorism, it was time to kiss your life goodbye. Those folks didn't mess around. A mere accusation was enough to peel the skin right off the target's back.

For a person like Alan, it wasn't appalling at all because he knew about aircraft, especially helicopters. He'd spent his whole life around IFOs, identifiable flying objects, first as an Air Force pilot, then as a commercial pilot, next as Wendell Caldwell's private pilot, and finally with his most recent gig in the Grand Canyon.

Alan checked himself in at the hotel and made sure he got the room he needed to get the view he needed. When he entered his room, he opened his briefcase on the bed and grabbed one of many beer bottles. He opened the curtains and looked out the window, then sipped his beer and wet his blond mustache. The bitter hops, yeast, malted grains, and refreshing carbonation went down smoothly. He nosed the malty aroma, rich and caramel-like, and piney hops, then sighed. His phone rang.

"Hello?"

"Hey, bottle vulture, you drinking that domestic piss water again?" Ben said over the phone.

Alan looked down at the Brewski in his hand. "No."

"Get rid of it."

"Oh." Alan stomped his foot, then chugged the rest of the beer and threw the dead soldier into the trash.

He had grown frustrated with people thinking he had an addiction, especially Ben, who periodically called him to ensure his "soberness." He admitted that alcohol tempted him, but he knew when to say when. He looked back to the time he started the habit: since his wife and child died ten years ago in a hiking accident.

Alan shrugged off his annoyance and somberness, then took out a pair of binoculars from his suitcase and saw more than he expected.

Screams of ecstasy accompanied loud bangs on the wall separating his room from the next. Portraits shook with passion and lamps moved as in redecoration. Alan looked over and thought, *what was that?*

Sex?

Oh, yeah. He smirked and put things together. These Wall Street ballers weren't satisfied with fat paychecks, drugs, fast cars, and big houses. They were playboys. They needed a spark, a little fun, midday or after work. Escorts and call girls, whores and prostitutes, all came rushing in like moths to the flame. Money could buy everything. Even the quieter ones couldn't hide from Alan. It was blatantly obvious when random visitors knocked on the door across the hallway or the room next door at odd times, accompanied with phrases like, "Hey, go ahead and take your clothes off," before the door slammed shut.

Despite the buzzing activity in his vicinity, Alan kept at his job.

He examined the timing of helicopters day and night, their markings and color, how many were in the air at any given time, where they came from, where they finished their duty, and the route between. Through it all, he snapped pictures with a professional camera and jotted down notes, his first tour at spy work.

Iago, at his desk in the Big Board with three computers spread in front, surrounded by a couple of professional hackers like himself and a bag of Cheetos, jotted down notes on a legal pad as his boss, Richard DuPont, Head of Security and Managing Director of Cybersecurity, the same man in the video displayed at the Plaza, stood over him.

"Trading floor computers are on, and they're not responding." DuPont tapped the computer screen as his subordinate, Iago, watched. "Traders shouldn't have to start their day on the backup emergency trading floor." He sighed. "Item 51 on the day's glitch list. We have all the major problems of a stock market and an auction house, and the markets aren't even open yet."

"Thanks." Iago adjusted his black, full-rim plastic glasses and scribbled a few notes. "I'll take care of it right away."

DuPont nodded.

Iago watched the head honcho leave to his right, then looked toward his left. The coast was clear. He set off doing a different type of work. As the rest of the floor worked, he wormed his way into the computer system. He kept his ears alert, listening to the room's cadence of keyboard strokes and computer mice clicks, and his eyes observant, making sure no one saw him, as he hacked into the Exchange's employee list and downloaded files onto his personal thumb drive.

In the evening, Kannada left the Plaza. He entered an apartment complex, red rose in hand, hoping to reacquaint himself and gain favor with his fiancée, Amara. He rang the bell of the residence.

A brunette opened the door. "Yes?" The woman sounded exhausted.

Kannada raised an eyebrow. *Is she a roommate?* The smell of cleaning materials and dust entered his nose. He looked past her at the many boxes inside. "Um . . . I think I have the wrong apartment." He knew he didn't. His fiancée had moved.

A tall man carrying a box approached. He noticed Kannada's carnation and grimaced. "What's going on here, Tammy?"

Kannada looked at the domineering man. The man stared hard at him.

"Someone was actually being romantic for once," Tammy said. "Why don't you bring me roses?"

"Baby . . ." The significant other sounded desperate.

Kannada's eyes darted from one to the other before he slipped out of the argument. He would have to find another way.

CHAPTER 12

Manhattan, New York

Under dim lighting, with an awning window partially open, Kannada, Ben, Rob, and Dilip hunched at the edge of their seats in the living room, surrounded by pizza boxes, coffee, laptops, notepads, and pencils, all the necessities to get work done. They'd been plotting the perfect getaway scheme, researching and discussing for several hours, since daybreak.

Kannada poured coffee into a cup, thinking of a country to hide money, then mixed in some sugar.

"Switzerland?" Ben asked, notepad in one hand, dull pencil in the other and another used pencil resting behind his ear.

Dilip shook his head. "Forget that. All the milk and honey are gone. The gnomes of Zurich aren't worth a pinch of coon shit. Dozens of Swiss banks are cooperating with the IRS. The Irritating Rotten Scoundrels have been prying open secret Swiss bank accounts since the financial meltdown."

Kannada didn't like the sound of that.

"They've all paid significant fines," Rob added, "and I doubt they want to pay more, not to mention FATCA."

"What's that?" Kannada sipped coffee.

"Red tape. It requires all foreign banks that cooperate with the

U.S. to report to the IRS on their American customers." Rob sighed. "Whatever happened to the American dream?"

Kannada grinned. The sweet coffee tasted as though it was black.

"But we're still doing overseas?" Ben asked.

"We have to," Dilip said, "but where overseas? No money is to be deposited in the U.S."

The group paused for contemplation.

Dilip rubbed his salt-and-pepper stubble with his hand and suddenly had a thought. "Hold on. We're getting to the hiding part, but what about the transfer?"

"We can wire transfer it," Kannada suggested.

"Oh no, we can't," Dilip said. "That requires a lot of identity."

"Automated Clearing House, or ACH?" Ben volunteered.

"The payments are processed automatically." Kannada put his drink on the table.

"Hmm." Rob scratched his scalp amid dark brown, curly hair. "I believe that requires batch processing. They'll put everything into batches; then they'll process it at the end of the day. It's not on a one-by-one basis."

"There's lag," Dilip said.

The group sat in silence, stumped. Paul came into the room, dressed for work as a bartender at the Dead Rabbit, and started to clean up.

"Uh . . ." Rob sounded uneasy. "You don't have to do that."

"This place is worse than a pigsty," Paul said. "Have to keep things tidy."

Ben looked at Kannada.

Kannada glanced at the midday pies that were held in loosely closed cardboard boxes. He wasn't ready to part ways with the aroma of leftover pizza.

"Don't worry about it, Paul. We're about through here." He fought to keep the intoxicating scent alive. "We'll clean up. Don't you have to get to work?"

"Ah, yes. I was just getting in the mood, I guess." Paul left his cleaning duties unfinished and headed for the bar.

"Okay, we'll come back to the transfer later. What method can we use? Form a shell?" Ben said.

"Maybe," Rob replied. "LLCs are used to buy property and investments, so that the company name, not the individual, appears in public documents."

Dilip ran his fingers through his salt-and-pepper hair and sighed. "Yeah, but LLCs require you to file tax returns with the IRS."

"Unless it's overseas." Rob grinned.

"What about a trust?" Kannada said.

Paul closed the door as he left.

"Trusts are useful," Rob said. "You can hide assets and keep your tax bills down, especially if you're a beneficiary. I mean, income is free from estate and gift taxes."

Dilip rubbed his chin. "And regular income taxes can be avoided if the trust pays the taxes instead of the individual."

"Gambling accounts?" Kannada inquired.

"That'll require small amounts to be transferred to avoid suspicion," Ben responded. "Plus, it's time-consuming and tedious."

The group looked at Ben.

"What?" he said. "I've tried it."

Those present looked at each other and smirked.

Paul exited the private elevator, put a piece of gum in his mouth, and waited for a normal lift alongside another man.

"Hi," the person said.

Paul looked over. A well-dressed, famous fashion designer named Louis Laurent stared at him with an expressionless face and gently stroked an Ashera cat in his arms. Paul didn't care that he was standing next to a celebrity; he never liked to put people above himself. "What's up, man?"

"What's up?" Louis sounded ritzy and confused. "Are you . . . visiting here?"

"No." Paul smacked gum. "I live here."

Louis nodded slowly, running his fingers through the cat's fur. The elevator arrived with a ding, the doors opened, and the two men entered and faced forward.

"I believe I'm your neighbor," Louis said. "You must know who I am."

Get the fuck off your high horse.

The fashion designer observed Paul's attire, blue jeans and a black Dead Rabbit T-shirt. He looked ahead. "Nice choice of clothing."

"Thanks."

"Are you going to the bar to get some drinks?"

Paul glanced at his inquirer. "I work there."

"You work there?" Louis sounded incredulous, and his eyes bulged. "You must be the owner."

"Nah, just a bartender."

"And you live in the multi-million-dollar, three-story attic?"

"Yep, that's me."

The elevator came to a halt on the ground floor and the doors separated.

"How?" Louis said.

"Good tips." Paul smiled, then left the fashion designer and his expensive cat alone in the elevator.

"Layering?" Kannada felt a whiff of cool, fresh air from the open window.

"I like layering," Rob said.

"Me, too." Dilip nodded.

"Okay, invoicing?" Kannada asked.

"That's a possibility," Dilip volunteered, "but it's typically not used in high amounts. You'll have to break the money down into smaller chunks and do it for intangible services like IT consulting."

"Legal settlement?" Kannada tried again.

"Take that behind the barn and shoot it," Rob chimed in. "Suing yourself can have significant negative impact. Trust me."

The group looked at Rob.

"Hey," he said, "you have to start somewhere."

The gang shared a few laughs at Rob's early futile attempt.

"Travel with the cash?" Kannada asked.

"Way too risky," Ben answered. "You have no insurance if you lose your bags." The wind whistled as the group sat quietly. "It's almost 7:00. I think we should call it a day. Maybe we'll get a—"

The door started to rattle, and heads turned. Iago walked in after work, dressed in a suit, his tie loosened and collar undone. His black, full-rim plastic glasses had slid down his nose.

"Set up a charity?" Kannada looked at the man who had given him the idea, the man who operated an elaborate mail and wire fraud disguised as a fraudulent charity.

"Hey, Iago." Ben smiled; then almost simultaneously, one after another, the greetings started.

"What?" A flush crept across Iago's cheeks as he positioned his glasses on the bridge of his nose.

The guys' planning stage was over for the day. They needed a break.

Iago held up his thumb drive. "I got the employee database. Give me half an hour and we'll go through it."

The four horsemen congratulated him on a job well-done, then unwound in the meantime. Rob headed upstairs, most likely to smoke on the terrace. Dilip cleared his throat loudly; he followed suit, except for the smoking part, to probably get fresh air and hurl mucus. Ben stretched and walked around.

Kannada yawned. "I'm taking a shower," he said to Ben.

Iago sat erect at his computer station in the penthouse office, surrounded by Rob, Ben, Dilip, and a clean Kannada, who had his towel slung around his neck. He wore a robe, his black hair still a little wet.

They needed the right working professionals at the NYSE, the proper appearance. Two traders, one who worked for Lemon and one who worked for Barney Trade, Inc., otherwise known as Barney's, the white-shoe investment bank and brokerage company that the group would use to execute their trades, would suffice. One after another, the group looked for the right match in the employee database.

"How about this one?" Iago stared at a black man on the screen. "He looks a bit like Walker."

"Nah," Ben said, "he's a police officer. We need traders on the floor."

A few more profiles later, everyone's eyes fixated on the screen.

"This one. Veronica Reyes." Kannada stopped Iago. "She looks a little like Zara. Add in some glasses, change up the hair, and there you go. Plus, she's on the trading floor."

"Right firm, too," Rob noted. "Barney's."

"Yeah," Iago said, "but Zara?"

The others looked at Iago. "Nah," all of them said, voting and laughing off the possibility.

"She's a sugar baby." Rob wiped a tear of hilarity from his face. "She couldn't pull that off."

"Yeah," Ben added. "She should stick to her day job."

"Never mind, bad idea." Kannada witnessed male chauvinism at its worst.

"Hey, don't count her out," Dilip stated as the lone defender of Zara.

As Iago continued to go through the profiles, Kannada noticed one looking similar to him, except for a small difference in appearance, but kept mum; the double had a juvenile chinstrap beard.

Iago pointed at the screen. "Lorenzo Moretti. He looks like you."

Kannada grimaced. "He does not."

Rob put his hand on Kannada's shoulder. "Get a beard like that, and you'd fit right in with the Jersey shore crowd."

The gang shared some laughs, except Kannada, who waited for the mockery to end. "Next."

"Him." Dilip coughed while looking at a tan, brawny man with brown hair and a mature hairline. "He works for Lemon. He should have what you need."

"We could take him out." Ben put his hands atop his dark brown, spikey Asian hair and interlaced his fingers. "He's a keeper."

"All right," Iago said. "Alistair Hawthorne."

"One more," Kannada said.

After combing through profile after profile, they landed at a trader who worked for Barney's.

"What about this one? Glen Radcliffe," Iago suggested.

Ben hunched over and put his hands on his knees. "Give Ricky some hair, and they're almost twins."

"I agree." Rob nodded.

"Me, too." Kannada put his hands at the sides of his waist.

"I think that about settles it," Dilip said.

"Everyone agree on these two?" Iago asked. "One Ricky sub, one Lemon trader."

"Yeah," the others in the room affirmed together.

"I'm going to get something to eat." Iago rolled the chair back slightly and stood. He straightened his pants as he turned to face everyone. "Who's up for some street meat?"

Ben stood erect. "I'm down. Are there any around here?"

"There're a few, six blocks away," Dilip said. "Let's go."

"You guys go ahead." Kannada viewed the monitor. "I'm going to stay back, take a look at some of this."

Ben looked at Rob.

"You can order room service anytime from the hotel side," Rob said. "I'll let the help know you'll be calling."

"All right, I'll see you guys in a bit," Kannada said.

Rob glanced at Ben and shrugged.

Kannada took to the computer as the others split. He was up to something, but the gang couldn't add it up. He made the impression that he was searching for better matches. He searched for Amara's profile; she had the same address that Kannada visited recently. It wasn't updated. He re-examined the profile he'd caught sight of earlier.

"Zara!" Kannada yelled.

She appeared in the doorway a few moments later. "What?"

"Can you do me a solid?"

CHAPTER 13

Manhattan, New York

Kannada picked up a white envelope on a circular, glass breakfast table. "Is this it?"

"I've got them right here." Rob pulled out a stack of credit cards from his coat pocket and handed it to Kannada. "That's some tickets for a dinner at the Guggenheim."

The embossed letters and numbers on the cards left imprints on Kannada's thumb, and the fresh plastic tightened his airways; the feel and smell of credit. "Are you going?" He started to distribute the cards to the other members.

"Eh, I should." Rob gave Ricky cash. "I need to keep up with my acquaintances, but I have to RSVP."

"How many guests are allowed?"

"I can bring up to three, a little unusual. Normally, these things don't allow more than one."

"What's the credit card for?" Zara asked.

"Shopping." Kannada grinned. He could tell this was what she'd been waiting for, though it wasn't what she probably had in mind.

She smiled.

Plainview, Texas

Alan and Zara flew into Lubbock, Texas and picked up a red Ford F-150 from a car rental agency. Alan had never been to the Lone Star State; it was somewhat similar to Arizona, where he worked previously. Plainview was removed far enough from the major cities, far enough from the densely populated areas, to provide nighttime artistry in the form of the Milky Way. Many scattered trees marked the terrain hither and thither and scenic fall foliage blew in the air, littered the streets, and added color to a flat portion of the state, as he drove the rental pickup truck to his journey's end.

They made it to Jerry Conway's hangar. It was basic and unobtrusive, built with metal and concrete, shaped like a dome, and opened via sliding doors. It was in the country, on a dirt road leading into the depths of farm life, and difficult to spot.

Alan discovered the seller Jerry Conway online, anxious to get his helicopter sold. He would probably be willing to make a deal to get this thing off his lot, as there were few shoppers.

In the air, Alan examined the potential purchase. He drooled over the sleek aerodynamic design, the gyrating wings, the loud, powerful motor, and the view as he took the helicopter for a spin.

In the hangar, Zara found Jerry Conway to be an Ed "Too Tall" Freeman-wannabe cowboy with a genuine Texas twang. He wore a sleeveless, unbuttoned flannel shirt, ripped blue jeans, cowboy boots, a leather belt with a huge buckle, and a ten-gallon hat. She had no trouble keeping Jerry's attention as she negotiated with him.

"You're one of those spicy Spanish señoritas, aren't you?" Jerry said. "Come from south of the border?"

Zara, at a loss for words, looked up at Alan, doing circles, giving her a thumbs-up.

"Venezuelan." Jerry corrected himself. "No, Indian?"

"Yeah, you nailed it." She smirked. *Sharper than he looks*.

"Yeehaw!"

Maybe not. "What's the asking price?"

"For that beauty up there? Uh . . . six-hundred fifty K is the best offer I can make you."

"Oh, I see." Zara licked her lips. She was only getting started. "That's a big, strong helicopter. Well, I guess I'll have to look elsewhere for something big and strong to play with."

"Jerry Michael Conway at your service." He stood a little taller, his chest out.

"Yes, Michael, like a god." Zara enunciated her words ever so smoothly and rubbed his arm. As she did, Jerry took a big gulp.

"I like a man with big biceps," she said. "Do you work out?"

"Uh . . ." Jerry's Stetson hat was about to jump off.

Zara squeezed the man's arm, grasping it firmly, as he tried to harden, to flex.

"Big, strong men are hard to find. I've never had a Southern charm, a real Texan. My sister says Texans are the wildest, especially in bed."

Jerry's face was reddening faster than a goby changing color, just as she had hoped. The goal now was to persuade Jerry to lower his price to score a date.

Zara edged closer to him and bit her lip.

"Miss, I think you mentioned you had a special Amex Black card?"

"Uh-huh. Are you single, Jerry?"

"Uh-huh." He swallowed.

"I'm so happy to hear that. What a woman really wants is to have some fun. That's the only way to keep one. And to satisfy her, she needs something to get on and ride, all the time . . . but that might be problematic for my body. I get these weird cravings to suck on things—"

"Miss, I can show you Southern hospitality. How about six-forty-eight?"

Zara ran her finger across Jerry's chest and left a red scratch mark with her nail.

"Six-forty-five," he said.

She gave him her patented puppy face.

"Six-forty." He sighed. "Plus, dinner with me at the steak house."

"Oh, you're so sweet." Zara gave him a hug and a thumbs-up to a returning Alan on the ground behind Jerry's back.

Chinatown, New York

In a parking lane, Rob and Paul closed the doors to their vehicle. As they walked a block to their destination, Rob struggled to maneuver around the many slender Asians on the sidewalk with his salad-dodging frame, but still managed to marvel at the neighborhood.

With each step, he guessed at the meaning of Chinese characters on red signs that smothered the passageways based on his observations of the interiors of buildings. A dragon's head cast his mind back to the surreal and oriental festivals he had enjoyed when he visited the Sleeping Giant.

Hole-in-the-wall restaurants, which Rob dined at from time to time, open-air fish markets, which carried a unique scent that he could do without, and charming souvenir shops, which sold just about anything that he had no use for, lined the streets.

They arrived at their stop, a gunpowder-filled, pyrotechnic shop that had enough firepower to blow any instant if ignited. Qin Dong had one of the highest-grossing specialty stores during three times of the year, Fourth of July, New Year, and Chinese New Year.

That was why Ben sent Paul and Rob to him in the first place; Qin Dong would probably have what they needed.

"All right, I got everything here," Qin said in a raspy voice. "Fountains, sparklers, smoke bombs, cones. You name it."

"Eh . . . what do you recommend?" Rob ignored the foul odor of nearby open-air fish markets.

"Eh . . . what're you looking for?" Qin asked.

"Explosive, man," Paul said, "explosive."

"Like a bomb." Rob's eyes burst out of their sockets.

"That's dangerous." Paul frowned.

"That's right." Rob grinned.

"Now what's this . . . and this?" Paul pointed to two nearby objects.

"That's a mortar, aerial shell, and that's a skyrocket. I don't sell those to the public. What about this?" Qin redirected their attention to something more feasible.

"That's what we want, the skyrockets and mortars," Paul requested.

"No, believe me; those are only used for aerial displays. It's for New Year's," Qin argued.

"Just give it to me," Paul urged.

"Yeah," Rob supported the bartender. "Don't build another Great Wall, Qin. We'll pay anything." He pulled out a wad of cash from his pocket. "We got the—"

"Yeah." Paul cut off Rob.

Rob didn't see any harm in greasing the man's palm. *The money's there. Why not take it?*

Qin nodded.

A bike's bell rang near them. Rob joined the others in looking in the direction of the noise. A car nudged the back tire of a bike messenger and knocked him over. The cyclist picked up his bike, then pumped his fist while mouthing something in Chinese.

Rob and the others resumed business as though nothing happened. *Just a typical day in New York.*

A couple of Asian Americans negotiated a good deal at a nearby outdoor market in a foreign language. Mindful of his surroundings, Rob asked, unworried, "Qin, you know of any particular Russian fireworks?"

Qin stared at Rob.

Rob stared at Qin. He was hinting at Russian firearms and explosives, illegal stuff. He was referring to the kind of stuff that could only be found on the black market.

Qin nodded.

Brooklyn, New York

"Yeah, I'll be in and out in a few minutes," Ricky said over the phone in the BMW.

He exited the luxury sedan and, just like the other people, marched up to an office supply store with a sense of purpose. *I'm going to get this, I'm going to get that, I'm going to pay for it, and I'm going to get back to my normal life, but with the added convenience of technology.*

He walked past the automatic sliding doors, struggled to dislodge a cart connected to another cart, and wiped the handlebar with a complimentary disinfectant wipe.

As he walked toward the back under hanging light fixtures, tube lights behind aluminum mirror louvers, the cart wobbled, and its wheels squeaked. A couple of patrons noticed his annoyingly noisy cart. *Dammit, I got this cart.*

Everywhere he looked, lost souls searched for the right electronic product. Some bit their nails; others rubbed their arms.

Ricky took a few more strides and became aware of the generic store music playing. *Would it kill them to get a better soundtrack?*

Five minutes later, he strolled into the aisle for printers, completely flabbergasted by the technological arsenal on show.

Wide-eyed and mouth agape, he looked up at the boxes upon boxes of printers to the ceiling.

An audio infomercial distracted him. *What aisle is this? Why'd I come here again?*

He quickly recovered and filled his cart with four laser printers. Ricky started to leave the aisle, but suddenly stopped, as a red tag signaling a markdown caught his attention.

"Hmm." He stared at a can of compressed air that could be used to clean a keyboard. *How does compressed air work? Wonder if they pushed the air down with something.*

Ricky snapped out of his trance, made his way around the store, and took a paper cutter, a few cans of hairspray, and a marking pen. On his way to the checkout counter, he remembered what else he needed, as new arrivals went to a specific area of the store, the ink and paper section, located in the front to the side. Tons of recycled paper and colored ink would do the trick, along with his other items. He gathered the printing supplies, then moved to the counter.

"I've been looking for cancer sticks all over. How much is that Newport pack behind you?"

The cashier, a round bald man with a black Van Dyke beard, turned around to look at the item, then faced Ricky. "Thirteen dollars."

"Thirteen dollars!" Ricky opened his wallet, and looking at it, he shook his head. "Never mind, it's just more incentive to quit."

He paid cash to avoid leaving any trail behind and escaped.

Bronx, New York

Walker entered a local paint shop. He walked around for a few minutes, trying to select what he needed based on a laundry list of items Alan had made for him. He examined different shades of paint, brands, and accessories, but chose nothing and shrugged. Having no experience, he took the easy route and gestured to a worker for assistance.

An employee approached. He had an orange cap, a flannel shirt, with the sleeves rolled up to his elbows, and an orange apron around his rotund girth. "Hey, how can I help you?"

"I need fifteen gallons of black paint, and one gallon of gold." Walker showed him two color swatches and a paper. "And everything on this list."

The employee viewed the required items with a tilted head, then straightened his neck. "Come on."

Walker followed him up and down the aisles and then to the counter, where primer, pigmented paint, clear coat, pinstriping tape, dust masks, sanding discs, paint guns, chemical strippers, and everything else that could be found in a body shop, were amassed.

Manhattan, New York

Simultaneously, at the Big Board, near the back entrance at the intersection of New Street and Wall Street, Ben anxiously waited in the shadows and peered through binoculars with the pictures of Alistair Hawthorne and Glen Radcliffe, the people they sought. He had to know about these men, where they were, where they weren't, if he was ever going to get Radcliffe's badge and Hawthorne's confidential knowledge.

Not far behind, Kannada was there also, keeping tabs on Ben and on the lookout for Lorenzo Moretti, his lookalike, at the Exchange's back entrance. He was equipped with binoculars, too.

CHAPTER 14

Manhattan, New York

The small, ornate, wood-and-glass private elevator to their townhome buzzed with an unfinished, pertinent conversation.

Kannada put his arms at his waist and leaned against a mirror. "So, is there a good place we can hide the money?"

Ben shook his head, the sheen of his short, spikey hair gone. "I've asked all over."

"So have I." Paul's blue eyes appeared dull.

Rob raised his brows. "Me, too."

Kannada frowned. "We all have." He lowered his head and viewed the mosaic tile floor, thinking.

"Nobody wants their banks known," Ben said.

"If I were stashing money overseas, I wouldn't tell anybody either." Kannada sighed and looked at the button panel. "Great, now I have to inform the rest of the group the jig's up."

"So, we're stopping?" Ben grimaced.

"I'm not saying that. We've got too much skin in the game."

The elevator bell dinged.

"So, what then?" Rob pressed, as the elevator doors opened.

The gang exited the lift and approached the doorman standing guard outside their room.

"Guess what else is new?" Ben said to Kannada.

"What?"

"Ricky's lookalike, Glen Radcliffe, is on vacation."

"We're pissing in the wind." Kannada shook his head and sighed as he walked into the gang's cave.

Rob and Paul hit the sofas, and Ben stood by the piano. Kannada headed toward the lower level, where he met Dilip.

"Hi, Uncle." Kannada had to pay homage to his relative by addressing him with the proper title; it was a cultural thing for Indians. Otherwise, he'd be scorned. His uncle's salt-and-pepper hair was wet. "Fresh and clean?"

Dilip plucked at his dress shirt repeatedly. He seemed to be experiencing after-shower sweat. "Don't call me Uncle."

Kannada twisted his mouth to the side. *Always with the secrets.*

"I'd like to talk to you guys for a second." Dilip buttoned the sleeve buttons on his shirt.

"We'd like to talk to you." Kannada was unsure how to break the recent bad news to him, but he had to tell him. He hoped the old man would have a solution.

He plodded up the stairs with his uncle behind him, gathered the others, and moved to the informal reception area. Kannada spilled his guts; fortunately, Dilip had ruminated on their issues during his shower. He expressed his water-time epiphany, the five of them seated together around a corner sectional sofa.

"That's your idea?" Kannada was shocked. He ignored a whiff of toiletries from Dilip, as cool wind blew from an open awning window.

"We've tried everyone we can trust, at the bars, on the streets, insiders." Dilip's shiny, wet hair had gradually dried to a matte finish.

"It's too close of a call."

"Originally, you wanted to act as the museum and pay the man for the NYSE's precious artifacts, the Czar Nicholas urn, the original clock, Buttonwood, hold them as ransom."

"I can see the writing on the wall. I don't think this will fly." Kannada stared at the fireplace across from him. *This is not part of the story I wrote.*

"The question is, how can we gratify him?" Ben said. "Lemon's not just going to divulge confidential bits of information."

113

Dilip turned to the burly financier. "Have you RSVP'd yet?"

"Not yet. I'm planning to mail it out today." Rob patted his coat's breast pocket.

"We'll use that." Dilip's gold stud earring shined bright.

Ben faced Kannada. "I think he may have something."

Kannada met Dilip. "I think you may have something."

Ben knew how to make Dilip's solution a reality. The diversity of New York meant that a person could shop for any occasion and buy clothing from every culture. Ben, Ricky, and Paul stepped into one of the Middle Eastern bazaars between Times Square and the West Side Highway.

Ben sat on a leather indoor storage bench, tapping his foot, and watched Ricky pose in new clothes. Ricky peacocked in front of three long mirrors in his latest dress, a red-and-white checkered keffiyeh held in place by a black head ring on top of a white thobe.

"I remember when this area was all hookers. It's all Giuliani's fault." Ricky sounded disappointed.

"He was good on 9/11." Ben checked the time on his phone.

"This looks good."

"It's from Dubai, Ricky."

"It might look better in leather." Ricky sounded flamboyant. "Do you think it fits?"

"They all fit," Ben said in a sharp tone.

Ricky turned toward Ben with a flair for the dramatic. He snapped his fingers. "Meow!" He faced the mirror again and posed. "You go girl! Work it!"

Ben looked at Paul, who stood against the wall with his arms crossed. Ben shook his head with his jaw misaligned, tongue pressed back against his lower gum.

Paul shrugged.

This has to be the worst shopping experience ever. Ben could see through Ricky's façade of courage; he was gay and looked like a real Muslim. In today's world, two things were working against him.

Ben waved off the tailor. "A few minutes, Khasim."

The tailor stepped away to tend to another customer.

"Have you done a foreign act before?" Ben asked.

Ricky turned to him. "Sweetie, you care too much." He went back to the mirror. "This keffiyeh is giving me life!"

Ben sighed. "All right, I think that about does it." He signaled Paul, the one with the credit card. They walked to the checkout counter from the fitting room together.

Long Island, New York

Kannada watched his large friend waddle down a flight of stairs.

"Here it is; Opera-ware." Rob gave Kannada a box of miniature binoculars at his residence in Great Neck. "You'd be surprised how many people want a pair of these."

Kannada looked at him strangely. "I doubt it. Maybe in your society." He opened the box and examined its contents. "You got them monogrammed, too. Where'd you get these?"

"Ben's connections in El Barrio. Alberto Romero Fernando Pablo José Ramirez."

"A group of people?"

"No, just one guy."

"Oh."

Rob shrugged. "I've got a whole room filled with them upstairs."

"A whole room of binoculars?"

"What'd I just say?"

Kannada grinned. "You rich people don't know what to do with your money."

"I just give them away as gifts." The real estate developer sounded nonchalant.

"Okay, now all we need is a limo or some nice car." Kannada looked at him expectantly.

"Oh, no." Rob sounded fearful.

"Oh, yes." Kannada grinned.

"Fine." Rob couldn't keep his babies from harm's way.

Kannada knew that if this job would go down correctly, by the end of it Rob could purchase a new lot of vehicles to add to his collection.

They walked the length of Rob's garage, which was practically a car depot attached to his mansion.

Kannada examined each car, one by one. Certainly, something in there could be of good use, instead of being on display at annual auto shows. He needed a specific car and Rob didn't have it. He turned to face Rob.

"No good," Kannada said, disappointed.

"I told you. I don't have anything." Rob sounded pleased. He shuffled his feet to block a car from Kannada's view with his rotundity.

Kannada looked past him and narrowed his eyes on a sleek, sporty, shiny vehicle with a prancing horse emblem. He fell in love with every inch of the aggressive low body, the spokes on the wheels, the aerodynamic design, the muscular front wing, the side air intakes on the flanks, and the long, flush headlights.

"This one." He gawked at the gold-plated Ferrari. "How much did you pay for this thing?"

Rob stomped his foot. "I got a special deal from a friend in Saudi. They drive those things like Fords and Chevys here."

Kannada inhaled the scent of recently waxed tires. "This would be perfect."

"There's no insurance on it." Rob sounded worried. "I just keep it in here. I don't even take it to auto shows."

"We'll drive safely," Kannada said, confident.

Rob sighed. "I wish that were true for the other eight million New Yorkers."

CHAPTER 15

Manhattan, New York

Kannada had kept close tabs on a NYSE worker named Lorenzo Moretti since he found him on the Exchange's employee database. He'd learned that the man was an after-work regular at a local watering hole through FriendBin and corroborated Lorenzo's status updates by following him.

Kannada conversed with Zara on the sidewalk across from the establishment, but kept his eyes peeled for Lorenzo. "That's him right there, in the light beige suit, dark hair, walking into the bar."

Zara focused on her prey. "You look like him."

"No, I don't." Kannada sighed, shaking his head. "He has a beard. If anything, he resembles me."

She gave him a look that said *yeah, right.*

He shrugged, then squinted in a different direction. "Wait, is that Jimmy Fallon?"

Zara followed his eyes, alert, ready to see the celebrity.

"Ah, who cares?" Kannada said, unable to determine if he'd seen the man who hosted a late-night television show. "Where're you staying?"

"At the Trump Hotel, room 419." Zara handed him one of her door cards.

"Shoot for 8:00."

She nodded, and the two separated. Zara casually crossed the road and walked past a crowd to get into the bar. Kannada dashed down the street to grab a quick bite to eat.

Inside the pub, Zara ordered dessert, then spotted her target, a man with a chinstrap beard. She sat across from him at the bar, made eye contact, and smiled; it was the perfect recipe to have him come over. She had to initiate; women always did with lonely, shy guys. She knew some men were too aloof to figure anything out for themselves.

He was a moderately handsome fellow, dressed to be noticed, not blending in with the wall, and standing in an area where he might be seen. He was lucky enough to catch Zara's gaze and smile, a warm invitation that let him know that he wasn't going to be shot down if he approached.

A male bartender gave Zara a slice of chocolate cake with a Maraschino cherry on top and a fork. "Here you go ma'am. Would you like to close your tab?"

She nodded.

"It'll be $15," the bartender said.

Zara looked at her credit cards and selected the Amex black card given to her by Kannada from Rob. "Here."

"We only accept cash."

"Cash only?" She twisted her mouth to the side, creating a crease in her cheek, and slanted her eyebrows inward.

The bartender pointed to a sign next to her on the bar table.

"The bar accepts cash only," the sign read.

"Ugh. This is why I don't like New York." She put back the card, took out enough hard-earned money to cover the bill, and gave it to the bartender.

Zara dove into the chocolate cake with the fork and took half of the dessert with her. She got her money's worth; it satisfied her sweet tooth.

"Hey," the man she'd spotted said.

Zara was looking at the muted television overhead, watching some college basketball game, taking a bite of the sinful cake. She twirled the fork in her mouth innocently as she tilted her head to face him.

"Hi!" She could barely hear him over the loud music and edged a little closer.

"My name's Lorenzo." The man extended his hand.

"I'm Candy." Zara kept her name hidden and accepted the handshake as a blonde sales rep popped a cork from a bottle.

Lorenzo took her hand and, staring deeply into her eyes, kissed the backside of it. "The pleasure is mine."

She raised an eyebrow and looked at him somewhat funny. *Forget about shy. This guy's a doofus.*

"Can I buy you a drink?" Lorenzo asked.

"Sure."

He signaled the blonde saleswoman amid some yelling in the background. She had just finished pouring a tray full of brimming wine glasses and handed them two.

"Hi! We're offering samples of a new sparkling white wine by *Le Riviera Gagner Société*. This is a light Champagne. It's on the house." The saleswoman handed Lorenzo a glass.

"Wonderful." He faced Zara. "Is this fine, or do you want something else?"

"I'm okay with this." Zara smiled at the sales rep. "Thanks." She took a glass bearing a collerette, bubble trains that had reached the surface.

"My pleasure."

The saleswoman's plate wobbled a bit; Zara parted her lips slightly.

"Do you live around here?" Lorenzo asked.

"I'm planning to," she said. "I'm staying at a hotel for the time being."

"Oh cool, what draws you to this area?"

"You." She smiled.

"Well, I'll take that." Lorenzo blushed. "Cheers to you." They clinked wine glasses.

"What about you?" Zara drank some Champagne and kept her tantalizing gaze on him.

"I live a block away actually." He sipped from his glass. "It's an awesome neighborhood. You should definitely check it out."

"Ah, sounds good." The beverage had gone down smoothly. Zara put her glass on a napkin. Alcohol wasn't her thing, but anything sweet was. She put the cake's wicked cherry into her mouth and sucked on it while holding the stem.

"So, are you here by yourself or with friends?" Lorenzo put his glass on the table.

"Uh, yeah, friends. They're over there." She turned to point in the general direction behind her. "Dancing."

She chewed on the cherry as a customer bumped into her and took his seat next to her.

"Sorry about that," the man said.

Zara remained focused on her target.

"Oh, do you dance?" Lorenzo asked.

"No, I think I'd break a leg, literally," she answered.

He laughed. "That's funny. I've tried, yeah, but I'm no good at it. But I do enjoy watching Bollywood dances."

"Really?" Zara's mouth dropped, and her eyes widened. *I think I'm starting to like this guy.*

"Yeah, you know Bollywood? Aishwarya Rai, Priyanka Chopra. Do you have a favorite?"

"Yes, I do. I love Hrithik Roshan. We should watch a movie sometime."

"It's fun. It has all these colors, and they do all these combos."

She chuckled.

"It's good." Lorenzo turned his head sideways for a glance, as a woman took the seat next to him.

Zara stroked Lorenzo's thigh with her hand and recaptured his attention; he viewed her arm, then met her eyes.

She removed the cherry stem from her mouth and placed it on the bar top with a smile; Zara had tied it into a knot with her tongue. "It's kind of loud. How about we get out of here? My place?"

Lorenzo stared with parted lips, then blushed and glanced at the bar top. "Uh, yeah, do you want to tell your friends?" He sounded off-guard.

Zara looked back as if she had real friends there, then faced him. "Nah, come on." She smiled, happy to snare her mark.

Brooklyn, New York

Under a cloudy sky, at an unoccupied warehouse with graffiti on the walls, a trio of waste bins in the corner and more than half of the glass window panes boarded up, Ricky had organized an assembly line. He was printing as fast as possible; not just for the sake of time, but to get the hell out of this place, while Walker cut the output as soon as it came out, and Dilip, wearing a facemask, sprayed the printed material lightly with hairspray on cue.

"That was the last batch." Ricky tested the final pieces of paper with a marking pen. There was so much hairspray in the air he could taste it.

"Geez, you even got the watermark in there?" Walker commented.

"Yeah. Didn't take that long." Ricky heard something scuffle around. "What was that?" *Maybe someone's on to us.*

The others looked around, then at each other.

Ricky tilted his head forward and narrowed his eyes. A squeak, then a loud bang, prompted him to look in the direction from where the noise came. They all sighed, as a couple of rats scurried away.

"Now what?" Walker wiped sweat from his forehead with the back of his hand.

"We'll have to get rid of all this stuff," Ricky said. "Break down the printers, then dispose of them."

"Why's that?"

"Take a look at the money under that light."

Walker followed instructions, as Ricky and Dilip crowded around him.

"What do you see?" Ricky asked.

"Dots. A bunch of yellow dots," Walker observed.

"Exactly. That's a code that's been sent to Big Brother that we're printing counterfeit money. We can't leave them any evidence."

Walker and Dilip nodded. They gathered the extra paper and ink cartridges, marking pen, hairspray, and paper cutter into garbage bags. When they finished, they smashed the printers with sledgehammers.

Simultaneously, Ricky gathered their belongings and packed them into the trunk of the Bimmer.

"Hey, pops," a child-like voice said.

Ricky glanced over to his right. A preteen white boy with sagging jeans and an oversized, puffy New York Jets jacket stood between two others, his posse, similar in age and clothing. The punk in the middle had rosy cheeks, a turned-up nose, and a backward cap.

"Got some change?" The central boy chewed gum.

Ricky faced the trunk. "Walk while you can." He reached for a lug wrench, then spun around and yelled, "Beat it, you little cherry-tomato-looking fuck!"

The thuggish wannabes gasped, and their hard demeanors turned nervous. They ran away.

After Ricky closed the trunk, he walked into the abandoned building and panicked; the broken printers were gone. He noticed an open side door ahead and quickly went there. Walker was carrying the garbage bags toward the dumpster, with Dilip holding the door open.

"Wait a minute. Wait a minute. Wait a minute!" Ricky said swiftly, outside, midway between Dilip and Walker. "What're you doing?"

"Throwing all this stuff away," Walker replied. "Just like you said, boss."

"Recycle," Ricky commanded flamboyantly. "I'm no punk. I'm a professional crook. I got standards. Be responsible and take care of your environment."

Walker did a double take. "Sure thing, boss."

Ricky headed for the car. Dilip and Walker held funny stares for a moment; then Walker ambled back with the bags. They scattered the printers on the corners of streets where other recyclable trash awaited pick-up.

Manhattan, New York

In the Trump International Hotel & Tower hotel room that would serve as Zara's net, Kannada moved the comforter and pillows to the side of the bed and dabbed the bed sheets with harsh chemicals. He heard light banter outside the room as the door handle started to turn. Kannada looked up; she was early. He hurriedly splashed the contents of the bottle onto the bed, quickly tiptoed to the shower, and hid behind the curtains.

The door opened with Zara in front, leading the poor sap.

"And then I said, 'Arty, the zoo called. They're running out of monkeys.'" Lorenzo guffawed at his joke.

She laughed, too, putting up her best charade while looking ahead toward the ground, her eyes widening. "You're such a riot." She rolled her eyes, and the door slammed closed.

"Is it all right if I take a leak?" Lorenzo asked.

Zara cringed. "Sure. I'll get comfortable."

"I'll be back in just a second."

While Lorenzo rushed into the bathroom, Zara retrieved a pill from her purse, poured two glasses of red wine, and slipped him a mickey. She quickly changed from her evening attire to a silky, lace red gown that showed her panties and bra.

Kannada was sitting as still as possible behind the opaque shower curtains. He became startled upon hearing footsteps and the restroom door close. *She didn't send him in here to take a shower, did she? Is Zara going to take a shower with him?* He cringed at the last thought. The intruder opened the lid of the toilet and started to urinate. *It's only him.* Kannada's muscles relaxed.

Lorenzo finished emptying his bladder. "Woody, meet Trojan. Trojan, Woody." He slipped on a raincoat.

Kannada's eyes dilated as he smirked. He nearly laughed.

Lorenzo threw his condom wrapper into the wastebasket, flushed the toilet, and left the bathroom. *That was close*, Kannada thought.

Zara heard the bathroom door open and put away her purse. She patted her wavy, chestnut hair, straightened herself a bit, and smiled as Lorenzo ambled into her view.

"Hubba hubba." Lorenzo grunted appreciatively as he looked her up and down.

"Would you like some, babe?" She handed the man a glass of red wine.

"No, thanks. I think I've had enough for the night." He started to return the drink.

"Oh, come on, hun." Zara pouted. "It sets the mood and makes it much more enjoyable." She raised her glass to her chin and led the way with a reassuring nod and smile.

"Okay. For you, anything."

She watched Lorenzo finish his drink and placed her own glass on the dresser.

"Ah. All done." He set his glass down next to hers.

"Go ahead and take your clothes off," Zara ordered. "And lie facedown."

The man undressed and did as she demanded. His face and body were rubbing all over the chemicals placed by Kannada earlier;

chemicals that would keep him out of work for a few days, if not weeks.

Zara searched for a way to make sure her skin avoided contact with the bed sheets. She took the pillows and placed them on either side of Lorenzo, then came over him, her lower legs on the cushions, and started massaging his back. "You seem tense. What's the matter, hun?"

"My job's killing me," Lorenzo said. "All this trading and all these young guns from college keep coming out ready to upstage you."

"Oh. Do you ever teach them anything?"

"Yeah, but I try not to say too much. You know, I want them to learn on their own, make mistakes."

"That's probably best. Have you learned anything from them?"

"I . . ." He yawned. "I . . ."

"Lorenzo?"

He was knocked out cold.

Zara got off him and quickly changed back into her dress, then walked over to his clothes and searched them. She found the man's NYSE access badge and took it before she started to leave. She met Kannada by the doorway and jumped, her right hand catching her heart.

"Is he . . ." Kannada whispered.

"Yes," she muttered.

"Come on." He started for the door.

Zara followed, then stopped. "Wait, I forgot something." She quickly rewound her steps, searched Lorenzo's pants, and fished out four Benjamin's from his wallet. "Got it." She held up the cash as she returned to Kannada.

He rolled his onyx eyes, and the two of them left the hotel room.

"Was he talking to himself in the little boy's room?" Zara returned to her normal tone of voice as they made their way to the emergency exit down the corridor.

"What happens in the john stays in the john."

Back at the Plaza condominium, Iago returned from work with a small shopping bag. He had stopped by a neighborhood electronics dealer on the way home.

"I got the walkie-talkie," he said, in the office. "Do you have the letter?"

"Almost done." Dilip coughed. "Proofreading it right now."

Iago looked at a package stuffed with money. "What's that?"

"One of Kannada's friends at the police station. He needs some money. Pack it up."

Iago packed the two-way radio in a cardboard box and sealed the package containing money with tape, while Dilip finished checking over his work and printed.

Dilip folded the paper into thirds. "Do you think we should put this into an envelope?"

Iago's eyes rolled up, his lips scrunched up to the side, and his head tilted to the opposite side. He weighed the proposition. "Nah, this is fine."

"I'll mail both of them on my way to work tomorrow at the SEC." The old-timer cleared his throat and spat phlegm into a trash can nearby.

The wastebasket thunked with the hit of mucus.

Iago stared wide-eyed.

CHAPTER 16

Manhattan, New York

The chump who took Candy's bait, sweet Lorenzo, in the suite upstairs at the Trump International Hotel & Tower, woke up from his stupor in the early hours of the morning, just before sunrise, and opened his eyes. It was dark in his room. The curtains were closed; they disallowed whatever glimmer of light there was outside.

"Candy?" Lorenzo called.

There was no response.

"Hello? Anyone here?"

They were lonely cries for help. He managed to get up with aches and pains.

"Ooh. Aah," Lorenzo muttered repeatedly as he hobbled to the wash area. He switched on the light and saw his disfigured reflection in the mirror. A rash and blisters covered his body. He screamed. *What'd that bitch do to me?*

Long Island, New York

On the eight acres that made up Rob's property, there was an outbuilding, akin to a hangar, but made of brick, that Rob never used. In fact, he didn't use a lot of his property. The separate construct had sliding doors that moved up and down like a garage. It could easily fit six cars. The previous owner used it as a gym.

Kannada felt it was wasted space, but Rob asserted that he'd put the garage to good use, determining David Lemon's deserved fate.

The helicopter that Zara and Alan acquired had been flown in from Texas and rolled into the outbuilding to rest on the estate's grounds. With it were all sorts of paint materials that Walker had bought.

"The next thing we need is to make it look like a DHS helicopter," Kannada instructed. "Alan has all the pictures necessary to get that done."

Alan placed a stack of several photo blowups of the helicopters that he'd shot with a professional camera during reconnaissance on a workbench.

"What's this for?" Zara asked.

"Special ops," Ben answered.

He wasn't lying one bit. This was starting to feel more and more like a military operation.

Kannada noticed Rob staring at his gold-plated Ferrari parked just outside the garage and approached him. A few tears rolled down the sides of Rob's cheeks as he tried to wipe them with a handkerchief.

"My baby," he lamented to Kannada.

Kannada patted Rob's back and comforted him. The thought of putting his precious car in harm's way without insurance was just too much to bear for Rob.

As the group toiled away on the body works, Kannada pulled Zara, Ben, Iago, and Walker to the side. "I need you guys to learn everything you can about Lemon. Other than Rob's details about him, we have nothing."

The gang nodded.

"Hold on," Walker said. "That's it? When do I get some action?"

Kannada glared at him. "As a boxer, you, of all people, should know that you have to know your opponent before you can strike him."

Manhattan, New York

At the corner of Fifth Avenue and East 89th Street, in the Upper East Side neighborhood of Manhattan, the permanent home of a continuously expanding collection of Impressionist, Post-Impressionist, early Modern, and contemporary art stood in a cylindrical vanilla building, wider at the top than the bottom. "The Temple of the Spirit" or, as everyone else called it, the Guggenheim, welcomed David Lemon to an annual gala.

He was joined by his best date yet, a blonde bombshell with enhanced breasts and augmented red lips. Lemon checked his watch, anxious, then looked at his partner.

Blondie admired the roses a few yards away. She glanced around the unique ramp gallery, which extended up from the ground level in a long, continuous spiral along the outer edges of the building to end just under the ceiling skylight.

Lemon's footsteps echoed as he quickly approached her. He gently but firmly pushed her along with his hand on her back. "Come on! We'll be late."

Two miles away, in the Plaza penthouse, Rob checked his watch and sighed. He and Walker, in tuxedoes, and Rob's date, his wife, in a navy-blue dress, were waiting for the last guest to their party.

"Where's Zara? Is she ready yet?" Rob snapped.

In his pajamas, Ben lounged on the sofa and flipped through the channels with the remote. "Judge for yourself."

Zara appeared in the living room wearing a velvety black dress that hugged her curves in all the right ways.

The men gaped. Rob's better half closed his mouth for him with her hand. He tilted his head to the side, shrugged, and half-smiled at his wife.

The dressed-up crowd headed to the Guggenheim for the award ceremony that Rob had RSVP'd earlier. A few minutes later, they moved into one of the many elevators in the museum.

"Whatever you do, don't be seen with me. Lemon hates me, and I hate him." Rob foamed at the mouth as he spoke to Zara about him.

She nodded.

"You're okay," Rob said to Walker. He held up his cell phone and showed them a picture. "This is what he looks like."

The lift shook, and the hoist's bell dinged.

As the elevator doors opened, Rob put his cell phone away. He stepped out with his wife first. Zara and Walker followed Rob's lead; Zara carried a small paper gift bag stuffed with tissue paper in one hand and held Walker's hand in the other. As they entered the ballroom, the double dates split to become single dates.

* * *

The award ceremony started to get underway. The guests slowly took their seats before dinner. Rob and his partner stood together with the other recipients on the dais and conversed with some of the other donors before the ceremony began. When it was time, he approached the only available seat left on the stage. It was next to Lemon.

Rob looked at his seated wife. "Let's switch seats."

She stared at him, wide-eyed, and gave him the impression that he'd better behave.

He took his seat next to Lemon, ungrateful.

"Ladies and gentlemen," the announcer said, "I'd like to welcome all of you to the Guggenheim International Gala, one of three major benefit events the Guggenheim hosts throughout the year."

One by one, each major donor was recognized and met with applause and cheers.

"Next up, Robert Prosperi," the announcer said. "A two-million-dollar gift to the museum."

Rob stood with his spouse as the light shone on them. Everyone applauded. His forehead perspired under the bright light.

Behind the appreciation, a fierce competition was brewing; a battle for bragging rights, for ego, and for power, which involved verbal jabs and prideful boasts.

"And last, our diamond sponsor," the announcer said, "David Lemon. A generous ten million dollars. The proceeds will go toward an Impressionist art exhibit, educational programs that benefit the community, and the museum's maintenance."

Lemon stood with his escort, held her hand, and raised it to the ceiling with his, triumphant. He looked down at Rob next to him and smiled. "The splendid things I do."

"Go fuck yourself!" Rob let his enemy have it.

Lemon stepped forward for a few words. "Today marks a day in which we celebrate art, the very thing that you don't see. Thank you."

The crowd clapped again.

Lemon covered the mic and turned to his blonde friend. "This is the easiest tax write-off ever," he said from the side of his mouth.

The trophy date stared at him with a raised eyebrow and parted lips.

* * *

After the recognition ceremony, the recipients and their guests mingled for a while before leaving. Walker nudged Zara to peek in the direction he was looking. She caught sight of Lemon. Walker took in the view of Lemon's date, dressed in a red evening dress.

"Wow, what money can buy," he commented as a waiter passed behind him.

Zara elbowed him in the ribs, like a true couple. *There're some things you just don't say in public.*

Walker winced in pain.

She stared at him, then looked back at Lemon. "When he's alone, I'll make my move."

Kannada's shadow grew, as he walked toward the balcony of the master suite to join Dilip, who was standing with his head down. He opened the door and leaned on the ice-cold glass fence next to the sexagenarian.

The two of them, uncle and nephew, hadn't had many conversations over the years, except for business.

The night was quiet. A few cars roamed the streets below. Lighted pathways serenely coursed through the dark expanse that was Central Park under a full moon.

"I didn't think you'd come along for this," Kannada said finally, breaking the ice.

Dilip stared into the distance. "Couldn't miss out on the opportunity."

"Why's that?"

"Simple. This is original. The investigators don't have anything to fall back on to figure this out. It's not an easy heist to trace. They don't know what to look for."

"How come you didn't help me get a job earlier, when I was let go by Caldwell Investments?" Kannada sounded bitter.

"What was I supposed to do?" Dilip turned to face him for the first time. "I couldn't help you. You were at the wrong place at the wrong time. Caldwell's Ponzi put everyone out of commission."

"You were here in New York at the time," Kannada said as a driver below urged someone to wake up with the horn. "And working for a bank."

"So? Banks are different. I didn't have the position I have now with the SEC. No influence. Is that why you're upset with me?"

"A little."

"What else?" The old man cleared his throat and hurled one sticky, heavy raindrop.

"A couple of us are getting tired of your llama act, spitting mucus everywhere. Here." Kannada pulled out a plastic bag from his pocket and handed it to his uncle. "These are cough drops."

Dilip looked at the bag of throat lozenges with raised eyebrows. "Hmm."

Kannada walked back into the townhome.

At the Guggenheim, Walker said to Zara, "It's your time."

She glanced in Lemon's direction. He was standing next to another man, deeply ensconced in conversation, with a drink in hand. Lemon's companion had left his arm, disinterested by the recent arrival of the man to their conversation, and had went to where many women were congregated.

Zara made her move. She stood near Lemon, as he continued to discuss stocks with the other man, possibly another hedgie, and waited until he would notice her.

Lemon's eyes darted back and forth. A few seconds later, he broke from his conversation to glance over.

This was Zara's chance. She extended her hand. "How do you do, Mr. Lemon? Shreya Aggarwal."

Lemon waved off his personal bodyguard.

"Nice to meet you." He shook her hand, then pointed his glass toward an athletic, black man with a goatee near the bar. "Is that your partner over there?"

She turned in Walker's direction, then faced Lemon. "Oh, him. He's just a friend. I didn't want to come alone."

"I wouldn't either." Lemon looked down at the gift bag she was holding. "What's that?"

"I wanted to give you these." Zara handed him the item.

He put down his glass on a tall cocktail table, looked inside the bag, and opened the box. "Opera lenses? My favorite."

"They're monogrammed, too," she said.

Lemon inspected his new toy. "Oh, why yes, they are . . . Made in Mexico. Must be of the finest quality." He sounded sarcastic.

Zara smiled nervously.

He looked into the distance and gave her the impression that he was checking on his blonde partner. He picked the miniature binoculars up, looked through them at Zara's breasts, and grinned. "These could come in handy."

Zara smiled, relaxed. Lemon appeared to be on the lookout for new women to add to his collection. *He's a horndog.*

Lemon put his gift away and placed the bag on the tall cocktail table. "Where'd you get these?"

"A Lawn Guyland connection," Zara said purposely with a smile. She did her best impression of a New York accent when she referred to Long Island.

Lemon chuckled. "So, what's on your mind? You got thirty seconds to make a good first impression. Beautiful women don't just appear out of thin air."

"I just wanted to let you know, Mr. Lemon, that I've read all about your business, the success of your company, and the work you do with the NYSE. And I think you're an incredible genius, something that amazes me. I've always dreamed of one thing; interviewing a man like you."

There was a moment's pause.

"What news are you with?"

"I'm trying to have my work featured in *The Wall Street Journal.*" Zara exposed her upper teeth with a smile and raised her lower eyelids to form crescent shapes.

"*The Wall Street Journal.* Everything's going digital these days. How's print coming along?"

"Eh, it has its ups and downs. The internet poses a challenge for circulation. Some prefer the original print; they like the feel of the pages. Others are moving along with the times."

"Shreya Aggarwal. Hmm, I don't think I've heard of you."

"I'm a freelance journalist, and I'm looking for my big break. And I thought who better than you?"

Lemon threw his shoulders back and straightened his tie. "Well, what can I say?"

Zara continued to talk and flirt with him for a few minutes.

Rob sipped his cocktail and watched Zara from thirty feet away. He and Walker were standing near another cocktail table, near the bar. The two of them shared drinks with a curly-haired man.

"Where do you work?" Rob asked.

"Bloomberg," the man said.

"Doing what?"

"I'm a reporter. What do you guys do?"

"Real estate and hedge fund." Rob met his wife's eyes across the room and pointed to his watch.

The news reporter looked over to Walker, who gazed in the direction where a bunch of women had assembled.

Walker refocused his attention on the man in front of him. "I work with him."

"Oh, okay, you guys come to these things often?" the news reporter said.

"Try not to," Rob replied. "My wife drags me every time."

The man laughed heartily. "Same here."

The three of them continued to bond over drinks and ultimately witnessed a smiling Zara shake hands with Lemon.

She walked in their direction and made eye contact with Rob on her way to passing the men. "Got the interview."

Rob sensed excitement in her voice and half-smiled.

The official reporter did a double take. "Did you see that?" Next time his pitch was a little higher, "Did you see that? I've been trying to get an interview with Lemon for months, and she just walks up to him and gets whatever she wants."

Rob shrugged. "Men just haven't made enough strides for equality."

The reporter looked toward the floor.

CHAPTER 17

Manhattan, New York

"I want to know how the NYSE works, when traders and brokers pour in, when they leave, etcetera," Kannada said to Ben in the living area of the Plaza penthouse.

Ben visited the Big Board, where George Washington, or at least his statue, watched over Wall Street as if guarding it, at Federal Hall, just across the NYSE. Outside, at 2 Broad Street, a small tent was set up where a security guard checked Ben in as a VIP guest of Iago Gonzales, all-access. Cleared to go, he descended a few steps to the entrance, a pair of glass doors, to the right of the Broad Street subway station and the iconic colonnades of the Exchange, draped in an American flag. He passed through security inside and waited to meet his tour guide.

"Hi, I'm Teresa," a lovely, perky brunette said. "You must be Ben." She extended her hand.

"Yeah, nice to meet you." He accepted the handshake.

"Nice to meet you, too. I'll be your VIP tour guide for the day. The tour is a little over an hour. I'll explain to you how the NYSE works and answer any questions you may have, and at the end of the tour, you'll be having brunch with Diego, right?"

"Yeah." *I got to hand it to Kannada. Passing Iago off as Diego is something I can't even do.*

"Great. This is for you. It's your access card. We'll be using it to get around different areas of the building. So, now if you'll follow me, we can start the tour." Teresa smiled.

"Thanks." Ben started to walk by her side.

Their footsteps echoed as they perambulated the modern lobby with old footage of the NYSE playing on the glass walls and artifacts like old tickers encased with glass nearby.

"First off, welcome to the New York Stock Exchange." Teresa spread her arms out, then returned them to her sides. "I always forget to say that, but I'm pretty sure you know where you are."

Ben faced her and laughed. *She's cute.*

"I'll take you up a few levels, so you can see what happens behind the scenes, and we'll save the best for last, one of the trading floors. Believe me, the trading floor is the coolest part of the tour; you'll be happy you came even if you find the other stuff boring."

He half-smiled. "Sounds good."

"So, how do you know Diego?"

"We met at a conference, then ran into each other in Vegas."

"A coincidence?"

"Yeah, you could say that." Ben smirked.

"Now, for the fun stuff, there're more than 3,500 companies listed on the NYSE and the average daily trading volume is over $170 billion."

"Is this the biggest stock exchange, or is that the NASDAQ?"

"Oh, yes, we're way larger than the NASDAQ. The NYSE's market cap, which is the total dollar market value of all outstanding shares, is over $20 trillion. NASDAQ is only around $7 trillion, same with the London Stock Exchange."

"So, that's why they call the NYSE the Big Board."

Teresa nodded. "Exactly." She continued to dump info on him as they entered an elevator and explored the rest of the building.

On the sixth floor, a few Andy Warhols and other artwork from pop culture graced the walls. They passed a small pantry room, then stopped outside an office. Behind French doors and down a hallway, the CEO's nest lay.

"That's the office of David Lemon, the Chairman and CEO of the NYSE," she said.

Ben peered through the French doors. This was his chance to acquire info about Lemon from Teresa. "Have you met him before?"

"Once; he's a nice guy and usually says hello if he sees you."

"What's his schedule like?"

"I couldn't tell you. He's very busy. Come on; I'll show you where all the important stuff happens."

Dammit. She has nothing. Ben held back asking more questions about Lemon to avoid being suspicious. He came across a large boardroom with a massive table that could easily accommodate forty people and a stained-glass skylight.

"Architect George Post designed the NYSE building in 1903. The desk in front of the wall clock is one of his furniture designs. Most of his work is kept in the archives room." Teresa pointed to a chair behind the desk. "The president used to sit there during the 1871 call market."

Ben observed the furniture, then the grandfather clock on the wall.

"This is the Wall Regulator Clock," Teresa said. "If you look closely, you'll notice the minute hand dominates the other two faces. During the call market of 1871, each stock traded in turn for five minutes."

Ben slowly walked around and took in the atmosphere. He looked at a red-stone-and-silver vase perched atop a green pedestal in one of the corners of the room.

Teresa followed him. "This is the Fabergé urn. It was gifted by Czar Nicholas II in 1903 and arrived in 1904."

He edged closer and viewed the silver eagle detail on the vase. "What's this made of?"

"I believe the urn is red jasper and the pedestal is green jasper."

Ben briefly marveled at the piece, then returned to her. "Are you a history buff?"

"Yes, I am." Her eyes widened, and she smiled. "My dad used to make me read history books, and I eventually fell in love with it. I majored in history in college and got this gig through a friend."

Ben nodded.

"Ready to move on?" she asked.

"Yeah."

The entire seventh floor was once home to the Stock Exchange Luncheon Club, or so the sign said, but he could only see its transformation, a conference center and an unoccupied gallery of archives, the Heritage Gallery, on one end and a restaurant named 1792 at the other. Down the hallway to 1792, on the left was the old card room where floor brokers once played cards and, in the restaurant, the NYSE Restaurant Bar.

The other floors were mostly offices and had much of the hardware behind the Big Board that was never seen. The fourteenth floor housed the Global Corporate Client Group, the Exchange's listings business, and had a futuristic feel to it.

The balcony, commonly seen on television, had a maximum occupancy of sixteen. Ben put his hands on the top rail and viewed workers pouring into the trading floor. He turned to Teresa.

"How does someone ring the bell?"

"This baby, right here." She pointed to an eye-popping apparatus with three distinct buttons. "They used to signal the start and stop of trading with a gavel, then a gong, then finally the bell."

When Ben saw the bell, he envisioned it ring and thought of what it meant.

A pro golfer dreamed of winning a major. A band hadn't made it until its album went platinum. An entrepreneur in business hoped to ring the opening bell at the NYSE. For every company, ringing the bell struck them as the most memorable experience; no other corporate milestone could compare.

"The green button is used for opening and closing the market for regular trading," Teresa informed. "The orange button is a single-stroke bell activated to signal moments of silence, and the red button is a backup bell used for green button failure."

Ben jokingly asked, "Can I ring the bell?"

Teresa smirked and looked down and away. "No, I'm sorry, you can't, but that would be pretty cool." She made eye contact. "Let's go down. You can watch them ring it from below."

They left and descended a few floors. Save for the balcony scene, none of that was interesting, just detective work. The entrance to the trading floor room, however, fascinated him, with its two pairs of glass doors under five electric panels that ran a ticker across them. It was the gateway to America's riches. Just steps away from the floor, no surprise, was a Starbucks, the fuel behind the country's wealth.

He headed for the trading floor around 9:10 AM, and opening bell was at 9:30 AM Eastern Time. It was noisy, all right, but not at a high, at least not yet. The day was just getting underway.

Ben saw an opportunity to observe the inner workings of the Big Board. He could feign nausea given the bright lights and his pale Asian skin. He put his hand on his stomach and grimaced. "I don't feel so good. Do you mind if I sit down?" He started searching for an empty chair.

"Uh, we really shouldn't stay in here. Do you think you can make it off the floor?"

He shook his head, then looked at an employee working on a computer. "Can I use this chair?"

The worker glanced at Ben. "Yeah, go ahead."

Ben grabbed the seat and turned it so that it faced the trading floor. He slowly perched atop the tall chair away from the action and made himself invisible.

"What's wrong?" Teresa asked.

"I don't know. I just feel nauseous all of a sudden."

Teresa put her hand on his shoulder and leaned toward him. "Yeah, you look a little pale."

Perfect. He bent over and held his stomach with both hands.

"Do you need medical attention?"

He rose and pursed his lips as in constipation. "No . . . I think I'll be fine. I need a few minutes."

She slowly retreated while observing him. "I was going to walk you through the floor and take you to the Ramp, but we can stop here if you want?"

"No, just continue the tour . . . without the walking." He rubbed his belly, then gazed at the hanging towers and computers from the walls of the Big Board.

"All right . . . the floor and ceiling are national historic landmarks. No one can drill into the floors, nor add support for any reason."

Ben sighed as if he were in pain. "What happens if you do?"

"I'm not sure, but it's illegal to modify them in any way, so you'd probably be in a lot of trouble."

There were trading posts with people stationed at them. People rushed around, trading, before hours, and took calls and electronic messages from brokerages around the world to small cubicle areas located at the sides of the trading floor.

"Can you tell me about the people who work here?"

"Sure, I was just about to mention that. The floor brokers execute orders for their clients, not for their own accounts, unlike floor traders, and provide information to their customers, such as banks, hedge funds, mutual funds, and some high net-worth individuals. They share rumors and opportunities for liquidity with their clients and begin taking orders at 9:00 AM." Teresa looked around the trading floor.

"The specialists are the market makers; without them, buying and selling can't happen at the NYSE. They match buyers and sellers, maintain liquidity by buying and selling stock easily to fill orders, and monitor trading."

At 9:15 AM, the floor broke loose. The volume of the room increased, and people scuttled. The difference between today's floor and that of several years ago, before computers started to take over, was that there was actual walking space.

Ben noticed some of the workers sporting handheld computer tablets. "What're those, iPads?"

Teresa placed her hand on the back of his chair. "No, they're special tablets that present continually updated news releases, show orders, and provide access to every order management system, algorithm, or computer program."

We may need to get one of these tablets. Ben stroked his stomach with downward motions and grimaced.

"How early do the floor brokers get here?" he asked.

"They start trickling in as early as 7:30 or 8:00, and that's just to prep themselves."

"What's their preparation like?"

"They read the news. The younger workers generally go to their Bloomberg terminals or tablets and check the news-wires, while some of the older generation still read newspapers."

Ben nodded and made a mental note. "Let's say I wanted to get a job here. What's required to work on the floor?"

"Well, it'd be best if you knew someone, which you do, Diego. Everybody here is a hard worker. You have to have a good short-term memory, so you can remember orders and instructions. You have to be good with numbers, be on time, and be able to put up with a lot of yelling. One more thing; you have to be fast, real fast."

"It sounds pretty sophisticated."

Teresa shook her head. "It's not. The floor isn't like the rest of

Wall Street."

Ben tilted his head to the side. "What do you mean?"

"Well, big banks and hedge funds are filled with over-achieving Ivy League school graduates. Most of the guys on the floor never attended college and usually arrive with unrelated experience from fast-paced environments, like that of Sotheby's."

Ben nodded. His hidden fears were laid to rest. He wasn't up against a floor filled with geniuses who could easily piece together the group's heist.

As scheduled, the bell rung at 9:30 AM.

"And there it goes," Teresa remarked.

Ben stared at the bell under the balcony with parted lips, and his face lit up. A few workers paused their work to look at the balcony and applaud, but most stayed glued to their monitors. *I guess after you experience the bell every day, it doesn't generate the same excitement.*

"Who actually presses the bell?" he asked.

"Usually some special guest, like a celebrity or corporate executive. It used to be the responsibility of the floor managers, but that changed in 1995."

Ben looked at the people on the floor. The traders hurried to the area of the floor where a particular stock traded and gave their orders to the trading specialist. Logos of investment banks were spotted on uniforms and trading posts, as investment banks competed to be the designated specialists for individual stocks.

"They move so fast; it's like a blur," he said.

"Yeah, the environment is fast-moving, but it's a bit slower now since electronic trading took hold. Computers do the bulk of trading and people chat online with their clients rather than use phones."

He noticed a few people slacking off, joking around. "They seem to be having a good time."

Teresa turned around and looked at the brokers, traders, and specialists. She faced Ben. "Oh, they're just playing pranks on each other. It helps them get through the day. Working here can get stressful. In fact, there's a heart attack on the trading floors almost every other week."

Ben blinked and made another mental note. *This could be useful.* "Wow! That's not good. Do they take breaks?"

"They can, but they usually don't. Most of them brown bag their lunch and remain at their booths while eating. It's too busy for them to leave, even to go down to the cafeteria in the basement."

Ben nodded, and Teresa continued to provide more details.

Starting at 9:45 AM, and for the next fifteen minutes, the mayhem died down, as algorithms and computer programs took the lion's share of trading.

In spite of the ongoing technological revolution, old-fashioned, face-to-face contact was still alive and present in trading transactions.

"It's almost time for brunch. Are you feeling okay?" Teresa said.

"Yeah, I think I am." Ben smiled and followed her.

By the tour's end, he had a feel for what happened in the Exchange, but there was still more to be known.

At the Plaza penthouse, Zara noticed Kannada move into the glass office with Walker, from down the hallway. They sternly stared at her through the glass, then turned the room opaque by pressing a button on the wall.

"Ugh." She rolled her eyes. "Boys and their toys." They had given her the impression that there was something else going on.

In 1792, the NYSE restaurant on the seventh floor, Iago put down his cell phone on the table and sighed, relieved to see Ben escorted to the establishment without raising any red flags. They ordered a pair of popular entrées and engaged in banter until the wait staff left them alone.

"The shrimp." A waiter gave Iago his dish. "And for you, the apple chicken salad." He gave Ben his brunch. "Enjoy."

"Thank you," Ben and Iago said, almost simultaneously, smiling.

The waiter returned their smiles in kind. As he left their table, a man of great dignity appeared in their view where the waiter stood. David Lemon had sauntered into the restaurant.

Ben and Iago watched Lemon's grace on display, as the don of dons on Wall Street made persiflage with a few servers, before making his way to a reserved table.

As the room worshipped Lemon, Ben resumed business. "Give me the dirt on Lemon."

"The guy's a big swinging dick and a Whartonite. He's ranked 33rd on *Forbes*' richest list, yet he seems to get along with everyone, even people not of his status," Iago reported, as his food cooled. "He's come into my office before several times. Everybody appears to like him, though my gut tells me he's not a guy to be crossed. He didn't get to the top without knocking some people over."

Ben nodded.

"Punctuality is duck soup for Lemon. He arrives at the NYSE, Monday through Friday, at 7:00 AM sharp, never a minute early, never a minute late. And he hates missing appointments," Iago said.

As he spoke, he remembered his scouting report of Lemon; Iago had kept an eye on how the big power brokers at the NYSE operated.

Iago observed Lemon arrive in a limo a few hours before the Big Board opened and discreetly followed him.

Lemon greeted employees and security guards on his way to the elevator.

"He goes straight to his office on the sixth floor. He stays there all morning unless there's a meeting or an IPO. When there's an IPO, he'll hit the big boardroom on the same floor at 9:00 AM on the dot, spend half an hour there talking with company execs who are about to present an IPO or some corporate milestone," Iago informed.

Taking long restroom breaks and trips to the vending machine on a different floor than his own, Iago saw Lemon come out of the French glass doors with two other men, other high-ranking officials. The great man, with his assistants, walked resolutely toward the large boardroom, where the company set to be introduced on the balcony enjoyed morning snacks and coffee.

Ben smelled his own food. He seemed ready to eat having walked around all morning with his tour guide. "What happens during the day of an IPO?"

Iago stood in the hallway outside the boardroom, quietly finishing his Cheetos bag, listening to, if not watching, what happened in the conference room. Lemon gave the company instructions, presented the history of the NYSE, and mentioned some of the novel things no one knew about.

"He welcomes them, instructs them as to the balcony scene, gives them a history lesson to be remembered, and talks to them about their industry," Iago said. "He's well-versed in every sector; healthcare, technology, energy, financials, utilities, you name it. He's not a guy who stays current with the news; he's ahead of it.

"When it's time for the opening bell, he heads for the balcony at

9:26 AM. While on the balcony, he steps to the side to speak with an assistant, at 9:28 AM, exactly, when pre-market trading stops, giving him a two-minute window before the market opens for regular hours."

A couple of glasses clinked.

"And that's when he gets the password?" Ben asked.

"That's when he gives the password, for the day," Iago said. "It's reset every day at 9:29 AM."

"What about pre-market trading?"

"Pre-market trading uses the previous day's password. He leaves at 1:00 PM every day for the Lipstick Building, his other roost, where his hedge fund operates, just after a couple of meetings in the Big Board at noon."

Ben nodded and checked his cell phone for messages as Iago tested the temperature of his meal, ready to fill his belly. Iago blew cool air onto his food as a man came up to Lemon and whispered something into his ear.

Upon looking up from his mobile device, Ben followed Iago's gaze.

"I've seen him do that every time Lemon's in here." Iago observed the man's muttonchops and slick, black hair. "I doubt he's a real waiter. He seems like an undercover security agent. This guy, Lemon, is slick and low key.

"When Rob refused to back down during the auction for the cables, this guy came back while Rob was being distracted by some fake employee at the auction house. He bribed the auction committee, paid cash on the spot, and signed the paperwork.

"Rob, the original winning bidder, couldn't even fight back. He sued Lemon, but the security company that recorded the auction supposedly lost the tapes during a business move. He sued the security company, but the case was thrown out. The appointed judge, it turns out, was Lemon's neighbor. He doesn't just wait to get an advantage; anything at all can and does happen."

Lemon waved off a waiter who came to take his order.

The restaurant's door opened.

A breathtaking Indian woman, middle-parted, straight, shiny, black hair with brown undertones, a flawless complexion, full pink lips, dark maple almond-shaped eyes, strode past them, trailing a whiff of heavenly scent, and took a seat across from Lemon.

"You see that lady over there," Ben said.

Iago followed Ben's eyes.

"That's the woman who got you a job here. Amara Sanon," Ben said, "Kannada's woman."

Iago narrowed his eyes, as Amara mingled with Lemon, a little too friendly. "You sure about that?"

CHAPTER 18

Manhattan, New York

Zara had arrived at the Lipstick Building. She was a bit surprised by Lemon's decision to operate his business here but made sense of it.

The Lipstick Building hardly embodied the definition of a skyscraper, given its short stature, standing at thirty-four stories, and was relatively new compared to other buildings in the area. It was a natural choice for Lemon to set up camp for his hedge fund; its shape and color were those of a lipstick tube, characteristic of his interest in women.

Zara flipped through a copy of *Inc. Magazine* in the waiting area of Lemon Group's headquarters. She looked nervously at the clock on the wall, which ticked loudly. It was almost 3:00 PM. She'd been cooling her heels for twenty minutes and was freezing; either the heater had failed to accomplish its one and only task, or Lemon intentionally kept the temperature down to keep him and his staff alert. Ms. Kwan, a slender, pale Asian secretary wearing a miniskirt and cat eye makeup, suddenly came out, expressionless.

"He'll see you now," Ms. Kwan said.

Zara attempted to make a cross-like gesture over her face and chest but failed miserably and shook her head. She brightened her face, grabbed her Coach purse, and followed Ms. Kwan down a hallway to Lemon's seventeenth-floor office.

She glanced around and took in the artwork and captions that graced the corridor's walls; paintings by William Holbrook Beard, the iconic *The Bulls and Bears in the Market* and *Wall Street Jubilee*, to Robert LeBron's famous *Wall Street* and Gayle B. Tate's *Time is Money*, to name a few.

Zara walked into a spacious room decorated with hypermodern gray and black furnishings. Black plastic trimming ran along the lower edge of dark gray walls, which rested atop gray-carpeted floors. At the center were two black wooden tables separated by a black leather chair, Lemon's. On the table facing her, a pair of monitors sat. In front of the table, a pair of black leather seats welcomed his guests. On the table away from her, a bank of computer displays rested. The windows had their curtains rolled up to the ceiling and showed nearby high-rise buildings in the backdrop.

Zara eased into a comfortable chair and placed her purse to the side. A mixture of cologne, sweat, smoke, and alcohol, the scent of a real man working, caused her belly to flutter and her mouth to flood with moisture as she watched her interviewee, a man with George Clooney's appeal.

David Lemon paced with the phone to his ear, his collar undone and tie loosened. His pinstriped coat hung off the back of his chair.

A long extension cord was attached to the blinking multi-line jet-black telephone held to one ear, and he wore a Bluetooth headset on the other ear. He answered calls from a myriad of people, and intermittently paused to issue commands to his aides, two young, leggy Latinas in short skirts.

Meanwhile, he kept his eyes split on stock quotes that ran across the several monitors, which carried everything from New York exchanges to Tokyo, foreign currency values, and commodities.

The secretary, outside the office, along with a busty blonde personal assistant in a miniskirt, inside the office, exited and entered with various messages written on pieces of paper, old-school style, which appeared to indicate a waiting party on the phone. Lemon determined whether he would take the call with nods of yes or no.

"What the hell do you mean, we haven't bought the stock?" Lemon pressed on one line.

He seemed unaware of Zara's presence; she looked away, bored.

"All the analysts say it's set to outperform. They say hold if you got it; buy it if you don't. Do you know the last thing that outperformed and people wanted to get a hold of? My twelve-inch shaft," Lemon argued.

He turned to the next line and continued. "Sell it. Sell it! Sell it, like your soul to the devil. Hahaha. I only want a thirty-percent stake because that's enough control for me to stop them from taking over that debt-ridden, no good, piece of—"

Zara was glaring at the framed tombstones on the wall commemorating Lemon's successful deals. She sensed Lemon stop himself at the sight of his new guest. The personal assistant handed him a note. Lemon shook his head no.

"Just sell it." He slammed down the phone, faced Zara, and picked up his cigar.

Zara looked at Lemon as a speck of ash fell to the lemon-shaped ashtray. *Whatever happened to building codes? Says whatever he wants and does whatever he wants.*

"This is the cupcake who brings me Opera glasses," Lemon remarked. "Thank you, sweetheart. Wants an interview with The Legendary Lemon. You should be at Page Parkes or doing a photoshoot with *Maxim*."

Zara blushed with a smile. *How does he get away with this?* If he had seen her earlier, he hadn't thought much of a freelance journalist.

Lemon took a puff of his cigar as the personal assistant brought him a new note. He went back to his phone.

Zara, like an angel, patiently waited for the man to finish his work. In the meantime, she observed a bull statue on his paper-cluttered table, which signified his lunatic lifestyle chasing the bull market.

"Look, Naren, they've got preferred stock, and they've got the drug of the future," Lemon contended. "You're telling me that it's not going to get up there? It's marijuana, for Christ's sake. I want to get high today, not tomorrow."

With that, Lemon stopped taking calls. His eyes drifted to Zara as he wore a genial, charming smile. Though he hopped from one topic to another, he appeared calm in the center of the melee. He was one of the few people for whom the stars and planets aligned themselves properly. He was doing what he was, what he wanted to do, and what he should do.

"Tell them I'm in a meeting," Lemon said to both his secretary and personal assistant, as he loosened his tie further.

They nodded.

"Mr. Paulson is on the line. Does a meeting on Thursday, December 18th sound good?" the personal assistant said, referring to George Paulson, the American business magnate, investor, and philanthropist.

"December 18th. Hmm . . . the Natural Gas Inventories will be released, as well as Leading Indicators, Initial and Continuing Claims." Lemon considered the day's important events. "Yes, I think that'll do."

The secretary and personal assistant left the room. The two young, model-like Latinas understood it was time to leave as well; their winter stockings whooshed as they departed.

"Shreya, right?" Lemon unbuttoned his sleeve's button.

"Yes," Zara answered.

"Pardon me. Sometimes I have to get after these folks. How're you?" Lemon took a seat and rolled up his sleeves.

Zara sat upright. "Fine, thank you."

"So, you wanted to interview me. I've got about half an hour; then I've got to get back to handling business." Lemon sipped from a glass that rested next to a bottle of vodka on his table.

"That's more than enough."

"Good, then let's begin," Lemon said, his attention undivided for the first time.

Kannada sat on the edge of the fountain in Washington Square Park with the arch behind him; loads of snow decorated the resting fountain in front of him. The gradient sky, purple at the top, blue in the middle, and orange near the earth, signaled the end of another day.

Despite his anger at Wall Street and the façade he had maintained of a confident white-collar criminal, doubts of what he was doing with his life and where he was going weighed on his mind. *Why am I really doing this heist? I'm not a crook. I have no experience. I'm not cut out for this type of life.* He sighed. *Well, you can't stop now. It's all about the money. No, that's only a part of it.* The loneliness of living in the subway momentarily gripped him. *It's people. I need people in my life.*

The squeaky, crumpling sound of snow stepped on approached. He looked over. "How'd you know I was here?"

"The gang told me." Ben took a seat next to him, faced forward, and hunched over on his knees. "What happened to Amara?"

"Nothing. Sweet as usual, last we spoke."

Ben sighed. "So, you want to steal Lemon's money?"

"That's the plan."

"And steal his girlfriend?"

Confused, Kannada faced his friend. "She's with Lemon?"

Ben glanced Kannada's way with raised eyebrows. "Mmm hmm."

Kannada looked toward the cold, snowy floor. His heart suddenly dropped. He couldn't believe the words he had just heard. He viewed the park in front. "News to me."

"I find that hard to believe. Tell me this isn't about you wanting to get back at the man who's getting his lemons squeezed by your girlfriend."

Kannada stared at him. "This is about Rob getting revenge on Lemon, and you know it. She just happens to be in the mix."

"Well, it can't be all just one big coincidence."

"She's not my girlfriend anymore." Kannada looked past the pedestrians, toward the park.

"Good." Ben faced the turned-off fountain. "I'm glad we got that settled."

"She's my fiancée." Kannada tilted his head to the side. "Or she was."

Ben looked at Kannada lightning quick. "Your what?" He sounded astonished. "You asked her to marry you? When did this happen?"

Kannada met Ben's eyes and filled in the details. "The day before the great layoff."

Ben stared hard. He was silent and gave Kannada the impression he was waiting for an explanation.

"The job market was rough," Kannada said. "Things gradually fell apart. Look, it's—"

"You're delusional. She's moved on."

A part of Kannada didn't want to believe that he had lost his mind. Amara was the one thing he had held on to through the difficult, homeless years.

"What about us, Main Street? What about Rob and the money he's got invested in this?" Ben sounded pissy, looked away to the park, interlaced his gloved fingers, and sighed.

"Losing my job was one thing, but losing her was different. I lost a part of me."

Ben tightened his grip. He continued to look out a long distance. "So, what're you going to do about it?"

"Well, I still have feelings for her and want to marry her. And if I can do that, I will."

"Feelings?"

Kannada sighed; he had to speak in Ben's language. Ben was somewhat of a horndog, frequenting escorts, like Zara, every now and then when his luck ran dry. Kannada tried a different approach. "Fine. You want the truth? Pussy runs the world."

"Now that, I understand. Tired of spanking the monkey." Ben paused. "The markets are an unforgiving place, my friend, and emotions always result in losses." He looked at Kannada. "The partnership's goals were about money, not what money might impress." Ben faced the park. "You can't stay here with Amara after we're done with the job; you know we have to leave."

Kannada joined him and gazed into the distance. They sat quietly for a moment.

"There's plenty of fish in the sea," Ben noted.

Kannada glanced at him, then went back to viewing the park.

"You don't have to worry about Amara." Ben sighed. "She won't stay with Lemon."

Kannada faced his friend. "And how do you know that?"

"Because Don Juan enjoys a new chick every month."

Kannada leaned back on his arms and stared at the ruthless snow. *Maybe Amara will scorn Lemon.*

Zara had taken her notebook and pen out of her Coach purse. She had no idea what she was doing but had watched some videos of interviews on YouTube to get a feel for how to conduct herself. She didn't know what was considered good reconnaissance but possessed a few questions the group had brainstormed for her. She glanced at the first question and paraphrased it in her own way.

"So, Mr. Lemon, what do you like about green energy?"

Lemon stopped squeezing a lemon stress ball he had taken out from his desk's drawer. He appraised her, and Zara knew it. She sounded like an amateur. *Stick to the script.*

"I mean, can you tell me about your interest in sustainable energy and what you're doing to make the world greener?"

"Ah, yes." Lemon placed the stress ball on the table. "Well, right now, I've been devoting a lot of my time to clean energy. As the Chair of Clean Future Ventures, a new billion-dollar fund that's—"

"A billion dollars?" Zara dropped her mouth in awe.

Lemon glared at her, and she apologized.

"As I was saying, it's focused on changing the way we traditionally view energy, finding innovative ways to alter our energy consumption, and combatting climate change."

She had a lead—great. *Just ask follow-up questions.* "That's a big deal. When did you start and what's the goal of this fund?"

"Well, it started about two years ago when I attended the November climate talks in Doha, Qatar. Two groups came together, one composed of several big governments, and the other, which I refer to as the Clean Future Group, a bunch of private investors, with the goal of making energy cheaper and as clean as possible. But two years later, and things are easier said than done."

Zara wrote a few key words as Lemon took a shot of alcohol.

"Where are my manners? Would you like some vodka?"

She kept her head down, thinking of another question to ask.

"No, thanks," she responded with a smile. She disliked alcohol, unless it was a sweet dessert wine or cocktail. "How do you plan to achieve this goal?"

Lemon put his glass down and sighed. "Well, there are two main approaches to achieving our aims. First, we need more R&D and innovation. And the reason is that there are still many players who aren't on board, such as China and India. If they have to pay a premium for clean energy, then they're not likely to change their habits. But clean energy can be cheaper than dirty energy with the right innovation. So, the question is: how do you get around a lack of innovation?

"Build new companies, invest and support the right startups, which brings me to my second point, legislation. A large part of accomplishing anything climate-related has to do with influencing policy. My initiative, the Clean Future Initiative, which you may have heard of . . ."

Zara nodded with a poised Botox smile as the pompous hedgie gave himself airs. "Oh, yes."

"Is concentrated on getting governments to spend more on R&D, on rewriting legislation, and making amendments to outdated rules and regulations that favor traditional methods of energy production. And, as you may have guessed, that involves putting the right people into power."

"That's all . . . so fascinating," Zara remarked, feigning interest. His lengthy response was over her head. Lemon had switched gears from being a wild, unrestrained man of the markets to a sophisticated, concerned citizen. She scribbled some notes.

"How much experience do you have in doing this?" he asked.

"Several years."

"Really?" Lemon's eyes narrowed into slits. "Kind of odd you haven't got your big break yet."

Zara paused writing, nervous, but came up with an explanation. "Writing is a competitive field." She smiled crookedly.

Lemon raised his brows. "Isn't everything?"

She faced her notebook and swallowed. "So, about this energy thing . . ."

"What'd you study in college, Shreya?" Lemon interrogated.

There was something about the way he addressed her that made her uneasy. "Fashion and business. Why?"

"And you're a freelance journalist?"

Uh-oh. Her eyes wandered away to the side. Zara accidently told the truth about what she had majored in. She searched the floor for answers and felt warm. "Career change. I'm a millennial." She shrugged.

"Ah." Lemon stared through her lies. He was on to her. "Still figuring out what to do with your life."

She nodded slowly with a grave face. Acting as a journalist was harder than it looked. She needed to level the playing field, play to her strengths, and use his Achilles' heel against him. Fortunately, she came prepared for the situation—she "forgot" to wear a bra and panties. She didn't want to bring out the big guns, but Lemon gave her no choice.

"It's a little warm in here. Do you mind if I make myself comfortable?" Zara put her hand up to her blazer's top button, ready to undo it.

Lemon stared. "No, go ahead."

Zara stood and took off her blazer, sticking her chest out in the process. She maintained a sense of innocence, not once looking at him as she exposed her top. Her nipples poked through her shirt, and Lemon ogled. But Zara wasn't finished; she turned around and pretended to drop her jacket on the floor as she tried to hang it off the back of her chair.

"Ooh, clumsy me," she teased. Zara bent over with one knee locked; the other leg hovered in the air. Her miniskirt rose and exposed her goods. She heard him shift in his chair and smirked. As she turned around, Lemon's gaze shot to one of his monitors. She returned to a sitting position and crossed her legs. Lemon bit his lip and gripped the stress ball as though they were her ass.

"What do you see as potential roadblocks?"

Lemon cleared his throat, looked down and away, and shook his head. The tables had turned, and Zara relished her new dominant position. *Come on, horndog. Continue the interview.*

Lemon regained his composure and dove into politics. *Good boy.* He talked about Obama, Hilary and the Democrats, Trump and the Republicans, and some politicians she hadn't heard of, then reverted to his initiative. He went on and on, boring Zara nearly to sleep. When he finished, she smiled to herself, happy to have taken a 5-hour Energy drink before arriving at Lemon's roost.

Zara put away her pen and notebook. "Well, Mr. Lemon, thank you for giving me an interview. I think I have everything I need to write a good article." She rose and extended her hand.

"My pleasure, Shreya." He smiled and shook her hand. "With me as your interviewee, I'm sure you'll have your work featured in *The Wall Street Journal*."

"What?" Zara was lost for the moment. "Oh, yes, of course." *He is full of himself.* She started to put on her blazer.

Lemon stood and circled her as she buttoned her suit jacket and untucked her wavy hair from under her collar.

Zara looked at her bag on the floor. She could bend her knees and pick it up like a conscious woman but opened her mouth, cracked a smile, and ventured to tease him again. She bent over in the same sultry manner as before and smirked as the silver fox tilted his head to get a better view. *What a naughty boy!* She covered her ass with her hand and pulled down her skirt. "Ooh. Forgot my panties." She giggled, sinless.

Lemon smiled from ear to ear. "Right this way." He gently but firmly pushed her along toward the exit, his hand near her lower back, and opened the door.

He leaned in. "Shreya."

Zara looked straight ahead. "Yes?"

"If you have any more questions or need to follow up with me, don't hesitate to call." His hand slid down to her apple bottom. He gave it a gentle squeeze and whispered into her ear. "Let's do this again sometime."

"Ooh." She winked and flashed an impish smile. "Bye."

Zara left, and Lemon closed the door softly. She moved to the reception area as though nothing had transpired between them. Ms. Kwan and the other girls loitered in the front like prostitutes and stared Zara out the door.

The hours passed through the day. In the evening, Zara noticed Kannada and Walker enter the office for the second time. They shut the door behind them and fogged the windows with the touch of a button. She reasoned something private was happening behind closed doors, then moved to the living area.

"Zara," Ben said, "a word with you."

He pulled Zara from the living room, where she was seated, posting an ad online for her services on her phone, as she hadn't had sex for a while.

She followed him to the skylit kitchen.

"I want you to distract Kannada," Ben ordered. "His ex-fiancée, Amara, works at the NYSE and is dating Lemon. I want you to make him forget about her. He'll blow this whole thing and take us all down with him. Here." He presented her with a wad of cash from his pocket. "Do what you do best."

Zara stared at the money, then at Ben. She didn't sign up for this. She didn't like to come between people. Kannada was a nice guy; he had given her a chance to make some real money, a way out of prostitution, and an upscale penthouse to reside in. But he could just as easily take all that away from her if he pursued Amara. Unsure, she nodded and took the money.

"Come on." Ben walked back out to the living room.

Zara stood frozen for a moment, then followed suit.

"What's the four-one-one, Zara?" Ben announced as the others were gathered around the central table in the living room. "What'd you find out about Lemon?"

Zara took her original spot on the sofa; her imprint was still fresh. "He's an eagle freak all about clean energy. He has this clean energy initiative that he's been trying to raise money for. He wouldn't stop talking about it. He wants to fund a political candidate who will support his initiative and others like it. He said he's trying to influence policy."

"Hmm, clean energy, dirty money," Kannada remarked.

Zara and the others giggled.

CHAPTER 19

Manhattan, New York

In the middle of cold December, Amara arrived early with her dance team at The Crossroads of the World in a dark blue sari and bright green dupatta. The streets of Times Square had been cleared over the weekend by political figures and donors for an international, spiritual dance festival, with performances including Argentine Tango, Indian Kathak, Russian Ballet, and much more.

She rehearsed with her group to sweat out the jitters in an area marked off with a metal fence, then joined fans lined up along the streets to watch. Music played, dancers danced, lights flashed, and cameras recorded. Amara stood captivated by the recent performance on stage as New Yorkers clapped, howled, and whistled.

"Their moves were perfectly synchronized. Everything was on point," she commented.

"It must have taken months, practicing in the right conditions," Amara's friend, Neha, said. "He choreographed it after his latest breakup." She sipped complimentary coffee from a white cup.

"You can see the tug-of-war," Amara observed. "Men, with their power and masculinity, try to impress us, and women, with their grace and beauty, seek to control them. We understand men; why can't they understand us?"

Neha sighed. "So true."

Amara bit her lip, desirous of Neha's steamy coffee. The weather forecast read fifty-five degrees Fahrenheit for the day when she watched the news last night.

"Where's David?" Neha asked. "We start in five minutes. Do you think he'll miss it?"

"David never misses an appointment."

As if the man heard their conversation, a chauffeur stopped in front of Times Square. The driver opened the door, and David Lemon stepped out, right on cue, decked in a custom-made designer suit, his chest out, abdomen in, and shoulders back. The only things missing were the red carpet and paparazzi. He examined the area, searching for someone, some sign.

Amara, with a bubbly smile, waved her hand repeatedly.

Lemon saw it, smiled, and made his way toward her.

"Did I miss it?" Lemon asked.

"No." Amara swept her shiny, straight hair to either side with her hands and tucked it behind her ears. "We're just about to start. I'd like you to meet my friend, Neha Kanuri."

Lemon turned to the dance mate. "Neha, you'll have to excuse me for not having more time to talk. I had some business suddenly present itself."

Neha's posture slacked. "I understand it's a busy time of year."

"Oh, with all the earnings, news releases, and last-minute IPOs, I guess it's true what they say; money never sleeps," Lemon remarked.

His joke was met with laughter.

"So, what made you choose Times Square for this event?" Neha said. "It's eye-catching."

"It's not completely my decision," Lemon explained. "The idea belongs to Amara and everyone she managed to sign a petition to get it to be here. Isn't that right, Amara?"

"Yes, David," Amara acknowledged.

Neha nudged Amara to look at the stage. The dancers waltzed into their positions.

Amara signaled to Lemon that it was time. "Here goes nothing. Wish me luck." She felt cold, but her muscles were still relaxed from stretching earlier.

"Break a leg," Lemon added.

Amara turned around swiftly. *What'd he say?*

"It means good luck." Neha clarified the cultural miscue.

Amara shook off her confusion and continued onward.

Lemon smiled and moved to the side, next to a councilman. As he did, he caught Amara in his glance as she was getting in place to perform. His smile widened. He shook hands with the councilman, went through the formalities, and looked at the myriad lights that beamed in every direction and the dancers' comfortable clothing.

"Splendid! I've been watching her for almost a year now. At last, she's getting a chance to showcase her skills."

"Yes, it's a great day for the city," the councilman said.

The performance began. With nimble moves as diverse as America's populace, Amara the lead dancer strutted her talent for New York to see, for America to see, for the world to see, as her performance would go viral. The music and dance, a synthesis of formal and folk Indian traditional music and dance traditions, in fusion with Middle Eastern techniques, was perfectly choreographed. The other great democracy, India, had carved a niche in the biggest, brightest, and best city in the world. Though Bollywood was based in Mumbai, it was quickly making its second home in New York.

Amara noticed Lemon watching.

"A lovely sight," Lemon said to the councilman. "When the lead dancer's not working as my PA, she's a choreographer on weekends and some weeknights."

"Yes, the Orient is cultured," the councilman remarked.

"It's hard to believe that this city has a secret obsession with Bollywood."

"You and me."

"Ah, this turnout, the funds, you couldn't ask for anything better," Lemon boasted. "But, enough meditation. I practically run this town; with you, of course."

The councilman smiled.

When the celebration was over, applause roared. Exhausted

dancers sought hot chocolate and fat, fuzzy jackets after the final bow.

Amara cozied up to Lemon, bright-eyed, optimistic, and still high off the rush. "What'd you think?"

"I think the same as you," Lemon said.

Amara paused, uncertain.

Lemon's photographer, a man with a ponytail and earrings, approached him, camera in hand. "We need you for a couple pictures, Mr. Lemon. The councilman has some other affairs to take care of."

As Lemon started to follow the photographer, Amara began to trail them, though she had already taken group pictures with the dancers prior to the start of the program.

The photographer halted her. "Only those who've made a financial contribution to the event."

Lemon shot Amara an indifferent glance over his shoulder. She comprehended her position and stepped back.

Lemon, the councilman, and a few other donors held their arms in front and posed together, phony smiles. The camera flashed several times. Lemon shook hands with the other donors, then broke from the pack.

"My dear Amara, there's been a change of plans," he said. "It appears that FriendBin has rescheduled their IPO for Thursday, December 18th, no longer on Tuesday of the same week."

"I'll take care of that first thing tomorrow," Amara said. "About tonight, where're we eating?"

He furrowed his brows. "Tonight? I thought that was next weekend."

"No, remember we made plans last Sunday to go out."

Lemon looked up, then returned his gaze to her. "Oh, yes, at Blue Hill."

She narrowed her eyes; Lemon was not the type to forget details. "No . . . at Gramercy Tavern."

He paused, then shrugged and flashed his perfect smile with dimples. "Just a slip of the tongue . . . I'm afraid I'll have to cancel and reschedule for another time."

"Oh." Amara's face sunk. "Why not? You're usually free on Sunday nights."

"I'll be out late for some live jazz at a bar." He looked down and away. "It's kind of a business affair."

Amara tilted her head to the side. "I didn't know you liked jazz. I thought you were interested in opera, classical music."

Lemon pulled out his phone from his coat's inner pocket and raised his brows as he viewed the screen, though the phone didn't ring, nor appear to vibrate. "I've got to take this call right now. It's a relative."

She nodded faintly and avoided eye contact. *Something's not right.*

"I'll see you tomorrow, babe." Lemon went in to hug her with one arm as he put the phone to his ear. "Hello?" he said into the mobile device.

Instinctively, she looked away, crossed her arms, and kept him at arm's distance.

"Hey, Mr. Lemon." A male dance choreographer popped into the scene at the right moment. "Thank you so much for closing the streets and sponsoring this event. It must have cost a fortune."

Lemon recoiled from his advance to tend to his fan. "What is money? The stuff that can buy anything."

Amara glanced up at Lemon. "Goodbye."

Lemon looked once more at the colorful ensembles and lights down on Times Square. "I think it's fascinating. Later sweetheart." He kept his phone to his ear as he walked toward his limo.

When the chauffeur opened the door for Lemon, Amara spotted the calf of a woman inside the car. Her head jutted forward, and her mouth fell open. *Who is that?*

The chauffeur closed the door and hopped into the driver's seat.

Amara watched the limo drive away with the man who seemed to be hiding something. *Kannada would never forget a date, nor fumble his recent memories. Oh, don't think of your ex, he's only trouble.*

She turned and watched the setup being taken down now that the show was over. The thoughts rushed in again. *It's business. Stop thinking so much. Lemon's a busy guy; he makes mistakes, too.*

She deserted her insecurities about Lemon's faithfulness as she joined the rest of the cleanup crew.

In the Dead Rabbit, Paul wiped the insides of a ten-ounce Pilsner glass with a towel, then put the glass away. He carried a tub of dirty glasses and dishes to the sink, where a barmaid washed them in the back, then came out from the back and started to make sure that the drinks and garnishes were well-stocked. He looked at his appearance, blue eyes and blond hair, in the mirror in front of him, then noticed a familiar large patron arrive and turned around.

A barmaid beat Paul to the punch and addressed the recent arrival.

This is my *customer.* "Hey, Sydney, I'll take it from here. He's a friend of mine," Paul intervened.

"Okay." She shrugged and disappeared.

Paul stood in front of the large man. "What can I get you, Graham?"

"Let me get a . . . actually, I'm not sure. What do you recommend?"

"What're you looking for?"

"I'm going on vacation next week to Hawaii for the holidays. I want to get in the mood with something light and fruity."

Paul slid a drinks menu some feet away on the bar top to his friend and pointed to a cocktail. "How about a home run? It comes with pineapple."

Graham viewed the menu. "Pineapple? Lay one on me."

"All right." Paul turned around and went to work, gathering the components of the mixed drink. "How's life?"

"Good. You remember Cindy all the way from Tucson?"

"Yeah, what about her?"

"She moved into my apartment building, two floors down."

"Small world." Paul grabbed a small silver bowl and poured salted almonds into it.

"Guess how much she pays . . . Three thousand per month for 866 square feet."

"Get outta here." Paul pulled out two Benjamins from his pants' pocket, placed them under the bowl, and served the salted nuts to Graham. He put his forearms on the bar top and leaned over. "Thursday, December 18th, what you got?"

Graham flashed a hopeless half smile. "Your money's no good here. I got nothing."

Paul sighed, stood erect, and slammed his fist down on the bar top. "Dammit. You and everybody else I've asked." He looked away. Another familiar face wandered into the bar, wearing a gray, three-piece suit and black sunglasses, chewing gum. Paul put his hand in the air, snapped his fingers twice, and called out, "Kevin."

Kevin approached and parked his caboose next to Graham. "You shouldn't use my name in public."

Paul looked around the bar and yelled, "Kevin. We've got Kevin. Look everybody, Kevin's here."

The scarce, distant patrons glanced at the commotion, then returned to their drinks.

Paul faced Kevin. "See, no one gives a shit . . . Nice shades." He took the sunglasses off Kevin's face and examined them. "If you didn't want to draw anyone's attention, you shouldn't be walking into buildings with these." He returned the glasses. "Thursday, December 18th, what you got?"

"Can I get a drink first?" Kevin chewed his gum slowly and put his shades in his coat's inner pocket.

Paul slid him the bowl of nuts with the two Benjamins underneath it. "Business first."

Kevin peeked at the blue cheese, then glanced at the drinks menu in front of Graham. He gave Paul a steely glare and a smug smile. "Don't get cheap on me, Paul."

Paul raised one side of his mouth. "Your drinks are on the house."

Kevin smiled and pocketed the lucre as the others leaned in. He looked around cautiously, then hunched over and spoke quietly in the huddle. "Milton Companies is going—"

A glass broke in the back. Paul shook his head as the conversation paused and his friends looked in the direction from where the noise came.

Kevin slowly chewed his gum, and his gaze prudently returned to the huddle. "Milton Companies is going to be taken over by UBT. The killer bees are trying to stop the bear hug, but I doubt they will."

With parted lips, Paul stared at Kevin for a moment. *Perfect.* He had been scouring the airwaves for the right insider information since Kannada tapped him to pull a heist on the NYSE. He returned to preparing the home run, his back against his friends, and grinned.

"What? Are you serious?" Graham sounded shocked.

"Yeah, heard it from some company exec at a party at the Empire State building," Kevin informed.

"No kidding? I knew it was going to happen one day, I mean, with their rapid rise and all. They probably don't want any competition."

"UBT's a monopoly."

"Yeah, and I'm Rich Uncle Pennybags."

"Mr. Monopoly. Hahaha. Pass Go; cash in," Kevin remarked.

The two laughed together as Paul added pineapple and lime to the home run. He turned around to give Graham his drink and nosed the sweetness.

"I think I'll be going to Hawaii soon, too," Paul mentioned.

"Yeah?" Graham said.

"Yeah." Paul smiled deviously.

CHAPTER 20

Manhattan, New York

Kannada flipped through the pages of a polygraph book, determining the main contents he would eventually read, as he hunched over the closed lid of the grand piano in the living area of the Plaza penthouse.

Zara approached. "I want you to show me around."

Kannada continued skimming the book and squished his brows together. "Show you around?" He looked at her. "We're busy here."

"Come on." She smiled, her Coach purse hanging off her shoulder, her chestnut hair recently textured. "Take a break. I'm your guest, and I've never been here."

Kannada viewed the piano's lid, calculating whether he had the time to take her somewhere, then looked up and stood erect. "Where do you want to go?"

"I don't know. You live here."

"I guess I could fit something into our schedule, maybe something nearby."

Zara smiled.

Zara and Kannada arrived at the magnificent Beaux-arts building, decorated with famous NYC statues and brilliant bronze and gold accents, Grand Central Terminal.

At the east end, from the main concourse, two sets of stairs on opposing sides led up to a central balcony, from which another flight of stairs led to the second level, or the East Balcony.

Zara and Kannada stood at the rail cap of the central balcony. Behind them were three large windows and in front of them another set of three large windows, all painted black. Across and below them was the central information kiosk, where several people rendezvoused, on top of which stood the bronze-plated Grand Central Clock.

They watched the thousands of busy commuters who passed through the main concourse daily. The squeaks of rubber soles on the recently buffeted floor interjected the quiet, even rumble and the flat footsteps that made their way up and down the stairs.

Kannada stared at the clock's crown, a bronze piece into which acorns were carved, then viewed a throng of people. "Is that Sarah Jessica Parker?"

Zara parted her lips and looked in the direction of the huddle to catch the actress.

"Ah, who cares?" Kannada shrugged, then faced Zara. "You've never been to New York?"

"No, well, once, but I hardly remember anything."

"How do you like it so far?"

Before she could respond, a pair of women walked up the stairs past them, talking loudly.

"Fuck him," a female rider swore to her friend. Kannada and Zara turned their heads to face them, their mouths open. "Fuck his girlfriend. You know what? Fuck everybody."

Kannada turned back to Zara. "What's there not to like about this city?"

She shook her head and smiled.

"Well, this is Grand Central Terminal," Kannada said. "A bunch of trains pass here. It's known for its architecture and sculptures. If you look up, you can see the constellations." He pointed up, stared at the blue-green mural, the nighttime sky, on the cathedral ceiling, and tried to discern the signs amid thousands of stars.

Zara followed his fingers and looked up.

Kannada wondered if she could see the imperceptible star clusters. "So, what do you think?"

"Sweet," she said, "but boring."

"What?" *How could she not like this?*

"Boring. You're like some old tour guide."

"No, no." He tried to meet her coolness.

Zara smiled. "Do you want to go to Brooklyn?"

Kannada squeezed his eyebrows together to make a slight wrinkle and curled his mouth to the side. "I don't do Brooklyn."

"What about Queens?"

"Queens? I don't . . . go to Queens."

She glanced around.

Kannada's mind became restless; he wanted to treat her to a tourist attraction she would like. There was something bothering him since he met her. She was attractive, why'd she want to be an escort?

"So, why do you do what you do?" he asked.

She hesitated, then replied brusquely. "Power. Autonomy."

He nodded. "So, what social good do your services provide?"

Zara raised an eyebrow, parted her lips, and lowered her face, awkward, then tilted her head back and looked up and away. She responded flirtatiously. "I've helped several boys become men."

Kannada's face dropped.

"I'm joking," she said.

Kannada laughed uneasily.

"And what about you?" Zara asked.

Kannada looked at the people below and mused on whether he should reveal his past. "It's not the case now, but I used to be homeless."

Zara grimaced. "You used to be homeless?" She sounded confused.

"Yeah. When people saw me, I think I reminded them of how lucky they were." He faced her. "Things could've been worse."

She stared into his eyes and smiled. "Well, you're certainly doing better now."

He nodded with furrowed brows, unsure.

"How'd you get out of it?" Zara asked.

"I'm still kind of working on that," Kannada said slowly. He expected her to be unhappy with his response, as he was ashamed of his financial difficulties and had put on the façade of an established crook when he first met her.

Oh? Zara silently mouthed to herself. She continued to stare, her eyebrows raised.

Kannada felt the need to explain. "When I first started living in the subway, I suffered from depression and hallucinations. My psychiatrist diagnosed me as insane, but I never believed I was crazy. I opted to speak with a therapist instead of taking meds, and it helped. Sometimes, talking about your problems takes the burden off you."

Zara nodded. "And then you decided to go out on a limb."

He chuckled. "Nah, I started writing to express myself and eventually turned to writing fiction to keep myself busy. What we're doing here is based on a book I wrote."

She lowered her head and raised both eyebrows. "A book?"

"Yes. I met Rob by accident, and he wanted to 'represent my work.'" Kannada made air quotes, then put his hands down. "It's not what I had in mind, but . . ." He sighed, shook his head, and moved his mouth to the side. "When you lose everything, you can do anything."

Zara held a gaze of disbelief. Her lips slowly formed a welcoming smile. "That's interesting. You like to write. What'd you learn from your experiences?"

Kannada's eyes drifted to the side for a moment, then returned to her. "Stability can only be found within."

She stared at his chest, where his titanium lay, then looked away.

"That and having company, friends, makes life easier . . . How'd you get into being a—" he caught himself, paused, and chose his words carefully. He wanted to say, 'call girl' or 'hooker,' but opted for something more pleasant. "Being an upscale luxury companion?"

"Oh, I was always a flirt," Zara said.

"I can tell."

There was a pause. The terminal died down in the meantime.

"Well, I graduated college, but then there was nothing, with the economy and all," Zara said. "I couldn't find anything reasonable for a college degree, and I was in debt. I felt cheated by higher ed."

"What'd you study?"

"Fashion and business."

"Do you ever think of going back to school?"

"Oh, God no, I hate school. I barely got by. I was happy to be done. And a part of me doesn't believe it's for me."

"Then what happened?"

"I worked at a couple of department stores for a while. The discounts were nice, but the pay was terrible for the work I put in. I hated standing on my feet all day."

"Mmm. So, you got into this profession?"

"Well, not right away." Zara looked down and away. "I worked as an exotic dancer for a few months in college and liked the attention and money, so I revisited that. My boyfriend for seven years didn't approve when I first danced, then rejected me when I went back to it."

She faced Kannada with slightly watery sea green eyes. "He was my rock during my post-college slump, so when he left, I really got hurt. But the final blow came when someone close to me passed away." Zara lowered her gaze and shook her head. "I just checked myself out of society, went down a destructive path from there." She crossed her arms and turned to the busy commuters below.

Kannada watched her for a moment. "It's . . . okay." He slowly moved his hand near her back, wanting to comfort her.

She flung herself onto him and hugged him tightly.

Kannada parted his lips and his head jolted back slightly, his forearms suspended in midair. He wrapped his forearms around her, caressed her with his hands, and felt her heart beat. "Can I ask you who died?"

Zara released her grip and stepped back, then looked away and wiped a tear under her eyelid with her finger. "I'll just get more emotional." She sniffed and cleared her runny nose. "A friend of mine suggested trying this for the money. It certainly pays a lot better, and is more fun . . . The first time I was so inexperienced. But the guys are worse. They're usually nervous. A lot of them cheat on their wives because they're not getting the sex they want." She shrugged.

The prostitution scene was foreign territory to Kannada, but her experience was entertaining. "So, what's an encounter with you like?"

Zara stared and hesitated. "I usually rush through the meeting; I mean . . . it's all about the money. I don't even try to act like I'm interested."

"What about your parents?"

"My mom didn't like it. I was meeting all sorts of guys, not settling down with one. But I was making money doing it. She thought I was just being used. And so, yeah."

Kannada moved his mouth to the side. "You no longer seek a relationship, do you?"

"No, I do, but I'm waiting to meet someone. A Prince Charming who could sweep me off my feet. Someone rich and powerful."

"The man of your dreams." He smirked.

"Well, I got close a few times, but I kept showing up late. I'm terrible with time. I did meet this one sweet guy who waited for me at the Beverly Wilshire."

"Oh?"

"He stole me away and took me to the Big Apple." Zara smiled.

Kannada grinned, acknowledging himself as the man who brought her to New York. He looked away. "Where do you get your clients? A professional escort service?"

"There're some websites where you can post ads. I like being independent."

"What if you meet the wrong person? Isn't it kind of dangerous?"

"I screen carefully."

Yeah, I remember that screening process. "Are you . . . disease free?" Kannada said, hesitantly.

Zara looked at him disapprovingly. "Very. I'm not a prostitute. I'm not a piece of meat. There's no full service unless I say so." She sounded serious.

"Mmm." He nodded. "What do you want from a guy?"

"Ideally . . ." She looked over the balcony. "I want someone who calls unexpectedly, who says I love you and means it, who I can talk to about anything, who will kiss me anywhere, who realizes that I say things but don't always mean them, who can tell me his problems and let me help, who will tell me I'm beautiful, who is mine to hold, who lets me wear his jacket—"

"Well, that's quite a lot." Kannada stared, wide-eyed; this could go on for a while. He looked away.

"It's not. What about you? Describe your ideal mate."

"Um, someone who looks moderately good and fits my personality."

"That's it? Someone who looks good and fits your personality?" Zara sounded shocked.

He nodded.

"That's exactly how I bought a dress last week. I went to the mall and looked for an item that made me look good and fit my personality," she said.

Kannada chuckled.

"You should demand more for yourself. Maybe you wouldn't be broke then," Zara advised.

"You should demand less for yourself. Maybe you wouldn't be single then." Kannada grinned.

She stared at him for a moment, then turned her attention to the people below scrambling to catch the next train. He joined her.

"You're not single?" Zara asked.

"Well, I am, but I'm kind of trying to fix things with my ex. She works at the NYSE and her name's Amara."

"So, what happened?"

"Well, it went something like this." Kannada recapped the last couple of years for Zara.

Near the New York Yankees' dugout at Yankee Stadium, Kannada was with his girlfriend, the two of them sporting Yankee uniforms in support of their baseball team, as the Yankees faced off against their arch-nemesis, the Boston Red Sox, a timeless classic, for a Sunday matinee.

"About five years ago, I took Amara to a Yankees game. We had been dating for about four years," he said.

In the middle of the third inning, the two of them and the surrounding fans were broadcast on the Jumbotron at the stadium and on national television for the viewers at home to see. He kneeled and searched his pocket for the engagement jewelry for what seemed like forever.

"During the game," Kannada continued, "I popped the question. I had been stalling. I wanted more stability in my job since the market bottomed out. And, she was waiting."

"Were you nervous?" Zara asked.

"A little. When I kneeled, I thought I had lost the necklace. But, after a minute, I found it in a crevice of my pocket. Everyone was watching on the Jumbotron, too."

A shocked Amara put her hands over her mouth and nose. Kannada didn't even mention that they were going to a Yankees game until that evening. He made it seem as if it was just another baseball game to hang out, enjoy some peanuts and cracker jacks.

"She was surprised," he said. "Smothering me with lipstick,

hugging and kissing me."

Amara had tears coming down her face while the crowd cheered. Kannada placed the diamond engagement necklace around her neck without any trouble. The hugging and kissing resumed as the fans hooted and applauded.

"We planned all night, where it would be, when it would happen, what the theme would be, etcetera, during the rest of the game, and afterward," Kannada said. "The weekend passed, and Monday arrived."

It was back to the grind. The next day, at work, a co-worker called Kannada's name and put his hand on his shoulder. Kannada looked up and ultimately followed the man to a conference room. Kannada took his position in front of the desk. The co-worker closed the door to the office and took his seat behind the table, the window behind him. He put his hands on the table and interlaced his fingers.

"A manager pulled me away from my work and let me have it," Kannada continued. "Gave me the walking papers. Straight to the point, blunt."

Resentment and fear filled Kannada. He believed the manager had similar sentiments. The manager looked as if he wanted to fix the situation.

Kannada, shaken, was at a loss for words. His face dropped. His posture drooped. His ego hurt. He avoided a scuffle, though a small part of him championed it.

"I don't think he wanted it to come to that, but yeah," Kannada said. "It felt scripted, kind of. I was shaken. But I knew it was coming."

"Why's that?"

"There'd been an investigation. Caldwell Investments was accused of operating as a Ponzi scheme. Thing is, they were, and the firm tanked. I wasn't a part of it. I'd done some insider trading before for them, but everyone does it; it's part of the rat race. It was the quants at the firm who were messing around and, of course, management."

The manager went over logistics with Kannada and helped him remove his belongings.

"They gave me a golden handshake, then booted me out," Kannada said. "My mind was warped. I mean, how was I going to explain this to Amara? I had just proposed. She'd been waiting for some time; the wedding would have to be postponed."

Zara maintained eye contact and nodded as he spoke. "What about your family? Couldn't they help?"

"Well, I've got an uncle here, Dilip, but we're not close. My parents passed away in my second year of college; a car accident. And Amara's family is not the wealthiest of people. They live on the other side of the planet, in India. So, yeah." Kannada shrugged.

"That's terrible. Plus, getting a job in New York is ultra-difficult, especially during the recession."

"Ben and a couple of the others worked there; now they can't find anything comparable either. Everyone's still waiting for that recovery to kick in."

At noon, Kannada emerged from the triangular Flatiron building, nice briefcase in hand, his tie loose, his collar open, his stance defeated, his hair a mess. He looked at his watch. It was time for lunch with his lady friend.

"How'd you break it to her?" Zara asked.

Kannada grinned goofily, as the moment unfolded in his mind. He had joined Amara for lunch at Tavern on the Green, in the glitzy, glass-enclosed Crystal Room, before the restaurant's 2009 closure.

"I got a new job." Amara sat across from Kannada under the green Osler chandelier.

"Oh." He was paying more attention to the conversations and clinks of porcelain and silverware circulating the room.

Amara was waiting.

Kannada wasn't budging. He stared at her food but focused on the waiter in his periphery who was pouring wine at the next table.

"Well . . . aren't you going to ask where?" Amara sounded impatient, yet excited.

"Oh," he said, "yeah. Where?"

"You're looking at the new personal assistant for David Lemon at the New York Stock Exchange," she said proudly.

Kannada put on his best happy face. "Wow. That's wonderful."

"I know. I can't wait. It's great. I was hoping for this position so much."

He squinted and poked his chin forward, a little jealous.

A few minutes passed without any conversation. Tears of condensation rolled down his glass of water as he watched her eat, his appetite gone.

Amara rooted around in her purse for something, then shifted in her chair. "You're awfully quiet." She picked up her fork.

"What's there to talk about?" he said.

She looked at him strangely, one eyebrow raised. "You look like you've been hit by a train. Are you okay?"

"I'm fine, really." Kannada's sloppy appearance had been drawing ugly stares from others and stirring gossip since he arrived. "Just a stressful day at work, that's all."

Amara stared with narrow eyes. She gave him the impression that she was trying to read his mind. "Did they give you too much work?" She waved the fork near her mouth, ready to take a bite.

"Yeah, I've got a lot on my plate," he said.

"I can see that. Aren't you going to eat?"

Kannada looked down at his untouched meal, beer battered fish and chips. It smelled stale, though a top chef prepared it. "I'm not hungry. I'll take it to-go." He raised his eyebrows, clenched his jaw, and gave her a glassy stare.

Amara looked vacantly at him. "Okay . . ." She resumed her lunch. "Do you want to tell me what happened?"

"Well, you know how these companies are. They want to keep everything under wraps until finally one day they just lay it on you."

Amara nodded slowly. She resolved to stay quiet and continued her lunch in silence.

Kannada continued to watch her and, likewise, kept mum. He was going to keep his unemployed state to himself, at least until his next gig.

Zara was waiting for Kannada to respond. "You didn't break it to her?" She sounded shocked.

"Not exactly," he said.

"Shut up! How could you not tell her?" Zara said with inflection in her voice, wide-eyed. She grinned and playfully hit him on the chest with her fist.

Kannada gazed over the balcony with a stupid grin. "Well, I mean, she found out. The Ponzi scheme was all over the news."

"Then what happened?" Zara asked.

He looked at her. She was completely engaged.

Kannada passed out resumes on the corners of streets as a last resort. His efforts were ignored.

"Slowly, days without a job turned into weeks, weeks turned into months, and months turned into years," he said. "Nothing, except for some McJobs. Not when they saw Wendell Caldwell. Taking his name off my resume didn't help much either."

"That's rough. How'd you make rent?"

"I didn't. I was kicked out. I moved in with Amara, hustled for a while, selling tomatoes and—"

"Tomatoes?" Zara interrupted him. Her head fell on Kannada's chest as she laughed.

He watched her enjoy herself.

"I'm sorry," she said. "I really can't picture that."

"Yeah, and now here I am doing the unthinkable."

"You're gutsy. And a handful." Zara shook her head. "All you guys think you're so macho, then life kicks your butt."

Kannada smiled. "Amara used to say the same thing."

"What?"

"That I'm a handful. Sometimes, I'm kind of overbearing when I'm with her."

Zara put her hands around his neck. "Well, I think anyone would be lucky to have a guy like you. You're handsome and charming."

He looked down and away. Her words were soothing.

"And crazy." She smiled.

Kannada met her gaze and nodded.

"When's the last time you two dated?"

"About a year ago. When she learned marriage wasn't a reality, things became complicated."

Zara edged closer to him and put one hand on his chest. "Well, I think you should forget about her."

"Yeah?"

"Sometimes things fall apart so that better things can fall together." Zara smiled with a sparkle in her sea green eyes.

Kannada nodded and processed her insight. He looked away.

"What do you like about Amara?"

His face beamed with strong color and sheen. "She's perfect, the kind of woman I'd want to bring home to my family, if I had one; smart and witty, well-cultured, pure, and caring. She's charitable and giving, and she stays in the kitchen."

Zara laughed, her head falling on his chest. "You're sexist."

He wrapped his arms around her. "I'm not sexist. She happens to be an excellent cook."

She looked up at him. "And what am I?"

"Trouble."

"I am not." Zara laughed.

"Yes, you are." Kannada grinned. "You're trouble. A gold-digger."

His comments cracked her up. *She has a nice laugh.*

"I happen to enjoy the finer things in life and like to dress fashionably . . . I haven't seen you wear anything but the same clothes since we met," Zara noted.

Kannada was wearing the same black suit he slipped on in the subway when he put forth the effort to attend a job fair. "Well . . . when you're homeless, you get used to wearing the same thing."

She stared at him with her mouth open. "No," she said emphatically with a slight shake of the head, "we're going to have to change that. Get you into something trendy. I know just the thing to cheer you up. There's one place I've been dreaming of seeing. Come on." She took his hand and rushed off with a smile, pulling him as a small girl did a wagon. "Let's go."

CHAPTER 21

Manhattan, New York

Zara and Kannada visited one of the major thoroughfares that went through the borough of Manhattan. Kannada hadn't set foot on Fifth Avenue, one of the most expensive and best shopping streets in the world, especially the section between 49th Street and 60th Street, since he fell into poverty. The affluent generously donated money, but usually through a charity rather than to his once dirty palms.

They stopped at Saks Fifth Avenue.

Kannada followed Zara wherever she led him; for some strange reason she knew where everything was without ever visiting the store, as though she had a special sixth sense that turned on during shopping. He boarded a few humming escalators and ascended the floors amid the smell of perfume and expensive, glossy shopping bags that rubbed against legs. With each change of escalator, he caught glimpses of luxury on the intermediate levels, as snobbish guffaws added pomp to spending sprees and wealthy shoppers meticulously examined clothes.

When they reached the women's section, Kannada winced at the price tag of a blouse on a rack. "You know this place is pretty pricey?"

"That's okay. I brought Rob's Amex black card."

Kannada looked past her, doomed. "Oh hell." He shook his head.

Zara chuckled. "All right, me first."

"Was it going to be any other way?"

She smiled.

They dropped by the women's Fifth Avenue Club without appointment, and the high-end store made sure to accommodate its customers on short notice. Zara collaborated with the style advisor to prepare a private suite, fitted with the appropriate size and style of clothing. Kannada stayed out of their way; a woman and her clothes was serious business.

Zara invited Kannada to join her in the changing room, but he opted to stay in the open seating area and kept his reason for doing so private. He wanted to avoid ogling her when Amara was on his mind.

New York Fashion Week had arrived, with Zara trying on several outfits to the tune of fashion store music in the fitting room. She matched hats and shoes, dresses and belts, and posed for Kannada in the open area.

Kannada sat on a sofa and watched, hypnotized by her sense of beauty and appreciation for haute couture. She possessed a certain *je ne sais quoi* that tamed any impatience he had to end the shopping experience early. Maybe it was her confidence, maybe her control of their outing, maybe her occasional hair flip, maybe her smile, maybe the eye contact she made, maybe the selfies she took with him whenever she unexpectedly pulled him off the couch, or maybe it was a combination of all this and more, but he couldn't say. For a few moments, his eyes turned dreamy and his heart melted.

"What'd you think of that last one?" Zara asked.

"Good," Kannada said.

"Good? Not great?"

He sighed, hammered by the show. "They all look great."

"Did it make my butt look too big?"

"No."

"So, my butt is too small; that's what you mean?"

"No, your butt is big."

"So, I'm a fat ass?"

"Uh, no." He touched the base of his neck and narrowed his eyes.

"So, you're lying?"

"Look, I like big butts, and I cannot lie." Kannada smiled.

Zara nodded, then turned away to gather the tons of clothes she had tried. She paused and spoke to herself. "Ugh, does teal go better with hazelnut or peach? These are the questions that keep me up at night."

Kannada grinned. "Why do you like to shop so much?"

"It's not what you guys think. It's not about shopping or spending money. It's about . . . decorating things, designing, mixing and matching."

"Artwork?"

"Yeah, art." Zara stared into his eyes and paused. "Sometimes I like to go to stores like Herman Miller and just walk around in my free time." She turned away.

"Why?"

"Just to dream of how I would decorate my home one day." She turned back around to face a smiling Kannada. "I know it's weird."

"It's not. I kind of do that, too."

"You do?" She sounded astonished.

"Except with Target. I love that store."

Zara lowered her head and raised her brows. "Target?" She chuckled a bit as she held her laughter, smiling.

"What?"

"You're a guy."

"So?"

She laughed. "Okay, whatever . . . I'm done. Now, it's your turn."

Instead of being a spectator, as Kannada had been, Zara was hands on. She decorated him as if he were her personal Ken and she, Barbie, giving him new outfits to try on, one after another, in a dressing suite in the men's Fifth Avenue Club.

Zara adjusted his collar, buttoned his shirt up, tied his tie, and did everything else that came with decorating a mannequin. She paused every so often to step back and view her grand design. She'd make a few adjustments, then start all over again.

"Do you have to jiggle?" Kannada had grown frustrated with the constant tugging of his pants.

"Yes, if you'd stop fidgeting, I could see whether these pants fit you or not," she said.

He stood frozen, acted patient, and kept his distance, as she put her hands in his pants. *What's she doing?*

"Not in my pants," he said.

Zara looked at him. "Why? I have to make sure they're not tight. And judging by the space, it doesn't seem like much is there."

He flashed a sarcastic grin. "Things shrink in cold weather."

"Ah," Zara said, lengthening the sound. "That's too bad. I'm sure you're well-equipped." She smiled.

Kannada put on a Botox smile. "I think we've got enough clothes. Let's go. It's getting late." As he walked away, he caught her reflection in a mirror.

Zara followed with a devious, childish look on her face.

Next morning, Ricky stood in front of the mirror and practiced in their Plaza townhouse. "Hello. I'm Prince Abdullah bin Malik al Saud," he said in his best Arabic accent.

He tried again, accentuating the short and long vowels, "I'm Prince Abdullah bin Malik al Saud."

He had been practicing for a few days now, nonstop. Ricky talked to himself in Arabic-English and held imaginary conversations while he showered, ate, and used the john. He trained his tongue and mouth and became familiar with the new sounds, listening to recordings and watching Arabic-English TV channels online.

Ricky embraced changing his tone from gay to straight; he felt like the other guys for once. He'd never done a foreign accent in all his acting days nor his con work. This was on-the-job training; it was something that could come in handy in the future.

Ben and Rob critiqued his voice and tone, mannerisms, and behavior. They rehearsed with him and made sure he could deal with any curve balls thrown at him; one hiccup and they were toast.

Ricky was dressed in the same red-and-white checkered keffiyeh, stabilized by a black head ring on top of a white thobe, which had pleased him at the Middle Eastern bazaar. This time, he had a black mustache glued to his face, a black hairpiece atop his bald head, foundation and bronzing powder wherever his pale skin would show, and photochromic lenses that were normally clear, but darkened with light exposure. He practiced again and again, raising and lowering his pitch, elongating and shortening his vowels, and twisting and turning his tongue.

"Hello. I'm Prince Abdullah bin Malik al Saud. The pleasure is mine." Ricky's latest attempt impressed him; he was sounding more and more like a native speaker.

"Remember the drill?" Ben positioned his sunglasses above his own pale forehead, atop his spikey, dark brown, Asian hair.

"Nose kiss, *as-salāmu ‘alaykum*, or *wa ‘alaykum al-salām*." Ricky pointed his nose in the air and wiggled his head. "Peace be upon you."

Rob slouched in a chair, his elbows on the armrests, his hands on his plump gut. "And?"

"Hold his hand," Ricky answered.

"Good," Ben said. "Keep this on you; it's a recorder." He gave him the device. "And here's the money." Ben handed him the briefcase Ricky had prepared earlier. "And the bad checks?"

Ricky patted his pants' pocket. "Right here."

Ben dropped the shades down and covered his eyes. "It's showtime."

CHAPTER 22

Manhattan, New York

Vehicular entrances to the key corridors leading to the NYSE were blocked by retractable posts on the road and NoGo blocks on the sidewalk. It was as if the automobile hadn't been created. On the other hand, people, mostly busy people, with a couple of tourists getting in their way to take photos, mobbed the narrow streets.

At the intersection of Broad and Beaver Streets, a gold-plated Ferrari flanked by two police officers, one in front and one at the rear, stopped a few feet away from the retractable posts and blocked traffic in the right-most lane. Ben Wu, the driver, calmly placed a phone call from inside the vehicle to the Big Board, amid the sound of car horns and angry stares from drivers who maneuvered around him.

Ben was dressed as a chauffeur in white gloves, a black driver's hat, and a black suit. He was calling to gain entry to the forbidden pathways.

The phone rang at the desk of Lemon's personal assistant, Amara. She picked it up while staring at her computer screen. "Mr. Lemon's office, Amara Sanon."

"Hello, may I speak to Mr. Lemon please?"

"I'm sorry, Mr. Lemon is not available. May I help you?"

"No, you can't. His Royal Highness, the Minister of Foreign Affairs, Prince Abdullah bin Malik al Saud, demands to speak with Mr. Lemon immediately." The caller sounded brusque.

Amara parted her lips and paused. It wasn't everyday a prince called and made commands. She handled the call courteously. "I know Mr. Lemon would want to talk to you. Could you please hold?"

"Make it quick."

Amara swallowed, put him on hold, and rapidly researched the prince on the internet.

Ben yawned as he waited on the phone. He checked out the two officers, Walker Mays through the front windshield, and Alan McGill in the side-view mirror. They looked authentic, wearing real police gear, uniforms, and helmets, and riding motorcycles; Ricky was their hook-up. Walker and Alan kept a lookout for any unusual activity that could endanger the person they were guarding.

It wasn't long before the parade caught security's attention.

Walker signaled a security guard to address the matter.

A guard with brown eyes and hair, under a winter hat, approached Walker, who directed him with his gloved hand to the back to speak with the driver of the Ferrari.

The window rolled down automatically as the guard stood to be greeted. The refreshing winter air cooled Ben's skin.

The guard exhaled warm breath. "Hey. This area is restricted access only. Is there a reason you're waiting here?"

Ben, shades on, reached for his wallet near the gear lever and withdrew some bills. "Good afternoon, sir. Yes. His Royal Highness, the Minister of Foreign Affairs, Prince Abdullah bin Malik al Saud, would like to have a word with Mr. David Lemon."

"Um. Does he have an appointment to see Mr. Lemon? Otherwise, you're going to have to move it."

Ben didn't like the security guard's haughty tone or his coffee-and-donut breath. The man looked like he was ready to call for backup. "His Royal Highness, the Minister of Foreign Affairs, Prince Abdullah bin Malik al Saud, doesn't make appointments. He belongs to Saudi royalty. Now, if you will . . ." Ben handed him a few hundred dollars. "Can you please inform Mr. Lemon that he's waiting?"

That cooled the guard. "Hold on. Let me check with security and see what we can do."

Normally, security wouldn't be so easily persuaded; however, Saud's gold-plated Ferrari, sturdy escort officers, and his chauffeur's fine etiquette were enough for the security guard.

Lemon, spectacles at the tip of his nose, peered over some papers at his cluttered desk. He sensed perfume. "Yes?" he said, without looking up.

Amara stood at the entrance of his office. "David, there's someone outside the NYSE who would like to speak with you."

He sighed heavily. "There're a lot of people who would like to speak to me. Some protester?"

"No, it's a foreign dignitary, a Prince Abdullah bin Malik al Saud from Saudi Arabia." She sounded hurried.

"Who's he?"

"Supposedly a royal of the House of Saud, the Minister of Foreign Affairs. and a professional investor as well. Invests mostly in the Middle East and Asia. He's impatient, but he's waiting at the retractable posts."

Lemon removed his glasses and looked at Amara's hand on the doorknob. "Saud? That's a big family."

"Yes, sir. That's why I looked him up, confirmed it was him."

Lemon looked at her. "He wants to speak to me? For what?"

"Not sure. Says it's confidential, paramount."

"I've got some other obligations to take care of shortly." He shook his head. "What's he driving?"

"He's in a gold-plated Ferrari, sir."

Lemon was moved; his eyes said it all. "Check him in."

He had no choice. Turn down a foreign dignitary? That was the same as instigating war. It was a *sine qua non* to welcome Saud to the NYSE and pay homage to him. Saud's gold-plated Ferrari had Lemon's attention; it could not be denied entry into the forbidden corridors that led to the building.

Prince Abdullah bin Malik al Saud, Ricky, received his entry into the Big Board, where almost no man, certainly not a nobody, went. Access to unchartered territory; his custom-made, gold-plated Ferrari parked right in front of the Exchange, below the colonnades, on the Euro-cobble. He made his entry at the VIP guest entrance.

Kannada knocked on the barrier to Zara's penthouse suite on the nineteenth floor.

Zara opened the door and peeked her head out. "Hey, come on in." She sounded sweet.

"Hey." He walked into the room.

She closed the door behind him.

Kannada continued walking and entered an open space in the room. An alluring scent permeated the air, sandalwood incense and fragrant jasmine ointments. Fresh, aromatic rose petals decorated the bed and lit candles flickered hither and thither. A well-chilled bottle of vintage champagne waited for its opening. He paid little attention to the set mood. His eyes searched back and forth quickly until he saw Lorenzo's confiscated NYSE work badge on a table to his right. He took the badge and turned around to leave. His path was blocked.

He was about to speak but hesitated upon seeing the rest of Zara's body. She was dressed in seductive red silk nightwear that accentuated her hourglass figure, flaunted her ample cleavage, and showed her shimmering light tan legs. He leaned away and swallowed, his gaze moving from head-to-toe-to-head.

"Uh, sorry, I didn't know you were occupied here." Kannada started for the exit.

Zara impeded him by putting her hand on his chest. "Stay. Relax a little."

He avoided eye contact. "I have to go."

"Come on." She took his hand and led him to the bed. "Have a seat."

Kannada settled down at the far edge of the mattress while she crawled onto the bed and sat on her knees behind him.

"Zara, I've got some errands to run," he said.

"They can wait. You're more important." She started to massage his shoulders.

"Ooh! That kind of feels good. Do I have to pay you?"

"It's free of charge. Just for you, this time."

"That feels even better." Kannada smiled, happy not to pay for her services.

She massaged his shoulders for a while as he dropped his head down.

He noticed a rolled-up, teal yoga mat in a corner of the room. "You do yoga?"

"How else do you think I keep my figure?"

"Makes sense."

"I've been going to this place near Park Avenue and 53rd Street."

Kannada frowned. "You joined a yoga studio?"

"Yes, yoga's all the rage."

"We're only here three weeks."

"Well, if you'd recruited more women, I wouldn't have to go there."

He paused to think about a yoga studio full of hot, sweaty women, then shrugged off the fantasy. *Estrogen Temple.* "That yoga studio used to be a dive bar."

"You seem tight. When's the last time you had a massage?"

"Too long ago."

Zara kissed his neck and back; then she licked his ear with a serpent's tongue while she caressed his chest and abdominals with gentle strokes.

Kannada got a hard-on.

"Lie down." Zara moved out from behind him and tried to lower his body. "Take off your shirt."

He went against the motion of her hand on his chest. "I don't want to get all oily now. I just took a shower."

"Okay, no oil." She moved off the bed and swayed her hips as she walked toward the front.

Nice body English. He lay on the mattress, propped up only by his elbows.

She stood in front, took off her sexy silky gown, and smiled in her birthday suit.

Kannada stared at her plump, perky breasts and pointy nipples. Her boobs were practically begging to be sucked. He gawked at her wet, outie vagina, decorated with a landing strip, and started to salivate. Pre-cum moistened his underwear and welcomed the inevitable. He hadn't had sex for years, and now it was readily available. His instinct was to bend her over, pull her hair, and fuck her hard, but when his gaze returned to her sea green eyes, he saw a lie.

The business world had warped Zara into a weapon of seduction.

Now she would say and do whatever you liked, if you just met her price tag. It was unfortunate because he liked Zara. His intention for coming into the room, Amara, flashed before his mind. He briefly compared the two, Amara and Zara; one was real, the other, superficial.

"All right." Kannada began to leave, exasperated.

"Wait!" Zara rushed to get in front of him.

"I don't have time for this." He clenched his jaw.

"Why do you want to leave?" She put her arm against the wall near the lock and blocked the doorway.

"I've got a friend to meet."

"You don't like what you see?" Zara sounded upset.

"No," Kannada said. "No, I mean . . ."

"Then what?"

"Can you please step aside?"

"You put me up here for three weeks. How come you don't want to spend some time together?" She sounded innocent.

"It's not that . . . I've got business to handle. Now, can you please step aside?"

Zara looked down, her eyes searching for a way to thwart his plans.

Kannada quickly grabbed the doorknob, turned it, and opened the door forcefully. Zara was pushed to the side, and he was gone.

Zara leaned against the door, crossed her arms, and let her head loll back against the wood as she looked up and sighed. "Ugh, he's impossible."

She couldn't stop him. Zara frowned and wiped a tear rolling down her cheek with her finger. For a moment, she felt hurt. He didn't just rebuff her specialty; he rejected *her*. Maybe he wanted bigger boobs, a juicier butt, or thicker thighs. She took care of her figure; was it not enough? Her experiences with cold, cheap men as an exotic dancer and escort ran through her mind. Kannada turned down a VIP session, sex. *It's what guys want, right?*

Her thoughts slowed down. *What does he want? What does Amara have that I don't?* She scanned her experiences with him; he stayed in the open seating area in Saks Fifth Avenue instead of joining her in the changing room. He used shorter words and talked less than her; suddenly and strangely, she felt attracted to him. His

186

strong, silent nature flashed before her, and it became obvious; he desired something more, something genuine, but she had given that up. She didn't want all the drama that came with a relationship. And he was far from being a made man. It was all about the act now; the money. *How am I going to give him what he wants?* Then it hit her; Kannada needed a girlfriend experience. Zara smirked with wicked eyes.

CHAPTER 23

Manhattan, New York

Amara finished her duties and tidied her desk at the NYSE in the event that the Prince might see it. She stood and straightened her outfit.

Lemon stormed out of his office to where Amara was standing. He stopped and straightened his tie, his broad forehead exceptionally shiny, his white-and-gray hair well-combed. "How do I look?"

"Dressed to impress." A whiff of conservative cologne with a professional and wealthy vibe tickled Amara's nose. *The Tom Ford Grey Vetiver I bought him.*

"I'm unaware of Middle Eastern formalities, Amara. Please, could you?" He rubbed his hands on his pants.

"I've already taken care of it. When he arrives, be sure to say *as-salāmu ʿalaykum*; it's the main greeting and address him as Your Royal Highness, the Minister of Foreign Affairs, Prince Abdullah bin Malik al Saud. And make sure to rub your nose with his, if he leans in."

Lemon repeated back, "*As-salāmu ʿalaykum*."

Amara smiled. "Perfect. That's only for guys. And make sure you hold his hand; it's a sign of friendship. I think I'll keep a distance."

Lemon looked at her outfit, black capris to her shins, green flats, a white shirt with black polka dots, and a yellow sweater. "You can go."

Amara raised an eyebrow. She didn't want to miss the once-in-a-lifetime opportunity to meet a royal member of the House of Saud. "Are you sure? I'd like to meet him if it's okay with you."

"I insist. This is business."

Amara got the picture; her casual Friday attire would not make a good impression. Dismayed, she forced a smile and nodded. "Would you like me to grab you some brunch?"

"Brunch is for wimps," Lemon scoffed.

Amara looked down. She turned away and left for the morning meal. As she walked the corridors upset and alone, she wiped her cheek with her hand amid the lonely echo of her footsteps.

Lemon met with the Prince, who was escorted by two solid police officers, Alan McGill and Walker Mays, and extended his hand. "Your Royal Highness, the Minister of Foreign Affairs, Prince Abdullah bin Malik al Saud, *as-salāmu ʿalaykum*."

Ricky shook his outstretched hand. "*Wa ʿalaykum al-salām*." The back of Lemon's hand was hairy, his palm was moist, and his handshake was firm. "And unto you peace." He leaned in, as did Lemon, for a hot nose kiss; then he smoothed his thobe with his hand to scour away the clamminess. Ricky stared deep into Lemon's eyes; frankly, he was a little turned on.

"Pleased to meet you," Lemon said.

"Oh, the pleasure is mine." Ricky smiled; his accent was on target.

A couple of corporate bigwigs took photos with their cell phone cameras while the greeting transaction took place; then they received Ricky graciously. Lemon and Ricky posed for a couple pictures as well.

"Right this way." Lemon directed with his hand. "After you."

Ricky put his hand out; he was expecting.

Lemon held his hand as they walked together.

Amara entered 1792, the NYSE restaurant, and sat in the same place she always did, at the table reserved for her and Lemon. She ordered, then glanced at her phone intermittently, distracting herself.

Someone approached from behind Amara. *The waiter*. She sensed

189

someone domineering in her presence, as the recent arrival stood close to her and wore a suit in her periphery. *Maybe the manager.*

"Full house," a man said. "Mind if I sit here?"

The voice sounded familiar. By judging the noise level in the room, she knew it wasn't packed. She looked up to address the person new to the scene.

"Kannada . . ." Amara glared into his eyes and searched for answers, lost for the moment. With an aroma of sandalwood and jasmine, he smelled as though he'd come from a massage parlor.

"Hi, Amara." Kannada smiled, standing tall in front of her.

Amara shook her head softly. For him to dine at the restaurant, he had to be a NYSE employee, invited client, or part of a listed company. "How'd you get in here?"

"I work at the NYSE. How else could I get in?" He took Lemon's seat.

Amara squinted. She didn't trust him; he'd lied to her before. How'd Pinocchio go from being homeless to being employed at the NYSE? Something seemed amiss. "Doing what?"

"Whatever they tell me."

She nodded with a grin.

"Never mind what I'm doing. I'm back," he said.

"Yes . . . you are." She watched his every move.

"So, how are you?"

"Good."

"How have you been after, you know, things didn't work out?"

She shrugged. "Okay . . . I guess."

"Remember our wedding plans? You couldn't have forgotten. They were extensive, to put it mildly."

Amara's nostrils flared and her teeth grinded, as she replayed the moment they started making plans on the night he proposed at the Yankees game. "Extensive? I was looking forward to getting married. I told everyone. I was so humiliated after Neha found you panhandling in some alley."

"Shouldn't have put the cart before the horse."

She parted her lips and flicked her gaze up, then coldly met him with narrow eyes. "All our wedding plans were for nothing. I planned for ten months and you're not even ready."

"Hey, you're the one who rushed into it because all your friends were getting married. I even tried to drop subtle hints that we should slow down. Patience is a virtue."

Amara sighed and shook her head. "Oh, yeah, it's my fault." She sounded bitter. "I stuck with you for years, hoping you'd weather the storm. How long am I supposed to wait?"

"I know. I shouldn't have brought it up. Let's . . . not talk about it."

Amara let her muscles relax momentarily.

"I wanted to personally thank you for getting Diego a job here. You've been helpful, more than you can imagine," he said.

"Let me guess, he got you in the door."

"You could say that."

Amara glanced at security, a man with muttonchops and slick, black hair, standing near the wall. She could call him over but decided not to; Kannada was overbearing but harmless.

"Well, I'm starving." Kannada waved his hand to the waiter.

"Don't even think about ordering."

"I have to eat. It's kind of hard to come by in the streets."

"Not my problem."

"And for you, sir?" a waiter said.

"He changed his mind. He's not hungry." Amara gave Kannada a dirty look. She had to be strict with him before he walked all over her.

Kannada met her gaze.

The attendant waited for a moment and looked at him.

"I'm fine," Kannada said.

As the waiter left, he shook his head.

Amara observed Kannada's chinstrap facial hair; it looked fake. "What's with the beard?"

"It's my new look."

"It's a bad look."

"The folks at the homeless shelter said I needed one to fit in. You have to follow the crowd."

"Ha, very funny." Amara folded her arms.

He grinned.

She looked around the room. No one seemed to care that Lemon's seat was occupied by someone other than himself. Amara made eye contact with her ex. "You have to leave."

"I was just getting started." He glanced at her collarbone. "You're still wearing the engagement necklace I gave you. I'm glad you

191

didn't lose it."

He remembers. Amara recalled telling Kannada about her dislike for rings; she always lost them in the sink. "I was planning on throwing it away." She unlocked the stare and looked elsewhere. A few patrons walked into the restaurant, conversing with one another. "And we're not a thing anymore." She faced him with a stiff neck and strained muscles. "I know you're not employed here. Did you find work?"

"I've created work."

"Oh, how nice," Amara said, sure this was going nowhere. "You're not still selling tomatoes on the side of the road, are you?"

"No."

"Still insider trading with your buddy down at the bar?"

"That comes with the territory, and no."

"So, what are you doing now?" She put her forearms flat on the table, her hands one on top of the other, near her chest, and leaned slightly forward.

"I've written a book."

She scrutinized his face and pointed her chin forward. *He wrote a book?*

Kannada continued. "I've developed an ingenious way to play the markets."

"Oh really?" She smirked. "And what does that involve?"

"A little deception." He winked.

Amara's posture stooped, and her facial features turned down. He was trying, but he was lost. She felt him rub her foot under the table and recoiled.

"Kannada, you can look, not touch. That seat belongs to someone else. You need to leave."

"I don't think Lemon would mind."

She stared sharply. He was aware of her relationship with Lemon.

"I believe he's in a meeting right now." Kannada smiled. "When'd you start dating him?"

"It's none of your business, but a while ago."

"Has he taken you anywhere special?"

Amara wondered how much she should disclose. "We've had a few lunch dates for your information."

"You moved."

Amara's eyes narrowed. "Yes, I did."

"The old apartment was nice. Good location, modern, affordable."

"Well, Lemon's place has all that, plus more."

Kannada's pitch rose. "You live with him now?"

Amara grinned. She wasn't under any obligation to give out personal details. "His building. We're not talking about my love life anymore."

He paused. "I saw you on YouTube, dancing. Lots of good comments. I usually don't like reading the comments. They can get nasty. Do you view them?"

Amara sighed. *He is such a handful at times*. "Kannada."

"The dance was terrific, colorful, and energetic. Although I would've done it in warmer weather."

"Yeah," she said, putting up with him. "I was freezing my butt off."

"Should've hosted it in Madison Square Garden."

"I thought about that, but Times Square—"

"—is Times Square," they said in unison.

She stared and wanted to express favor but held back. There was an awkward silence. She wasn't going to let Kannada slip back into her life. He was a bum.

"You know what I miss about us?" Kannada said. "It's the little things that we have in common. I know what you're thinking; you know what I'm thinking."

"I think you should—"

"Do you know how much I missed having conversations with you for the last year?"

"You just don't quit."

Kannada snickered. "Yeah, I liked our meaningless talks." He looked deep into her eyes with a smile.

She glanced at security, then looked down at the table. "Sounds like you had a lot of time on your hands."

"You were always fun to be around."

Amara kept her gaze elsewhere. "Yep, there's nothing like being with a dancer."

"All right." Kannada sounded as if he was no longer interested in flirting around what he was getting at. "I fell and now I'm picking myself back up and making a return. For *you*. That's the only reason, and I want it to be like old times."

193

"Who do you think you are? My knight in shining armor? You're broke without a job and want me to carry your weight."

Kannada narrowed his eyes.

She felt sorry for a moment, as her words were resentful, but brushed off her pity.

"I'm worried about you," he said.

"Why?"

"You look . . . comfortable."

Comfortable? What does that mean? If I'm comfortable, I'm relaxed. If I'm relaxed, I'm at rest, not active . . . Oh my God, he just called me fat. The nerve of him. "You think I've gained weight."

Kannada's brows rose. "I didn't say that."

She held back her accusations; she didn't know what he was hinting at.

"Just out of curiosity, what'd you order?"

Amara avoided eye contact, leaned back, and spoke with a weak voice. "Three entrees."

"Three?" He gave her a crooked smile. "You're not happy with Lemon and you've been binge eating. It's what you do, Amara."

Amara glowered; she'd been caught with her hand in the cookie jar. *Well, he didn't have to say it like that, but he's right; I've been binge eating lately.* "Ugh, I'm with a better person now, an individual who doesn't have to resort to selling tomatoes and insider trading for his survival."

"No, he's much worse."

"Okay. He doesn't hold a sign for a living, and he's not homeless."

"The correct term is minimalism."

Amara snickered.

"Did you stalk him and read his bio like you did me?" Kannada asked.

She scowled.

He grinned. "What do you see in him anyway? All you young women going with older men."

She thought of Lemon's power and prestige, his grace and manners, and her opportunity to be with someone great. "He knows things, understands, stays in shape. He's stable. I know he'll be able to support me."

"Of course, he will." Kannada sounded sarcastic. "He's as old as the hills."

"He is not."

"He's a dinosaur."

She sensed him trying to claw her back into his reality, but there was something romantic about being with an older, wiser man.

"He is not," she repeated with a chuckle.

At last, Amara broke her resistant, obstinate disposition. She gazed at him, somewhat nostalgic, and cracked a smile against her will, but that was the best she was going to give him.

"You know what you're missing?" she said.

"Nothing anymore."

He thinks I'm playing hard to get. "Structure. You're a hopeful, spoiled dreamer. You think you can get whatever you want, whenever you want."

A waiter came out from the back with a large round serving tray in one hand and a mahogany folding tray stand in the other.

"And Lemon doesn't." Kannada paused. "Do you want to go somewhere?"

She rolled her eyes. "I'm at work, for one. And two, I'm in a relationship with David now." *I'm not playing hard to get.*

"You're into him for the money." Kannada came off as abrasive.

Amara considered what he said while she placed a linen napkin on her lap. She backed down. "Well, at least I'm not into a bum who lied to me about his job loss. Lemon doesn't hide things from me."

"Are you sure about that? He has his secrets."

The waiter arrived with Amara's entrees and set the food down before her.

Lemon and two of his aides had welcomed the Prince into the large boardroom on the sixth floor. They made chitchat on the way there.

The Prince's escort officers, Walker and Alan, stood outside the doorway. They were serious, armed and dangerous, or so it appeared. They had a job to do, at all costs. A close inspection, or a test of their duties, would quickly reveal that they were a deception, unloaded and harmless. They kept alert as businesspersons walked by with wary eyes.

When the coast was clear, Walker smelled alcohol. He looked over to a sweaty Alan and caught him drinking from a hip flask.

"Alan, not now." Walker shook his head with furrowed brows.

Alan sighed heavily and quickly put away his flask.

Inside the boardroom, Lemon and the Prince laughed together, over coffee.

"I always see you on TV, that CNBC channel." Ricky's accented Arabic-English was working well. "They always talk about you, Chairman and CEO of the NYSE, founder of Lemon Group, Hedgistan's best hedgie. Always provide good returns for clients. Always one step ahead. Thank you for taking the time to see me."

"Anytime," Lemon said.

"And, do I have to ask? My blood sugar is running low."

"I'd love to join you for some refreshments, Your Royal Highness. However, I do have some important meetings soon."

"What? No time for some *ma'amoul*? You're the Sultan of Wall Street, and you can't have them wait for you?"

"I'm sorry." Lemon gave Ricky the impression that he swiftly remembered his status in relation to the Prince. "It was just short notice." Lemon leaned over to speak to one of his aides, a female. "Get him some Arabic food, *now*."

The assistant nodded and split.

Ricky sipped his coffee and wetted his mustache.

"What brings you to New York?" Lemon asked.

"Eh, meeting at the United Nations." Ricky patted his lips with a napkin. "It is my understanding that you are interested in clean energy. Correct?"

"Correct." Lemon's gold college graduation ring from the Wharton School of Business shined.

"Tell me a little more."

"I started a private energy initiative not too long ago, aimed at reducing environmental problems, mostly here in the U.S., with some global reach. Decreased fossil fuel production and consumption, energy conservation, the use of renewable—"

"Yes, that all sounds superb to me." Ricky yawned. "You see, this is also a great benefit to me, both financially and environmentally. My family wants, eh, less interference from the U.S. in the Middle East. There is still much oil, but it is being depleted quickly. And my family, we are looking to make a shift in policy, eh, less dependence on oil to maintain our political influence.

We, too, believe in climate change, eh, and feel changes are necessary."

Lemon glanced down at his watch, then got to the point. "What're you proposing, exactly?"

His true nature came out. He was a businessperson. He liked his conversations succinct and direct. The Prince, a political dignitary, beat around the bush, stalling and in no rush.

"I'd like to fund your efforts. To show you that I mean business . . ." Ricky opened the briefcase, turned it, and showed Lemon the contents. "A donation."

Lemon looked at the money as a roar started from the trading floors.

"That's only a small token," Ricky said. "I am ready to write you a check." He pulled out a small book with bad checks.

Lemon paused and observed the table; his actions suggested he was processing the situation. He signaled the other aide, a male, and whispered something to him with his hand covering their conversation. The male aide departed.

"What seems to be troubling you?" Ricky asked.

Lemon gave him a long, fixed look and drummed his fingers on the table. "Respectfully, I'm not sure I'm totally convinced."

Ricky met Lemon's piercing stare. He appeared poised, but inside he felt a shiver. "I can assure you, you won't be disappointed." The shouting from the trading floors tapered off.

Lemon narrowed his eyes and studied him. "And what do you want in return?"

"Advice. Financial advice."

Lemon turned silent again. His face looked puzzled.

Let me clarify. "You see, with all this crackdown in Switzerland, it's difficult to . . . what do you say? Manage my assets," Ricky continued.

Lemon nodded. "There are a few countries that you can manage your assets in. They keep a low profile. The chances of them being discovered and raided are slim."

Ricky stared sharply into his eyes. He slowly moved his hand to his pants' pocket, then tapped the recording device that Ben had given him. "Each country you provide, eh, is additional fifty thousand."

Lemon grinned widely at the advantageous position he was in. He paused again, but Ricky couldn't tell why. Lemon's male aide returned and whispered into his ear.

Ricky observed the presents under a lit Christmas tree in a corner of the room in the meantime.

"One. Samoa. National Bank of Samoa. Ask for Fetu Tuioti." Lemon cleared his throat and faced his male aide. "Give him the minutes at the end."

Now, Ricky knew why; the Prince's money was good. Christmas came early, and he smiled like the Grinch.

"Two. Nauru. It's a small island northeast of Australia. Bendigo Bank. Search for Yaren Waqa. Three. Labuan. It's excellent for holding companies, and it's in an autonomous province in Malaysia. Go to Maybank International Labuan Branch and ask for Salman Rahman.

"Four. Estonia. Taxes are only on the distribution of profits, ideal for a holding company. Coop Pank. Look for Kaisa Ratas. Five. Uruguay. Banking secrecy is quite intense. No public records of company officials. Only the company's finances are available for inspection. Santander. Seek out Carolina Vázquez. Six. Comoros. East of Africa in the Indian Ocean. Zero tax agreements. Zero taxation for international business companies. Zero controls. And, limited government. Go to Exim Bank and ask for Said Jaffer. Seven. Bahrain. You must know about Bahrain."

"Eh, yes, yes, Bahrain," Ricky said, stroking his chin. "Bahrain."

"Eight, and my final destination. Maldives. HSBC Malé Branch. Ask for Ahmed Anil."

"Very well then." Ricky smiled with delight and whipped out his pen. "Four hundred thousand it is." With the stroke of his pen, he closed the deal. He tore the bad check at the perforated dotted line and slid it to Lemon.

Lemon's male assistant gave the minutes of the meeting to the Prince. The female aide, the one who'd gone on the errand to fetch some Arabian delicacies, returned, box in hand, and provided the Prince with the gift. "Courtesy of Mr. Lemon."

Ricky opened the container, smelled dates and cinnamon, and tried one of the treats. His taste buds screamed for help, as he was allergic to the nuts inside. Instinctively, he dropped the pastry and reacted with folded arms. "Oooo, those don't look so good. I think not," he whined, picky and ungrateful, uncommon for a foreign dignitary. Worse, it was in hybrid form, high-pitched Arabic-English with a drop of gay.

Lemon and the others looked at him suspiciously.

Ricky realized his faux pas instantly and perspired. His fake mustache was about to quit its job. He dabbed the phony hairs with a napkin to ensure the piece didn't fall off. He regained his composure and returned to character. "I apologize," he said, in his broken Arabic-English, deeper. "It's not often that I can come out of the closet and show my true self."

Lemon nodded slowly with narrow eyes.

Ricky watched Lemon scrutinize his facial features.

Lemon's concerned face broke into a smile. "You had me. Should go to Hollywood."

They laughed together.

Behind the guffaw, Ricky was touched by Lemon's comment; he was a failed actor. *Was that close?* The most active supporter of the lesbian, gay, bisexual, and transgender movement would have lost everything for the group if it weren't for his quick thinking and relentless practice.

The conversations were at a low murmur, and the patrons were a scarce few. Only Amara, Kannada, and a few waiters cleaning up remained in 1792, the NYSE restaurant.

"You know what your problem is?" Amara said. "You're careless. You don't even try anymore. You think everything will just fall into place. It won't. You have to get off your backside and do something."

Kannada sighed.

"I had to explain to every single person that the wedding was off," Amara continued. "People think I chickened out at the eleventh hour or that I made a bad choice and got entangled with the wrong guy. I don't want to believe it, but maybe I did choose poorly."

"You didn't, okay. And don't blame yourself; it's my fault. I can tell you one thing. A dream wedding doesn't mean you'll be with someone forever. It takes love and respect, trust and friendship, and most of all, faith and understanding to make it last."

"Then why weren't you straight with me from the start?" Amara jabbed him with his own hypocrisy.

Kannada took a deep breath and sighed. "Because I didn't want you to see me hobbled, unable to protect you. I made a mistake, but I'm humbler now and I haven't moved on yet. And a part of me believes you haven't either. And if you ask me, Lemon will probably hurt you."

"Hurt me?"

"He's a bigger player than you know, Amara."

"I'm not being played." Those were her words, but she wasn't sure she believed them. Lemon had been acting shady around her lately, especially when he was leaving the spiritual dance festival she had performed in. She wondered why Lemon had avoided taking her to social functions, like the Guggenheim International Gala, and said it was business. But her relationship with Lemon was new, and the line between his work and his pleasure was blurry.

"He's a wolf on Wall Street."

"He's a perfectionist. He just wants to get it right."

"You think he'll get it right on his fifth marriage?"

Amara sighed and stared. She couldn't ignore his last statement.

"There's no such thing as a perfect marriage," Kannada said.

Amara nodded, unable to avoid his wisdom. She changed her posture from her forearms flat on the table to having them stand up with her head resting on her hands. "I think your advice is tainted with your own personal bias."

He shrugged. "Maybe."

"Do you remember what I told you when we separated?"

"Yes. You told me I'd better get my act together."

"Well, you should definitely get it together now."

Amara's eyes flickered. She straightened herself a bit, as her boss approached the table.

Kannada looked at her strangely. "I've gotten my act together."

"Then why're you here?" her boss inquired.

Kannada's eyes widened, and his face changed color. He glanced up and behind him.

Lemon was standing over them, absolved from last-minute duties with the Prince.

"Catching up with an old friend," Kannada said, looking up at Lemon.

"David," Amara said, "this is my ex-fiancé, Kanny." Her eyes widened as she recognized her flub.

Kannada looked at Amara, quick as lightning.

"Sorry, I mean Kannada," Amara said, swiftly recovering. With her elbow on the table, she put her hand on her warm forehead and covered herself from Lemon's view, embarrassed. *I can't believe I just said that. Maybe I haven't gotten over him.*

"Don't apologize for saying what you feel. You're just being honest," Kannada said.

Amara uncovered her face from under her hand and looked at her ex.

He smiled and stood. "Hey, David."

"Kannada." Lemon stared coldly at him. "Sorry I'm late. A major deal was in the works."

"Kannada was just inquiring about my Bollywood dancing," Amara explained.

"Is that so?" Lemon said.

"Just happened to bump into her. Who would've thought?" Kannada smiled.

Lemon raised an eyebrow. "Of all places, here, in the New York Stock Exchange?"

He was on to Kannada. They glared at one another as some of the wait staff glanced at them.

Lemon looked down at Kannada's name tag, unclipped it from his lanyard, and held it. "Lorenzo Moretti?" he said as he examined it.

Kannada swallowed and turned pale.

Lemon continued. "Kannada? That wouldn't be a middle name, now would it?"

"Yes," Kannada answered. "It's my middle name."

Amara didn't say a word. She knew he was caught.

"You know," Lemon said, "Amara had mentioned that her ex asked for her hand in marriage at a baseball game. The way she remembered it was that you bailed, couldn't handle the pressure of being a man. Not up to your old ways again, are you?"

"Remind me, how many of your marriages ended in divorce?" Kannada stabbed Lemon with his own question.

Lemon's eyes narrowed.

"Kannada," Amara said, not interested in where this was going. She removed the napkin in her lap, stood, straightened her clothing, and looked at Lemon. "He was just about to head out."

"I came to say hello," Kannada said, "and to see if I was dance

201

material."

A waiter started to clean a nearby table, though it looked spotless.

"I'll wait. Go ahead, continue," Lemon said.

The three of them stood in silence. Lemon looked at the intruder. Kannada glared at Amara. She watched her ex. Her eyebrows rose.

Lemon signaled a security guard with slick, black hair and muttonchops to address the matter.

"I was on my way out," Kannada said.

"So," Lemon said, "I guess we won't be hearing from you anytime soon."

"Well, I happen to pop up every now and then."

"You should see to it that you don't. This is my exchange, and I know everything that goes on in it."

"Maybe I should go back to the subway."

"Maybe you should, schmuck."

Her ex smiled. "It was nice to see you, Amara."

"Bye. Hope you find a good dance partner," she said.

Kannada walked away. Lemon stared at the recently confiscated badge.

Amara watched Kannada leave, bit her lip, and thought, *he came back for me? How sweet.* Her maple brown eyes said it. She waited until he was no longer in view. When the door closed, she quickly recovered from her wistful feelings. "I'm not sure what to do with him."

"I do," Lemon said powerfully.

Amara swallowed; Lemon's remark shook the ground.

CHAPTER 24

Manhattan, New York

The group had congregated for lunch in the penthouse's dining area. Plates with crumbs, glasses with varied levels of alcohol, and dirty, scrunched napkins marked the gathering. Ben held one of Rob's top hats, stood quietly under dim lighting, and listened.

"Thanks to Ricky, and after some research, we've found a few banks in which we can put our money overseas," Kannada said to the entire assembly. "In this hat, there are ten pieces of paper, like this one." He took out a small folded piece of paper during show-and-tell. "Each details a different path in hiding your money. You'll follow exactly what it says."

Ben gave the hat to Zara first to be passed around.

"In general," Dilip added, "no money will be deposited in the U.S. The money will be split up in ten unique ways. Some might open a bank account in the name of an offshore trust, some might do it in the name of a foreign company, and all of you will have false identities. Ben and Rob will set up everything. The offshore jurisdictions we chose don't require disclosure, so your identity will be protected. In the event your name is uncovered, not to worry: you're still under an alias. Two layers of protection."

The hat was making itself around the crew. Different facial

expressions characterized different roads to be traveled.

"The exception, Iago and his charity," Kannada joked. "Of course you're going to hell, but we'll probably see you there one day, too."

Iago grinned. The group chuckled and giggled.

"And the method of transfer," Ben said, "will be a mix of layering and invoicing. The layering portion; the money will first be moved to a good tax haven, like the U.K. Then it will be redeployed to a reputable tax haven, then again one more time to a jurisdiction with far stricter secrecy laws. There will be absolutely no crossing of layers, and the banks are different. The invoicing portion; your offshore company will issue itself invoices for intangible goods and services, web hosting, IT consultancy, etcetera."

It was Kannada's turn. "Then, and only then, can that money be converted to actual hard cash. I'd buy gold and ship it to the U.S. You'll incur some fees along the way, but you'll be virtually unrecognizable in the end." He collected the hat. There was one paper left for him.

"All we need is the right guy to do the paperwork." Ben looked around the room to see how the group was taking the news.

Dilip grimaced and rubbed his chin.

"What's with the long face?" Ben asked the old man.

"It's just fascinating to me," Dilip noted, "that you guys, all this time, aren't afraid of the SEC, but the IRS."

"Hey, they're no joke," Ricky said, seriously. "Took down Wesley Snipes."

Zara put her hands behind her head and started to tie her wavy, chestnut hair into a ponytail. "Sophia Loren."

Alan crossed his arms. "Judy Garland, too."

"Don't forget Pete Rose," Walker said in his deep voice.

A low rumble sounded from the group.

"Yeah, and Tom Coughlin." Rob sighed and shook his head.

"Nicholas Cage," Paul added.

Iago started to clear his black, full-rim plastic glasses with a microfiber cleaning cloth. "The great Annie Leibovitz."

"And my personal favorite, Al Capone," Kannada said. "I think we have a reasonable fear."

A few hours later, Kannada was sitting at the end of a couch, his back against the corner, reading under the lighting of an end table's lamp. Zara walked into the living area.

"What're you doing here all by yourself?" Zara pressed the book down. Dressed in tight leggings and an oversized men's shirt, she exhibited a camel toe and, with an unbuttoned look, cleavage.

Kannada gaped at the outline of her vagina. "Um . . . reading."

She giggled, staring at him with her chin down. "What?"

"Uh, some polygraph book." He made eye contact and tried to focus. "Is that my shirt from Saks?"

"I didn't think you'd mind." Zara smiled.

Kannada stared at the shirt; she was braless and nipping. She was also cloaking herself in *his* property, *his* scent. "How come you didn't join the others for dinner?"

"I felt like staying in and ordered a pizza."

"Where from?"

"Emmett's."

"That place got a great write-up in *The New Yorker*."

"That's why I stayed in. How come you didn't join them?"

He held up his book. "Research."

Zara plopped herself onto the sofa and leaned her head on Kannada's shoulder, her hair cool and wet from a recent shower.

Kannada felt an invasion of privacy but opted to stay silent. He kept reading.

"I'm bored," she remarked.

"You look bored," he observed.

Zara took his arm and wrapped it around her neck. "I'm so bored." She rested on his chest.

He dog-eared the page he was on and closed the book; a few dust particles floated under the light. "I don't think I'll be getting much reading done tonight."

"Let's play a game," Zara said.

Kannada absently looked at the central table in front. *A game?* He sighed. "What do you want to play?" He put the book on the end table.

"You ask me a question, and I'll ask you a question."

"And how do you win?"

"Whoever runs out of questions first, loses. The loser has to give the winner a kiss."

"On the lips?" He was sure that she'd deny him; when they first met, she had made it clear that she wouldn't kiss him on the mouth.

Zara hesitated. "Yeah."

Kannada blinked. *A kiss from Zara? Or a kiss to her? This is a win-win situation. Wait a minute! She isn't trying to seduce me again, is she? Maybe she likes me, but then again, she's a hooker. I still think she has STDs.* He twisted his mouth to the side and shook his head gently. *Why don't you carry a condom, dumbass? She probably has a stash of them buried in her purse.*

"Okay, you first," he said.

"You go first."

"I'm a gentleman. Ladies first."

Zara laughed, then scolded him playfully. "Oh, please, stop." Her soft, manicured hands gently caressed his arms. "How come you don't have any hair on your arms?"

"Because I had them waxed at the spa downstairs."

"You wax your arms?"

"Yeah."

"Your back, I get. But your arms? You're a guy."

"So? I can get pretty hairy and Amara doesn't like it."

"You should just let it be. Be yourself. I like hairy guys."

Kannada raised an eyebrow. "You do?"

"Yeah, there's something masculine about it. It makes me feel more like a woman." Zara nestled her head against his neck and chest.

"Oh . . ."

"Now, your turn," Zara said.

Kannada paused and took a deep breath. *She smells good.*

"You can't take all day," she pushed.

He half-smiled. "Do you have any siblings?"

"Two sisters."

"A house full of girls . . . must be fun."

"You mean your fantasy." Zara sounded naughty.

Kannada chuckled. "No, well, maybe. Do you ever get into fights?"

"Mmm, sometimes, but we make up pretty quickly."

"Your turn," he said.

"What about you? Do you have any brothers or sisters?"

"I'm an only child."

"Nice. You get all the attention." She started to run her finger down his well-built chest.

He parted his lips, watching her hand's downward motion. "That's not always a good thing. What's your passion? Besides shopping."

Zara grinned. Her hand came down to his groin, and she lightly squeezed the tip of his crotch bulge. "Mmm, I like horses."

Oh God! Kannada stared ahead with droopy eyelids, his mouth open, his tongue pressed against his cheek. His penis hardened in an instant, and his heart raced. "You ride horses?"

"Yeah, it actually builds leg muscles, and they're so fun." She crossed her legs, and her body shifted toward him even more. "What's your passion?"

Kannada gazed at her shapely thighs; he appreciated the inventor of leggings. "You know, you can't just ask me the same questions I asked you."

"It doesn't say that in the rules."

"And who makes the rules?"

Zara looked up at him. "I do."

Kannada smiled and laughed. "I guess I like to read and write."

"What do you like to read?" she asked.

"Mmm, politics."

"Yuck."

"Yuck?"

"Politics is boring. They all say the same thing, and nothing changes."

"I guess. And what do you read, might I ask?"

"Magazines like *Cosmopolitan*, *Femina*, mmm, *Harper's Bazaar*."

Kannada rolled his eyes. "Those are all women's magazines."

"Uh, hello? I'm from Venus," Zara quipped.

He chuckled. "I forgot. Whose turn is it?"

"Most likely yours."

"Way to put the pressure on me."

"Mmm hmm."

Kannada looked down at her cleavage. He brought his hand to her breast and circled his finger around her nipple, then squeezed.

"Ooh, that feels good," Zara ejaculated.

He was wet now. He made his move and tried to kiss her, but she pushed him back with her hand and looked down.

"You can't give up that easily," she teased.

What? I don't get her. He stared, confused and disappointed. "Um . . . what's the craziest thing you've ever done?"

"No." Zara shook her head softly. "We're not going there."

"Why not?"

"It's too . . ."

"You can be honest with me. I won't judge you."

Zara put her hand on his lap. "Fine, but you have to promise not to laugh." She sounded serious.

"Okay, I won't."

"I got wasted in Vegas and married some poker player hit by the deck."

He burst into a guffaw.

"See, I told you!" Zara said, amid his amusement.

"I'm sorry. That's just hilarious. Then what happened?"

"Well, we only went to the altar, no papers."

Kannada smiled. During an unplanned break, a strong breeze whistled from a few open awning windows and the light buzzed evenly. He viewed her manicured hands; her nails matched her light mauve lips.

"I like your nails."

"Thank you." She returned to the silence.

He nudged her. "Well?"

"I'm thinking. I'm thinking . . . What're your dreams?"

Kannada's eyes veered down. He twisted his mouth to the side and thought about Amara. "I wish I could do this more often. You?"

"Finding Prince Charming and . . . maybe have kids one day."

She wants to settle down? Oh, yeah, she mentioned she was waiting for someone special in Terminal City. He nodded. "How many kids?"

"At least two; otherwise, one would get lonely."

"Like me."

"That's not what I mean."

"I know," Kannada said. "What kind of movies do you like?"

"A good heist or a good love story," Zara replied.

"Well, I guess you're in the right place."

"It's like I'm in a movie."

"Life's a movie."

Zara paused.

Kannada's eyes settled on the central table, on the corner of a piece of notepad paper that undulated because of the draft, but he focused on his thoughts. He enjoyed the game so far, though it was unusual. He could end it, properly, and kiss her, but playing with her was more fun. He was a little surprised that she could keep a conversation going and started to see there was something more to her than going belly-to-belly, locking crotches, and swapping gravy. He half-smiled to himself. *I like this side of her. It's real.*

"What are you afraid of?" Zara said, after a while.

"Too many things."

"Like what? You can tell me."

"Just stupid stuff."

"If we're going to be in a relationship, you can't keep secrets from me."

A relationship? Whoa! He rubbed his forehead, his thumb at one temple, his fingers at the other. For the first time, he was split between Amara and Zara. *Do I want this? Zara's hot. The sex would be unbelievable, but . . . she's not the sharpest tool in the shed. Amara's my equivalent, education, morals. Zara's got a degree, too, but if I have sex with her, it'd be like exploitation. I mean she's a—*

Zara cleared her throat.

"I had career expectations," he said, "but things haven't worked out. I'm not as clever or special as I thought I was."

"Same here."

"I'm not exactly a crook, so we might end up in jail."

"You'll be fine. This is a white-collar crime."

Kannada raised a brow. *She's right.* "There's a lot of shit pay out there, and with the rising cost of living, I'm not sure how I'll ever own a home or live a normal life." He sighed.

Zara slowly turned her head up and looked at him. He made eye contact. She kissed him on the cheek, then nestled her head between his neck and chest.

Kannada half-smiled to himself again, then returned the favor, but on her head. "What do you absolutely not like?"

She hesitated. "Being tickled."

He grinned. "You're ticklish?"

"Yes, in some places."

"Are you ticklish over here?" He tickled her armpits.

Zara curled her neck toward his hand and squeezed her arm against her body. "Ah," she screamed. She grabbed a pillow and hit him with it.

Kannada blocked the blow with his arm, then leaned over and tried to tickle her again. "What about here?" He aimed for her stomach this time.

Zara screamed and fought back, hitting him with the pillow repeatedly. She tickled him under his chin to no avail. He stroked her stomach again. She grabbed his shirt with one hand and hit him with the other, then fell off the sofa and took him down with her.

Kannada landed on top of Zara and smiled. "I think I won this game."

Someone rang the doorbell, and she shoved him off her.

Kannada hit his head on the leg of the sofa. "Ouch," he said, wincing in pain.

"The pizza's here." Zara sounded happy.

"Wait a second." Kannada got up, holding his head. "You let the delivery man come up here?" he asked with a concerned tone.

She shook her head innocently and shrugged. "Yes, I told the people downstairs to bring him up."

He grimaced. "This penthouse is accessible by private elevator for a reason."

"Oh my God," Zara said, rolling her eyes. "He's just here to do his job."

Kannada looked away, anxious. "I'll pay. What's the damage?"

"Fifteen."

He went for his leather wallet, pulled four fins out, and gave them to Zara.

"Thank you." She took the bills, then returned one. "Oh, you can keep this." She headed to the door.

"But he'll need a tip." Kannada went back to his wallet and started to reinsert the five.

"I'll take care of it."

"You sure?"

"Uh huh," Zara said, nodding.

Kannada put away the money and wallet while Zara answered the door.

A young man with freckles presented her with the pizza. "The pepperoni?"

"That's me." Zara exchanged the money for the pie.

The young man stared at the money, only fifteen dollars. He looked up, extended one of his hands, and rubbed his thumb and forefinger together.

Zara smiled and winked, molded her lips into a kiss, and kissed the air. "Thank you."

The pizza delivery boy foolishly smiled and tried to catch the kiss in the air with one of his hands as she shut the door.

That sexy, irresistible bitch, Kannada thought, upon witnessing Zara's actions. "Are you serious?"

"What?" She nonchalantly walked down the hallway, toward the kitchen. "He wanted a tip, so I gave him one."

Kannada followed her and shook his head in disbelief. "Pretty women get away with everything."

She slightly turned her head to the side. "Hush, I just saved you some money."

He shrugged, and they dined in the informal reception area. Across the fireplace, Zara sat on the floor, leaned against the corner sectional sofa, and used the center table. Perpendicular to her, Kannada sat on the same couch hunched over with a paper plate.

"It's good." He chewed, his mouth stuffed. The tomato sauce was tangy. "You like pizza?"

"I love pizza," Zara said, elongating the word of affection.

Kannada half-smiled, then looked down with pursed lips. It was clear the game had ended, and without the coveted kiss. *The pizza boy was a minor disruption. That's all.* Kannada was a little desperate to restart the Q&A session but hesitated, not wanting to force anything.

"Have you had Emmett's before?" she asked.

"No, this is my first time." His heart lit up, and reasons to hold back disappeared. "Do you have any childhood memories that stick out to you?"

Zara snacked on her slice and ruminated for a moment. "When I was a little girl," she said with her left cheek full of dough, "my sisters and I would take turns taking piggyback rides on my dad. I kind of wish I could stay a little girl forever. I think that's how I fell in love with horses."

He watched her eat for a while. She was being herself, her cheeks stuffed, unladylike. She was certainly on her good behavior, not trying to lure him into sex like the last time they were alone, when she got naked in her room. But the night was still young; maybe she would after dinner. Or maybe not; she seemed innocent today. He hadn't had anyone to talk to, fool around with, for years, and it felt good, damn good. During his days in the subway, he never thought he would have a date, if tonight could be called that, like this again, especially not with someone other than Amara.

Zara finished chewing, looked at him, and beamed.

She has a lovely smile.

She bent over and fetched a napkin from the central table.

"Do you like to travel?" he asked, finally.

"I love to travel." She wiped the edges of her mouth.

"Where do you want to go?"

"Everywhere," she said. "There're so many beautiful cultures I want to see and things I want to do. Where do you want to go next?"

She took a bite of her pie; the cheese stretched before her. Zara simpered as she looked at Kannada.

His head lowered, his lips parted, and his eyes ogled. He flashed a wistful smile, as she reminded him of the many times he and Amara had dined at Prince Street Pizza.

Zara disconnected the string of cheese from the slice with her free hand and put it into her mouth.

Kannada turned his head down and to the side, looked at the floor, and rubbed the back of his neck.

"Mmm . . . Alaska. I want to kayak with the whales." He noshed his pizza and left teeth marks in the bread.

"You like adventure?" she said from the side of her mouth.

"Yeah."

"Me, too." Zara continued to chomp. The food swished around with saliva in her mouth.

"What do you think the meaning of life is?" Kannada licked his finger, repeatedly dabbed his plate to collect the crumbs, and put them into his mouth.

"Enjoying every moment, experiencing everything. You?"

He sighed. "When I was writing this caper, I thought the meaning of life was to give it meaning, create something. Now it's just seizing opportunity, taking risks, even if that amounts to stealing." He frowned.

"That's deep."

"I'm a deep guy." Kannada grabbed another slice.

"What do you think you are?" Zara asked.

He gazed deep into her innocent sea green eyes; she quickly looked away, but why? They had good chemistry tonight. There was little tension between them since her arrival to New York. Was it a coincidence? Kannada tried to think of a response, but his mind wandered about lingering doubts of her intentions.

Where is this conversation going? The memories of their visit to Terminal City and Fifth Avenue surfaced; she asked a lot of questions then and recently came up with a game to ask him more questions. *She's inquisitive for a hooker. Oh, don't call her that. She's a person . . . just with a troubled past.* The enticing massage she had given him and the free sex he had declined also came to mind. *What is she after?*

Zara moved her head forward, and her wavy, balayage hair oscillated softly on either side of her face. She raised her threaded brows.

He was taking too long to answer. "I don't know. Everything, the whole creation." Kannada gorged on his pie.

Zara stared into his eyes. The edges of her mouth crept up, her lips pressed together tightly, and her cheeks swelled.

"What?" Kannada said.

She pointed to the side of her face.

"Ugh." Kannada wiped the smudge of sauce on his face with a napkin. "I always do that."

She bore a Duchenne smile as he wiped his mouth.

After dining with the group, barring Kannada and Zara, Ben resumed business. He departed the subway and arrived at his destination, Madison Square Garden, slap dab in Joe Louis Plaza.

"Come on, Knicks!" an ardent fan shouted during a New York Knicks match against a Cleveland Cavaliers team. For the sold-out occasion, he was sitting courtside, below the two new Chase Sky Bridges in The Garden, near the one-and-only original regular, Spike Lee. "D-fence, D-fence, D-fence," he yelled, joining the rest of the crowd.

A Cavaliers player missed a shot from the right side of the court as Ben walked down the steps.

"You couldn't hit a jump shot even if you were open," the fan yelled, beer in hand.

Ben approached the empty seat, the only one in the house, next to him. Basketball shoes squeaked on the hardwood as he sat on the thick cushion of the courtside chair. "Mr. Hawthorne?"

Alistair Hawthorne, a well-built man with brown hair, sat with the top button of his dress shirt unbuttoned for after-work comfort, fresh bait from Wall Street. He was the same Alistair Hawthorne who worked for Lemon Group, as discovered by Dilip when Iago and the others were going through employee profiles. He turned to face the man who called him.

"Great returns, I hear." Ben presented his business card as a referee blew his whistle. "Sorry to disturb your little get-together here."

Hawthorne took the card from Ben's hand and put his beer down. "TradePlus Investments. Never heard of it," he said, examining the card. He looked at the players on the court, then furrowed his brows and folded his arms. "I've got a pretty sweet gig here. What're you looking for?"

The crowd started to boo. Hawthorne looked up at the Jumbotron.

"We're a private white-shoe firm catering to the richest two percent, and we're looking for traders of the top two percent. We were hoping to hire you. We've been tracking the impressive trades you've made," Ben said.

"Bullshit. Quit crying like a baby," a fan yelled in the background.

"In Chicago," Hawthorne said, looking at the card.

"You just made four billion on a single trade for your company," Ben noted.

"I've had some lucky stretches."

"That's exactly what we want from you. We'd like you to come to a presentation we're holding in the Dead Rabbit in two days. Help us invest."

"I don't know. It's hard to beat what I'm making now. You'd have to have something phenomenal in store to make me want to leave."

Before Ben could speak, a sweaty Cavaliers player ran into Hawthorne. "My bad. You good, baby?" the player said.

"Yeah." Hawthorne beamed, his eyes wide and glowing, as the player returned to the game.

Amid the lingering tang of body odor, Ben wiped a speck of perspiration from the player off his face, then continued. "We'll give you two weeks. All expenses. First class airfare and temporary housing until you find your own place."

Hawthorne watched the game; the buzzer buzzed for a twenty-four-second shot-clock violation. "You're pretty sure of yourself."

"Here," Ben said, handing him an envelope. "Your sign-on bonus. Go ahead; take a look."

Hawthorne opened the flap and peered over a bad check, courtesy of Ricky, as a couple of fans waved orange and blue foam fingers down the row and *Get Ready for This* by 2 Unlimited started to play. He looked at a smiling Ben in disbelief.

It was late at night and the group had returned to their quarters, ready to hit the sack before taking on the next day. Zara walked into the living area and retrieved her phone from the centerpiece table. She started to leave but paused upon hearing commotion from the office. She edged closer to the noise and stood outside the doorway in her pajamas. Zara put her hand on the wall and lowered her chin.

"I want the truth," a man with a deep voice yelled, in the office, behind closed doors and opaque glass.

Zara narrowed her eyes. Who was doing the yelling and who was taking the scorning, she couldn't say. There was something else going on as part of the operation. She tiptoed away and met Paul in the hallway as he wandered around with an electric toothbrush in his mouth.

"What's happening in there?" Zara asked.

Paul took the toothbrush out of his mouth. "Training." He continued brushing.

CHAPTER 25

Bronx, New York

In the projects of the borough, a 1980 Toyota Tercel, with Rob and Ben inside, pulled up to the curb of a street to park. Rob looked through the windshield, past several layers of dust on the dashboard and an odorless, tree-shaped car air freshener that dangled from the rearview mirror, at their destination ahead to the right.

A large mural, paint chipped and hardly readable, marked the dilapidated building as Terrell "Rainbow" Jenkins Law Offices. "Call for a FREE Consultation. 1-800-119-BRONX. No fee if we don't collect," the sign read.

Rob readjusted himself in the crack-laden, old, leather seat and glared at the crumbling building. "This, no wonder you wanted to take my Tercel. This, what the hell is this shit?"

Ben looked out the windshield, too. "What? It's a legitimate office building."

Rob gave him an unpopular stare.

Ben faced him. "Kind of."

Rob rolled his eyes.

"Hey, if you want to leave without getting caught red-handed, this is it," Ben said.

"This, this is your connection?" Rob sounded incredulous.

"He's not my connection. He *is* the connection. He's the guy who knew the guy who knew another guy who found the guy with the speed last time we did business together."

"Ah," Rob said, lengthening the sound. "He is the connection."

Rob was still unimpressed. He inhaled fungal odor and sighed.

"Look," Ben continued, "every lawyer knows how to bullshit. If you want to stay one step ahead of the pack, one step ahead of Lemon, you have to go to the source of the bullshit, the asshole."

Rob continued to gaze at the surrounding area, battered housing units and other edifices and degenerate streets.

"Come on; come on. It's not that bad," Ben said. "Trust me."

"All right." Rob manually rolled up his window. "I don't know what drives me to take such risks."

Rob and Ben exited and shut their doors.

A gunshot sounded in the air, and they ducked. Rob gave Ben a disapproving gaze over the rooftop of the Toyota Tercel.

Despite the inherent danger, a few minutes later they stepped into the office.

The smell of fried chicken and malt liquor welcomed Rob. He surveyed the dark room. A pair of college degrees amid posters of rappers and porn stars hung on the walls, and empty forties rested on the desk. *Why'd I set foot in here?* His attention turned to a vertically challenged man as a whiff of flavored cigarillos hit him.

Terrell "Rainbow" Jenkins had a dark complexion, full lips, and a cube-like head, and wore red plastic frames, a blue-and-orange camo cape over a dark brown trench coat, a yellow-and-white striped shirt, bright green jeans, and basketball sneakers, Air Jordans.

Rob stared. *This guy's a walking rainbow.*

"Rainbow, this is Rob," Ben said. "Rob, Rainbow."

Rob put his hand out for shaking as someone quickly stomped on the floor above and slammed a door.

Rainbow looked at his hand, then at Rob, wide-eyed.

Rob swallowed, uneasy.

"He's new around here," Ben explained. He gave Rob the impression that there was some miscommunication.

"Ben told me you went to Harvard?" Rob smiled.

"Oh, yeah, Howard, best black college." Rainbow's African-American roots were evident in his speech.

Rob's face dropped.

"Ben tells me you guys need a little help," Rainbow said. "Before we begin, I got some questions to ask you guys. Since they locked me up, I had to institute a two-part screening process, all right?"

"Okay," Ben and Rob said in unison.

Loud rap music started to play from the floor above.

Rainbow patted both of them down, Ben then Rob.

"Let me see your pockets," Rainbow demanded.

They showed him the contents of their pockets.

"All right, you guys passed the first part," Rainbow said. "Now, your loyalties. Which lives matter, black or everyone?"

Ben looked at Rob with parted lips. Rob looked at Ben with raised eyebrows. Ben spoke first. "Black." He sounded uncertain.

"Yeah, black." Rob followed his lead, nodding, sure of himself.

Rainbow cross-examined them. He looked from one set of eyes to the other, then back. Rob swallowed, again. Ben seemed calm, his hands in his pockets, his posture loose.

Rainbow broke out laughing. "I'm just messing with you guys."

Ben's and Rob's faces showed relief, with both of them sighing.

"All right, all right. What you guys need? Fake IDs?" Rainbow opened one flap of his trench coat. "Fake passports?" He opened the other side of his trench coat.

"We need to hide some money," Ben said.

"All right, all right. I got exactly what you guys need. Gentlemen, let's begin," Rainbow said.

The three of them signed papers. They set up false foreign trusts, LLCs, and identifications. They opened overseas bank accounts in the countries that Lemon had provided for the group, some of which were unheard of by Rainbow. Just as Ben said, the man had connections, and if he didn't, he had connections to connections; Rainbow would find a way.

Manhattan, New York

In the NYSE, Amara typed an email on the computer as classical music played from the speakers. She paid little attention to the visitor who came into her office.

"Ms. Sanon, this just came in, express delivery." A postal employee held out a box.

Amara's dark maple eyes hesitated to leave the monitor. Within seconds, she glanced at the rectangular prism for a package and took it without worry, as it had undergone a grueling inspection process before reaching her, then looked up at the postman. "Oh, thank you."

"Have a good day." He tipped his hat, then went on his way.

"You, too." As Amara stood to give the package to her boss, her eyes settled on a framed photo on her desk of her and Kannada when she had won a Bollywood dance competition. She twisted her mouth to the side and fondly stared at the picture, then strode to Lemon's office with the package and knocked on the partially open door.

Lemon was busy reviewing papers with reading glasses on the bridge of his nose. "Come in."

"David, this just came in for you." Amara handed him the parcel.

"Hmm, wonder what this could be. Thank you."

Amara exited his office.

Lemon observed the parcel; it was from the FBI.

He opened his drawer, took out his box cutter, and cut open the package. He uncovered a plain black box and a letter. Lemon opened the container, found a black two-way radio, and examined it, leaving his fingerprint on the display.

He unfolded the letter.

"Dear Mr. David Lemon," Lemon read aloud. "Blah, blah, blah," he skimmed through, then continued. "Please dispose of the NYSE cell phone with two-way capability you currently use. It has been compromised. Due to heightened terrorist activity during the holidays, your life may be in danger." His brow furrowed. "Please keep this phone with you at all times and respond immediately in the event we need to contact you." Lemon stopped reading; that was all he needed to know. He stared at the paper with raised eyebrows. "Can never be too safe."

Kannada sat alone in the afternoon on his bed, leaning against a bunch of pillows. An empty glass and an open, clear, plastic bag of green leaves rested next to him on the nightstand. He took in the aroma as he penned a journal entry.

Zara walked in, leaned against the entryway, and ogled. She was wearing her Playboy pajamas, a tank top and short shorts.

His eyes veered up, though his head remained facing the notebook. "Can I help you?"

"No."

Kannada readdressed whatever he was writing. Zara continued to amorously gaze.

He couldn't ignore her inviting sea green eyes for long. He looked up again, this time with his head veering up, and sighed. "What?"

"Oh, nothing." She genuinely smiled and twirled her loose curls.

"So, you're just going to watch me?"

"I'm just observing."

"Well, observe somewhere else."

"Ooh," Zara said. "The leaves. You're four-twenty-friendly. So am I."

"What?" Kannada looked at the bag of green leaves next to him on the nightstand.

"I'm hip to the whole scene. Money, drugs, me." She winked.

"What scene? This is mint. I have a cold and just had mint tea."

"Oh."

"What's four-twenty-friendly mean?"

"Marijuana friendly."

He brooded over her drug use as he nodded. "Ganja."

She smirked as though she had found a new dopehead to get high with. "Yeah, ganja."

"I don't do drugs . . . Where do you learn all this from?"

"It's just the world I live in, but Urban Dictionary's a good place to start."

"There's an actual dictionary in the study. I think it might help you more."

Zara chuckled and tilted her head, then started to approach him. "What're you writing?"

"It's none of your business." Kannada covered his notebook with his arms.

"Do you keep a diary?"

"Do you?"

"Yes, but I keep it in my head."

"That explains a lot."

She giggled. "What's that supposed to mean?"

"Nothing. Now, if you'll excuse me, I can get back to my writing."

Zara put one knee forth, slid onto his bed, and sat with her back against the pile of pillows. She peered over his shoulder.

"Hey, this is private."

Zara brushed her cheek against his and spoke into his ear. "Remember, no secrets." She rested her head on his arm.

Kannada tilted his head back and sighed. *She said she wanted a relationship. I still don't know. Everything's happening so fast.* "It's just my life, nothing spectacular."

"'Zara entered the room,'" she read aloud from his journal. "Sounds interesting to me."

"That's because you're in it."

"So, you're writing everything that happens here?"

"Yes. When people can't hear you, the paper and pen always will."

Zara lay silent for a moment. "I never thought of it like that. But isn't that the same as leaving evidence behind?"

"Do you even believe we're about to pull off one of the greatest heists ever?"

"No."

"Exactly. It's pure fiction."

Zara smiled and cozied up to him. "You're really not a good crook."

He parted his lips to say something but held back and pursed them. Her nostrils flared. *What'd I do now? I don't understand women; one minute they're flirting with you, next minute, they're mad.*

"What cologne is that?"

"Uh, the Yves Saint Laurent we bought on Fifth Avenue."

"It smells good." She playfully grabbed his chin and turned his head slightly, then kissed his cheek.

He looked straight ahead at their reflection in the dresser mirror, deadpan. *This girl is amazing.*

"How'd you get started on Wall Street?" she asked.

Again with the questions. "Well, actually, I was kind of like you."

"Oh," Zara said, covering herself with the comforter.

Kannada was distracted by the inquiry. "I graduated around the same time as you, and worked in Chicago for a while, met Amara there. She stayed back while I moved over here. Ben was working here and tried to get me a job at his firm, but it didn't work out. He introduced me to his connections, including Paul, and I started getting insider information and slipped it to traders for money.

"Slowly, I became like everyone else around here, and Caldwell Investments hired me. I got Ben a job there; they had a nice referral bonus. But I was always swamped with work, burning the midnight oil, taking drugs to stay focused. And I hated my boss. He always needed more results, more growth. I think he felt the pressure to perform, so he set up a Ponzi scheme."

"So now playing fair isn't an option?" Zara said.

"In this town, if you're not cheating, you're not trying."

"Wall Street sounds terrible." She reached over him to take the mint bag.

"You could ask?"

"Then I couldn't annoy you." She brushed off his latest comment, then took a mint leaf from the bag and put it into her mouth.

He tilted his chin down and frowned. "I still don't understand how my life fell apart. It's strange when all your effort amounts to nothing."

She stared in front of her, listening to him. "It's not your fault."

Kannada readjusted the sheets as a couple of birds shuffled around on the rooftop. "It's like everything's an illusion now. Money, possessions, jobs, friends. They're all gone. I can see them, but I can't have anything."

"Kannada." Zara put her hand on his chest and looked up at him. "I'm real." She sounded like it, too, with her young, attractive breathy voice, and made him feel as though he mattered.

He met her gaze, then looked away. *She cares for me. Not many people do*. The droning sound of an airplane came and went as he meditated on his life.

His faultless eyes settled on her wrist. "You have a tattoo."

Zara held up her arm for greater visibility. "Oh, this, it's a memory."

"Of what?"

"My dad."

"What does it say?" Kannada asked, unable to decipher the cursive ink.

"Daddy's Princess."

"So, you love your dad?"

"Yes. I miss him so much."

"I'm sorry. What happened?"

"He had a heart attack a few years ago."

That's the person she was talking about when we visited Terminal City. He was at a loss for words and stared at the ambiguous shadow of the window's grilles on the white comforter in front of him.

Zara snuggled against him, resting her head on his chest, her eyes closed.

Kannada sat quietly in silent stillness, not writing, but contemplating death, the ruler of life. He thought about his family and how they had passed away in a car accident. He looked at her, then at his journal. "Life is short."

"Mmm," she muttered, her eyes still shut. "It's difficult to love again after loss."

"Yeah . . . it's no longer natural. Even my relationship with Amara feels inorganic."

Zara opened her eyes. "It's not natural?" She sounded kind of elated.

Kannada sighed. "It used to be. But now it's like I'm trying to catch up to her."

"Don't chase love. If it isn't given freely, it's not worth having."

He paused for contemplation. "Do you ever find yourself chasing?"

She chuckled. "I'm wiser now. It's just about going with the flow. People don't realize what they have in front of them before it's gone."

He paused again. *Zara's in front of me; how strange is that?*

"Are you nervous around her?" She closed her eyes once more.

"Sometimes. It wasn't like that before. I think . . . it's a little awkward now."

"I read that when you meet your soul mate, you'll feel calm. No anxiety."

Kannada looked out the window. A pair of birds flew away from the roof amid a blue and pink sky. He sighed, then gazed at her reflection in the dresser mirror, stupefied.

Zara opened her eyes and kissed him on the cheek. "How do you feel now?"

He grinned. "Calm."

"I think you should move on." Her eyes started to droop.

"Why?" He looked at her, not wanting to hear her latest vision.

"It has to be natural." Zara yawned. "If it doesn't feel right, it's not."

Kannada thought about her words for a moment. *What she said is true.* He had lost enough as it was and didn't want it to come to losing Amara, too. The two logs that had met and swum together in the water, Kannada and Amara that is, were slowly moving apart with the current. He flirted with the idea that Zara may be a worthy partner for the circumstances. *Zara is right. Maybe I should start a relationship with her. She's interested in me, so why not? I guess I have a new girlfriend.* He half-smiled to himself.

"I have to give you credit," Kannada said, finally. "You're deeper than I thought."

She remained quiet.

"Zara?" He bent his neck slightly forward; she was asleep. He smelled her flowery scent, then looked at her wavy, long bob hairstyle and the small goosebumps on her soft, light tan skin. He smiled and put away his diary and mint bag on the nightstand, turned down the lights, and crashed with her, his head resting on hers.

A few hours later, Kannada and Zara woke from their midday nap together. They joined the rest of the group, minus Paul, Ben, and Rob, in the living room. Zara looked out one of the foggy windows through a space she had cleared, her nose nearly pressed up against the glass. So cold it was, a single breath could frost the entire window. Lightning flashed, and her face lit up. Thunder followed.

"Looks like we're going to have rain." Zara looked at Iago.

"You know what that is?" Iago put on his black, full-rim plastic glasses after cleaning them.

"What?" Alan asked.

"The weatherman called it bombogenesis," Iago said to Alan.

"Bombogenesis?"

"Bombogenesis."

"You like saying bombogenesis, don't you?"

Iago grinned.

Zara rolled her eyes and looked out the window again. "A few more days," she said to herself.

She quivered, leaning against the side casing of the window, and rubbed her arms with her hands to smoothen the goosebumps.

"You're really going to town with those Cheetos." Alan sounded amazed.

Zara turned; empty bags of Cheetos littered the living room table.

"Hey, all I ate today was a bagel," Iago said.

"Oh no." Alan shook his head. "You're turning into one of them."

"Into what?"

"A New Yorker." Alan sounded disappointed.

Iago shrugged. "Cheetos are good. Want one?"

"Yeah." Alan stuck his hand into the extra-large bag. He bit into a Cheetos snack. "Mmm, these are good. Wonder what makes them so tasty?"

"It's the monosodium glutamate," Iago replied. "Can't live without it."

Ricky frowned and flicked his wrist. "Ew, gross," he said with inflection in his voice.

Alan looked at Kannada. He seemed as though he was expecting Kannada to laugh with him.

Kannada was watching the clock on the wall. "Quiet, all of you. Where're Ben and Rob? They should've been back hours ago."

Bronx, New York

Rob and Ben were still at Rainbow's law office, long done with the paperwork. All three of them slouched on leather sofas, barely recognizable now, with semi-dense smoke permeating the air. They were laughing and getting high as the ceiling. Rainbow had loosened their nerves.

"All right, all right." Ben tried his best to enunciate his words, bombarded by jokes. "We should get going." His words were interspersed with laughter. Ben laughed so hard, his sides hurt.

Rob was no better, reclining on a sofa, laughing and smoking.

"Thanks for hooking us up, Rainbow." Rob struggled to get his words out, too, amid the guffaw.

"Hahaha, yeah. Hahaha," Ben said.

"All right, I'll see you guys later." Rainbow's words were sparse.

Slowly, but surely, Rob and Ben recovered from the fun spell and showed themselves out of Rainbow's laugh factory.

Manhattan, New York

Paul listened to the messages on his answering machine in his apartment while sifting through some days-old mail before heading out to work at the bar.

225

Someone banged on his door. Paul looked up at the entryway. He put down his mail, walked to the door, and glanced through the peephole. A large, intimidating police officer was standing outside. Paul looked down and wondered whether he should let him in. *Are they on to us?*

The officer pounded again. "We know you're in there!"

Paul sighed; he had no choice. He opened the door and gaped.

CHAPTER 26

Manhattan, New York

The workday was over. A cold Iago barged into the Plaza suite, his brown forehead wrinkled and his jet black, curly hair disheveled. He slammed the door behind and let out his frustration in the living area.

"All that terrorist activity, all those new cables, comes with an added feature to the NYSE." Iago faced Kannada. "Bulletproof cybersecurity."

He witnessed blank stares.

"The NYSE has a geographically dispersed fiber optic routing backbone, the SFTI, or 'safety,' connecting all the major financial services firms," he explained.

Kannada raised an eyebrow. "Safety?"

"Secure Financial Transaction Infrastructure."

Just then, the door opened. In poured Ben and Rob, straight from Terrell "Rainbow" Jenkins' office, smiles on their faces, a soupcon of flavorful smoke in their aura.

Iago continued. "The safety is a private extranet. It provides a secure means of market data distribution, trading, clearing, and settlement thanks to an uninterrupted telecommunications system."

Confusion marked their faces.

"They're not running circuits directly to the SIAC. They don't need to rely on a single route because users are linking themselves to multiple access centers."

Standing between Alan and Dilip, Rob squished his eyebrows together and turned his large frame to the left. "Um, what're we discussing?"

"I don't know." Alan, beer in hand, shook his head.

Dilip coughed.

Iago continued, frustrated. "All of safety's power supplies, connections, etcetera, are redundant. Its architecture features are independent. Ugh, it has these stupid, self-healing fiber-optic rings."

Rob glanced at Ben; he looked focused.

Iago put his hands on his hips and leaned on one leg. "Ergo, if one safety fiber pathway is compromised, financial data will continue to move uninterrupted along another pathway."

Rob turned his head to the right. "Am I the only one who's lost?"

"He's getting there." Dilip took a cough drop.

"Damn IT beefed up security." Iago smashed his fist into his palm. "They've built redundancies into everything. Two ISPs, instead of one, a backup for when one system crashes."

"So, what does that mean?" Kannada asked.

"It allows equity brokers to maintain connections to the markets, no matter what." Iago's body temperature was returning to its normal state.

Rob still looked confused. The rest of the group seemed puzzled, too.

Iago threw his hands up in the air. "We're fucked!" he exclaimed, simplifying his concerns as much as possible.

"Gee, why didn't you just say that?" Rob remarked.

Dilip flopped down into an armchair. "What were you originally going to do again?"

"I was going to put in a glitch," Iago explained. "It would stop trading and buy me a ten-minute window, during which I could search for and delete the trades in the system, as far as I can. Otherwise, there's like a million trades coming in, and it's impossible to find the trades I need to delete. The problem is, with all this security, I'm leaving a trail.

"I'm going to attempt to cover my tracks. But let's be realistic; there's one of me and an army of them. They'll most likely break through the barrier I set up."

"What's the solution?" Ben asked.

"I need to wipe out everything."

"And how can you do that?"

"Shutting down the system, the mains electric current to the NYSE, is the only way to wipe out everything I plan to do, then . . ."

"Then what?" Kannada dug further.

"Then there's probably a contingency plan," Iago said, "backup generators or some way to access what I've done, and a contingency plan to the contingency plan. It's like an onion; the more layers you peel, the more it stinks."

Dilip leaned back, extended his legs, crossed them, and put his hands behind his head. "That's where I come in."

"How can we shut down the system?" Ben asked.

Iago shrugged.

"Nothing short of a terrorist attack," Ricky remarked.

"Contingency plan for that," Iago responded.

"We're not going there." Kannada deepened his tone.

"Kannada," Iago said, "I can't introduce a glitch into the system and delete the trades. They have far too many security plans built-in. If we're going to get away with this, the system has to crash."

Kannada crossed his arms, pursed his lips, and stared at the floor.

Kannada paced, trying to figure out something. Ben plopped onto the sofa, joining the rest of the gang, and sighed with a frown. They'd put in too much work to leave without the fruits of their labor, but they were stumped.

Moments later, Paul came rushing in, his blue eyes icy and his blond hair messy. He slammed the door.

"That's the second time someone's slammed the door," Zara commented. "This is starting to look like a bad hair day."

"I thought you had work?" Ben said.

"Called in sick," Paul replied.

Kannada and the others glanced at each other; then they looked at Paul with curiosity.

"Wu," Paul addressed Ben Wu, "we have a problem."

Kannada smirked, then shook his head. *The irony.*

"What happened?" Ben asked.

"This is what happened," Paul said. "A complaint has been filed

229

with the NYPD." He glared and pointed at Kannada. "He's alleged to have committed criminal trespass, impersonation, and larceny."

"This *is* a bad hair day," Zara chimed in, twirling her loose curls.

"What?" Kannada looked down and away. His blood reversed direction and his mouth turned dry. Hope started to disappear, and regret began to take its place; this mistake was his fault. He looked up slowly and saw the group staring at him; a flush of embarrassment marked his face.

The lights in the room seemed dimmer. This was another hiccup to getting in on the unfairly protected, inaccessible IPO.

"The police have probable cause to arrest you," Paul said to Kannada. "The officer told me all of this in case you dropped by. He said you'd put my address in as your primary residence."

"What'd you tell him?" Kannada investigated.

"I told him I hadn't seen you for a couple of days, didn't know where you went."

Ben turned from Paul to Kannada. "What's going on?"

Before Kannada could respond, Zara swooped in. "I know what." Looking at Kannada without hesitating, she said, "He visited her at the NYSE, and Lemon caught them. That's the only explanation. That's why you wanted me to get that badge a few days ago."

Kannada stared hard at the hip-shooter. He appreciated Iago Gonzales' intelligence to keep mum. He, too, was an accomplice to Kannada's transgression for providing details to him about Amara's brunch routine.

He turned to Ben and blanched. "I've seen Amara once. I knew she didn't want to cross paths again, but how else was I going to reacquaint myself with her? Lemon probably exaggerated the whole event."

Ben looked pointedly at Zara. "And you helped him? I told you to distract him."

"I—" Zara started.

Ben growled at Kannada. "I knew this would happen. I knew it when I confronted you at the fountain."

Kannada narrowed his eyes. Something Ben said stuck with him. The flirting, the massage, the date; it all added up. He raised his voice. "Distract me? You paid her to hustle me?"

Ben sneered. "You just had to see her."

"Amara's here?" Ricky said.

Rob tilted his body toward Kannada. "Who's Amara?"

"His ex-fiancée," Zara clarified.

Ben's gaze remained on Kannada. "I'm not about to let you mess this up. I knew you couldn't stay rational." He looked down at the restraining order, then back to the group's Judas. "You can't stay here. Your presence brings too much attention to us."

"We can't stop now," Kannada objected.

"Who said we're stopping?"

"You can't do this without me. This is my story."

"It's mine now."

"You can't just take ownership of my work."

"Yeah, that's infringement," Ricky remarked.

"Sue me." Ben grinned at Kannada. "You know the difference between us? You never had the 'it' factor. Never could bounce back, you worthless bum. Now go!"

Kannada heard the most unexpected words imaginable. Stabbed in the back and in the heart by his close friend, his eyelids drooped, and he nearly fainted. "What?" he said, his back against the wall of opposition.

"You heard me. Get your ass out of here, you fucking waste of time!"

Kannada sighed as he experienced *déjà vu*; he was reminded of the moment he was kicked out of his apartment, then the instant Amara got rid of him. Today's expulsion was worse; he mostly believed in his plans since he committed himself to the caper, but an ominous, inconceivable power had played him like a puppet all this time. The door of opportunity was closing, and darkness was encroaching, again.

"You need another place to stay in New York?" Rob winked at Kannada.

"Either that or he leaves." Ben looked away. "You know where the subway is."

Ricky's eyes protruded. "Don't be ridiculous. He can't live there."

"He's been calling it home for the last year," Ben bristled. "Why not?"

Ricky gasped.

Kannada and Ben held a fierce stare, stopping just short of going mano-a-mano, one frustrated with the effect, the other with the cause.

"This isn't your choice to make," Kannada pleaded.

"You're right. It's the law's choice when you think with your dick and not your head." Ben arrested Kannada's fight with his own stupidity.

Kannada watched his chance to make a better life slip away, and the group, one by one, assemble on Ben's side. Kannada was in the wrong. So close he was to leaving poverty, yet so far away. Recovery was nothing more than an illusion.

Singled out, he glared at Zara—traitor—and stormed past the others out of the room. "How could you?" he said, passing her.

"Kannada . . ." She sounded apologetic.

He was gone. He moved to the private elevator, to the receptionist area on the ground floor, for solitude and time to think everything over.

"Wait a minute. He's the author," Rob noted. "How's the tale going to go on?"

Zara stared at the floor, regretful for speaking up.

"Sugar baby, you ready to right your wrongs?" Ben asked.

Zara looked at Ben with her mouth open, then glanced around the room. They were waiting on her. She was a flirt, not a person of the markets. She didn't want Kannada out of the loop; they gelled with each other, and his way of playing the system impressed her. She gulped, unsure what would be required, then nodded hesitantly. She was in.

"Everything depends on you now," Ben said.

Zara froze; this was more responsibility than she wanted.

The others in the living area except Ricky and Zara staggered back to their rooms, moping, down-faced.

"I'm going to check on him," Rob said.

Zara watched Rob walk out the door. Kannada's struggles weighed heavily on her mind; he faced three new battles in the war, the power, the law, and perhaps worst of all, his love. It was all crumbling, on the brink of crashing down.

"Amara's dating Lemon now?" Ricky asked an audience of one.

Zara stood there, musing on her new burden. She said nothing.

"Sour taste, she's got," Ricky quipped.

CHAPTER 27

Manhattan, New York

Matters had cooled off after a couple of hours. People regained their composure, as the mighty clouds held back the snow, rain, and lightning. The group went to address the challenges that lay ahead. They'd come too far for everything to collapse.

On the terrace, a focused Iago sat on patio furniture with his arms crossed. He needed some cool, fresh air to clear his mind. Rob leaned over the glass fence, smoking a cigar. The others stayed warm inside, except Kannada, who'd left the penthouse.

Physically, Iago appeared to be doing nothing, but he was hard at work mentally, trying to restart the ignition to their plan.

Pull the massive switch on the central circuit breaker. Useless; they'd just turn it back on. Operate outsize vehicles; disconnect the power lines for their passage. The cables are underground. Destroy power lines. He shook his head. *Too big of a task. Call the power company; have them switch the power off for some maintenance or safety reason.* His brows rose. *During trading hours? They're not going to believe you. Unpaid debts? They'd contact you. Conduct a whole building shutdown test. But they know what to do.*

Iago adjusted in his chair, as his extremities teetered on the brink of numbness. *Maybe we should call it a night.* Suddenly, something hit the table in front of him and fell onto the floor. Rob turned his head for a peek, then returned to face Central Park.

Iago bent down to pick the item up from where he was sitting. His eyes squinted as he lifted the small rock-like object and held it near his face. "You know what this is?"

Rob faced him.

"It's an acorn. There're squirrels nearby," Iago observed.

Rob narrowed his eyes. They moved to the living area and met the group.

"It's too cold for squirrels to be out. Don't they hibernate?" Alan took a sip from his beer bottle.

"Not exactly," Iago said, sitting on a sofa, "but they do sleep a lot. On the flight to New York, I sat next to a biologist who studied squirrels. When it's freezing, they stay hunkered down in their den."

Ben was pacing behind a couch; he had taken Kannada's spot. "So?"

Iago rotated the acorn with his hand, near his face. "Mother Nature."

Ben stopped pacing and looked at Iago.

Walker sat up, hunched over, elbows on his knees. "What? We can't just wait for another snowstorm."

As Iago envisioned his plans for Mother Nature to take over, the natural disaster he thought of was perfect. It would leave no evidence, was guiltless, and was entirely incidental.

"Squirrels," Iago said. "They're small but pack a huge punch."

"Squirrels?" Ben sounded doubtful.

"Yeah." Iago cracked a smile. "Squirrels chew wires all the time, creating fire hazards or, in our case, power outages. Just put them near a transformer and they'll step on a pair of hot wires and cause a short circuit. And it's worse if they're wild and haven't eaten for a couple of days. They'll gnaw on the wires so fast."

Rob, sitting on the sofa, leaned forward and clasped his hands. "Okay. Sounds like a plan." His head bobbed up and down. "Bushy tails shutting down the system."

"How long until things return to normal?" Ben asked.

"Could be anywhere from half an hour to four hours, depending on their discovery," Iago answered.

"Can squirrels literally halt trading and shut down a building?"

Ricky asked.

"The NYSE?" Iago grinned. "Yeah."

"It's happened before," Rob added.

Ben placed his hands on the back rail of the sofa and leaned forward. "Okay, first thing tomorrow morning, we go to the nearest pet shop."

"Not so fast," Iago curbed his enthusiasm, "they're not pets. I'm not sure where you could get them."

"I do," Paul said, standing behind a sofa. "I know exactly where we can get them."

"Where?" Ben asked.

Paul hesitated. "The Ass Woman."

With two dog crates filled with live traps, Iago, Walker, Alan, and Ben arrived at Central Park, located just north of their hideout, the Plaza. They split into pairs and walked the trails among the snow-scattered trees and walkways, hunting for the elusive Ass Woman, as though there was an egg hunt afoot in a freezing fifteen degrees. The gallant souls promenaded their utter disregard for the unpleasant weather with a Presbyterian-like purpose. A few minutes in, Alan fell behind his partner, Walker, and reached for his stainless steel, leather wrapped hip flask; the cold stillness of the engineered park gave way to painful memories.

When the weather was polite and when he was Wendell Caldwell's private pilot, Alan used to anguish over his dead wife and child as in summertime sadness, somewhere along the many pathways of Central Park, as lively New Yorkers buzzed with excitement, took horse rides and engaged in alfresco activities around him. He slugged along the snow-covered pathways and wondered whether he would find another soulmate and whether dating was worth the effort. *Being single's not all that bad.*

Some people, dressed in several layers of winter gear, lifted his spirits as they braved the icy wind from the eastern ocean and enjoyed the serenity of the atmosphere. Alan caught up with Walker and the rest of the gang near the *Alice in Wonderland* statue at their meeting time. One hour had passed with no luck.

Alan unscrewed the lid of his hip flask and looked at White Rabbit hold a pocket watch. "Maybe we're too late. Are you sure she's out here?" His breath covered his vision momentarily and the strong scent of alcohol entered his nose just before he tipped in a mouthful.

"Maybe she doesn't exist anymore." Walker warmed his palms by exhaling hot air into them.

Ben looked every which way. "She's here. Somewhere." Then under his breath, "Hopefully."

"Out here?" Iago stared at the flask.

The others looked at Alan.

"What?" he said. "It keeps you warm."

"No, it doesn't." Iago sounded frustrated. "That's a myth. It moves warm blood closer to the surface, so your skin feels warm, but your core loses heat. You'll get hypothermia."

Alan stared at Iago, stumped. He looked past the computer nerd, unmoved, and processed the science in disbelief, then faced him. "Oh."

"Yeah." Iago nodded with wide eyes.

Alan put away the hip flask as Iago and Ben watched, and Walker continued to search the area.

Ben narrowed his eyes at Alan. "Let's stick together for a while."

Alan looked down and away. *There he goes again, monitoring me.* "I don't have a drinking problem."

Ben rolled his eyes, and they continued onward.

Within minutes, Ben stopped, as the susurrus of something approached. "You hear that?"

The others remained quiet.

A couple of wheels squeaked, and an animal bellowed in the dark archway of an overpass.

As if prompted, a pair of eyes with dark bags below them appeared, watching, from under a bridge. They peered out from beneath the brim of a felt rain hat wrapped in a dark blue scarf on the open crown, forming a band, and above a red-as-Rudolph nose. The figure was covered in several layers of thick wool clothing, with a dark blue wool overcoat on top.

The woman sat on a four-wheeled, wobbly, shanty carriage pulled by two donkeys draped in blankets. She was gray-haired with harsh, red cheeks and dead blue eyes. The bags under her baby blues, chapped lips, wrinkled skin, and withered hair told a story of a life rode hard and put away wet. She wore a necklace with a dirty release dove pendant, originally white.

Ben was wide-eyed, beaming with awe, as she approached them. The two parties looked at each other without saying anything. Ben hesitated and started to breathe from his mouth; she came with an unforgiving smell of feces.

Walker stepped forth. "Look, sister, Halloween was—"

Ben overcame her stench, drew closer to the woman, and put his hand on Walker's chest as to restrain him. "Let me handle this." He cleared his throat and let his bullshitting skills take over. "We're volunteers with The Humane Society of New York and we've been searching the park for the last hour for stray and injured squirrels. We would like to give them the attention they deserve and a home, and would appreciate it if you could help us in finding them. The longer they're out here, the worse they're off."

The lady looked down and away before she addressed him in an Irish accent. "Oh . . . I was just heading back to the stable."

Ben suddenly recognized his flub; she couldn't have those donkeys out here in this weather. "You're okay."

The woman glanced at the ground. "At this time? Squirrels?"

Ben cringed at her discolored teeth. "We're looking for squirrels, and you see squirrels. Do you know where they go in the winter?"

The Ass Woman returned to her downward gaze. "There." Her eyes trekked in the direction of what she was hinting at. "In those trees." She pointed as a few pigeons fluttered away from on top of her snow-covered coach. "They're nestled away from the cold."

Ben looked over at the trees. Iago, Alan, and Walker approached, surveyed the towering branches, and began positioning live traps at the bases of many trees and on a few horizontal branches. Some of the traps had their trigger plates coated with peanut butter, while others had unshelled peanuts placed inside them.

A cold breeze whistled past Ben; leaves rustled, and globs of snow dropped to the ground. "It's pretty cold out." He attempted to shoot the shit with her; she did help them after all.

"It's lovely." The woman dismounted her coach with a blanket, her breath visible. She placed the blanket on a shivering donkey, giving it two layers of protection, and glanced at Ben with a smile that said she was trying to stay optimistic.

"So . . ."

"What's your name?" the woman asked.

"Ben." He folded his arms and snuggled his hands into his warm armpits. "And you?"

"Sarah, but you may know me by my alias, The Lady of Donkey."

He nodded. *That's not the only name I know you by.*

"Where do you stay, Ben?"

"Over there." He turned his body to point. "At the Plaza." He glanced at Alan and Walker in the trees, with Iago below to catch their fall, if it came to that, luring the squirrels into several one-door and two-door live traps.

Ben needed to keep the focus off him; otherwise, he might slip up and reveal the truth. "How long have you had those donkeys?"

"Oh, about six years. Bought them when the market went south. The jack's twenty-five, and the larger one, my jenny, she's eighteen. The jack will probably expire soon."

"Then what?"

The woman sighed. "Then it's just me and my big ass."

He smirked, wanting to laugh, as the jenny started to excrete feces. "How come you drive at night?"

"I don't usually. Just started late today. Have to make up for lost time." She looked at the ground. "Stupid bureaucracy. It took forever to renew my license."

He nodded slowly. "How long do you stay out here?"

She uncovered a pouch under her garments and reached into it with her right hand. "I live out here. I love nature. It's been years since I first started living under the moon in New York." The Lady of Donkey fed her animals with several handsful of grains.

Ben frowned; he didn't think she liked nature like this, homeless in an unforgiving cold.

"But I stay in the subway," the woman muttered.

Ben turned his head in the direction of some light shuffling of comforters from the coach and found a small boy tucked under an army jacket. He parted his lips, then returned to the woman. "Where do you keep your animals?"

"On the West Side, at the Clinton Park Stables. It's always been a dream of mine to own a stable like that. They made an exception for me, said I was unique for having donkeys."

"Yeah, that is unique."

"People wanted to take my ride when I started; it was new. But everyone reverted to the horse."

"How's the money?"

"I make some, but not enough to keep a roof over two heads. Money comes, and money goes." The Lady of Donkey sighed. "I haven't had much to hold on to the last few years, except Luke over there." She pointed toward the small boy in the carriage with her head. "And these donkeys."

Ben nodded slowly.

"I didn't always use to live like this. I had things, a better carriage operation, a man, but I lost them and ended up here."

Ben twisted his mouth to the side. "How'd that happen?"

"Scam artists. Bogus websites charge fees for planning ahead, customizing rides. None of that fee money trickles down to us, and the ride is the same whether you book ahead or walk up to a carriage driver."

His brows rose. "I had no idea."

"All these animal-rights groups keep fighting to shut down our industry, and de Blasio wants to replace the animals with electric-powered replicas of vintage cabs."

"Yeah, I read about real-estate interests wanting to develop the West Side."

"It doesn't help that the economy is down. Damn Bush! Tax cuts for the rich. Borrow, borrow, borrow. Idiot!" She sounded bitter. "Then Obama came; he was a spectacle to see. Hope and change, more like despair and pain; 47 million Americans in poverty later, hope didn't change a thing."

"Yeah. Times are tough, but I hear The Donald might run."

The woman rolled her eyes.

"You know, blaming people for your problems won't help you," Ben counseled.

The woman covered her nose and sneezed. "There's some truth in that." She wiped her dirty hand on her rags.

Ben felt his ears and nose become numb. "I've never been out in nature much. How's it out here?"

"It's not terrible." The woman sighed. "Might lose a few toes this winter though."

Ben stared at her teary eyes. He turned away and saw a fallen tree. "Well, everyone's been hit by the recession, but the economy will pick up."

"What I need is a horse, a better carriage. It'd be nice to have a stable, but that'll never happen."

There was a moment of silence as the two watched Iago, Alan, and Walker struggle to get squirrels.

The woman faced Ben. "What do you do?"

Ben thought before responding as some pigeons fluttered around. He turned to face her. "I play the game of life."

The stillness of icicles on the trees characterized another moment of silence as they both looked on at the other three. The donkeys huffed.

"You know, I haven't had many heart-to-heart conversations over the years. You can only ask, 'How's it going back there?' or talk about the park so many times. People want to be left alone when they're on the carriage."

"You'd be surprised how many people open up if you open up yourself." He inhaled her foul scent through his nose. "I think you just need to wear some perfume; I mean you sit behind two asses."

The woman laughed. "I guess I haven't been the most accommodating driver." She bent over, shook her head, and scratched behind her ears, like a dog with fleas. She stood erect. "It doesn't help that I haven't taken a shower in weeks."

He slowly turned his head away, his eyes leading the way. "So . . . where do you wash yourself?"

The Lady of Donkey glanced at him, then turned back away. She rolled her eyes and sighed.

Ben saw no harm in his innocent inquisition; she brought up the topic of bathing.

"I don't take many showers," The Lady of Donkey said. "Sorry. I'm like the environment I live in. When it rains, there's water. That's my shower. Sometimes it doesn't rain, so there is no shower. The clouds see me, but they try to ignore me. 'Send forth rain,' I say. They prefer not to hear me."

"Uh, yeah." Ben humored the absurdity in her response. "It's like that in my apartment. Sometimes the water turns off; then the super sees me. 'Send forth the maintenance guy,' I say. He ignores me."

The woman looked at him strangely with one eyebrow raised. She turned back to watch Iago, Alan, and Walker make their way back to Ben. "No one wants to be a dirty tooth. Everyone judges a book by its cover."

"Yeah, you can shower all you want . . . and still feel dirty."

"What's the story, horse? Not clean inside?"

Ben looked down and away. "Yeah."

"Something weighing your heart down?"

He sighed, and his gaze turned gloomy. "A lot of things."

The woman lowered her chin, expecting.

"It's my friend, a co-worker. He's just . . . been very difficult and jeopardized our project."

"So, what're you going to do about it?"

"I fired him."

The woman's brows rose, and she hesitated. "I'm sure your friend had good intentions. Everyone makes mistakes. It's what you do afterward that counts."

Ben recognized two dog crates stuffed with bushy tails as a couple of pigeons flew away from the trio's path. He rocked back and forth on his heels. "Guess it's time for me to go." He faced her. "I warned him beforehand not to chase a woman, but he doesn't listen."

"Oh, I see. He has a glad eye and is acting the maggot." Her head tilted back. "Forgive and forget. Maybe you don't understand your friend."

"Probably, but I don't know if forgiveness is worth it."

"Of course, it's worth it. Where's your holiday spirit?" The woman smiled. "Forgiveness is the cornerstone of friendship."

Ben pursed his lips, and the squirrel hunters returned to him.

"Ready to go, boss?" Walker asked.

Ben nodded, then sighed and addressed the woman. "There's a good chance we won't see each other again. Good luck and stay warm."

"Goodbye," she said.

Ben pulled out his wallet and sifted through the bills, some counterfeit, marked with discolored, smudged ink, and some real. He twisted his mouth to the side, took out actual money, and gave it to her. "Merry Christmas."

The Lady of Donkey smiled. "Merry Christmas."

CHAPTER 28

Manhattan, New York

It was just another day at the NYSE on Wednesday, December 17th, the day before FriendBin's much-anticipated IPO. The market was buzzing with activity; traders and brokers were scrambling to fulfill trades or orders. Gains and losses were realized, and for those who held their positions, unrealized, as stocks fluctuated, up and down, like ocean waves. Some went long, others short. It was a relatively calm day, a little yelling, a little hair being pulled out, and fewer cigarette butts on market grounds. The day's regular trading hours were nearing an end.

Iago had left his office. He was down on the trading floor.

He spotted his target, a woman whose hazel eyes were glued to a set of monitors, and approached. "Hi, Veronica." Iago's heartbeat quickened, and he couldn't get quite enough air.

Veronica Reyes was the woman Iago had come across while searching the employee database of the NYSE a few weeks ago. She was the Zara lookalike that Kannada had a vision for, except for a few minor adjustments, cat eye glasses, a mole, and a bun hairdo. She was the blessing that worked for Barney Trade, Inc., the white-shoe investment bank and brokerage firm that held the group's investment account. The group had all but dismissed the notion of

242

Zara taking Veronica's part, except for Dilip, the wise guy. Oh, was he right.

The woman turned to face Iago. "Hi."

"My name's, uh, Sergio and I, uh, work in the security department." Iago fidgeted with a pen in his pocket. He was using a second alias on top of his first moniker of Diego Sanchez. "There's been a, uh, breach in the security system and some identities have been compromised."

"Oh." Veronica sounded worried. A brunette in a business suit walked toward and behind her.

"We would, uh, like you to use this badge starting tomorrow." Iago flashed her a new badge. "Oh, it may not work on the first swipe. You might have to, uh, swipe it a few times to get it going. And that's because the system might take a while to update. You might not be able to check in right away."

Veronica nodded as a couple of traders and brokers in blue and green jackets walked away from and behind her.

"Who's up for some drinks at the Dead Rabbit?" a man in a blue jacket asked.

The other men replied, "Sounds good," and "I'm in."

"So, uh, can I please have your old badge?" Iago was shaky given that he was swimming in a shark tank of brokers and traders who could sense his unusual activity any moment.

"Oh, yeah, sure." Veronica unclipped the badge from a badge holder at the end of her company lanyard that hung around her neck, then took the one Iago gave her and clipped it on. "Thank you."

Iago's confidence rebounded. "No. Thank you." The closing bell sounded. His heartbeat and breathing returned to normal. *She actually fell for it? Easier than I thought.*

A few hours later, Paul met Ben in the Dead Rabbit, on the third floor, the Occasional Room.

Paul noticed the twelve-ounce Pilsner glass he held had a few drops of water at the bottom and dried it with a towel. "I was sorting out some old clothes for donation yesterday and found a subway token in one of my pants; it had a cut-out 'Y' in it."

Ben sat on a bar stool's bottle green upholstery amid bare brick walls. "No kidding. That's old school."

Alistair Hawthorne, the top producer whom Ben had recruited on behalf of TradePlus Investments, a nonexistent company, showed up. He gazed at the audio-visual amenities.

Paul directed Ben with his eyes to look at the burly newcomer.

Ben, dressed as a company representative, had booked the room with Paul being the designated bartender for a private presentation, an orientation for potential employees and new hires. In reality, there was only one candidate, Alistair Hawthorne.

Ben rose from the bar stool and greeted the recent arrival while Paul pretended to clean the countertop with a white rag.

Hawthorne glanced around the empty room. "Am I a little early?"

"Better to be early than late, right?" Ben remarked. "They should be trickling down any minute. In the meantime, why don't you join me for some coffee?"

Hawthorne nodded. Ben and his guest sat on a pair of bar stools.

"What can I get you?" Paul asked.

"A regular," Hawthorne replied.

"I'll have one, too." Ben turned to face Hawthorne. "Did you get a chance to look at the company website?"

Paul placed two napkins on the table, then started his preparation of a New York regular, coffee with milk.

"Yeah," Hawthorne said. "I was impressed. How come you guys haven't gone public?"

"I think management wants to keep it a family business," Ben said. "They've been doing it for the last sixty years, and that's what works. But we'll get more into that in a couple of minutes. So, what're your hobbies?"

"Boating. I recently entered a sailing competition."

Rich people. Paul feared that Ben wouldn't be able to hold a conversation.

"What's the format?" Ben asked.

"Fleet racing, One-Design. You race?" Hawthorne said.

"Hell yeah. The company participates in team racing."

"Sweet."

Paul was impressed. *Where does Ben come up with this shit?* While Ben made small talk, distracting Hawthorne, Paul grabbed the coffee carafe and milk and poured one cup. Before he poured the other, he slipped a strong, fast-acting sedative into the first and mixed it with a spoon. He poured the second cup and left it drug-free.

Paul brought the drinkware out on top from under the bar table. "Here you go."

Ben raised his cup. "Too much Wednesday, not enough coffee."

Hawthorne laughed and clinked his cup with Ben's. "Cheers."

Alan and Ricky had just arrived at Crosby Street between Prince and Spring. Ricky parked behind a van at the southern end of the alley, but kept the Bimmer running, lights off. Darkness engulfed them, and graffiti on some buildings surrounded them. Cardboard boxes, overfilled steel garbage cans, and snow lined the sidewalks, and trash blew in the street.

"This is it," Ricky said. "Mugger's Lane. Qin sure picked a nice spot to meet the Russians."

"You better bail if things get ugly." Alan opened the car door.

Ricky nodded slowly, worried for the desert pilot.

Alan left with a briefcase of counterfeit money, and Ricky looked straight ahead and gulped as Alan closed the door.

Alan treaded the wet, cobblestone byway amid blustery winds. He vigilantly peeked about for the other party to his transaction and continually glanced over his shoulder to ensure his safety. A police siren sounded in the distance. His muscles tensed; criminal element lurked in the shadows and waited in silence to take his briefcase and life.

A few people stood on the fire escapes mounted to the outside of the buildings. Some panhandlers sat on the steps leading to the stores and murmured pleas. Alan sighed; he had witnesses.

He avoided making eye contact with a few Hispanic men who had assembled on the sidewalk. Their conversation slowed, and they stared at him. Alan swallowed.

"Lookin' for somethin', ese?" A man with slick, black hair and a black leather jacket asked.

"Uh . . . isn't Solar Antique Tiles on this street?" Alan said.

The man frowned. "Tiles? Need somethin' hard." He cracked his knuckles, and the gang closed in on the passerby who appeared to be in the wrong place at the wrong time.

Alan held his ground. *What's he going to do? I was in the Air Force.*

The man pointed to the end of the road and looked in that

direction. "What you want to do is walk all the way down. It's right before the intersection. Ask for Pedro. He's the owner." He smiled.

The former airman nodded slowly with parted lips, lost for the moment, and the group retreated.

Alan continued and reached his rendezvous spot. He looked around. *Where are they?* He checked the time on his phone, made a call, and started to retrace his steps.

Ricky looked in the rearview mirror, the side mirrors, and ahead. His eyes twitched from one scene to another. The phone rang. He picked it up.

"Looks like they're a no—" Before Alan could finish his sentence, someone from behind put him in a choke hold and dragged him into a building's indoor fire escape. The attacker took away his phone and briefcase, then released him.

"Hello?" Ricky said, then louder, "Hello?"

"He call you later," a man replied with a Russian accent.

Alan turned around slowly. There were three of them—the leader, who'd taken Alan's phone away, and two behind him—all balding with widow's peaks. The man on his left was holding a gun and a duffel bag, while the man on his right had another gun.

"*Proveryat' den'gi,*" the leader said in Russian. He handed the man to his right the briefcase.

The money handler put away his gun, fumbled with the suitcase, opened it, and took out a random stack of bills. The man fingered the bills, then checked a few other stacks.

"*Khorosho,*" the money checker said in Russian.

The leader directed the man on his left to give Alan the duffel bag.

Alan took the bag and his cell phone and escaped without checking the contents of his bag. He rushed to the car, entered it, and slammed the door shut. "Go," he ordered Ricky. They sped away.

Ben watched Hawthorne's head hit the bar table. Only Paul, Ben, and Hawthorne occupied the third-floor Occasional Room of the Dead Rabbit. Hawthorne needed help. Ben and Paul would give it to him.

Paul finished cleaning his last two cups, Ben's and Hawthorne's.

"Let me tell my boss I'm out of here."

"All right." Ben tried to pick the man up over his shoulder in the meantime, seeing if he could carry Hawthorne by himself. He couldn't; Hawthorne was a relatively heavy person, especially when he was involuntarily comatose.

Paul returned; his assigned duties for the night were over. Ben and Paul carried Hawthorne on their shoulders, his feet dragging, to the Parlor on the second floor, through the Taproom on the ground floor, and out the bar.

Some regulars enjoying late-night booze noticed and smirked at the sight.

Ben started to sweat; the last thing he needed was witnesses. "Two drinks." He shook his head. "Can't hold his liquor."

Ben and Paul were outside, lugging Hawthorne along through the New York Vietnam Veterans Memorial Plaza, as they made for a nearby pier. Fortunately, the Dead Rabbit stood at the southern tip of Manhattan, near the many harbors that lined East River.

A whipping wind swept through the plaza and brought smoke to Ben's nose. He looked over to his right and noticed a pair of lit cancer sticks. A couple of prostitutes were smoking across from them, near the snow-covered, black granite fountain, to stay warm.

"Hey," one call girl said, "you boys lookin' for a good time?"

"Not with your stanky, rachet ass," Paul hollered back.

"We don' need you either," the hooker returned.

Ben was stunned and afraid that a pimp might pound their faces. "What're you doing?"

"Eh," Paul said, "she's a regular around here. It's how we communicate."

Ben shook his head, then glanced over his shoulder.

"Long live the hooker!" the other prostitute yelled, her fist in the air.

Long Island, New York

The gate to Rob's eight-acre estate opened. Alan unbuckled his seatbelt, eager to take on the next task, and Ricky drove in. Snow littered the sidewalks, and gargoyle lamps lit their way. They arrived at the brick outbuilding that had transformed to a body shop in the last three weeks. The sliding doors to the construct that housed the helicopter rose slowly; the only thing missing was introductory music.

In pristine condition, the beauty waited to be approached. The paint job, decals affixed and all, was complete. The DHS helicopter was ready to go.

They walked up to the aircraft, and Alan opened the door. His mouth dropped, as there was someone in the back seat.

"Hey, guys." Kannada smugly smiled. "The fireworks are set to start."

Alan and Ricky looked at each other. Plans had changed.

Kannada revealed he'd been staying at Rob's estate on Long Island since he'd abandoned the Plaza for losing his focus, since he'd been confronted with criminal trespass, impersonation, and larceny, since he'd put himself before the good of the group, but he was back.

Manhattan, New York

In the Plaza penthouse, Zara watched the Market Choice (MC) channel on television in the informal reception area with Iago. She splurged on a bucket of Vermont's finest Ben & Jerry's ice cream as Iago munched on some Cheetos.

"Want some?" he said.

Zara declined with a slight shake of her head.

On the show, two large big screen televisions on the sides, with a creamy orange backdrop and a logo in their displays, were recessed into dark green wooden walls. One smaller television between the two larger ones, with a silver display and a similar logo, was positioned just below a, "Mo' Money, Mo' Problems," sign.

Their trademarks had an Italian woman with shoulder-length brown hair sporting a black business suit and a white dress shirt, unbuttoned at the top. Her arms were crossed, and she looked directly at the viewer. The trademark had a sign under the woman that read, "Miss Market w/ Stevoni Romano."

Miss Market, a jersey shore girl, a guida, wore tight, flashy, designer clothes and excessive jewelry and had scrunched hair that looked wet and wavy but was dry and hard.

She stood at one end of her set, on the right side of her long rectangular desk from the viewer's standpoint.

The table rested on a circular light green carpet, which had a stock's squiggly chart design in front of the table. Portraits of economists and the current Chairman of the Federal Reserve decorated her set.

"Let me give you some color on one of the most-hyped IPOs in recent memory," Miss Market said in an eccentric New York accent. "The soon-to-be-hot FriendBin Corp., which will trade under the symbol F-B-N. The social media company taking the world by storm. Investors have been waiting *on line* for this. FriendBin's going to be a huge IPO when it comes public tomorrow, Thursday. Right?"

Zara looked at Iago. "On line?"

He shrugged.

"Wrong. Listen, all you guys out there, I want you to know the difference between—" Miss Market started counting on her fingers as she walked off the set to a trading floor at the NYSE, "—a mad IPO and a mad stock so that you can smile at the nice sun shower without getting drenched by the rain after this baby comes public.

"You see, FriendBin is a . . ." Miss Market paused and allowed her word of caution to sink in as she walked around a terminal. A couple of sturdy, square-jawed men dressed as traders appeared from behind the terminals. "*Sell, sell, sell,*" they said repeatedly.

Zara's gaze turned dreamy upon seeing the men.

Miss Market continued. "That's right. It belongs on the sell block. Don't get junked up on it. You're going to love it, then hate it. It's only good for," she said, as she approached a cashier with a green see-through visor, purple glasses, and a cigarette butt in his mouth, standing at one of the terminals. He sounded the cash register three times. "Thank you sweetheart," Miss Market said.

The cashier smiled and nodded.

She continued, unmatched and fiery. "A quick buck or two, and then fuhgeddaboudit!"

Zara and Iago looked at each other and chuckled.

"You don't want to own this stock; you don't want to lease it— heck, you don't even want to socialize about the darn thing. Maybe you could buy some sneakers with it, but it's not a long-term play. Don't bet your country house on it. You with me? I'll tell you why."

Iago turned off the television. "No spoilers."

This was the first time Zara saw the MC financial show and heard an authentic, thick, female New York accent. "I didn't . . . understand a word she said."

"Nobody understands New Yorkers." Iago crashed on the couch; it was time for bed.

Near the pier at the intersection of South Street and Gouverneur Lane, Ben and Paul schlepped Hawthorne along. The walk to the jetty wasn't terrible, having an extra body on to keep them warm.

Ben had looked over his shoulder more than once to see if anyone had noticed their fishy behavior. They were in the clear so far, as the streets were empty at this hour.

He smelled Eau de Garbage. Trash bags piled high against a wall to his left. Red and blue flashing lights, accompanied by a siren, lit the heap. He looked to his right; a police car rolled up with two men in blue. *Shit!*

An officer with a dark brown Fu Manchu and a winter hat rested his arm on the windowsill. "What seems to be the problem here?"

"Uh . . ." Ben said, "our friend got a little tipsy."

The policeman's eyes darted back and forth between Ben and Paul. "Where're you folks headed?"

"To his apartment," Paul replied.

The officer glanced at the ground. "Where's he stay?"

"East Village," Ben responded.

"Seems like you guys could use a lift."

Paul parted his lips and glanced at Ben.

Ben looked to the ground and ruminated on the welfare of their plans; then he faced the officer. "We wouldn't want to trouble you. In fact, our car is just around the corner."

"Who said I was giving rides?" The officer sounded stern. "Which car is that?"

Ben and Paul didn't have a car with them. They'd ridden the subway to get to the Dead Rabbit.

Ben looked at a car across the street. "That blue sedan."

The officer raised an eyebrow. "Thought it was around the corner."

Shit. Ben swallowed. "Uh . . . I didn't realize we were so close."

The officer's radio went off. The policeman glanced at his dashboard.

Ben and Paul looked at each other. The weight of Hawthorne was bearing down on them.

"You know what?" The officer narrowed his eyes and lifted his chin. "I have a reasonable suspicion that you guys are committing, or are about to commit, a crime. I want to check his breath."

Ben's eyebrows rose. *Fuck! Hawthorne's got coffee breath.* "Okay, yeah, sure."

The officers stepped out of the patrol unit as other cars passed in the background. Their name tags read, "L. Boggs," and "C. Harding." Officer Boggs, the man with the Fu Manchu, approached them, and Officer Harding, a burly, clean-shaven man with a similar winter hat, stood a few feet away.

"Set him on the ground against the wall, then step away," Officer Boggs commanded, referring to Hawthorne.

Ben and Paul did as they were told, while Officer Harding kept his hand near his trigger.

"Doesn't smell drunk from here," Officer Boggs observed. He moved toward Hawthorne and stooped low to get his nose near his face, then opened his mouth and sniffed, searching for an alcoholic scent. "Must be a lightweight." He shook Hawthorne's shoulder and checked his eyes. Hawthorne mumbled something. Officer Boggs stood and looked at his partner. "He's been drinking."

Ben cracked a smile; fortunately, Hawthorne didn't have noticeable coffee breath.

"You want to call EMS?" Officer Harding asked.

While Officer Boggs hesitated, Ben's eyes widened, his diaphragm nearly collapsed, and his heart and lungs almost fell to his stomach. He swallowed. The whole operation hinged on this moment; Hawthorne's information was the key to everything. Paul trembled and fell to his knees.

"Nah, he's still conscious, not vomiting," Officer Boggs said.

Ben sighed, and his muscles relaxed.

"Get up!" Officer Harding demanded.

Paul returned to his feet and smiled at Ben.

"Can we go?" Ben started to approach Hawthorne.

"Just stay here. Turn around." Officer Boggs sounded intimidating.

"What'd I do?"

"Listen to me." Officer Boggs grabbed Ben's arm. "You're not free to leave. Turn around." He twisted Ben's arm behind his back, spun him around, and pinned him against the wall. "Hands up."

Ben followed orders, and his heart pounded to a blur. "You can't run a stop-and-frisk. I don't have anything."

"Trying to meet your quota," Paul yelled.

"Shut your fucking trap," Officer Boggs shouted.

Officer Harding closed in on Paul and stared him down. Paul gasped and looked robotically straight ahead.

Ben felt the shivers, and it wasn't because of the cold weather. They didn't have anything that could be confiscated, but an officer running a stop-and-frisk was just as good as being accused of a felony or penal law misdemeanor in this city.

Officer Boggs grasped Ben's nape and spoke in his ear. "Look, our job is to look for suspicious behavior. When you keep looking back at us, we think—"

"I was just trying to see if—"

"Listen to me, when you're walking the block, carrying a drunk person, and you keep looking back at us, we think you're up to something. Now, spread your legs."

Ben sighed and gave up. Officer Boggs aggressively patted him down as Paul watched, and Hawthorne fell over. Ben felt the coldness of his pants with every touch of his lower extremities. The officer found nothing, proceeded to Paul, and slammed him against the building. As he frisked Paul, curious drivers and passengers slowed down to rubberneck at the happenings. Ben looked away, frustrated, and focused on the officer conducting the Terry stop.

Officer Boggs finished with Paul. "Names. I want names."

"We don't have to give you our identities," Ben argued, still facing the wall.

The officers glanced at one another.

"I know my rights. That's within the law." Ben sounded tough but feared the officers would confiscate their wallets. "I don't get this, man."

Officer Boggs softened his tone. "I understand you're upset, and I'm sorry for the inconvenience. But—"

A rushed voice came through the officer's radio. "We have a 10-30 at Front and Water. Suspects armed and dangerous. All NYPD in the area report immediately."

"That's a few blocks away." Officer Harding went to address the call of duty.

Officer Boggs glanced at his car, then faced Ben and Paul and hesitated. "All right, you guys are free to go." He walked back to his car, sat down, and closed his door. "This better not happen again."

Ben and Paul slowly turned around.

"The last time," Ben said.

Officer Boggs rolled up his window, leaving only a small crack to allow cool air to enter, then started his engine.

Ben waited until he wasn't within earshot of the officers. "Damn police state," he said to Paul.

Ben and Paul watched the officer drive away, then picked up Hawthorne and moved toward the pier. They kept their eyes peeled for any other cops who might think they wanted to dump an unconscious Hawthorne into the heavily trafficked East River, where the mob threw dead bodies. They reached their boat, Rob's yacht, where they met a waiting Walker.

Walker had placed a bottle of champagne on the dashboard near the helm. He came out of the cockpit as the waters crashed gently on the side of the boat during low tide.

"You got him?" Walker sounded elated.

"Yeah," Ben said. He and Paul set Hawthorne down on a chair in the bow, then simultaneously sighed. They had unloaded their cargo.

The wind carried a funky odor that wreaked havoc on Ben's nose. "What the hell's that smell?"

Paul sniffed the air and looked at him. "We're in the East River, the most polluted waterway on the eastern seaboard. What'd you expect?"

Ben grimaced at the briny tang of clams and scallops with excess metal. "Fish, trash, dead bodies, but not this."

"Well, you better get used to it. You've got a long night ahead of you."

Ben shrugged.

"I'll see you guys back at the Plaza," Paul said.

Ben's face turned down. "Eh."

Behind schedule, Paul quickly departed and headed for the penthouse to begin the next step.

Ben looked at Hawthorne. "I'll tie him up."

While Walker released the boat, Ben searched the icy deck; he almost slipped more than once. "Where's the rope?"

"On the starboard next to you," Walker answered.

Ben carefully moved to the right side of the boat and, behind an inflatable life raft, found what he needed. "Start her up."

Walker nodded, then went to the cockpit to start the engine.

Ben fastened Hawthorne to the chair with the rope and chained his feet to an anchor.

CHAPTER 29

Long Island, New York

Alan, Ricky, and Kannada had rolled the helicopter out of the garage into an open area on Rob's lot. They had changed their clothes; Alan sported a flight suit, and the other two wore black jumpsuits, gloves, and beanies. Alan sat in the pilot's seat, Kannada took shotgun, and Ricky moved into the back seat.

Alan fastened himself in. "Seatbelts?"

"Yeah." Ricky's buckle clicked.

Alan looked at the passenger next to him; Kannada grinned, ready to go.

Alan adjusted the collar of his flight suit, as it chafed his neck and chin. *Should've got the low-cut neckline.* He ignored the discomfort and put his hand on the collective, comprised of the start button, fuel cut-off button, and a throttle twist grip, then went through a series of steps to start the engine, all second nature to him by now. He got an adrenaline rush, as there was nothing like liftoff, and kept his eyes on two main gauges, the turbine outlet temperature, or TOT, and revolutions per minute, or RPM. He pressed and held the start button on the collective.

The fuel igniters ticked several times.

He covered the fuel cut-off button with his thumb. He waited a few seconds for the RPM to increase to fifteen percent, which signaled him to introduce fuel by advancing the throttle twist.

He had to time this perfectly; introducing fuel too early would damage the engine and too late would drain the battery. The needle on the TOT shot to the yellow. Two seconds, that was all he had for the temperature to take a dip. It stayed too high.

Alan's heart sunk; he had to abort the start. He twisted the throttle grip to fuel cut-off and brought the engine to ground idle. "Dammit," he said in frustration.

"What's wrong?" Ricky sounded apprehensive.

The three of them exchanged glances; they all had the same scared shitless expression.

"There ain't nothing wrong. Just need to give it some more juice." Alan gave it a second try, nervous.

Manhattan, New York

Paul had caught up with Rob at the Plaza. Rob was on the snow-capped rooftop when Paul opened the door to the top. He was scattering the tons of fireworks they'd obtained from Chinatown.

Rob pointed to his watch. "Where've you been?" He sounded impatient.

"Thank the Po-Po and thank the MTA," Paul said, disappointed. He was referring to the police and the Metropolitan Transportation Authority, respectively.

"What happened?"

"We got pulled over, Ben and me."

"For what?"

"Damn Terry stop." Paul shook his head.

"They're still doing that in New York?"

"Apparently." Paul sighed. "Then the subway took forever. But Ben's on the boat with that Lemon trader now. What about Alan? Did you get a call?"

"Not yet. Let me phone them."

Long Island, New York

Alan had the same result. The second attempt to start the helicopter failed.

"Do you even know how to start this thing?" Ricky sounded irritated.

"Get it together, Whiskey Delta!" Kannada glared at the pilot.

Alan turned his head to the side so that Kannada and Ricky entered his field of vision. "Third time's a charm." He forced a smile, trying to stay positive.

The passengers frowned with their arms crossed and looked out the window.

Alan's brows furrowed. *What's wrong?* He'd started the helicopter before. He didn't want to join the Whiskey Delta hall of fame; members were notorious for caving under pressure. The three of them were excited and ready to go somewhere, but their mode of transportation was failing them last minute.

Alan went through the same motions as before. The temperature soared high on the TOT gauge. One. Two. The temperature dropped, just enough to start the engine.

Alan started to vibrate with the machine. "Yes!" he screamed. "You see that?"

Kannada faced Alan. "What?"

Ricky sat up, his head between Kannada and Alan, attentive now.

"It worked." Alan released the start button. "The temperature is in the right zone."

He turned his head to the side again; his passengers had relieved smiles.

The engine revved loudly, the rotor mast churned vigorously, the main rotor blades, paddles on the flybar, and tail rotor blade revolved faster and faster, to a blur.

"Here we go." Alan grinned. He put on his noise-canceling headphones, as did the others.

The helicopter lifted off the ground from Rob's estate and fled toward Manhattan, laying low in contrast to its seeker, the actual DHS copter.

Manhattan, New York

Rob held a pair of binoculars near his face, on the lookout for the real DHS helicopter that hovered around the NYSE.

The government helicopter continuously looped the NYSE high in the sky in clockwise fashion, from a few miles south of the bottom tip of Manhattan near Governors Island all the way up to Midtown, just south of Times Square, and kept watch over New York and the financial markets like a guardian angel.

"Yeah. We just left. Do you see the DHS chopper?" Kannada said over the phone.

"Yeah," Rob replied. "I see them. It looks like they're making their way to the Financial District. Where're you?"

Long Beach, New York

Kannada had taken his headphones off but covered his free ear with his hand. He paused to process what Rob said over a line that was breaking up; it was difficult to hear him in the loud helicopter. He looked below through the window; waves broke and crashed on a shore. "Over Long Beach."

Alan piloted the helicopter in a U-shaped pattern, stretched horizontally, with Rob's chateau on one end and the NYSE at the other. He reached the base of the "U."

Upper Bay, New York

At sea, Ben, Walker, and a sedated Alistair Hawthorne were passing the Statue of Liberty in Upper Bay just west of Governors Island, heading toward Lower Bay, which opened up to the Atlantic Ocean.

Walker was outside the cockpit with the boat on autohelm for the moment. He and Ben stared at the brightly lit national monument in the middle of the night.

Ben smelled the air. Either he was getting used to the foul odor, or it was fading away.

He approached Hawthorne and hunched over him. Walker left the statue and stood over Ben. "Wake up," Ben said to their captive. "Wake up." He tried to shake Hawthorne from the spell he was under as they passed the monument in the background, but Hawthorne was out cold.

Ben took off his glove and touched Hawthorne's right cheek. It was red and cold. He looked at Walker. "You brought a hat and comforters for him, right?"

"Yeah, they're in the cockpit." Walker went inside to retrieve the headgear and bedspreads.

Ben put his glove back on and slapped Hawthorne's right cheek. Hawthorne's head moved to his left. His cheek turned redder, and he stayed asleep. Ben slapped Hawthorne's left cheek; it also changed color. Hawthorne's head moved to his right. He didn't respond. Ben sighed and stood.

Walker retrieved an Alaskan fur hat and a few comforters. He put the hat on Hawthorne's head and wrapped him with the bedspreads to keep him warm. He stepped back. "He kind of looks cute."

Ben shook his head. "Don't go there."

"How long until the pill wears off?"

"A couple of hours. You want to play good cop, bad cop when he wakes up?"

Walker smiled.

East River, New York

Kannada looked through the helicopter's windshield at the New York City skyline. "We just passed the Brooklyn Bridge," he said to Rob over the phone.

"They're in the Financial District again."

Kannada peered through binoculars. "I see them. Is everything set?"

"Yeah. We're waiting on your word."

"When they're heading in the direction of Times Square, begin."

Manhattan, New York

"Get ready," Rob said to Paul on the Plaza rooftop. Rob kept watching the DHS helicopter. "Now." He let the binoculars droop from his neck and joined Paul in setting the fireworks. Rapidly lighting fuse after fuse with lighters covered by their hands to avoid the wind's effect, they ignited a huge fireworks show.

Bright blue, royal purple, neon green, hot pink, and the rest of the color spectrum burst into the night sky in fascinating shapes with bangs and crackles, treating folks everywhere in New York City and its surrounding areas.

Rob ignored the smell of rotten eggs, sulfur from the fireworks, and repeatedly glanced up to enjoy the aerial masterpiece.

Bronx, New York

A mother held her son's mitten-covered hand as they walked home. She heard faint pops from above but brushed off the noise.

"Happy New Year's, Mama," the boy wished his mother.

The mother looked at the child; he was staring at the sky. "Oh, don't be ridiculous. It's not New Year's, dear," the mother said, straightening out the boy.

He continued to gawk and pointed to the sky.

The mother looked up and gaped at the flashing lights. "Maybe it is New Year's," she said slowly.

Manhattan, New York

Eddie Yeager, a clean-shaven rookie co-pilot in the genuine DHS helicopter, pried his eyes off the city's buildings, including the NYSE. The fireworks show distracted and captivated him.

"Why're there fireworks today?"

"Maybe they're practicing." Dick Lindbergh, the chief pilot and a man with wrinkles, watched also.

"Shish. That's a lot of fireworks just for practice."

Kannada unbuckled his seatbelt and noticed some late-night workers peer through their office windows at their helicopter. Alan had flown low into the jungle of skyscrapers. He rounded his way around buildings, turning left, then right, then left. He edged corners until he reached the tall tower affixed to the north end of the NYSE. He hovered there for a second and tried to get the landing skids as close to the rooftop as possible without actually coming to rest.

"How far is it?" Alan asked.

Kannada opened the cabin door and glanced over the edge. A blast of cold wind hit him. "Looks like seven or eight feet from the roof," he yelled back over the loud engine.

"You think you can handle that?" Alan yelled.

"Yeah," Kannada shouted back. He turned around to face Ricky. "Come on."

"Did you get your lunchbox?" Alan said.

Kannada rolled his eyes. "Yes, Mother." He grabbed the duffel bag that Alan had acquired from the Russians and a second bag with accessories—a professional lock pick set, a spray bottle, a crowbar, a two-way radio, string, and electromagnetic climbing clamps.

Kannada and Ricky departed the helicopter and jumped onto the snow-covered rooftop. Kannada landed on his feet, came out in front of the chopper, and gave Alan the thumbs-up he needed to leave. Alan flew away just as he'd come.

The advancement in time and the altitude made for an even colder night. The skyscraper's antenna wobbled dangerously in the wind.

"Ouch." Ricky winced in pain, lying on the ground, holding his ankle.

"You okay?" Kannada checked.

"My ankle."

"I'll nurse your wound once we get inside. Being a doctor runs in my blood."

Ricky stared; he didn't get the joke, but he wasn't Indian-American.

Kannada brushed off his damp squib, then opened the accessory bag and took out the professional lock pick set. He unlocked the door to the rooftop, then tugged on the door; it remained closed. Water had seeped between the seal and doorframe. *Dammit!* He applied pressure on the door to break the ice around its seal, then jimmied it open with the crowbar from his bag. Once inside, he helped Ricky loosen his ankle joint by warming up the surrounding muscles with some light stretching.

Ricky was moving again, though with a slight limp.

CHAPTER 30

Lower Bay, New York

A bucket of freezing water splashed onto Alistair Hawthorne and made for a rude awakening; it was an ice bucket challenge to remember. He was drenched.

"Wake up," Ben demanded.

Hawthorne may have crashed hard earlier, but he was awake. He repeatedly blinked, trying to get the excess water off his eyelids, amid the bay's briny funk. "Oh God!"

"Rise and shine," Ben greeted him.

Hawthorne shivered. "Are you out of your mind? That water's freezing cold."

"I know. Sucks."

Hawthorne's gaze turned down; his body was fastened to the chair with rope, and his feet were chained to the anchor. Comforters were on the floor next to him. *What's going on?* His adrenaline spiked. He looked at his captors and gasped with wide eyes, then tried to break free, his legs and arms wriggling for a way out. He rocked from side to side, trying to tip the chair over, but a black man with a goatee held him in place.

"Stop that," Ben ordered.

"Where am I?"

"You're in the Lower Bay."

Hawthorne looked around with a frown; he was in the middle of nowhere. There was no land in the night sky. A cry for help wouldn't be heard. His heartbeat had run away, leaving him to fend for himself. He started to hyperventilate, staring at the floor.

He faced Ben with a shrill voice. "What is this? All I remember is that we were at the bar last night."

"You had a little too much to drink," Ben said.

"Mmm hmm," the black man added.

A trace of coffee lingered in Hawthorne's mouth, but his breath was still a far cry from being bad, which happened whenever he got smashed with alcohol.

He looked at the black man who stood over him next to Ben. "And who're you?"

"Your worst nightmare," the black man answered, in a deep tone.

Ben nodded. "Don't let Walker scare you; he's just a boxer."

Hawthorne looked away toward the floor of the boat, perplexed by the new revelations. His wet face had nearly lost all feeling. *Is this a dream?* He fidgeted and squirmed, trying to escape the rope that bound him. "What do you want?"

"What we want is the password you use to make trades at the NYSE for Lemon Group," Ben stated.

"I don't have that. I don't even work for Lemon."

"Yes, you do," Ben said. "Rule number one; lie, and you'll be sleeping with the fishes."

Walker cracked his knuckles.

Hawthorne swallowed.

"We know there're two passwords," Ben said. "The one Lemon provides for the whole exchange to use daily, set right before the market opens, which you get on your phone, right here." Ben waved Hawthorne's confiscated phone. "And the one that he's given you to trade on his account. I want the previous daily password, today's daily password, and the one you use to trade on his account."

Hawthorne's posture deflated. *How's he know about this?* Two goons, for all he knew they were probably members of the mafia. They'd kidnapped him and held him hostage in the middle of the ocean for a trio of passwords. Maybe they had guns. He wouldn't be surprised. Thoughts on the video he'd first watched when he joined the Big Board as a floor trader ran through his mind, as well as thoughts of how organized crime had infiltrated Wall Street previously and was a threat to the smooth, honest functioning of the markets.

"I'll make you a deal," Hawthorne negotiated, finally piecing something together. "I'll pony up whatever you want, millions. I have millions—a yacht, too—if you let me off this boat."

"Rule number two," Ben declared. "We make the rules, not you."

Hawthorne turned to the floor again and wondered how he could keep the passwords protected, as well as his life. He sighed. *Maybe you could give them a fake password. They'd let you off the hook and wouldn't know. You could then report them to the police and get the hell away from New York.*

"And if you're thinking of giving us a false password," Ben stated. "Think again. We're going to hold you at least until the market opens."

Okay, that option won't work. What else do you have? Come on! What else can you say to appease this guy?

"All you have to do is tell us the truth," Ben said.

The Asian captor was feeding Hawthorne answers to his thoughts.

"You know what they say," Ben said. "The truth shall set you free."

Manhattan, New York

In the government helicopter, Lindbergh spotted a chopper that was passing the Brooklyn Bridge; it appeared as a vaguely discernible blurb to the naked eye in the dark.

"You see that? Probably one of the CEO's helicopters. These Wall Street tycoons work crazy shifts, chasing the money. They've got helipads on top of some of the buildings. That's some life."

"That's insane." Yeager put up his binoculars to look.

"Yeah. They make billions, trading here and in overseas markets."

"That's not a CEO's helicopter. That's one of ours."

"What? Let me see those." Lindbergh looked through the binoculars to the now clearly visible duplicate helicopter running off course. He couldn't believe his eyes. He returned the binoculars to the rookie co-pilot.

"Chip," Lindbergh said over his radio headset. "You let another one out to cover the NYSE?"

He waited, listening, while continuing to follow the other helicopter.

"No," Chip responded over the radio headset. "Just you tonight, roger."

The DHS pilots watched the similar helicopter flying over South Brooklyn Marine Terminal on the outskirts of Brooklyn. The real DHS chopper edged closer to the southern tip of Manhattan on its return route.

"Hang on. Something's not right." Lindbergh homed in on the other helicopter.

Lower Bay, New York

"Now, I'm going to ask you one more time," Ben demanded on the boat. "What're the passwords?"

Hawthorne looked at the floor and heard the gyrating wings of a helicopter far away; he'd nearly run out of novel ideas to get himself out of the sticky situation he found himself in. *I knew what he was offering was too good to be true*, he lamented to himself. *TradePlus Investments. It was bogus. And that check! Come on, Hawthorne. How'd you fall for that? It didn't even have enough time to clear.*

"Well?" Ben said, sounding impatient.

"I hate to break it to you," Hawthorne said, "but I'm part of the mafia." He pointed his chin and stuck his chest out.

"Oh really?" Ben sounded sarcastic. He faced Walker. "Give me his wallet."

Walker retrieved Hawthorne's wallet and tossed it to his accomplice.

Ben examined its contents, then tilted his head and twisted his mouth. "Money's not in a broccoli band, but he's one of the wise guys."

"Now it makes sense." Walker nodded, playing along. "He doesn't want to snitch on them. They take care of him."

"Ah," Ben said. "I never would've imagined. Our lives could be in danger."

Hawthorne slumped as much as the rope allowed, frowned, and looked from one captor to the other as they teased him. "Look, you won't get away with this. They'll piece it together, the authorities. Security, forensics; it's so advanced today."

"We can do this the easy way or the hard way." Ben smiled.

* * *

Atlantic Ocean

Alan's helicopter trembled unusually. A rumbling noise came, louder and louder, and momentarily rendered his noise-canceling headphones useless. He viewed the gauges; everything appeared normal. *What's happening? Is the engine going out?*

He was now overhead Rockaway Park, west of Long Beach, the base of his U-shaped trajectory.

Alan looked to his left during the apex of the deafening turbulence. An airplane flew overhead, circling around John F. Kennedy International Airport. The waves generated by the plane had nearly thrown his chopper for a spin. It was close. As he turned back to face the front, he caught sight of a DHS helicopter following him in his side mirror.

The DHS helicopter was hot on the target's tail, cutting across Brooklyn, cutting the distance in half.

"He just dodged that plane," Yeager observed.

"Got lucky." Lindbergh's heart was racing; they had action tonight. He licked his chops while eyeing their prey, then glanced at the gauges on the dashboard; he was going as fast as possible.

Their target swerved the duplicate helicopter off its trajectory and went southeast, toward the Atlantic Ocean.

"What's he doing?" Yeager asked.

"Looks like we've got an HWI," Lindbergh said, confident.

"HWI?"

"Helicoptering while intoxicated."

Alan needed to shake the DHS pilots, but how? He couldn't outfly them by going high in the sky above the clouds. They could do that, too. He'd have to slow down to land. Either they'd land nearby or put that darn, ultra-powerful searchlight on him and contact local authorities while he ran like a criminal. There was only one way out of this—and that was getting out of the helicopter. Most helicopters didn't have an ejection system. He had to improvise, using the old-fashioned method of leaving an aircraft.

Alan hyperventilated and unbuckled his seatbelt swiftly while he flew lower, toward the earth. He took off his headphones and unlatched the cabin door. The alarm sounded as cold wind blew hard in his face. He dove out, head first, to avoid the sharp, fast-turning, rotor blades, and prayed for safety on his way down. He hit the ice-cold water at the western edge of the Atlantic Ocean. The helicopter followed suit a few hundred feet away and exploded on contact with the sea.

The DHS pilots stared with open mouths. Yeager cleared the fog built up on the cockpit's windshield with his hand.

Lower Bay, New York

Hawthorne absorbed a shovel hook in the gut, his first blow, courtesy of Walker. He gasped for air and nearly fainted. The shock compressed his innards, but they quickly recovered, owing to his burly size. He heard the soft reverberation of a distant crash but couldn't decipher whether it was his stomach churning or something else.

"That must sting," Walker remarked.

"Don't you have to prep yourself before fighting?" Ben asked the boxer.

"It's mostly mental. It's about having a positive emotional profile."

"You hear that?" Ben said to Hawthorne. "Stay positive, pal. You might come out on top."

Hawthorne wasn't going to give up that easily. He'd go down with a fight even if that meant being the punching bag for Walker's blows.

Walker made second contact, this time on Hawthorne's side, above his hip.

Hawthorne leaned toward the injured side and struggled to breathe. *That really hurt!* He recovered, but slower than before. He swung his head back and slouched.

"I'm waiting," Ben said to Hawthorne.

Hawthorne gathered himself, his rib cage almost broken. The combination of brutally cold weather and Walker's punches hurt more than words could describe; he stayed silent.

"Don't you ever feel guilty for hitting someone?" Ben asked Walker.

"It's important to desensitize yourself to the effects of inflicting injury," Walker said in his deep tone. "In fact, seeing the opponent in pain is actually motivation."

"No mercy, huh?"

"Exactly."

Hawthorne took another hit in the stomach and shuddered. His resilience started to wane, and his wall of reluctance to fork over the information saw its first cracks.

Ben took out a Blow Pop, unwrapped it, and sucked it once. "How many hits does it take to get to the center of Alistair Hawthorne?" he taunted, looking at the candy.

Walker struck Hawthorne's jaw with a haymaker. Hawthorne readjusted his jaw slowly and painfully and realigned it to its normal position, though with a little crookedness.

"Ready to throw in the towel?" Ben said.

Hawthorne stared at the floor and didn't respond. *Give up. They're going to kill you.* Despite his thoughts, he shook his head slightly.

"Don't your hands hurt?" Ben said to Walker. "I mean, that's bone-on-bone."

Walker shook his head. "No."

"What about you?" Ben asked.

Hawthorne looked up and tried to muster a battle cry. "Bite me."

Walker fed him a knuckle sandwich. He had first blood.

Hawthorne's lip had torn open. Blood dripped down his chin, to his Adam's apple. He tasted the iron in the hemoglobin and smelled a smidgen of copper. He shook his head back and forth, reeling from the recent hit, trying to put his eyes back into place. He saw birds circling his head now.

"All right, all right. I give up."

Walker wiped the blood from his hand with a towel.

Ben inched closer, on the edge of his seat. "What's the password?"

Atlantic Ocean

Lindbergh's mouth had fallen open. "There's no way he could've survived that."

Yeager looked through the binoculars. "He must've jumped out last minute."

"There's only one way to tell." Lindbergh turned on the powerful searchlight and started to examine the crash and surrounding areas.

"Call the Coast Guard. Even if he made it out, he wouldn't make it through those cold waters. He's got five minutes, tops. It's forty degrees down there."

Yeager followed orders as the chief pilot kept searching.

Alan's head rose up from the sea, and he wiped the excess water from his face with his hand. Waves rolled violently and carried him without permission. He was freezing; he would surely be sick if he reached shore. He breathed heavily, his respiration heightened, and his lungs hurt. The DHS helicopter flew ahead, and a whale, rare for this time of year, lifted its tail flukes to his right. He shivered, and not just from the cold; there could be less-friendly underwater creatures.

Alan ducked back into the water, went down a few feet, and swam underneath to evade the searchlight. He came back out every minute to get some air and hoped his flight suit would prevent his muscles from locking up.

Manhattan, New York

Kannada and Ricky had made it into a pitch-dark elevator shaft. They turned on their LED headlights; bright white light flooded the space and cast harsh shadows. Cold cement walls, cords, electric boxes, and metal bars of a ladder spanned the length, as did the smell of oil and metal. The shaft had spaced out bulbs, too, but they had been turned off. Somewhere, there was a switch for the lighting. There was an elevator more than a hundred feet away, near the bottom. At this hour, there were no riders.

They made their move.

On the ladder, Kannada glanced over his shoulder. "How's the view?" His voice echoed.

Ricky looked up between Kannada's sturdy legs. "I wouldn't mind if you ran into me."

Kannada stared at the wall, gulped uncomfortably, and processed Ricky's response. *Just one fry short of a Happy Meal.* He looked down with furrowed brows. "Shut up. Not me, I mean down there. Is everything clear?"

Ricky looked down the tunnel. "Oh, yeah, sure."

Rob and Paul, dressed as maintenance workers with tool belts around their waists, hoodwinked the doorman of an apartment building and slipped in. They pussyfooted quickly to someone's residence with a large rectangular wooden board under their arms. They stopped in front of room 123.

Rob selected a few nails from a small box filled with them. "You bring the hammer, Tim?" he joked.

Paul whipped out the tool from his belt. "A Binford. You remember who hired you, Al?"

Rob smiled, and they got to work boarding up the doorway of room 123.

Lower Bay, New York

"A3B2C1D0E-1F-2," Hawthorne said. "All letters are in caps. That's Lemon's account. And you'll get the other one when they send it to me by text."

"I also need the one you used to log on yesterday," Ben said.

Hawthorne looked at Walker, then back at Ben. "Redfern100. All lower case, no spaces."

"See, that wasn't so bad." Ben patted Hawthorne's face with a towel to stop the stream of blood that emanated from his lip.

The cold air felt good on Hawthorne's broken skin.

"I'll take the boat off autohelm," Walker said.

Ben nodded as Walker started for the cockpit. Smudges of blood marked the towel he held.

Hawthorne hadn't lost as much red juice as he'd thought. "What're you going to do now?" he asked with a shaky voice.

Ben faced the captive. "Nothing. Just wait, until we can verify your passwords."

"Then you'll let me go?"

Ben chuckled. "Sure."

Hawthorne frowned, and his head sagged. He started to wet himself and groaned. His head pounded from the blows to his jaw and the cold weather, and rule number one began to haunt him. *I'm going to be sleeping with the fishes.*

CHAPTER 31

Manhattan, New York

The phone rang next to Zara's head in the penthouse. She felt around the nightstand without opening her eyes and picked it up.

"Hello?" Zara mumbled, groggy.

"Hi, this is your wake-up call for 4:30 AM," a jubilant man said from the hotel's reception desk on the ground floor.

"Thanks," she drawled.

"You're welcome. Have a great day."

Zara attempted to hang up the phone but missed the base. The phone hit the nightstand and landed on the floor. She turned her head away from the table and continued to sleep on her stomach.

Kannada and Ricky had made their way into the ventilation system. It had four metal walls and a square cross-section. There was enough space to crawl. They tread prudently, though made loud clunks with every move, especially when they used their electromagnetic climbing clamps for vertical progress, until they reached the main trading floor's ceiling. As they wormed their way through the air duct, Kannada worried whether anybody heard them. He peered through a vent near a catwalk with Ricky and sighed; they hadn't set off any alarms.

The trading floor was deserted. The electronic communication networks were in full use in pre-market trading.

Kannada and Ricky spotted one male security guard standing near the entrance. They watched for a minute to see his pattern of movement.

Kannada inhaled dust from the surrounding walls. He covered his nose and mouth with his arm and sneezed. His cold was flaring up.

Ricky looked at him, then went back to viewing the security guard with Kannada.

"He's not even moving around," Ricky said. "What's he doing, taking a standing shit?"

Kannada sighed. Drops of sweat formed over his eyebrows; it was warm inside the ventilation system. "Where's the duffel bag?"

"Here." Ricky uncovered a bag underneath his jumpsuit.

Kannada opened the bag and held one type of small can. "Sleep agents . . ." He took another weapon out from the bag and said, "and EMP grenades. The electromagnetic pulse generated from the grenade should confuse the security cameras. It'll jam the electronic system, at least for a while."

"Oh, reminds me of video games."

Kannada smirked. "Where do you think I got the idea?"

"Yeah, good stuff."

"Yeah, love shooter games," Kannada said. "All right, anyway, we need to chunk this over there. Then we can get on the catwalk, then on the trading floor."

"Sounds like a plan."

"Give me the sleep agents."

Ricky gave them to him, then popped open the vent cover and held it in place to prevent its fall.

Kannada took out string from the accessory bag and tied it around a few canisters that contained sleeping gas. He lowered down the sleep agents via the string attached to them. The canisters landed on the ground level and dispersed gas into the trading floor.

Within minutes, the security guard yawned. Kannada looked at his watch and counted the seconds while he listened. Ricky peered through the vent. A few moments later, the guard hit the floor with a thud, incapacitated.

Iago walked into Zara's room. The phone rested on the floor and beeped. He picked it up and put it on its base.

He shook Zara's body by her shoulder. "Wake up, Zara."

Dilip leaned against the doorframe.

Iago stooped over the bed, and Zara opened her eyes while resting on the pillow. She turned her head around to face him. He receded.

"Didn't you set a wake-up call?" Iago asked.

Zara's eyes widened. She sat up immediately. "What time is it?"

"Relax. It's only five. You still have enough time to get ready."

"No, I don't." Zara started to rush to the bathroom. "I have to take a shower. I have to put on my face. I have to—" She was gone.

Iago looked at Dilip with parted lips.

He shrugged.

Kannada held a cold cylindrical canister, the EMP grenade. He took a deep breath. "Okay, I need to get this over there, in that chair." He unhooked its safety pin and threw it into the air with an arch onto the chair.

He pumped his fist softly; the grenade was heading toward the target. It bounced off the seat, landed with a thump on the computer desk at a terminal, and rolled around a bit before coming to a stop.

Kannada shook his head; they'd already made enough noise as it was crawling through the vent.

"Isn't it supposed to do something?" Ricky asked.

"Maybe the fall damaged it. Let's try another way." Kannada tied string around an EMP grenade, mimicked the same procedure to trigger the detonation, and gently lowered it down to the catwalk.

The EMP grenade touched the narrow walkway. Nothing happened.

Kannada stared at the canister intently with Ricky and sighed in frustration. "Just great. They're defective."

Zara had dyed her hair black and had finished her shower. She was preparing her appearance, matching her face to that of a taped picture of Veronica Reyes on the mirror. She contoured her face to achieve a narrow effect, powdered her cheeks a rosy hue, colored her mouth with Ferrari-red lipstick, attached a mole on her cheek between her nose and lips, tied her hair into a messy angular bun, put on a pair of warm hazel contacts, and wore cat eye glasses. She looked at Veronica, then back at herself, comparing the two. The mole was on the wrong side of Zara's face. Her posture deflated as she sighed. It was close enough.

She was dressed in a gray business suit and a blue trader jacket and wore a lanyard with Veronica Reyes' badge around her neck, just like Veronica Reyes.

In the dining room, Dilip heard a Taylor Swift song play from his phone.

Rob raised an eyebrow. "Nice ringtone."

Dilip smiled and nodded. "She's soothing." He answered the call and put it on speakerphone.

On the other end of the line, Kannada sounded panicky. "Looks like the Russians screwed us. The EMP grenades were nothingburgers. I need an alternative route to the trading floor."

Dilip was holding the phone near his face. "You get what you pay for. Hold on a second." He looked at Iago. "Get the schematic."

Iago brought the set of blueprints from a corner in the room and placed them on the table.

"Where're you now?" Dilip asked.

"I'm at the main trading floor, in the vent, by the catwalk near the entrance," Kannada responded.

"Okay, I've got the blueprints here. I think if I follow this, I can walk you through it. Can I put you on a different floor?"

"No, it has to be on this trading floor, where there're no cameras, if that's even possible. I need a badge to get into the trading floor otherwise, which I don't have."

Dilip searched the map, tracing different paths with his finger. "Wait a minute. I don't see an area with no cameras . . ."

Iago pointed to a small enclosure on the map.

Dilip continued, "Ahead of you, in the direction of the entrance, there should be an intersection. Go toward it."

He narrowed his eyes and listened carefully; the duct creaked and swayed in the background as Kannada and Ricky bellied to the open space where four passageways met.

"I'm there," Kannada said.

"Can't you crawl quieter?"

"We're trying our best."

Dilip shook his head. "Turn left. After maybe thirty or forty feet, you'll come to a T-junction. Take a right."

"Come on. Just have him use the crawl space." Iago sounded hasty.

"Just a second. I understand how to read a map." Dilip wanted to be a part of this as much as him.

Kannada crept along with Ricky. "Okay, going right . . . okay . . . dammit! Dead end. It goes up from here."

"Uh . . . wait a second. Wait a second." Dilip squished his brows together. His old age was kicking in. "There should've been a left back there somewhere."

Iago signaled for the phone; Dilip gave it up.

The hacker held the phone near his face. "Kannada, retrace your steps to the elevator shaft. Climb up the ladder; there should be a small opening in which you can get into the crawl space."

Crawl space? Kannada and the gang had overlooked this option when viewing the map for a route to the trading floor. He craned his neck toward the back. "Hey, we got to go back to the elevator."

Ricky sighed. "Fuck!" He started to crawl in reverse.

Traveling at a slower pace than before and being more skilled the second time around, they made less noise in the ventilation system. Several minutes passed until they reached the crawl space, a dark, shallow unfinished space under the roof with pipes and wiring. They ducked their heads and squatted.

"Okay, we're in the crawl space," Kannada said over the phone.

"You can walk in either direction," Iago directed. "There's an exit point on the other side of the building from which you can get back into the air duct."

Kannada and Ricky started to lumber side by side. A rat crossed their path, and Ricky screamed and bumped his head on the low ceiling. Kannada widened his eyes, and his heart fluttered. Ricky's sudden outburst startled him more than the rat.

Ricky hyperventilated and rubbed his head, then moved his hand to his chest. "Oh God, oh God." He fanned himself with the other hand.

Kannada tilted his head and pursed his lips. *Hopefully, nobody heard him.*

"Rats in the NYSE?" Ricky sounded confused.

"It's New York. What'd you expect?" Kannada continued onward.

"Wait!" Ricky bristled. "If you leave me, I will hunt you down and kill you."

Kannada stopped and sighed. He waited for Ricky to recover, about thirty seconds, then resumed business. They encountered a few rats along the way, and Ricky handled them with squeaks. They exited the crawl space and emptied into an air duct.

"We're on the opposite side. I just saw the trading floor through a vent," Kannada said.

Dilip snatched the phone and his command back. "Good. Keep going now. You'll get to a T-junction. Go right."

Kannada kept moving. "Turned right, following your directions. Okay, the passageway narrows. Could you guys keep talking to me? How much longer do we have?"

Iago yanked the phone away from Dilip. "You're almost there, another twenty feet. You'll fit, right?"

Kannada chuckled. "Yeah, we'll fit."

Dilip was annoyed yet mature enough to let it go and not show his dissatisfaction. Proper, succinct, directions were a young man's game, he figured.

Kannada continued along fast, Ricky not far behind, and followed the duct to the end of the corridor where he saw a grid-like frame below him and a passage above him.

"Look for a vent opening below you," Iago said.

"Okay, I see the vent grid."

"Open it."

Kannada opened the vent and looked around—mops, wash buckets and basins, trash cans, vacuums, a floor waxing machine, and a stench. He was above the janitor's room. He paused to appreciate their fortune; they had found another way to get into the trading floor. He was also pleased that they would no longer have to deal with hot, dirty, confined spaces.

He dropped down quietly, grabbed a ladder in the room, and helped Ricky descend, careful of his sore ankle.

They stretched, then looked at each other; debris covered them. As they dusted themselves off, Kannada sneezed into his arm. He pinched his nose and scrunched up his face.

Ricky shook his head. "That's the second time."

Kannada shrugged. "Okay, I'm down," he said on the phone. "Are there cameras outside the room?"

"No," Iago replied. "You're in a small crevice of the trading floor. The restrooms are next to you."

"Okay. We can take it from here." He hung up.

Kannada and Ricky stripped out of their robber gear, black jumpsuits, gloves, and beanies, and revealed the clothes underneath, dress attire and trader jackets, somewhat wrinkled with creases from all the twisting and turning in the maze-like ventilation system. They took out the spray bottle and two-way radio from their accessory bag, then stuffed their two bags and robber gear into a garbage bag and dumped it in a trash can.

Zara took a deep breath, hoping she resembled her alias, then appeared in the dining area of the penthouse, where she met Rob, Dilip, Iago, and Paul peering over blueprints.

"How do I look?" she asked.

The four men turned to face her. Rob and Paul stared, their mouths agape, their brows raised. Dilip and Iago glanced at her, then looked away.

"Ms. Veronica Reyes," Paul commented, finally.

"Perfect," Rob remarked.

Zara smiled.

"All right," Rob said. "It's straightforward. When you get into the NYSE, scan the backside of your badge. Don't make any eye contact with the security guards. Just keep going, as if you were in a rush."

"They're all in a rush," Dilip interrupted. "You'll fit right in."

Rob continued, "You'll have to scan again into the trading floor. This is the floor you want to go to." He pointed to the designated area on a diagram of the building. "It's the main floor. Same process, don't make eye contact. Then, you'll get a text message from Ben. He'll give you the password to log into the computer."

"Reset daily." Dilip coughed.

Rob took over. "Then, when you're on the computer, log into our account and dump—that is, sell—all of the FriendBin shares you have. There'll be millions of shares. Get rid of all of them with a market order. Not a limit."

Dilip butted in again. "That's the order type." He took a cough drop.

"How come we can't do it here?" Zara asked.

Dilip shifted the throat lozenge to the side of his mouth. "It's too many shares, institutional level. That's why."

"Then get the hell out of there," Rob commanded. "Got it?"

"Got it." Zara nodded.

"Don't talk to strangers, either," Dilip cautioned.

Zara chortled at Dilip's comprehension of her flirtatious ways.

Lower Bay, New York

Ben and Walker had drifted into the region between Sandy Hook, New Jersey and Brighton Beach, approximately twenty miles away from 11 Wall Street. They'd been in the wintery waters for a few hours now. They were seated, playing a game of chess at a table in front of Hawthorne, passing the time until the market opened.

Ben noticed a misty fog encircle them during sunrise; then he readdressed the game board.

Hawthorne was wrapped in comforters and allowed to have hot chocolate. He sipped his mug occasionally while his captors duked it out in the two-player strategy game.

"You play chess, Hawthorne?" Ben moved his queen into position.

"Not since college. Used to play."

Walker stroked his chin with his hand; he gave Ben the impression he was deciphering the move's implications.

"How come no more?" Ben asked.

"Busy with work," Hawthorne replied. "My girlfriend."

Walker hovered his rook over one of the squares on the chessboard. He put it down, waited a moment, and let go of his chess piece.

Ben stared at the game board and examined Walker's advance. He made a move with his queen, again. "Checkmate."

Walker tipped his head to the side and stared for a moment, comprehending the move. His countenance said *Is it really checkmate?* "That's one-to-one. We need a tiebreaker. One more?" He sipped hot chocolate from an insulated stainless steel bottle.

Ben checked his watch, 7:00 in the morning. "I guess we have time for one more."

As Ben looked up, he noticed something wrap its wet arm, or tentacle, around the port side of the boat across from him through the heavy mist. His face turned serious.

Walker seemed to notice Ben's demeanor, put his bottle down, and turned around.

In his periphery, Ben saw Hawthorne look to the side as well.

A second tentacle came up and gripped the side rail. The object pulled itself up. It was a person, a recognizable person. Its face appeared over the rail. It was a man. It was Alan McGill.

"Alan?" Ben cried, worried.

Ben and Walker rushed to his aid and pulled him out of the frigid sea.

"What're you doing, joining the Polar Bear Club?" Ben said to Alan.

Cold as ice, Alan shivered. His lips and fingers had turned blue, and his face, pale. His skin was blotched with red lesions, and his ears, nose, and hands were swollen. Ben reasoned the only things that'd kept him alive in the freezing ocean were the body heat generated from his swimming, his flight suit, and his ferocious will to survive. Alan didn't say a word. Ben realized he couldn't.

Ben addressed Walker. "He needs warm clothes."

They looked at Hawthorne and the comforters he was utilizing.

Hawthorne rolled his eyes. "Just when I was beginning to like you guys."

Ben and Walker took Alan into the cockpit, denuded him, wrapped him with the comforters that Hawthorne had been using, and gave him a cup full of hot chocolate.

CHAPTER 32

Manhattan, New York

The door to a janitor's closet in the corner of a trading floor at the NYSE opened slightly. Kannada peered through the opening. Likewise, Ricky looked at the outside traffic, his head just above Kannada's. The passageway was empty.

Kannada checked his watch. It was 7:30 AM, two hours before U.S. markets opened for regular trading.

Kannada and Ricky had time to kill. They went to the adjacent men's restroom, their hideout, and filled the stalls.

"Veronica Reyes" and "Diego Sanchez," Iago's alias since he'd been hired to consummate bug bounties, prepared to leave the townhome, on their way to the NYSE. Rob, Paul, and Dilip stood in the living area, watching.

Rob, wearing a navy blue robe and slippers, was weary, having pulled an all-nighter. He leaned against a sofa with his arms crossed and sipped caffeinated coffee from a mug.

"Badge?" Iago said to Zara.

She flashed her badge for him to see. "Check."

"What's the first thing you do when you get there?"

"Read the news on my tablet. Pretend I'm busy."

Iago nodded. "See you guys at lunchtime," he said to the rest of the group at the apartment.

"Wish me luck," Zara said.

"Bye." Rob smiled; he was glad that things had worked out so far because he was paying for the operation.

"Good luck." Paul waved.

Dilip slipped on his suit jacket, unable to neglect his duties. "Hold on, I'm leaving, too."

He was going to work as the Securities and Exchange Commission's Regional Director at the SEC's New York office at 3 World Financial Center, a couple of blocks away from the NYSE building. He took out a comb from his coat's inner pocket and started to arrange his salt-and-pepper hair.

The door to the group's penthouse closed with Rob and Paul left behind.

"You think we should pray for them?" Paul asked.

Rob sighed, tired of unanswered prayers. "You think I want to waste my time?"

Charles Frasier, a well-dressed trader who worked the Big Board, rushed into the bathroom near the janitor's closet. His footsteps echoed. He ducked his head and looked under the first stall; it was occupied. He walked farther and looked under the second stall; it was also occupied.

Frasier snapped his fingers. "Shoot. Every time I have to take a shit."

The back of his pants bulged, and a look of horror marked his face. He put his hand on his butt to prevent the accident and hurried out of the lavatory in search of another stall where he could unload himself.

Iago and Zara reached the back entrance to the NYSE, at the intersection of New Street and Wall Street. Zara stood in line behind her accomplice and noticed the guards.

Security seemed lackadaisical, leaning back in their seats. The guards performed the same monotonous task, watching the same monitors, all day, every day. If someone were to sneak in under a disguise, they most likely wouldn't notice, especially during rush hour, unless there was a major difference between the entry person and the image that showed on their screens, which flipped continuously, almost to a blur, according to Kannada's reconnaissance. Zara reasoned that was exactly how he had made it into the Big Board a week prior.

They scanned their badges swiftly, one after another. Despite being warned to not make eye contact, Zara peeked at security as several workers passed through the turnstiles.

A security guard studying the monitors opened his mouth. Zara gasped, looked away, and suddenly felt warm. She faced forward, but her eyes crept to the side to see if she had been caught. The guard's cheeks swelled, and he blew out air.

Zara smiled—she made it. *One down, one to go.* She and Iago went through the turnstiles and blended in with the other workers by walking quickly to the bank of elevators ahead.

Bennet Rothschild, another well-dressed, dapper-looking trader, entered the trading floor bathroom. His footsteps echoed as he walked to the sink. He checked his appearance in the mirror and adjusted his brown hair.

"About thirteen inches." The words sounded like they came from a straight male.

The newcomer glanced at the stall from where the voice came but paid little attention.

"How big is yours?" the straight male asked.

"Ten inches." The pitch sounded gay.

Rothschild's face grew disgusted as he made sense of the ongoing conversation.

"That's too small," the straight male commented.

Rothschild started shaking his head in repulsion.

"Well, it's still worth the view," the gay man said.

Rothschild was utterly startled by the lack of taste shown by the two stall users. He'd had enough. "This is a workplace, you know," he yelled as he charged out of the bathroom.

In his confined space, Kannada furrowed his brows and tilted his head to the side. *What's wrong with talking in the restroom? Is there a rule here that says you can't?* He looked toward Ricky's stall. "What's your laptop's resolution?"

* * *

Veronica was ready to go to work. She put on a thick mink coat and buttoned it down, then grabbed the final accessory to her wardrobe, her purse. She unlocked the deadbolts on her door and opened it. A wooden wall impeded her progress. She couldn't leave, at least not so quickly.

What's this? Her eyes wandered about the wall, and her blank face wore a frown. She rushed to her landline home phone and dialed the number of the maintenance office. Veronica leaned on her left leg, put her left hand on her waist, and sighed, as she waited for someone to come on the line.

"Yes, this is Veronica Reyes in room 123. Why's my door blocked off this morning?"

Zara scanned her badge a second time, just outside the trading floor. She made no eye contact with security and continued.

"Ma'am," a male security guard called.

Zara wobbled on her heels, her eyes dilated, and her stomach flipped upside down. Her heart never had beat this hard, not even during sex with johns. The entrance to the trading floor, a few feet away, suddenly seemed miles apart from her. She slowly turned around and gulped, unprepared for the interrogation and her arrest.

The guard pointed with his eyes. "Did you drop that?"

Zara saw a tube of lipstick on the floor. She sighed, and feeling started to return to her legs. "Oh, no." She half-smiled as her hand flew to her chest. *Ben would've killed me.* She spun around, walked in, stopped, and gaped. It was her first time in the New York Stock Exchange, on the main trading floor, a modern marvel.

Housing computers, wires, and round trading terminals, the NYSE carried a distinct aura. Slips of paper scattered the floor as in mosaic prose; symbols accompanied by numbers of unique shapes, sizes, and colors decorated screens and tickers; and men and women in suits and uniforms scurried in madness. This was what fueled the city, what fed the country, and what established America as a global leader.

This was the most important thing she'd ever been assigned to do. Her resume was filled with "time and companionship" experiences, nothing to be thought of seriously, nor respected by most people. She inhaled the fragrance of money, perhaps ambient scenting, and continued onward.

Iago entered his office in the NYSE building, ready to get to work. There was a large pile of files on his desk, waiting to be addressed.

The co-worker who sat across from him, another hacker-type, hadn't arrived yet. Iago took advantage of the situation by passing the buck. He opened a drawer, took out an already-prepared sticky note, which read, "Needs to be taken care of ASAP. Give to Diego for final review. Thanks, DuPont," and stuck it on the file. He glanced around, then placed the file on the hacker's desk across from him.

He opened a bag of Cheetos, stuffed a few into his mouth, and began to put the finishing touches on the program he'd been working on in secret for the group.

Lemon's watch beeped; the time was 9:00 AM. Lemon, followed by three other men in suits, two on his right, one on his left, entered the large boardroom on the sixth floor to greet FriendBin's executives, right on cue. "Welcome, welcome, ladies and gentlemen, to the New York Stock Exchange."

Lemon and his top executives at the NYSE shook hands with FriendBin's leaders and congratulated them personally. Shortly after that, Lemon gave a lengthy introduction to the Big Board, a bit of history mixed in with the magnitude of their accomplishment. During his speech, the company's team indulged in a few breakfast items that were on a table at the end of the room: milk, coffee, apple juice, French toast, fresh fruit, muffins, potatoes, scrambled eggs, sausage, and pancakes with syrup.

Iago noticed the co-worker who sat across from him arrive.

The overweight, scruffy-haired, dirty blond hacker wore thick purple-rimmed glasses and carried a leather satchel and cup of smoking hot coffee. He placed his coffee cup and shoulder bag on his desk and observed the stack of files and the sticky note. "Shit."

Iago kept his devious smile on the inside as he maintained a foolproof poker face and worked on his personal program.

Kannada stood in the restroom near the sinks with Ricky and tried to call Ben. "I can't get reception in here. I'm going to have to go outside."

The two of them left the lavatory and walked down a hallway on the floor above the primary trading floor.

On one end, a few people were hunched over a gaudy metal railing talking to each other or on their phones as they overlooked the main trading floor. Ricky blended in with them.

On the opposite end, large tinted glass reached high to the ceiling, outside of which were the iconic colonnades of 11 Wall Street. Near the bottom of the stained glass were several sets of double glass doors.

Kannada stepped outside onto a balcony two stories above ground level and leaned on the metal railing between two tall stone columns. His eyes widened, as a wind tunnel destroyed hairdos and caused pedestrians to stagger across snow-covered Broad Street to lampposts for support. He comfortably made his phone call.

Lower Bay, New York

On Rob's boat, in the cockpit, Ben felt his phone vibrate in his pocket. He picked it up. "Hello? . . . Hello?" He looked at his phone. The screen was blank. He sighed. "I think my phone just went out. Let me see yours," he said to Walker.

Walker took out his phone and glanced at it. He slowly looked up, mouth agape. "It's dead, too."

Ben stared at him. His worst fears were being realized; they couldn't communicate with Kannada at the Big Board.

Walker turned his head to the side and looked through the cockpit's windshield. Ben followed his eyes and noticed Hawthorne clearly amid minimal fog.

"Try his," Walker suggested, deep-toned.

Ben checked Hawthorne's phone. "It's still good, but the battery's running low. We still need it for the password. Now, what?"

Manhattan, New York

As Zara weaved her way through several workers to get to her station on the trading floor, she saw Ricky standing above her in the distance. He spotted her, too, and waved, his fingers together, moving up and down, like a hinge on the heart line of his palm. She smiled and motioned similarly.

A trader on the floor mistakenly waved to her as well.

Zara recognized this was a prime opportunity for an interested male to acknowledge a pretty girl. She didn't want to bring attention to herself, so she ignored him.

The trader turned around and looked up toward the balcony where Ricky stood. He shook his head in defeat and went back to his post.

She reached her trading post and took out her tablet, flipped to a news article, and pretended to be consumed by it.

Lower Bay, New York

In the cockpit, Walker furrowed his brows. "What about the two-way?" He sounded worried.

"Let's see." Ben swallowed as he tried to reach Kannada at the Big Board using the two-way radio. His eyes held a glimmer of hope, and his heart beat hard enough to give the transceiver life. "Dammit!" He slammed his fist on the dashboard and almost knocked over the bottle of champagne. "We're probably out of range. These things say thirty miles, but that's only under ideal conditions."

"What's wrong?" Alan's teeth chattered with the cold. He spoke his first words since coming on board, and his skin had regained some color.

"The phones are out; won't turn back on. The two-way is too far away." Ben clenched his jaw.

"Maybe they're not out." Alan sounded shaky. "Maybe it's the batteries. It happens in the Canyon all the time. They don't last long in cold weather, and the battery meter becomes inaccurate. The phone will shut off suddenly and not turn back on, but if you warm it up, it should continue operating as usual."

Ben stared for a moment; he couldn't believe what he had just heard. Something mysterious in the night sky had looked out for them; if Alan hadn't come on board, they would've been doomed. His eyes regained their poise, and his frustrated face broke into a smirk. "Kind of like you?"

Alan smiled and nodded, holding a mug of hot chocolate.

Ben and Walker tried to warm up all the phones in their possession. They had only fifteen minutes until the opening bell.

Manhattan, New York

Veronica stood behind the door to apartment 123 with her arms crossed and shook her head. She listened to a worker remove nails on the wooden wall that blocked her doorway. Her blood boiled, and she envisioned telling management off. Light from the hallway seeped in through the peephole.

Veronica swung her door open as someone rang the doorbell. She stepped out and restrained her rage; three idiots, a police officer, the super, and a maintenance guy, surrounded her. She glanced at the wooden piece that had been placed next to the entry and rummaged in her purse for her keys.

"Everything's set, ma'am," the super said. "I'm not sure how your room got boarded up, but I apologize."

"You don't know?" She foamed at the mouth. "Of course, you don't. Move. I have to be at the NYSE." She whipped out her keys.

"The officer would like to ask you a few questions."

Veronica sighed. Her eyes darted from the super to the officer with disapproval. She locked her door and started to leave. "Stop by later. I don't have time for this."

"Ms. Reyes, I insist you answer a few questions," the cop ordered.

That stopped Veronica dead in her tracks. She quickly answered his questions, then stormed off to work, her eyes watery.

Lower Bay, New York

Walker checked his watch, then glanced up at Ben. "It's nine twenty-one. You think we should try them now?"

Ben nodded, picked up his phone, and turned it on. He waited one slow, enervating minute, hoping for the best. His face lit up with glee, and he smiled. "It works, forty percent." With new life, he started to text the two passwords in his possession to Kannada and Ricky.

Manhattan, New York

Kannada viewed his phone, then his two-way, with a furrowed brow as the wind howled in the architectural landscape. Neither device could reach Ben and Walker on the boat. He looked up at the sky for a sign as sunrays showered the NYSE, then turned to go inside the Exchange, staring down at his phone. He stopped suddenly, startled. Someone stood before him.

CHAPTER 33

Manhattan, New York

Kannada sighed upon seeing Zara on the balcony, and his muscles relaxed. "Don't do that."

She smiled and stood under one of many sunrays.

"I think you should go to your post." He headed for the door, focused.

"Kannada, I'm sorry."

He stood adjacent to her and craned his neck. "Now's not the time."

"I know, but all we can do is wait. Can we talk?"

Kannada stayed silent.

"I'll be leaving tomorrow, and you'll be rid of me." Zara stepped back to be in front of him. "I'd like to see you again. We can stay at a hotel, get dinner, and shop." She held his hand and tilted her chin down.

"Then what? You'll be gone when I wake up? I don't buy sex." He retracted his hand and disregarded her inviting sea green eyes.

"It wouldn't be like that."

"Then how?"

"Kannada, what do you want?"

He remained unresponsive, thinking of the right words to express himself.

Zara searched his eyes. "What'd you think would happen between us?"

"I don't know." Kannada sighed and turned around. He put his hands on the cold rails and looked over the balcony. "When I was living in the streets, most people ignored me, some laughed, and even less provided something, maybe a few coins, a few dollars, whatever they could, given their situation.

"But one time a couple shared a meal with me and gave me some company. I watched them walk away and hug each other before separating. That's when I realized I needed affection more than money. Surviving on the streets . . . is very lonely."

The door to the balcony clicked, as someone opened it. He turned around swiftly and noticed Ricky, his head popped out.

"Ben just texted me the passwords. It's 9:24," Ricky said.

Zara never turned around; she continued to face Kannada. She looked down and away. "He'll be in soon."

She was suddenly calling the shots. Ricky looked at Kannada as if he expected him to say something in return. Kannada met Ricky's stare but hesitated.

"Better listen to the boss, Kannada." Ricky smiled.

Kannada smiled crookedly, and Ricky went back inside.

Zara went in to hug Kannada, but he pushed her forearms down, his eyes unforgiving. She swallowed, looking at his chest, then met his cold stare. "I want you to know that I understand everything you said. And I do care. Some people fall in love with each other but aren't supposed to be together. It's normal for people to have feelings for me in my profession, but I'm not real. My history, the way I live . . . Amara would be better for you. I'm—"

"She would." Kannada said it like he meant it, but his heart sank. *How can Zara be so self-centered?* He clenched his fists, pursed his lips, and narrowed his eyes, disappointed.

Zara stared and finished her sentence. "I'm just . . . a wreck."

"That's too bad." He looked at her with affection one last time, then tried to sever his feelings for her. "It was good while it lasted, though you took advantage of me." He twisted his mouth to the side, bitter, and pierced the hooker's double-dealing soul with his gaze.

"I never played you." She furrowed her brows. "What was I supposed to do? You're hung up on her."

Kannada gave her the cold shoulder as ruthless, bleak wind blew behind him. He walked back into the Exchange and left Zara on the balcony by herself.

In the offices of Morgan Sachs, the institutional bank underwriting FriendBin's initial public offering, Kate Hollingsworth took a breather from her work and watched business professionals scour over paperwork and computers. The underwriters looked at all the subscription requests and decided how to allocate the shares to their clients, the institutional investors.

The day before FriendBin's public offering, Kate received a phone call from the company. The corporation set its IPO price at $33 for its institutional investors. She gazed in awe at the amount FriendBin would raise from the offering, $6.6 billion.

Kate came across the Lemon Group account on her monitor and moved the pointer over a link that read, "Allocate the shares." Once a member of the team, now the leader, she hesitated in clicking the button on her mouse. She didn't handle IPOs every day. Her experience with them topped out in the millions. She sighed. Everything had to be perfect. If anything went wrong, it would be her fault. Her stellar resume, years in the making, would lose its brilliance, and demotion would follow.

She took a deep breath, mustered the required courage, and allocated 1.19% of the total two hundred million shares outstanding, or 2.38 million shares, to her client. Lemon's shares were valued at $78,540,000. Her worries started to dissipate, and her stern face cracked a smile; she did it.

Kannada sighed on the trading floor; Zara crossed his mind, but he couldn't let rejection get in the way now. He checked his watch; the time was 9:26 AM. Within seconds, his body temperature rose, his lungs required more air than the room had to provide, and his palms became sweaty. He never felt so alive; the next few hours would determine his life, as well as every accomplice's. He looked up and saw Lemon come out on the balcony with FriendBin's executive team.

Ricky was on the trading floor, too, not far behind.

Kannada moved toward a Lemon Group trader who was busy looking at his tablet. He took out his phone, covered his mouth with his hand, and furtively spoke into the phone. "I got something for you." The trader craned his neck to the right, and Kannada continued to fake a conversation. "You didn't hear this from me, but UBT is about to acquire Milton Companies today. Pump it."

The trader suddenly paused what he was doing and stared ahead, activated. He rushed to the monitor directly across from him and acted on the insider information that Paul had overheard at the Dead Rabbit, buying millions of shares of Milton Companies.

Kannada raised an eyebrow, surprised that the trader took the bait, and smirked.

Ricky wetted his face and neck with water using the spray bottle from the accessory bag, away from people's view, before staggering to the Lemon Group trading terminal and feigning a heart attack. Under the façade, he was giddy with delight; this was a live performance. He imagined acting on Broadway with naysayers in the crowd; he had to prove them wrong.

Ricky clenched his left breast with one hand while trying to find something to hold onto with the other. He visibly made the impression he was under duress, sweating and lightheaded. He tightened his upper body and became zombie-like. He used his free hand to grab a trader's shoulder. "Help . . . burning."

The trader and a few others surrounding him gaped and temporarily stopped their work.

"Call 9-1-1," the trader yelled amid a noisy room. "Anyone know CPR?"

Ricky was dragging the trader down with him with one hand and clasping his heart with the other.

Another nearby trader urgently stooped low and caught Ricky before he hit the ground. "That's the second one this week."

While Ricky was doing his best Red Foxx, *Sanford and Son*, "I'm coming, Elizabeth!" heart attack act, Kannada approached a computer behind the traders and began his work. He tried to log into the computer using the previous day's password given to him by Ben but failed on his first attempt. The flow of blood to his heart nearly stopped. *Do I have the right password?* His fingers were trembling, and he repeatedly opened and closed his hands to restore feeling in them. He took a deep breath. *Take it slow; you have time.*

Kannada's second attempt was successful; he sighed. Then he logged into Lemon's account with the other password. The FriendBin shares were there. He transferred them to the group's account at Barney Trade, Inc., deleted the confirmation email, and smiled. He was done, free to leave, except there was one minor issue. A trader was standing over him.

Paul and Rob were at the penthouse watching *Trade Time*, a live Market Choice (MC) news broadcast. The show's set stood at one end of the primary trading floor of the NYSE, with the floor in the background. An anchorman and anchorwoman were interviewing a *New York Times* best-selling author, a professor of financial mathematics, and the head of another exchange, the NASDAQ, according to the labels at the bottom of the screen.

Rob yawned with droopy eyelids as he slouched on a sofa; he needed more coffee but was too lazy to get up and go to the kitchen.

"Hey, look! That's Zara." Paul sounded excited. He pointed out a woman in the background on screen.

Rob squinted. "It is not."

"It's the back of her head. You want to make a bet?"

Rob shrugged. "Eh, I don't like to gamble."

Paul narrowed his eyes and shook his head slightly. They continued to watch the talking heads.

"Do you believe the markets are rigged?" the anchorman asked the author.

Rob moved to the edge of his seat, his elbows on his knees, his fingers interlaced. This was a hot-button topic worth watching. Debates on whether the stock market was rigged or not had been going on for years, especially with the advent of high-frequency trading. Nothing interested financial industry experts more than this question.

"Yes," the author replied. "There's no other explanation."

The anchorman looked at the professor. "And you?"

The professor cleared his throat. "Well, Larry, given the gravity of the situation and the full spectrum of data available to investors, when I look over the horizon to determine the triumphant response, we actually need to go beyond the charts and technical analysis, fundamentals, which introduce a series of limitations to the average investor due to their widespread accessibility, and—"

"Hold on, hold on." The anchorman took off his tortoiseshell glasses and rubbed his eyelids and brows with his thumb and fingers.

Rob scratched his dark brown, curly hair, and his mouth fell open. *English, please.*

The anchorman put his glasses back on. "In 'Dishonest Gains,' published in the *Journal of Financial Mathematics*, you state, 'I know the markets are rigged.'"

The anchorwoman tilted her head to the side and raised her eyebrows. "You are quoted as saying that."

The professor smacked his lips. "Well, in order to accurately express my concern, we should focus on the servers and networks and their integration of fundamentals, starting with the multitasking, multiuser input system, which has been configured to predict the interaction an investor has with the markets. If we innovate here and incorporate new technology, we can stop the market interface from mapping user activity and capitalizing on user data. Then—"

The anchorman slashed the air with his hands and cut the professor off again, shrewdly. "Cut the technobabble; is the market rigged or not?"

Thank you. Rob smirked.

The professor adjusted his glasses. "I have to say that you're a little out of space, but the markets are rigged."

The President of NASDAQ frowned. "Oh, please, the markets aren't rigged any more than carnival games."

The author pointed at the leader of NASDAQ. "I've done my research, and in my book, *Getting High on HFTs*, I detail exactly how the markets are rigged."

The anchorman intervened. "And how's that?"

The author raised his hands, palms up. "It's the quants! All this algorithmic trading."

The professor nodded.

Meanwhile, the leader of NASDAQ shook his head. "It's a bogus claim to bring attention to yourself and sell your book. The markets have been around for centuries."

"But not computerized trading." The author pointed to the Ph.D. "And what about the professor here?"

"Publish or perish," the NASDAQ leader scoffed.

Rob grinned; he stayed awake and watched.

* * *

Kannada swallowed and perspired as he stared at the trader standing over him. His heartbeat accelerated, and his legs almost gave way. *What do I do now?* He needed nothing short of a miracle. He heard the *Trade Time* debate and looked at the television screen above. "It's rigged."

The trader glanced up, too. He was distracted for the moment; divine providence.

Kannada wiped the sweat off his forehead with the back of his hand. *Was that close, or what?* He looked over to Ricky; he was lying on the floor with a broker over him performing CPR.

The broker opened Ricky's airway using the head-tilt, chin-lift maneuver. He checked for normal breathing. Ricky appeared to hold his breath. The broker went in for mouth-to-mouth resuscitation and gave him two rescue breaths.

Ricky smiled wide when the broker finished breathing into him. With his recent dating history, that was the closest thing to a kiss Ricky had in a while.

Kannada sighed, rolled his eyes, and walked away.

Lower Bay, New York

Hawthorne's phone vibrated on a table in the cockpit at 9:29 AM with a new text message from the NYSE. Ben viewed the message; it held the password to the computers on the trading floor for the next twenty-four hours. He texted Zara the password, then looked out the window and sighed. He smiled and glanced at the accomplices on board. "We're done."

Alan yelled in excitement. Walker popped the cork on the champagne, poured two glasses, and gave the bottle to Alan.

Manhattan, New York

A floor broker tapped a trader's arm. "Hey, look," he said to Bennet Rothschild. "There she is."

Rothschild turned in the direction he was advised. He saw a woman with black hair, cat eye glasses, and a light, rosy complexion viewing a tablet. "Not bad."

"She's all yours," the floor broker said. "You better trade ahead before someone else gets to her."

Rothschild, a young bachelor, coolly brushed the side of his brown hair with his hand as he approached the woman with exaggerated swagger. "Hey, Veronica, how's it going?"

The woman stared ahead. She slowly turned to face him, glanced at the name tag on his lanyard, and looked up. "Great, and you?"

"Not too bad myself." He scrutinized her facial features, especially her mole. Her voice sounded breathy, in contrast to her usual plummy tone. "You look . . . different today."

The woman swallowed. "What're you saying, I don't look good?"

"Oh, no, no." Rothschild raised his brows and put his hand on her shoulder. "You look great. Wonderful." He smiled and winked, but he couldn't get over her voice. *Leave it. You're already in hot water.* "Rough weather, huh?"

She cleared her throat. "Yeah," she said slowly. "I think I'm getting a cold."

"Yeah, you sound a little different today."

David Lemon, Chairman and CEO of the NYSE, clapped on the Mussolini-like balcony with FriendBin's corporate management team across from the MC set below him, as the opening bell rang with the pressing of a green button at 9:30 AM sharp.

The bell was the crowning spectacle that normally made heads turn from screens chock full of numbers and symbols to the balcony, but not today. Floor workers hardly noticed, so ensconced were they with whatever ran on the monitors and televisions.

Lemon ignored the less-than-welcome reception and continued applauding and celebrating the moment. Behind him and his corporate guests was a large banner that displayed FriendBin's company logo. In front of them, attached to the balusters of the balcony, were three digital signs. The left-most read, "FriendBin." The middle read the date. The right-most read, "FBN LISTED NYSE," from top to bottom.

FriendBin's shares could be officially traded on the public market starting now. Orders from all over the world came into the NYSE, from both institutional and retail investors. Each order was either a bid, "I want to buy FBN," or an offer, "I want to sell FBN."

The designated market maker, or specialist, working for Morgan Sachs on the trading floor on behalf of FriendBin, swiped his blond hair out of his eyes and pushed up his tortoiseshell glasses while he viewed all the bids and offers in the electronic order book. He gauged the buy and sell sides by entering one price point after another. Taking a glance at the first numbers appearing, the specialist reported the prevailing price might be in the $36 to $40 range. Standing next to him was the underwriter's lead trader; he relayed real-time data to Kate Hollingsworth over the phone.

The monitors around the specialist showed every business news media outlet except MC report this interval. MC, which was ensnared in an epic battle to settle the un-settle-able on *Trade Time*, opted to run it in a side screenshot for its television viewers.

Veronica entered the Big Board at the intersection of New Street and Wall Street. She checked her watch; to her surprise, she arrived three-quarters of an hour earlier than expected after being barricaded in her apartment. She scanned her badge into the system and pushed the turnstile. She was denied. She scanned again. She was denied again.

"Ma'am," a man said.

Veronica looked up. A tall security guard signaled her to come over to him with his hand. She approached.

"Let me see your badge," he requested.

"It's probably not activated yet." She held her badge, affixed to the lanyard. "Somebody told me that it would be ready around this time, but it may not work right away."

He narrowed his eyes, squished his eyebrows together, and tilted his head. "Who told you that?"

"Some guy who works in security. His name was Sergio, I think."

The security guard held her badge while it was attached to her lanyard and stared at it. "Hmm. Why's that?"

"He said that some identities had been compromised. So, he gave me this new badge yesterday."

"Hey, Ron," the security guard said to a muscular officer reclining in a chair. "Did you hear about some identities being stolen?"

Ron shook his head. "Nope."

"Can I see your badge, ma'am?" the first security guard asked.

She nodded and took off her lanyard, holding her badge.

The guard examined it, front and back, with a furrowed forehead. "I need some ID."

Veronica sifted through her purse and retrieved her license.

He held the two items side by side and compared them, then picked up the phone and appeared to call security upstairs. "Hey, I have a Veronica Reyes here, says she was issued a new badge yesterday. It doesn't work . . . Yeah, I'll hold."

Veronica crossed her arms; she had to wait.

Zara laughed with the trader who had approached her moments ago. She was relieved that she hadn't been caught red-handed. When she regained composure, Rothschild made his move.

"My weekend's open. What about you? Do you have any plans?"

Before she responded, through a small aperture in the pool of workers who were scrambling everywhere, Zara noticed Kannada standing with crossed arms, staring at her. His displeased countenance gave her the impression he was ready to blow steam. She was off task, and she knew it. She addressed the trader once more. "My boyfriend and I are going to the movies."

Rothschild stared incredulously and shuffled back a step or two. He went from being steps to miles away from scoring a date thanks to rebuttal. He nodded and retreated. "I gotta take care of some work." He hung his head as he returned to his workstation.

The specialist for Morgan Sachs worked fast to set an opening price. He was attempting to balance supply and demand as much as possible, a process coined by financial gurus as price discovery.

The underwriter's lead trader leaned toward him and kept one ear to the phone. "Discover a price yet?"

"Thirty-eight dollars," the specialist reported, surrounded by individuals that pressed him to work quickly. "I'm freezing the books."

After deciding an opening price of $38, he froze the books; in other words, he blocked any new electronic orders from coming in.

The underwriter's lead trader relayed the information to the office of Morgan Sachs over the phone, then turned to the specialist. "Kate says open the stock at 10:20."

Zara checked her phone and witnessed the new daily password. She quickly logged into the computer and the group's account at Barney Trade, Inc. She put in her order to dump the newly acquired position in FriendBin, all 2.38 million shares at an elevated stock price.

Within seconds, the trading floor erupted as workers noticed the large number of shares that were sold, triggering a domino effect. A massive selloff of FriendBin's shares ensued with virgin retail investors across the globe growing anxious to sell their positions. Zara quickly learned that human emotion drove the stock prices, second by second.

Her brow furrowed, as hand signals made a temporary return. Traders and brokers pushed their open hands away from their bodies, which was followed by corresponding numerals made with the hands, palm facing out near the face. One, two . . . a hundred. Some were tapping their heads to say, *How many?* Others pulled their open hands toward their bodies, which was followed by corresponding numerals made with their hands, palm facing in near the face.

Zara gaped at the workers' speed and multitasking abilities; this experience was unlike any other.

"Sell FriendBin. It's going to sink!" a trader screamed.

"It's going to pull the tech sector down!" another yelled.

Traders and floor brokers in cotton jackets, dark red, dark green, and dark blue, rushed to the specialists for Morgan Sachs who handled FriendBin's shares.

The specialists did their best to match up two brokers, one willing to buy and one willing to sell, and settled differences by purchasing and selling shares themselves.

"Bidding for five thousand shares, a hundred eighty K," a specialist said to a broker on his left. He turned to another broker on his right. "Five thousand shares offered at a hundred eighty-two five." Then he turned back to the person on his left. "You want six, six thousand shares? I can guarantee you six."

Dilip watched the shitshow on television from his office at the SEC, reclining in his chair, hands atop his gray hair. Traders and brokers ran all over the place, yelling, screaming, and fighting to get their orders met. "Idiots," he mocked, shaking his head.

CHAPTER 34

Manhattan, New York

Through some unknown impulse, Zara turned her head to look behind her during the commotion. A pair of security guards was approaching fast, with Veronica directing them.

Zara slowly turned her head back around, appeared calm despite a racing heartbeat, and walked away swiftly. She weaved through the mosh pit of traders and brokers scrambling for the best trades. She didn't bother to look back for fear that it would bring more attention to herself, and she didn't want to see them again. She exited the building at 18 Broad Street, under the colonnades, as an ambulance rolled up inside the gate that encircled the Big Board. As she strode toward Exchange Place, she discarded her glasses and fake mole, undid the bun, and let her hair loose as though she were a model in a shampoo commercial.

Paul, dressed as an electrician, weaseled his way into the electrical unit that supplied power to the NYSE building. He had the two dog kennels full of squirrels with him. He coated some of the wires and transformers with peanut butter and set the bushy tails free.

The squirrels, left hungry overnight on the penthouse's cold

299

balcony, rushed into the dark space filled with wires and began gnawing at them.

Zara hastened and nearly lost her footing, as her heels almost gave way. She glanced over her shoulder, hoping for the best. The paramedics worked as fast as possible to remove the stretcher and a plastic medical box from the back of the ambulance. They rushed into the entrance at 18 Broad Street.

"Move it. Move it!" a paramedic yelled to a group of security guards. "We've got an emergency."

The emergency responders slowed the security guards' pace. Zara turned the corner onto Exchange Place and narrowly escaped. She smirked, and her heartbeat gradually returned to normal.

Lower Bay, New York

A few vessels traveled to and from New York in the distance and a couple of quiet gulls perched atop the edge of the yacht as Ben stood over Hawthorne. Away from the captive's view, Walker finished filling an inflatable life raft with air and tossed it into the freezing cold waters.

"Good news. The passwords worked." Ben squatted and started to unchain Hawthorne's stiff legs from the anchor.

"Where're you going?" Hawthorne sounded worried.

Walker moved behind their captive and started to undo the rope that bound him to the chair.

"We're going back to New York," Ben replied.

Hawthorne sighed. "Thank God."

Ben looked at a standing Walker behind Hawthorne. "Did I say he was going back to New York?"

"I didn't hear that," Walker said.

Hawthorne pissed his pants.

Ben stood, patted him on the shoulder, and smiled. "You're free to go."

Walker picked up their captive and started to carry him to the opposite side of the boat.

"What? What're you doing?" Hawthorne sounded panicky and fidgeted, kicking his legs in the air.

"Sending you home." As Walker threw him overboard into the inflatable life raft, the only witnesses, gulls on the gunwale, flew away.

Manhattan, New York

The aroma of savory dishes tickled Amara's nose as she walked in the corridor that led to 1792, the NYSE restaurant, for brunch. Suddenly, she gasped, and her hand flew to her chest, as her ex-fiancé came out of the old card room. "Kannada, you have to get out of here."

"Give me a second." He kept his head low and sounded desperate.

"David will press charges. You're not allowed in here." Amara could report him to Lemon or security but resolved not to get involved for the moment. She continued toward the restaurant.

"I came back for you, and this is the thanks I get."

She stopped on a dime and turned around. Her hair tossed over her shoulders. "You're going to get me fired. What we had a few years ago is no more. We're just . . . not on the same level." She immediately regretted her words.

Amara froze and looked past Kannada. A man was approaching.

Kannada glanced over his shoulder and remained quiet.

She flashed a Pan Am smile as the man walked past them.

"Good morning," he said.

"Hi." Amara looked at the floor. Her stomach growled as she waited for the sound of the stranger's footsteps to fade away.

"You're right." Kannada frowned, nodding. "We're not on the same level."

"Kannada, I didn't mean it that way," she said, apologetic.

"I'm leaving the country tomorrow."

"Where're you going?"

He hesitated. "I can't say. It's business."

Amara shook her head, then rolled her eyes. "Whatever. Just go."

"It's complicated."

Her eyelids drooped. "With you, always. Take care of yourself."

Kannada went in to hug her, but she recoiled, crossed her arms, and looked away. He stared and hesitated to speak. She headed for the restaurant, weary.

He reached for her hand and held it.

Amara gasped and looked over her shoulder. "The only thing between us is that wall you keep putting up." She gave a despairing little smile from one side of her mouth and released her hand from

301

his grip.

Kannada sighed. "Bye." He started to leave.

Amara nodded, then turned to watch him walk out of her life. He trudged the hallway alone with his head hung toward the elevator. "Ugh. Why does he always drive me crazy?" she whispered to herself. She missed him already but shook it off and resolved to go to brunch.

The emergency responders Brett and Colin worked on a pale, bald heart attack victim while the broker who performed CPR stood over them. The former paramedic checked the sufferer's heartbeat as the other set up the defibrillator.

Brett was sitting on his knees. He finished examining the patient's radial pulse with two fingers. "We won't need that. His heartbeat's steady."

Colin nodded and put away the defibrillator. He opened the plastic emergency drug kit that contained several medications in separate compartments. He administered an aspirin as Brett watched and wiped perspiration off his brow with the back of his hand.

"I need you to chew this, okay?" Colin took the patient's jaw and moved it up and down. "It'll prevent blood clotting. Good," he said as the victim chewed. "Keep chewing."

Brett sighed, then viewed his surroundings. The mayhem had slowly died down from the time the paramedics arrived.

"Did anything trigger your heart attack?" he asked.

"I don't know." The patient sounded weary.

"Do you smoke?"

"Not lately."

The first responders glanced at each other, then put the patient on the stretcher, strapped him in, and gave him some nitroglycerin to reduce his heart's workload and improve blood flow through the coronary arteries. They connected him to an electrocardiogram, then sped off to the New York Presbyterian Hospital at 35th and 7th Streets.

At his desk in the Big Board, Iago rapidly typed a program and reviewed the code he'd started weeks ago. He appeared to be working, searching for bugs in the system and correcting them, but he was preparing the computer glitch that would jam the computers on the trading floors, buying him time to search the database of trades and delete them on the NYSE end.

"You got to leave," Dilip shouted into the phone.

"No, no, no," Iago said anxiously over a headset with a microphone.

"Kannada says we got to go, we got to go."

"I need ten minutes. That's it."

"Paul's already dumped the squirrels. Lemon could find out any minute."

"At least five to ten minutes. Give me five minutes; I'll have it done."

"I can't stop security from coming after you."

Iago glared at the monitor. "I did a test run on this thing, and all I need is five minutes."

"No guarantees."

"The redundancy kicks in in ten minutes."

"There's not enough time." Dilip slammed the phone down.

Iago looked to his left at the other workers and his boss under the dim lighting and sighed. The pressures of programming were something only he and others alike understood, not the outside world.

On the trading floor, trader Charles Frasier furrowed his brows at his computer screen. "That's odd. Take a look at this, Wes."

The nearby broker ignored him, preoccupied with his handheld device. "I'm busy. Market research."

"Would you stop watching YouTube?"

Wes glanced up. "What?"

"The FriendBin IPO is missing," Frasier said, looking at the screen. "The shares aren't on our account."

The broker smirked. "What?" He viewed the trader's monitor.

Frasier wasn't bluffing. This was no laughing matter, not part of the jokes and camaraderie the traders and brokers enjoyed occasionally. Several ideas of what could've happened ran through Frasier's mind, as well as thoughts on the best way to act.

Wes stared with his mouth open and slowly said, "Oh my God."

"Call Lemon's people," Frasier ordered, "in Sutton Place."

In the back of the ambulance, Colin monitored the patient's ticker on the electrocardiogram. "Where're we?"

Brett drove the emergency vehicle. "On 34th Street, near Penn."

"I checked all his vitals, blood pressure, oxygen saturation. He seems to be doing just fine. I'm not sure if he even had a heart attack. Either that or he recovered."

The patient lifted his head from his supine position on the stretcher. "You know what they say. Miracles happen on 34th Street."

Colin stared at him with a bewildered expression. He looked into the rearview mirror and saw Brett glance at him.

Near his desk, Iago nervously stood in front of developers, programmers, and white hat hackers. "Anybody want a snack or drink or, uh, anything? I need to get something spicy to, uh, keep me going."

The manager, DuPont, rolled his eyes. "More Cheetos?" He seemed as though he was aware by now that while the rest of America ran on Dunkin,' Iago ran on Cheetos.

Iago swallowed slowly as the others watched, then continued, "Oh, I, uh, finished troubleshooting the computers on the backup trading floor. Uh, yeah, uh, the bugs are fixed and, uh, the backup computers are okay to use if something were to happen. Oh, and I should probably tell you that a few computers on the trading floors may, uh, see an error message momentarily, as new software has been added, nothing to worry about." He rubbed his sweaty hands on his pant legs and surveyed the crowd from right to left, hiding his true intentions.

The rest of the room appeared to pay him little attention, their eyes darting back and forth. Some looked at each other with devious smirks as if there were some inside joke circulating the office. They seemed to have come to expect poor performance from Iago; he had made the impression that he was a substandard hacker because his priorities were divided at work and he was a Cheeto-holic.

He sat down and typed, "The Bull Option," on his command prompt window. He set his watch for ten minutes, then pressed 'enter' on the keyboard. The program ran with the remainder of the room unaware.

Lemon was marching to his office down a hallway with two other men, Thomas Pembroke, a top executive, and Ken Winston, an assistant. "I want everyone in on the IPO questioned, starting with the underwriter."

"Who?" Pembroke said.

"Morgan Sachs."

"Winston, get them on the phone," Pembroke barked.

Lemon barged into his own office, through the double French doors, and stopped at Amara's desk, where Frasier was standing.

Instead of retrieving snacks, Iago jogged up a few floors and walked with a brisk pace down a couple of corridors, glancing over his shoulder every now and then. He leaned against a wall, whipped out his smart phone, viewed the reflection of the security camera at the end of a hallway on his screen, and waited for the camera to stop functioning.

The camera's red light turned off. Iago turned the corner, paced the corridor nervously, and sneaked into a room that housed large mainframe computers; they stored the data of trades on behalf of the Big Board. His stature as a bug bounty hacker granted him access to the area, but he wasn't supposed to be here unless requested.

Amara watched Lemon boil as he peered over her computer screen and viewed his trading account.

He stood and faced Frasier. "What do you mean, the shares aren't here? Today's the day of the IPO. You know that, don't you?"

"Yes, sir." Frasier avoided eye contact.

"Then what're you saying, Frasier?" Lemon glanced at Amara's monitor, then faced him. "Are you saying that Morgan Sachs just forgot about me, The Legendary Lemon?"

Frasier looked down. "No, sir."

Lemon moved closer to his top executive, Pembroke, who was standing across from Frasier, holding some documents.

"What about you?" Lemon said to Pembroke. "Tell Frasier what you've got." He pointed to the papers his top executive was holding.

"The subscription agreement and allocation confirmation," Pembroke said.

"Mmm hmm." Lemon examined the copies of documents and recently printed papers the top executive was embracing, then pointed to an area on a paper. "Here, look, FriendBin's shares, requested 2.5 million, allocated 2.38 million, paid nearly 79 million. I sure do. See? It's right there." Lemon paused to look back at Frasier. "The shares were documented as having been credited this morning."

He turned toward Amara's desk, his back facing Frasier, and put his hands on the table. "Can someone explain to me why they're not there two hours later?" The room was silent. Lemon spun on his heel, faced Frasier, and pointed his finger at him. "I want those shares found, and I want them found now!"

"Yes, sir." Frasier rushed out.

Lemon moved behind Amara; he paced one direction, then back. She felt an invasion of her space, and her face flushed.

He reached over her shoulder, picked up the framed photo on her desk of her and Kannada at a Bollywood dance competition, and viewed it. "It all makes sense now." He turned to Amara. "Well?"

Amara avoided eye contact. "Don't look at me. I'm not on the trading floor." Fearful of Lemon's ensuing wrath, her eyes darted back and forth, and she gulped.

Lemon walked around her desk, stood in front of her, and put the picture down on the table.

Amara slowly glanced up; his face and eyes were red.

"He's your ex-fiancé." With the flick of a finger, Lemon knocked over the framed photo. "He was in the NYSE the other day. He wasn't here for nothing."

Amara stared at the picture frame. *He's accusing me of a conspiracy? How dare him.*

She shook her head, afraid for her job. "No, David," she said innocently. "Don't put this on me. Not a word. I don't associate with him anymore." She looked away. Those were her explicit words, but implicitly her thoughts raced too fast for her to gather and make sense. *Last week was one thing; why's Kannada in the NYSE today? It can't be just to say, "So long, see you some other time." He's involved! He has to be. But he can't be. Can he?*

Lemon's face underwent spasms of disagreement and shock. "How chivalrous. Man drops out of the sky into the most highly protected place on the planet to say 'Hello.'" He shook his head.

Winston whispered into Pembroke's ear.

"Sir, Morgan Sachs is on the phone. Kate Hollingsworth," Pembroke said.

Lemon, staring at Amara, snatched her desk phone from Winston with a total disregard for manners owing to the heat of the moment. "Put it on speaker." He changed his mind.

Winston followed his order and put down the phone.

"Lemon here," he said.

"Mr. Lemon, I can assure you that we credited the shares to your account," Kate stated, for everyone to hear.

"Then where the hell are they? Shares don't disappear like Houdini's elephant."

Amara propped the picture frame on its easel. *Lemon's not mad at you. He's just upset and trying to make sense of the matter.*

"I can double check for you." Kate sounded calm.

"I'm waiting," Lemon said.

On the trading floor, Rothschild gawked at his screen, then at other people. One by one, computers on the trading floors received an error message. They no longer functioned properly, and the screens froze.

"I'm in the system," Iago said over his headset in a restricted area of the Big Board. The room was dark and empty, except for a couple of computer stations. He had logged into the computer and the database of transactions with a set of usernames and passwords shared among his peers. He perused the contents of the computer screen briefly and experienced a nerdgasm. "It has all the trades recorded; everything. What time did he make the transfer?"

"About 9:26, 9:27," Dilip said from his SEC office.

"How many shares?"

"Two point three eight million."

Iago faced hundreds of thousands of pre-market trades and transfers. With his mouth agape, he momentarily sifted through the trades, scrolling down the list with his mouse, then ended his awe. He used the find tool, narrowed down his search, and stared at one transaction.

"You got it?" Dilip asked.

"Yes, this is it." Iago deleted the data for the transfer. "I got it, yes."

"Okay, you'll have to manually clear and settle the trades we made," Dilip explained. "Otherwise, it'll take until the end of the trading session."

"We went over this at the Plaza." Iago shook his head. *Old geezer.* "I need details, details." He looked at his watch anxiously; he only had three minutes left until his ten-minute window gave out.

"The other order; Zara flipped the shares around 10:22," Dilip informed.

Iago searched quickly as before. "Okay, I see, cleared the first and cleared the second."

"Get out, *now*," Dilip ordered.

The underwriter returned to the phone. "As far as I can see, the shares were allocated to you from our end," Kate said over speakerphone. "We'll continue to investigate and let you know of any new developments."

"You distributed them?" Lemon sounded surprised that the reputable underwriter wasn't going to take the blame. He pursed his lips and clenched his jaw. "If we can't find where they went, I'm suing the living sh—" Lemon stared at Amara. "I'll see you in court." He hung up.

Lemon leaned on Amara's desk with crossed arms, his back facing her, and sighed. "The shares were allocated from our end," he mocked Kate. He looked at a wall that had two side by side portraits; one featured a bull, the other, a bear. He focused on the bear and continued his tirade. "Let's ask him. Maybe he knows. Hey, Yogi Bear. Care to share? Oh, look, he won't talk. Maybe that's because he's in on it. Maybe I should fire his ass, too. That's what's going to start happening now."

No one said a word.

Lemon craned his neck toward Amara. "Maybe it's best you leave." He stood and turned around fully.

She opened her mouth. "David—"

"I insist. It'd be best for you and me."

Amara didn't bother to argue against a gorilla-tempered Lemon. She gathered her purse and stalked out the French doors of his office.

Lemon looked at the floor; he hadn't seen this kind of market malpractice before. "This is going to get worse," he said to the rest of the people in the room.

CHAPTER 35

Manhattan, New York

Iago closed the door to the secure room as soon as he was finished. A window on the door read, "Clearing House Trading Data. Restricted Access." The security camera was still out. He checked his watch; his ten-minute window was coming to an end. The camera would turn back on within twenty seconds. Workers at the Big Board would soon discover his well-timed computer glitch that halted trading. He started to leave.

Lemon's two-way radio, the one he received in the mail recently, buzzed. He picked it up. "Hello?"

"Hi, David. How's that IPO of yours doing?" a man ventured.

Lemon's face turned bitter, more than before. "Who is this?"

"The Main Street investor who got even." The perpetrator sounded happy.

Lemon paused. It wasn't Morgan Sachs' fault. It wasn't Amara. It wasn't any of his traders and brokers at the Big Board, nor at his Lipstick Building office in Sutton Place. It wasn't Kannada; his voice didn't match—and Lemon remembered Kannada's voice.

The perpetrator continued, "Every share of that IPO that was yours is now ours. We deserve the same privilege as you. And by the way, it gave us a nice little profit, too. Your behemoth hedge fund isn't so big anymore."

Lemon leaned over to his top executive. "How high did the shares go?"

"As your assistant crunches the numbers," Iago said, walking past Lemon's office outside the French doors, "you'll notice that the shares went up to thirty-eight dollars before the selloff. That's a five-dollar gain from the price you paid, or a profit of $11,900,000. Not to mention what could've happened if you went long. Let me ask you something, David. What's the purpose of the stock market?"

Lemon remained quiet.

"To make fools of as many men as possible," Iago answered. "Learned it from Baruch, you know."

Lemon hunched over Amara's computer and viewed his account. What the thief said was true. He stood erect and addressed the crook. "Bravo. You've turned an otherwise bullish day into a bearish one."

"I don't think so," Iago said. "If you haven't noticed already, we didn't spoil your day completely. We left you a little token of appreciation. There's a trade on an acquisition that one of your traders made for you."

Iago scanned his badge to get on the trading floor and proceeded. "If you let us go, you can save face in your own little world of who has the most yachts, biggest homes, and fastest private jets. And if you come after us, we'll notify all your clients, movie stars, athletes, politicians, banks, the whole shebang—and I know you wouldn't want to disclose that, now would you?"

Lemon had been figured out. He wouldn't disclose such a loss.

"Mr. Lemon," the perpetrator continued, "Are you ready to break the unwritten code of silence on Wall Street?"

Lemon understood. He'd been set up somehow.

He turned to face the assistant, Winston. "Find out who this asshole is. Nobody squeezes Lemon the wrong way and lives to tell about it." He marched past Winston.

Pembroke narrowed his eyes and smirked, holding in laughter. The assistant stood frozen, unsure what to do next.

Lemon's rage went up another level. "Get the SEC on the line," he yelled.

He returned to the two-way radio and took charge of the conversation. "Now you listen to me. You can run, but you can't hide. I'll have the whole city, the whole country, looking for you."

"Really?" the perpetrator mocked.

"You won't get away with this. You don't actually believe that you'll go unnoticed with the SEC, the FINRA, the clearing houses, the regulatory measures, not to mention the IRS and the U.S. banking system, do you?"

Iago was no more than a level or two away from Lemon on the main trading floor. He walked nonchalantly as workers passed behind and in front of him. "Actually, you've already helped us with that."

"Oh," Lemon said. "And why would I venture to do such a thing?"

"Because global warming is the new golden egg, the next big bubble for the markets to take in profit."

Lemon knew it. Technology combatting global warming had been popping up everywhere. Startups jumped on it. Established companies shifted gears for it. In time, that momentum would lend itself to a bubble, so much so that he even had his own initiative to change people's minds about how they viewed the world. For him, there was a calculated profit-making motive behind the push for a greener future. That greener future he envisioned was nothing more than a greener bank account. He liked the notion of a cleaner world, but he wasn't the conservationist he portrayed.

Lemon's sharp brain connected the dots; what the thief said about global warming and Prince Abdullah bin Malik al Saud and the suitcase full of money and large check he had discovered to be counterfeit after the barter for information.

In the background, someone yelled, "Sell!"

Lemon snapped back to the present and processed the commotion. "He's on one of the trading floors," he said to Pembroke. "Make sure no one leaves."

Lemon rushed to the balcony to see if he could determine where the crook was.

* * *

Iago overheard Lemon's conversation with his executive while heading for the exit at 18 Broad Street. "Of course, I'm on the trading floor. And one more thing; a message from my boss. Don't ever underestimate a bunch of schmucks." Iago casually walked out of the Exchange, his fifteen minutes of fame over.

Lemon surveyed the trading floor from the balcony with two of his assistants looking around for a man on a two-way or some phone. Unfortunately, the entire floor was covered with market players on phones; he was pursuing wind. He wheeled around and turned back toward his office.

"Very well then," Lemon said, striding purposefully. "We'll just see who makes it out of this a free man." He hung up the two-way device upon entering his office, his complexion red as the devil. He stopped in front of the bear portrait, yelled in frustration, and threw the radio at the painting, shattering the glass and damaging the picture.

Winston, the assistant, stood near the door, watching his boss go apeshit. He was holding the phone on Amara's desk. "Mr. Lemon, Dilip Patel from the SEC."

Lemon grabbed the phone. "Dilip."

Dilip reclined on his chair in his SEC office, waiting for this moment. He sat erect. "Mr. Lemon."

"There's been a theft," Lemon said.

"Is everyone okay?"

"Everyone's fine. A couple of hackers got into the system. Send the investigators."

"Sure." Dilip hung up the phone, picked up his coat from the rack near his doorway, and left, closing his door behind.

Kannada strutted casually along Wall Street toward Trinity Church but entertained distressful thoughts of Amara and Zara. Even if the group escaped with the money, the two rejections within the last hour would bother him for some time. He turned the corner onto Broadway; seconds later, he dropped his preoccupation with the women and turned back to the direction from which he came. His gait became anxious and swift. He avoided eye contact, flexed his arm near his head, and scratched his ear to cover himself from view from the NYPD vehicle that was passing.

"Hey, you," a man yelled.

Kannada stopped racing and looked up.

"Yeah, you!" the man shouted.

Kannada turned around as the cop in the passenger's seat came out.

"Kannada Khan," the cop who left the vehicle barked. "We've got a warrant for your arrest."

Kannada put his hands up. "I didn't do anything."

"You and everyone else we cuff." The police officer put Kannada's arms down, spun him around, handcuffed him, and escorted him to the back of the squad car.

A central trading floor leader who monitored the level came into Lemon's office. He spoke to Pembroke as Lemon watched.

"David, we've got a problem," Pembroke reported.

"What now?" Lemon inquired.

"Computers are failing all over the NYSE."

Lemon instantly thought of the consequences. If the problem persisted, workers would have to move to the emergency backup trading floor. For them, as well as their clients, a breach in trading would amount to millions and billions in losses. The system had to go on; the markets had to continue.

Computer failure was no coincidence; the perpetrator who taunted him moments ago came to mind. The punk had to be responsible. There was only one man who could explain what was happening.

Lemon stared past the French doors. "DuPont."

He and Pembroke moved fast to the cybersecurity office.

"It must be one of those mangy hackers," Lemon said, as they made their way down a hallway. "I knew we shouldn't trust those people."

Lemon approached a trio of computers that idly sat on a messy workplace with Pembroke and Richard DuPont, the Head of Security and Managing Director of Cybersecurity.

"Look at this desk!" DuPont slid the empty Cheetos bags and soda cans at the workstation into a trash can at the end of the table. "What garbage!"

Lemon's brows furrowed. "Whose computer is this?"

"Diego Sanchez," DuPont answered.

Lemon faced nearby workers. "Find Sanchez. Check the vending machines."

"Whatever he did, there should be a trail left behind," DuPont said.

"The emergency trading floor is still working, right?" Pembroke asked.

DuPont turned to one of the computers, functioned as the administrator, and clicked his way through the Trading Computers folder to check. "Yeah, it's still fine."

Lemon frowned at Pembroke. "Then why the hell did he disable the ones on the trading floors?"

Iago hurriedly boarded the Bimmer and sighed as rain started to pour lightly; he couldn't believe he escaped. He looked straight ahead, past the screeching wipers that moved back and forth; he had accepted Kannada's challenge in Vegas and now felt the exhilaration of victory. The group wasn't done, but his part, perhaps the most important step, was complete. He looked over to his left.

Paul acted as the driver. Zara occupied the back seat, sat at the edge of the middle hump, and hunched over, her head between Iago and Paul.

"Finished?" Paul asked.

"Like a bag of Cheetos." Iago smirked.

They started for the Plaza but stopped immediately, as some tourists with umbrellas and cameras walked in front of the Bimmer.

"Damn tourists," Paul cursed.

"I hate tourists." Iago shook his head.

"Ugh." Zara's eyes flicked upward.

Pembroke stood next to DuPont while Lemon peered over the manager's shoulder.

"Main trading floor." DuPont clicked on the folder.

Accompanied by the appropriate sound, the computer returned an error message: access denied. Lemon let out a long sigh, and his head dropped.

DuPont rewound his steps and tried another folder. "Trading floor grid."

A similar error message appeared, and Lemon pursed his lips and shook his head.

DuPont went to the directory of computers and scrolled down the list. "Computer 352."

Lemon noticed a sticker with that number on the Trojan horse's monitor.

The computer denied access, again.

DuPont looked at his boss. "He's changed the permissions."

Lemon stood erect and suspiciously glanced around the room at the other workers.

The speaker started to beep. His attention returned to the computer; the subtle noise corresponded to several error messages that popped up all over the screen.

A cartoon of Santa Claus suddenly appeared, carrying a red bag over his shoulder with Diego's face in place of the animation's face. He stomped forward from the back of the screen in the middle and stopped. "No, no, no. You've been a naughty boy this year," it said, in Santa Claus' accent, an old, fat Greek man.

The manager slammed his fist onto the table. "Fuck Santa Claus!" he yelled.

Lemon went to touch the screen. "What about that?" He pointed to a pair of discreet words in the corner and tapped the screen.

The monitor flickered.

"Okay, what'd I touch?" Lemon asked.

The lights went out. The backup security lights turned on. The room was darker.

"Uh, you didn't touch anything," Pembroke said. "The mains went out."

CHAPTER 36

Manhattan, New York

"The power is returning," Pembroke noted, seated near Diego's chair, which was occupied by DuPont.

Lemon had his elbows on the table and his hands on the sides of his face. He gloomily looked past the desk at the floor as the light, soothing keystrokes in the room tried to put his worries to rest. Dilip viewed the computers in Lemon's peripheral vision.

"So much for the biggest IPO of the year," Lemon lamented. "Shares disappear, the stock collapses, computers are hacked, and the power goes." He continued to stare at the floor, teary-eyed.

Pembroke scrunched up one side of his mouth. "At least you didn't take the loss on the shares. It could've been worse, David; much worse."

Lemon sighed; there was a moment of silence, of mourning.

"Everyone, stop what you're doing," Dilip announced to the room. "The computers, phones, and records are SEC property." He directed his team, a blue-eyed blond man, a goateed black man who looked vaguely familiar to Lemon, and a spikey-haired Asian man, to seize the items, then approached a standing DuPont.

"Richard, I'll need the hardware on which the clearing house trading data is kept, if not here."

DuPont sighed, hands at his waist. "Sure. I'll take one of your men there."

Dilip nodded, then moved to the man in charge. "David, where do you think your FriendBin shares went?"

Lemon turned to face the SEC's Regional Director and leaned back in his seat with his arms crossed.

Dilip took a cough drop, holding a folder.

"Hackers?" Lemon said. "This Diego Sanchez. Maybe some others."

"The only thing that could've happened," Dilip said, "if the underwriter allocated them, is the shares were transferred, which is illegal prior to the IPO. That's always stated in the prospectus."

Lemon didn't like where this was heading.

Dilip continued, "Obviously, it doesn't show up here on the computers. Let me ask you another question; how'd you find out about this acquisition?"

"One of my traders must have made a good trade."

"Well, three red flags are cause for concern."

"Oh?"

"One, this acquisition is an all-cash deal. Two, the anticipated lift in stock price was large. And three, there are several parties involved in the deal."

Lemon furrowed his brows. "What're you saying?"

"I'm saying that it's more than likely that someone couldn't resist taking a position that would earn him or her a bundle."

"So?"

"So, from today, Lemon Group is under investigation for insider trading on the acquisition and perjury on the transfer of shares."

"No, that can't be!" Lemon countered defiantly. His bad day turned into a terrible one. He'd been set up somehow. There had to be several people involved to pull this off, perhaps a few from outside the Big Board or, worse, maybe a few inside the Exchange, like Diego Sanchez—or worse, perhaps a few inside his firm yet to be determined. He realized he should've never contacted the SEC. He'd broken the unwritten code of silence on Wall Street and now was paying for it.

"David, I've been doing this for a long time, and I'm going to be blunt with you," Dilip said. "You know what it looks like. And I'm not accusing you, but the conditions point to the telltale signs that your firm knew ahead of time that there would be a massive selloff of FriendBin. Your hedge fund didn't want to take the loss, so your company disposed of it somehow and hedged the loss of that potential gain with the acquisition." His gold stud earring and salt-and-pepper hair shined, as though he was sticking it to Lemon.

Lemon sighed, and his shoulders slacked. "No. No, not at all."

"David, I've seen all sorts of things in the markets over my twenty-plus years working at the SEC, on Wall Street, and this is by far one of the best con jobs I've seen. Of course, nothing is final now, but it doesn't look good. My advice is not to hide anything; it'll turn out in the wash. If you come clean now, I can get you to pay less in fines, if that's what happens."

"I stand by my original statement that there was no insider trading, no perjury, at least not that I'm aware of. But I'll speak to my staff and see what they have to say, and I'll let you know."

"Okay," Dilip said, staring him straight in the eye.

"How long do you think the investigation could take as far as my lost IPO?"

"Could be weeks, could be months. It depends on how well these rogue hackers hid their tracks. We'll have to get a search warrant for Diego, interview witnesses, and subpoena records. There's nothing I can do right now, but we'll stay in contact to figure this out. All right?"

Lemon's eyelids drooped, and his lips pursed. "Thank you."

Dilip and his team confiscated whatever they deemed as evidence, then departed.

At Lemon's office at the Lipstick Building in Sutton Place, George Paulson, the American business magnate, investor, and philanthropist, and a few other executives had arrived.

Ms. Kwan, Lemon's Asian secretary, calmly sorted some files on her desk as Mr. Paulson chewed her out for failing to notify him of Lemon's absence earlier.

His face was craggy, and he had wrinkles above his aviator frames. "What's this I hear? Lemon makes an appointment to meet with me, and he's not even here?"

"He sends his apologies." The secretary avoided eye contact as she pasted a sticky note on one of the files. She was doing her best to pacify the pushy man and cover for Lemon.

"We're facing heat from the government for the contributions we made to his little energy initiative, and he can't even bother to see me?"

"He had to stay at the NYSE." Ms. Kwan put away the files in a drawer to her right. "He had a major loss today."

"Well, I understand that." Mr. Paulson's tone softened, but it picked up where it left off, sharp and fast. "It'd be well advised for him to see me now. The Justice Department thinks the money is going to political campaigns. I even brought an auditor."

"Mmm hmm." She picked up the phone to call Lemon.

Kannada arrived at a police department, just blocks away from Wall Street, in a patrol car. The arresting officer escorted him to a desk officer seated at a cluttered table in a room filled with several desks and police.

"Take a seat," the arresting officer snarled.

Kannada, cuffs on his wrists, slouched in a metal chair across the desk officer. The name tag on the cop's chest read, "H. Bates."

The arresting officer addressed the man behind the desk. "I'll speak with an ADA."

The desk officer examined the complaint as the arresting officer left, then viewed Kannada's profile on his computer.

Kannada's eyes wandered around the room. Police peered over paperwork, some conversed with each other over donuts and smoking-hot coffee, and others occupied meeting rooms, investigating crimes.

"Where've you been?" Officer Bates demanded. "We've been trying to reach you for the past week."

"I was in the Poconos, and I lost reception."

"Poconos? In this weather?" The man in blue paused and studied the arrestee.

Kannada restrained his urge to react and responded calmly. "So, now what?"

"You'll be arraigned in criminal court within twenty-four hours for the allegations against you."

"Don't you guys issue appearance tickets?"

The officer ignored him.

Kannada pursed his lips. Distracted by some commotion, he turned to his right.

A man escorted in handcuffs twisted his body. "I'm a clean skin. I don't know how it got there. I thought it was powdered sugar!"

Kannada recalled a photograph Walker had showed him after his spy work was complete. He was the same Wall Street player who bumped into Walker just moments before he exchanged money for drugs with a drug pusher near the Big Board. *Small world.* Walker had mentioned that he would send the photo to the NYPD.

"That's funny, real funny," the escorting officer said to the drug user in custody. "Hey, Jimmy. One kilo of coke," he said to another officer.

Kannada turned back to Officer Bates. "How long could I be sentenced?"

"The judge will decide that at your trial."

"Can I post bail today?"

"Not until you're arraigned."

Kannada froze and stared blankly past the cop as the room continued to move around him. He would have to spend the night in jail. He felt sick and swallowed; rapists and murderers crossed his mind. *I'm going to die in there.* Another officer came into his view; he wore a suit, appeared to be someone of rank, and looked directly at Kannada as he approached them.

"I'll pass," the arrestee said.

"You'll what?" Officer Bates raised his voice.

"Pass. I don't want to go to jail."

The cop stared at him as though he was ready to smash Kannada's head on the table. Before he could respond, the ranking officer was at his desk.

"I'll take care of this," the new officer said. "You can take your donut break." He looked at a smirking Kannada. "Come with me."

Officer Bates stared hard at Kannada, lowered his chin, and grinned evilly. "Good luck."

Kannada rose and faced the new officer. His name badge read, "Lt. Frank Napoli." He was the same man who had set up a fake ID for Iago "Smarty" Gonzales. Kannada began to follow the lieutenant. A few surrounding cops faced their dialogist but side-eyed him.

Kannada entered the lieutenant's office and sat down in a wooden chair in front of the desk. The office was chock full of papers; they were on his desk and bulletin board.

Lt. Napoli shut the door, then closed the blinds. He went behind his desk and occupied a worn-out, squeaky chair that had tears in the maroon leather.

"What're you trying to do, create a brouhaha? You'll get in even more trouble."

"You get the cookies I sent you?" Kannada asked.

Lt. Napoli flashed a smile. "All fifty grand."

Kannada was pleased to hear that the package of money that Iago and Dilip had prepared a few weeks ago had reached its destination. It was now in good hands.

"How're the kids?" Kannada asked.

"One's going to college next year, the other one the year after."

"And Debbie?" Kannada said, referring to the lieutenant's wife.

"On this new gluten-free diet. Looks better than when I married her."

"Yeah, I was thinking about trying that."

In the boardroom, Lemon curved his back and bowed his head as he sat on a corner of the large table, one foot on the ground, and listened on the phone to Ms. Kwan at the Lipstick Building.

"Tell Mr. Paulson we'll have to reschedule." He hung up and frowned at the thought of a missed meeting.

Lemon had assembled the Lemon Group staff who worked at the NYSE, a bunch of aggressive traders and brokers, in the boardroom. A guard stood next to Lemon with his arms crossed.

"Which one of you was responsible for the trade on the acquisition?" Lemon folded his arms across his chest.

A young stud, a former college football player with a square jaw and perfect teeth, stepped up with a smile to claim ownership. "Me, sir."

Lemon feigned a smile. "It was a good trade. How'd you do it?"

The employee stuck his chest out, boastful. "Well, I've been hunting elephants, researching the markets, working late, looking for the black edge."

Lemon continued to appear affable. "Looking for the black edge? This trade you made. It's almost as if you have no idea how Wall Street works. We're under investigation for insider trading."

"Well, I was trying to get ahead."

Lemon nodded and smiled. "Get ahead?" His demeanor turned serious. "You're fired. Get him out of here."

The worker's mouth dropped, and his eyes froze. Just like that, he went from hero to zero.

The guard approached the prep and grabbed his arm. "Let's go," he ordered, his back against Lemon.

Lemon looked at the floor with no emotions.

"Have you been training?" Lt. Napoli asked in his office.

Kannada thought of the several practice sessions he'd had with Walker behind closed doors. "Yeah, I think I'm ready for it."

"Well, only if the prosecution presses charges, we'll strap you in."

Kannada nodded.

"Does he have anything against you?" Lt. Napoli asked.

Kannada pursed his lips and looked down. "Maybe on tape, but I kept my head low."

"Gotcha," Lt. Napoli said, nodding. "Anything else?"

"Timing of my arrest."

"Gotcha," Lt. Napoli repeated, nodding again.

"That's it, I think."

"I still have to take you in."

Kannada let his eyelids droop, turned his attention elsewhere, and raised one side of his mouth. "Yeah, I know.

CHAPTER 37

Manhattan, New York

In the penthouse, MC's *Miss Market* with Stevoni Romano ran on the TV. Zara watched and enjoyed a cherry lollipop, surrounded by the remaining members of the group, except Kannada and Ben.

"Oh my God, was the market volatile today or what? First, let me give you some color on Milton Companies. The stock skyrocketed today, hit the moon it went so high," Miss Market said in her New York accent, this time on one of the trading floors in the NYSE. Cartoon bulls charged forward from behind her, representing the bullish rise in price. The bulls bellowed.

"You know why? Bear hug. UBT acquired Milton Companies. What does that mean for you? UBT is a long-term play."

A couple of tall, square-jawed men dressed as traders appeared from behind the trading terminals. They yelled, *"Buy, buy, buy."*

Zara smiled; the hunks were cute.

Miss Market walked to one of the computer screens on the floor and looked at the chart of Milton Companies. "And hold. If you missed out, don't be all sour grapes about it. So, why the bear hug?

"Okay, when you have the cheese, why not? Make it rain, make it rain. So, UBT went out, made a godfather offer, and bought the manufacturer that wanted to compete with them. Of course, now they're facing a lawsuit, but whenever you make it big, somebody's always after you.

"Did they pony up too much, or what? Maybe, but sometimes you have to squash the menace before it threatens your survival. You guys in New York know what I mean. UBT will have a greater share of the market when it comes to pecans, almonds, mayonnaise, syrup, soda, everything they sell in bodegas, and that two-billion-dollar price tag won't seem like too much in the end."

Miss Market continued to walk.

"Now, turning to the main attraction, and I know you've been waiting for this. I hope you didn't lose too much money; if you did, take the bridge, not the tunnel. You with me?"

"Take the bridge? Suicide?" Zara thought aloud.

"Luckily, the circuit breakers didn't kick in. We had a dead cat bounce afterward; thank you, underwriters. Did you see what happened to FriendBin, F-B-N?"

Dead cat bounce? Zara chuckled, struggling to understand the television personality. She started to rotate the candy in her mouth one way, then the other.

A man in a black trench coat with matching fedora hat, a mafia man, appeared from the right of the screen. An innocent man stood on Miss Market's right. The mobster took a machine gun out from underneath his trench coat and fired several consecutive gunshots. There was smoke from the gun's barrel in the air as the bystander fell to the ground.

"He's going in the East River. Okay? Somebody died today," Miss Market said.

Zara's eyes widened; she paused twirling the lollipop in her mouth. A few others laughed.

"Or, rather, some company died today. You with me? People get clipped every day. That had to be the biggest blunder in IPO history, and just before Christmas," Miss Market said.

A couple of cartoon grizzly bears appeared on the trading floor, signaling a bear market, and roared.

"It was sweet as caramel when it came public. Cost the first owners thirty-three dollars per share; went up fifteen percent to thirty-eight dollars. Dumb guap, right? Couldn't even last the day, not even the first hour of trading. Settled a dollar, a dollar, above the IPO price. What're they doing? Tripping. What do you do?

Fuhgeddaboudit!"

Zara took the lollipop out of her mouth. "Thirty-eight dollars per share. How much is that, Iago?" She asked the question everyone else in the room seemed to be trying to figure out with their cell phones.

Iago looked up and appeared to calculate the numbers quickly in his head. "Because we didn't pay for the shares, it's $90,440,000, or divided evenly among ten people, $9,044,000 per person."

"Not bad for a day's work." Dilip took a cough drop.

The others nodded nonchalantly.

Zara stared, mouth open, trying to get her head around the amount. She almost dropped her candy. This was truly dumb guap.

"FriendBin had the same trajectory as Roxin, remember that company from Long Island, much faster, which we told you Monday would have a huge first-day pop when it came public, but then would be a dud afterward, and that's exactly what happened," Miss Market said.

"How's this lady know everything?" Zara asked Iago, who was seated next to her. She maintained her gaze on the television.

Rob leaned over from behind the sofa. "Fuhgeddaboudit." He clicked the remote and switched off the television. "Come on, let's go."

One after another, they walked out of the penthouse toward Rockefeller Plaza as darkness settled for the evening. The sound of handbells rung by the Salvation Army beckoned them over, and everyone emptied their wallets and purse, feeling generous. They continued past the twelve wire-sculpture angels facing each other on opposite sides of the fountain, now turned off. The angels held long brass trumpets angled toward the Christmas tree, amid snow-covered shrubs, flowers, and small fountain statues. The figures, along with sparkling wire snowflakes that decorated the buildings on either side, glittered from thousands of tiny lights.

At the base of the Rockefeller Center, they stood side by side directly across the illuminated centerpiece, the Christmas tree, crowned with a shining star, its rays in every direction, erected for the holidays.

Two large wreaths graced the walls of the building on either side of the tree. There were trees on their level, too, on both sides, with red, green, and gold flags nearby, those of the world's countries now replaced to make way for the season. Light peered through some of the windows of the surrounding buildings, late-night workers or janitors starting their shifts, and added to the merriment.

Zara watched a crowd of New Yorkers frolic around on the ice below her, the dining tables with umbrellas and chairs now removed. The skaters glided in front of the bronze gilded statue recumbent at the sunken Lower Plaza while others stood still at the far edge of the waist-level, glass enclosure of the ice skating rink as they talked among themselves and marveled at the effigy.

She vaguely discerned the carved words on the red granite wall behind the statue, behind the fountain, then looked to her side, down the line of thieves.

From one end to the other, Dilip took a cough drop, Walker massaged his knuckles, Rob lit a cigar, Ricky rubbed some lotion on his hands, Ben checked his hair in the reflection of his smart phone, Paul raised his beer bottle toward Alan and mouthed cheers, Alan sipped from his hip flask, Iago chomped at some Cheetos, and Zara, at the other end, smiled at the other eight fraudsters.

Skaters slushed ice and people voiced their merriment as snow started to fall. Despite the joyous setting, Zara felt sad and nostalgic. Her three weeks of fun were ending; this was their last night together before their flights the following day.

Worse, she experienced an unusual and rare longing for a companion, as she missed the mastermind, Kannada Khan. She maintained a solemn expression as strong feelings surfaced, and the noises in the background left her alone for brooding. *Why am I stressing over him? When we first met he was so, what's the right word, awkward. A few weeks together and I'm attached? He can't leave me like this. Get over him. I can't. But you have to. Escorting is a business. Things would never work. He's not promiscuous. He'll return to Ama—*

"Hey, Zara," Ben called.

She parted her lips, lost for the moment.

"Let's go."

The others had already walked away. Zara nodded and joined Ben.

CHAPTER 38

Manhattan, New York

Back at the NYSE, Lemon worked overtime. He viewed the security tapes with DuPont and Pembroke for the day on the trading floors, peering over DuPont's shoulder.

DuPont played the digital playback. "I still don't understand where those two came from. They keep their heads down the whole time."

The tape showed two men walking out of a hallway that led to the trading floor restroom and janitor's closet.

"A few workers reported hearing some noise from the air duct," Pembroke noted. "Could be related."

Lemon furrowed his brows. "What happened to the security guard who collapsed before market open?"

"He's doing okay," Pembroke replied. "The guards found some sleep agents on the floor and a grenade-like object at a workstation; they're still investigating the matter."

"What about the man who had a heart attack? Any word?"

"Nothing. The hospital said he left his bed."

Lemon turned back to the digital playback. DuPont exited the full screen mode; the monitor displayed several thumbnail views of surveillance cameras throughout the exchange.

Lemon stared at the thumbnail for the hallway to the NYSE restaurant and pointed to it. "Expand that." He narrowed his eyes on two people on the screen and waited a moment, trying to discern the happenings. His heart jumped, as he caught the perpetrator. "It's him. Kannada Khan."

"How can you tell?" Pembroke asked.

"He met Amara." Lemon wore a Grinch-like smile. "That's how."

The video showed Kannada's meeting with Amara.

Kannada had been moved to a holding cell in some criminal court building. He was sitting with crossed arms on a hard bench that hung from the wall. The walls were similar to that of the subway, minus the colorful tiles and artwork. The odor wasn't much different; he was used to it. Street music was replaced with a few inmates talking to each other in blue language and making unnecessary noise. His initial worries started to dissipate; as long as he avoided eye contact and didn't show any fear, he'd make it through the night.

He reminisced on his attempt to leave poverty as he stared at the dirty cement floor. Something held him down and brought him back, if not in a worse position. He was hampered by a lack of money before, but he was restrained now by security cameras and guards. He had to ask permission to do anything and felt like a schoolchild unable to take care of himself. His arraignment was tomorrow; he prayed without showing it that the charges levied against him would not be too serious.

Kannada snapped out of his reflection as a fly buzzed around the room in front of him. He followed it for a while, challenging himself to see how long he could keep track of its aerial path.

At the 1st Precinct police station, Lt. Napoli perched atop a corner of his messy desk and viewed the security tapes from the Big Board with Lemon, Pembroke, and DuPont.

He held a coffee mug and scrunched up his face. "You said this happened earlier today?"

"Yes," Lemon insisted.

Lt. Napoli paused the video. "I'll give you credit for your detective work." He sipped coffee. "He does look a bit like Kannada, but there's only one problem."

"What's that?" Lemon demanded.

Lt. Napoli put his mug down on a paper on his desk, next to a coffee cup stain. "He was in our custody yesterday." He stretched the truth for Kannada's sake. "Unless he escaped overnight, stole your money, and came back here, you've got nothing."

Yesterday? Lemon mouthed to himself, staring past the officer, at the wall behind him. His eyebrows scrunched together. "Oh." His pushy demeanor receded, and he looked down. "I still want to press charges."

Lt. Napoli stared at him. He was dealing with a man who wouldn't take "no" for an answer. Before he could respond, Pembroke spoke up.

"Will you excuse us for a second?"

"Sure," Lt. Napoli said.

Pembroke, DuPont, and Lemon walked out of his office and stood outside. Lt. Napoli moved behind his desk and sat on the worn-out, squeaky, maroon office chair. He read a report in the meantime.

Outside, DuPont hitched up his pants slightly, kept his hands at his waist, and stood between Pembroke and a bitter Lemon. The police station was dark and deserted. Most of the blinds were drawn, some were rolled up halfway, and a few were still open. It was dark outside. A few officers with reading glasses peered over paperwork, lit by lamps, at their desks.

"David, maybe we should just let this go. Maybe we've got the wrong guy," Pembroke said.

"I agree," DuPont backed.

Lemon shook his head in shock. He looked from DuPont to Pembroke and foamed at the mouth. "No, this guy is it. He's responsible. I just know it."

Pembroke glanced at the floor. "Look, I believe you that he was in the NYSE the other day, but the cop says he was here, so he was here."

"I'm telling you this guy's protected by the Prince of Darkness," Lemon argued, pointing his finger at Pembroke as if scolding him. "I'm not going to let this go until I have evidence that says otherwise. He's guilty until proven innocent." With that, Lemon paraded back into Lt. Napoli's office.

Before following their boss into the room, Pembroke and DuPont, sharp minds, exchanged a look that said they were losing faith in

Lemon.

Lt. Napoli heard his door open and put down the report he was reading.

"I still want to press charges," Lemon asserted.

Pembroke and DuPont came into the office, one after the other.

Lt. Napoli rose from behind his desk and put his hands on his waist as his old office chair squeaked. "Mr. Lemon, it's not worth the time and cost. I'm not sure why you have it in for this guy, but you can't just file charges because you don't like someone."

"I'll prove he's involved with one phone call." Lemon took out his phone. "That schmuck met his ex-fiancée, my personal assistant, before he left." He made the call and put the phone on speaker.

Lt. Napoli hesitated, and his eyes froze. *What's he got that Kannada didn't mention?*

CHAPTER 39

Manhattan, New York

At the 9/11 Memorial, Amara walked alone with the other three thousand or so restless souls around the edges of one of the two pools, human-made waterfalls that muted the sounds of the city and provided a contemplative sanctuary.

In a black overcoat and dark red beret, she felt lonely and lost during one of the most festive seasons of the year in the Big Apple. Her gaze remained down and away, toward the pit of the Memorial where cold, ruthless snow was beginning to accumulate. She crossed and held her arms and mused about the might-have-beens with Kannada. What irritated her most was that he kept falling short of her expectations. Her mind jumped from him to Lemon. Her relationship with Lemon was sour at best. She forgave his meltdown but remained uncertain whether she would try to make it work with him.

Her phone buzzed. She put away her feelings, cleared her throat, and brightened her face. "Hi, David. What're you up to?"

"Oh, just working late, trying to sort out the day's mess. Are you busy tonight?" He sounded affable.

Lemon was never available on Thursday nights; he always had some business to take care of. "Hold on. I think I'm going out with

331

my girlfriends . . ." She didn't want to seem like she had nothing to do and rocked her head back and forth a few times. "Nope, looks like I'm free."

"Would you like to go out for dinner?"

"Sure."

"Great. Meet me at the lobby of our apartment building in an hour."

"Will do." Amara smiled. "Bye."

"Oh, before you get ready, could you help me with the investigation by answering one question?"

"Ask away."

"Did you meet Kannada today near the old card room?" His voice was sharp.

Amara swallowed. The conversation she had had with Kannada flashed before her. She didn't want to turn him in. She knew Lemon would eat him alive if he got the chance. But she worked for the NYSE; it was her duty to be ethical. She also felt the urge to stay faithful to Lemon.

"Amara?"

She hesitated.

"He's cheating on you," a voice said.

Amara slowly turned around with parted lips. An old black man walked behind her. Her brow furrowed, as she paused to process the sign. *How'd he—what?* She couldn't tell whether she had taken the man's words out of context or not. Lemon's shady behavior at the spiritual dance festival came to mind. *He is cheating on me.*

"Amara?"

"Uh, no, I didn't meet him. That was some random guy." She felt bad for lying to her boss, but the resentment she harbored for Lemon's dishonesty outweighed her duty to abide by moral principles for the sake of her work. There was no point in waiting to catch him cheating on her again; she had enough evidence to resolve the uncertainties of their future together.

Lemon's eyes lost their vigor, and he hesitated before returning to the call on speaker. "Very well, then. This investigation might take longer than I had hoped."

"David, about tonight . . . maybe we should see other people."

Lemon paused and felt warm, as the people in the room heard the rejection. "I'll see you tomorrow." He hung up and faced the lieutenant. "She's covering for him." He ground his teeth.

Lt. Napoli pursed his lips and shook his head.

"Can't you at least question the man as a suspect?" Lemon whined.

"He has an airtight alibi," Lt. Napoli countered.

"Fine. I demand to talk to the Chief of Police first thing tomorrow morning."

"David . . ." Pembroke and DuPont said one after another with frowns.

"Mr. Lemon—" Lt. Napoli began.

"What's going on here? I'm the head of the New York Stock Exchange, and everyone is suddenly taking this punk's side?" Lemon pointed his finger at the lieutenant and raised his voice. "I make more money in one day than you will your whole life. I am owed the respect to speak to the Chief of Police."

"Don't forget whose house you're in." Lt. Napoli stared Lemon down. "I'll tell you what. Finish giving me your written accusation, then before you proceed with the charges, we'll put him on a polygraph as part of the investigation to see if there's a chance that he committed a crime."

"Do those things actually work?" Pembroke asked.

DuPont nodded. "Mmm hmm. Ph.D. backed."

"Yes, their efficacy is so good that we won't hire people without having them go through a polygraph," Lt. Napoli asserted.

"Fine," Lemon said. "Where's the pen and paper?"

CHAPTER 40

Manhattan, New York

The sun rose quickly the next morning, and Zara overslept. Ben called her name and nudged her arm; she hugged a pillow and felt around the sheets for the man in her dreams, but Kannada wasn't there. She motioned Ben away, then wondered if Kannada missed her the way she did him. She gradually got out of bed, readied herself alone, and hurried to the airport with the group; she had packed the several bags she had arrived with the previous night, as did the others.

The gang had flights to different parts of the world to manage their stolen goods, except for Kannada, who was in custody, and Dilip, who would continue working at the SEC for another few months to impede the investigation before retiring.

Zara sat in the airport next to Rob and addressed her phone. "Who's going to handle Dilip's share?"

"His lucre is under my supervision," Rob replied, looking over a newspaper.

"And Kanny's?"

Rob glanced at her with one eyebrow raised. "Ben."

Kannada had made it through the night in jail; it wasn't as bad as he had thought it would be. With a court-appointed lawyer, he came before a judge in criminal court for his arraignment. An assistant district attorney stood off to one side and spoke first; the allegations dated back to the time when Lemon had caught him impersonating Lorenzo Moretti and visiting Amara. There were no witnesses, no evidence, and no trial.

He was charged with criminal impersonation in the second degree—class A misdemeanor—criminal trespass in the third degree—B misdemeanor—and petit larceny by acquiring lost property—A misdemeanor. He and his court-appointed lawyer negotiated a plea; Kannada knew that Lemon had digital security recordings of him wandering the hallways and meeting Amara in 1792, the NYSE restaurant. Moreover, he wanted to get his punishment over with and remove the uncertainty that would eat away at his sanity until his trial. He pleaded guilty, and the judge sentenced him on the spot—six months up the river and $500 in fines.

The bailiff escorted him away, and another officer took him to the precinct. Instead of occupying a jail cell, Kannada was taken to a hallway of offices.

He entered a dimly lit, soundproof, interrogation room, slouched in a metal chair, and tapped his foot. He wasn't planning on fleeing but wondered if it were even possible. A table in front of him posed the first obstacle to breakout, a two-way mirror to his right likely hid interrogators, a pair of cameras on the walls kept watch, and a heavy door with the silhouette of two men in a small window across made escape impossible. Lt. Napoli and one of his cohorts stood and conversed outside the door.

Kannada sat erect as one finished briefing the other.

The door opened and the man, bald with an eagle's nose and blue eyes, barged in, carrying a portfolio, as Lt. Napoli turned his head to the right and gave the prisoner a wink.

The man took a seat in front of Kannada; the chair screeched on the floor. "We received a tip that you were involved in a financial crime. You're here on suspicion that you participated in the theft of FriendBin's IPO from Lemon Group. We'd like you to take a polygraph as part of an interrogation process. You're not obligated under law at this moment. It's your choice."

Kannada nodded. Just as he'd envisioned from the start, he was a suspect. "I'll do it. I have nothing to hide."

The man looked at Kannada with unwavering eyes. He opened his portfolio and pulled out a few papers and a pen. "I'll need you to sign these papers before we can proceed."

Kannada nodded and signed the papers.

"You're not going to read them?"

"No," Kannada answered nonchalantly.

The man remained stone-faced as he collected the papers. "The polygraph examiner will ask you a series of questions relating to the crime in question."

Kannada nodded.

"Follow me," the man ordered.

Law enforcement stuffed Kannada in a dull room devoid of pictures. The seamless, dobby fabric texture of the dark gray walls made sure no sound escaped. A polygraph machine sharpened its needles, ready to judge him. A box of tissues on a dark gray L-shaped desk with hutch to his right waited for his meltdown. The room possessed an unusual deafening silence that made Kannada cringe.

"Nice office," he remarked.

Muscles, a short, stocky polygraph examiner, grinned. "Yeah. No sudden movements, no movement at all. Breathe normally and consistently. No deep breaths. Keep your eyes open the whole time or keep them closed the whole time. No blinking. Only respond with a 'yes' or a 'no,' okay?"

"Okay." Kannada sat uncomfortably in a leather chair on a special sensor pad while his feet rested on a similar mat. One arm was elevated above the other, his fingers were connected to electrodes, and his chest was strapped with a cord.

"I'll be asking the same pre-interview questions we went over just a while ago," Muscles said, "but before we get into that, I'll ask you some basic questions to get you acclimated and the machine ready, okay?"

"Okay," Kannada said.

"Are you thirty-five years of age?"

"Yes."

"Were you born in Chicago?"

"Yes."

"Is Chicago in the state of Pennsylvania?"

"No."

In Kannada's peripheral vision, the examiner appeared to go over the polygraph's output.

"We'll begin now," Muscles said. "Did you steal David Lemon's IPO?"

"Yes." Kannada bit hard on his tongue, to elicit the specific physiological response; nervousness.

The machine's accusatory needles scratched the paper, signaling a lie.

"Did you work alone?"

"No." Kannada bit again.

The needles flew again, making a similar noise.

"Keep still. Did you work with a group of accomplices?" Muscles said. He gave Kannada the impression something was amiss.

"Yes." Kannada pressed his foot softly on the sensor pad below it and bit again.

The bucket list of lies was growing.

"Did you trespass the NYSE building on the 18th of December this year?"

"Yes." Kannada moved his finger slightly and bit his tongue again.

"Did you meet Amara Sanon in the NYSE building on the 18th of December this year?"

"Yes." Kannada gently moved his knee. The needles zigged and zagged.

"No movement. Did Amara Sanon conspire with you?"

"Yes," Kannada responded. There was no need to bite his tongue this time. This was a real lie. He was telling lies upon lies.

"Do you know where the money went?"

"Yes." Kannada moved his elbow discreetly and bit again.

"Okay, hold on just a minute. I'm going to print the results and go over them with you."

Kannada was fatigued by the postural misalignment, but his tongue was recovering. He sat quietly while the printer etched out a bunch of lines. "Can I move around now?"

"Yes, do you need to take a break?"

"No, I'm fine." Kannada stretched his fingers and legs, craned his neck one way, then the other.

Meanwhile, the examiner went over the paperwork, trying to decipher what the lines meant. "My polygraph is showing that you're not telling the truth."

Kannada leaned over to look at the results, a bunch of squiggly lines. If there was any abnormality, it was barely discernible.

"Looks all the same to me."

"Hey," Muscles shouted, "do you know how to read a polygraph?"

"No, but—"

"Okay then. I'll do the reading, got it?"

Kannada nodded and rolled his eyes.

"Let's try this again. Sit still, no movement at all. This time, I want you to make a slight nod for 'yes' and a gentle shake of the head for 'no.' Okay?"

"Okay." Kannada went through the same questions, with the same answers, with the same amount of fidgeting. Upon completion, the examiner printed the results and reviewed them again.

"Mmm, my test is showing that you're still not telling the whole truth." The inspector rolled his chair out in front of an exasperated Kannada, loosened his straps, and started pressuring him.

"Tell me the truth. Did you have a hand in stealing the IPO?"

"No," Kannada said.

Muscles rolled a bit closer and slapped the back of his hand on his palm loudly.

"No? You just told me 'yes' a while ago. Which one is it? Tell me the truth!" he yelled. His muscles bulged, and the buttons on his shirt struggled to contain them. "I'm only trying to help you."

"I don't know." Kannada's eyelids drooped. The walls appeared to move in waves.

"I want to help you. But to do that, I need you to come clean. I want to paint a whole picture of you, so we can help you, okay?"

Help me? Give me a break. "Okay."

"Tell me what happened in your own words."

"Since I decided to make something of myself again, I recruited about nine people; then we tried to steal the IPO. And we shipped our money overseas to different countries."

"Which countries?"

"I don't remember."

Muscles leaned back in his chair and watched a struggling,

338

exhausted Kannada. He went to his desk and started making some notes.

"What're you doing?" Kannada asked.

"Recording what you said."

"What do you do with all this stuff?"

"Send it to the appropriate authorities to look at."

Kannada started to recover as blood was returning to his brain.

The examiner moved back out in front of him. "Tell me more."

"There's no more."

Muscles looked at him carefully.

"Really, there's nothing."

The examiner continued to watch him struggle. "I don't think you're telling me the truth." He rolled his chair back to where it was behind the desk. "We're going to do this again with more questions."

"Oh, I get it," Kannada said, recovering himself. He leaned back against the seat. "You just want me to say whatever you want to hear."

"No, I'm doing you a favor," Muscles countered, shaking his head. "Come clean now, and you'll face less time."

"Yeah, right, I see you guys do that kind of stuff on television all the time."

"No . . . we never do that." Muscles deflated; his voice was unsteady.

Kannada recalled the book he had read on polygraphs and made sense of what was happening. The examiner was trying to ensure confidence in the system. He was trying to keep the polygraph going and get him to his breaking point. After all, the polygraph measured guilt, not deception.

"I want to cancel this polygraph. This whole interrogation process."

"No, you don't want to do that." Muscles about to lose evidence.

"Yes, I do," Kannada said emphatically.

Muscles put his hands on the table and clenched his fists, his face red. "Believe me. That'll make things worse for you."

"I said I want to cancel this."

"You sure you want to do this?"

Kannada looked down and paused as though he were thinking about it. "Yes."

The examiner's fists loosened as if he could no longer hold on to something. "Give me a moment. I need to speak with my manager." He rushed out of the room.

A few minutes later, Stache, a man with a thick, brown mustache, entered the dark room. "Hey." He took Muscles' seat. "The examiner tells me you want to stop the interrogation process."

"Yes, he gave me the third degree, and I just started saying things." Kannada felt better now, no longer nauseous.

"Did you say something that wasn't true?"

"Yeah."

Stache stared at him and plucked the hair above his lips. "Well, we won't put you through any more of this. We'll end the polygraph here for now, but the examiner will come back and go over everything you said. Just let him know what isn't true."

Kannada nodded.

Stache left, and Muscles returned.

The examiner reviewed his paperwork. "Okay, so you stole the IPO with a group of people and hid the money overseas, correct?"

"Actually, that's not true," Kannada replied.

"What's not true?"

"All of it. I made it up."

The examiner's eyebrows rose. "All of it? None of this was true?"

"No. How can it be true? I saw it in a movie."

Muscles eyeballed him.

"I'm a devout religious person. How could I do anything wrong?" Kannada said, toying with him.

The examiner stared at him for a moment, then crossed out his paperwork feverishly. He slammed his notebook close, stood stiffly, and opened the door for Kannada. "Thank you for your cooperation."

Kannada stood and walked toward the door. "When do I get the results?"

"It'll take us a couple of weeks. We'll have to run it across some other examiners," Muscles explained.

"Thanks." Kannada left with a police officer who was waiting outside the door.

Kannada smiled as he was escorted down the hallway. All that precautionary simulation he had undergone with Walker yelling at him behind closed doors paid off, as did reading a book about polygraphs. Kannada had the machine figured out. He had a hunch that he passed the test.

Back in the polygraph room, the examiner was gathering the results of the exam.

"How'd he do?" a man asked.

The examiner looked up and saw Lt. Napoli holding a coffee mug. He put his hands on his waist and sighed. "Never seen a bigger liar. Failed his tests altogether."

"Well, the homeless are delusional," Lt. Napoli remarked.

CHAPTER 41

Manhattan, New York

In January 2015, one month after the heist, in his SEC office, Dilip slouched in his chair with his feet propped up on his work desk. He cradled a phone between his ear and neck and dipped a samosa into a cup of hot chai.

"David, David, I've got my hands tied . . . I understand, but I'm busy right now . . . Yes, yes, don't worry. We're hot on their trail."

He blew air onto the wet samosa and took a bite as David Lemon continued ranting.

Long Island, New York

Rob examined his latest credit card bill. "Forty-seven thousand at Saks Fifth Avenue," he muttered. His eyes narrowed, and his brow furrowed, trying to remember that purchase. Suddenly, it made sense. "Zara!" he yelled.

Honolulu, Hawaii

Zara relaxed on a stool at a tropical beach bar. Wearing a floppy hat, she took a sip of her margarita through a straw.

"Is everything all right, ma'am?" a bartender asked.

"Perfect." Zara smiled.

* * *

Manhattan, New York

Two months later, Dilip stood with a couple of darts in one hand to his side, a slender projectile in the other hand near his face, and the phone on speaker.

"David, David," he said as he squinted and took aim at the dartboard, "I'm on his case right now, targeting him as we speak."

Dilip threw the small arrow onto the dart-covered board. It was the closest hit he'd had thus far, just outside the red bull's-eye. The other pointed missiles were scattered about the edges of the board.

"We've never been closer."

Rikers Island, New York

In June, a heavy metal door swung open at the base of a brown concrete building. Kannada followed Rob's chauffeur out the doorway at the Eric M. Taylor Center, a men's medium-security facility. They approached the Plaza Hotel BMW, and the chauffeur opened the back door. Kannada entered the vehicle and met Rob in the back seat, where a tan leather bag rested on the middle hump.

"How was prison?" Rob asked.

Kannada looked ahead and sighed. "I think I prefer the subway."

Rob grinned. "I've got just the thing to cheer you up." He lifted the bag and put it on Kannada's lap. "Here. Ben pulled that out of your share earlier, so you'd have some money when you got out until you found a place."

Kannada looked at the leather bag with several hundred-dollar bills and smiled. "Not bad, not bad at all." He paused to think of the right words to express his gratitude. "I wanted to say thank you for everything you've done. I mean, backing this heist, planning it based on my novel . . . and just giving me a second chance."

"Oh, don't mention it. I should be thanking you. Lemon got what he deserved, and my finances are in better shape. You got any more ideas like that?"

The mastermind smirked, then laughed as the car started to move.

Manhattan, New York

Kannada returned to the Plaza. The rental property he and the gang had used as their hideout was occupied; Rob had found a tenant. Kannada set foot in a Carnegie Suite on the hotel side of the building, placed his tan bag on the sofa in the living area, and headed for his room. He glanced at the brass handle as he slid open the door to the bedroom. Once he entered, he looked up. He was expecting an empty room, but someone was standing in the distance, on the mini terrace, waiting for him. He vaguely discerned the silhouette of the shapely figure through the semi-transparent curtains. He approached the balcony.

Kannada parted his lips, not disappointed. "I didn't expect you to be here."

The woman turned to face him, looked into his eyes, and pulled a red lollipop out of her mouth. "I said I wanted to see you again." Zara smiled.

"Did you get your money all right?"

"Yeah, no problems. You?"

"Ben has my share."

There was a moment of awkward silence. Their eyes stayed locked on each other.

Kannada looked away, toward Central Park, then stared at her bosom and hesitated. "I'm pretty tired. I think I'll take forty winks." Zara lowered her head to be in his view and appeared to search for more of a response. "Alone."

She retracted her head. "What happened to Amara?"

"Uh, she quit her job and returned to Chicago."

"I know. Ben told me."

Kannada acknowledged that she'd asked just for conversation's sake, to see his reaction. Unsure of what to make of Zara's surprise visit, he looked around the floor, thinking of how to proceed, and sighed. "I guess I wanted to show her I was still somebody." He faced the escort.

Zara shook her head slowly. "You are somebody, just not to her. You're always somebody to someone." She gave him a warm smile.

She's just saying that to lighten the mood.

Zara cleared her throat and put her hand on his chest. "Kanny . . ." He looked at her with new life, as his pet name reverberated in his ears. "Things change for a reason."

He stared at the ground. "Things used to be perfect. We were a perfect match."

"You know, you're not exactly her type, perfect and all. At least not anymore. You're a robber now."

Kannada grinned. "What's the difference? You're a gold-digger."

Zara smiled, staring deeply into his eyes.

The right side of his lips veered up. "Why're you here?"

"I thought you could use someone who cared."

Kannada nodded slowly and recalled her last words at the NYSE balcony. "I thought we weren't meant to be together."

"Look, this isn't easy for me either." Zara scrunched up her face, then released it with a heavy sigh. "A part of me is afraid to get close to someone because I know he'll leave. It happens all the time. It's just my reality." She edged closer to him. "But I want to try." She cradled him in her arms and looked up at him.

Kannada nodded. "I'm not planning to leave you." He gazed into her eyes. "I wanted to tell you earlier that your performance was incredible."

Zara leaned in and kissed him on the lips. "*I* am incredible," she said, beaming.

He stared, then smirked. *I'm going to get laid tonight.*

Zara seductively licked and circled her top lip. "Taste good?"

He tasted cherry and recalled his first meeting with her in Beverly Hills. "Very. I thought you said no kissing?"

"That's when I was an escort. I think I found my Prince Charming." Zara smiled.

He blushed and lowered his chin.

She embraced him even more. "What're you going to do with all that money?"

Kannada looked out over the balcony. A couple of birds hovered over Central Park. "I don't know." His gaze returned to her. "I can't spend it alone."

"You want to go shopping?"

He laughed. "Maybe . . . I've got one last thing to take care of."

"What's that?"

Kannada walked with Zara at his side, his arm wrapped around her, in Central Park. The summer evening warmed his heart. It was a gorgeous, beautiful, sunny day in New York's pristine, natural preserve. Young men and women frolicked in the greenery, played games, and enjoyed the outdoors, as coach drivers steered horse carriages around the paved pathways and squirrels chased pigeons.

"Hey, Kannada," a jogger said, sounding energetic.

Kannada noticed him running toward them just before he passed. "Hey, man, how're you?"

"Great," the jogger replied, now behind them.

Kannada looked at Zara, uncertain. His voice weakened, embarrassed. "I forgot his name."

She chuckled.

A few minutes later, Kannada spotted some donkeys and approached them. A pair of squirrels chased away a group of pigeons behind the coach, and a small boy and girl screamed and ran toward the rodents. He grinned at the scene as the carriage came to a stop.

"Ben told me about you," Kannada said to a woman in a carriage pulled by donkeys. She was sitting next to her small boy in the jack-and-jenny carriage ride. "I think I've seen you before in the subway."

The Lady of Donkey nodded and squinted. "You look familiar." She sounded Irish.

"Thanks for the squirrels."

The woman parted her lips, and her eyes gravitated away from him.

Kannada tossed the woman the tan leather backpack that Rob had given him earlier.

She flinched. "What's this?"

He smiled. "A new start."

With his arm wrapped around Zara at his side, he looked at her; she was smiling, too.

The Lady of Donkey opened the holy sack of green; her face glowed. "A long life to you!"

Kannada winked and continued with Zara as The Lady of Donkey sifted through the bills.

He looked into the distance as a couple walked past them with their child in a stroller.

"Oh look, they're filming *Law & Order*."

Zara gaped. "Where?"

He shrugged. "Ah, who cares?"

Zara faced Kannada and playfully hit him on his chest. "You always do that," she said, smiling.

Kannada grinned. "You want to take a piggyback ride?"

"Sure."

Kannada stooped low, and Zara climbed aboard.

She wrapped her arms around his chest. "How'd you beat the polygraph?"

"I told the truth."

"Right . . ." Zara sounded cynical. "You must have sold it pretty well."

"You think Lemon bought it?" He looked up at her.

"When there's a seller, there's a buyer."

Kannada laughed. "You're learning."

The End.

www.ingramcontent.com/pod-product-compliance
Lightning Source LLC
Chambersburg PA
CBHW051327250626
47155CB00007B/2478